Sweet Millions

Maria Antokas

ISBN 978-0-578-74436-0

Cover design by Camille Rossi Petruccio, Impress Graphic
Design

Atalanta Publishing

First Edition: June 2021

Acknowledgements

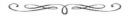

This book started as a minor hobby when I was asked to join a writers group being formed at our church. I had no idea what I was going to write about and whether I was going to stick it out for longer than a few months. But our leader, Patty Apostilides, was a true inspiration and after years of playing around with it, I finally had a finished product.

I want to thank all of the members of this group, who with their loving and thoughtful feedback over the years, made me a confident writer. We went through quite a lot together and I have become very fond of this extended family. So, to my special friends at the Hellenic Writers Group of Washington D.C. – Patty, Calliopi, Diane, Stella, Andie, Toula, Karen, Steve, Ann, and the late Dr. Peter Paras, thank you!!!

I also want to thank my amazing husband, Jim, whose encouragement helped me get *Sweet Millions* over the finish line.

When I started writing *Sweet Millions*, I had no idea where it was going to go. As a former banker, I just wrote what I knew. Danielle Mendow is obviously a bit of me – especially when it comes to adventure and chocolate.

Table of Contents

Chapter 1

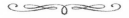

Wilhelm Schmidt arrived at Dulles on the overnight flight from Munich. Since he wasn't carrying any luggage, he beat everyone to the taxi line and was in the lobby of the Willard Hotel in a little over an hour. He was quickly checked into room 1016 by a young, efficient male receptionist who, in true Washington D.C. manner, did not ask many questions before handing him his key card. Hanging tightly to his briefcase, he made his way to the bank of elevators, wading expertly through the usual Capitol Hill crowd of manic lobbyists, self-important businessmen, well-coiffed trophy wives, and neatly dressed employees.

The long flight exhausted him. All he wanted was a shower, a Scotch, and a soft mattress.

The ride up to the tenth floor seemed to take forever as guests and workers kept coming off and on. He sighed and caught the attention of a dark-haired woman wearing a stylish fedora hat and raincoat who smiled back at him. He sensed they were sharing an "I feel your pain" moment as he tried to catch her eyes through her smoke-colored "cat-eye" sunglasses.

They both got off on the tenth floor. He mumbled

a good night to her as she ambled down the hall–
her small, tight hips swaying one way as the bottom
of her tan Hermes raincoat swayed the other. He
watched as she read the numbers on the doors, her
full red lips mouthing 1018, 1020, 1022 as she
continued looking for her room. She seemed like a
class act. He would have loved to share that Scotch
and a snuggle with her, but at that moment his key
card clicked and his door opened.

"Not meant to be the story of my life," he thought
to himself as he ambled through the door.

The room was comfortable with a bed that was
bigger than his car back home. He put down his
briefcase and removed his raincoat. He threw his
jacket on the bed and loosened his tie. The trip left
him feeling every one of his 58 years. He looked at
himself in the mirror that hung over the modern
built-in desk. He was sweaty from the humid
September air. Thirty years ago, the woman in the
elevator may have done more than smile at him.
But tonight to her, he was just another aging male
with too little hair, too much stomach, and glazed,
tired eyes.

"Where did the years go?" he asked himself, while
opening the minibar. He pulled out two tiny bottles
of Johnny Walker. It was fun then–the international
travel, exotic locales, the fat envelopes full of cash,
the women, and the fancy hotels. Those were the
years they were writing the book on international
banking, making it up as they were going along.
Nobody understood it back then, and nobody

knew they were making it up as they were going along. They were untouchable. Governments, businesses, other banks never got in their way. They didn't have a clue. It was like stealing money from the blind.

There was a knock at the door.

"Who is it?" he asked, as he walked to the door. He waited for the response before opening it. You can never be too careful–even at the best hotels in Washington D.C.

"It's me. The lady from the elevator."

'Well, well,' he thought, and opened the door.

She was wearing a mischievous grin and holding up her key card. "I'm having a bit of trouble with this," she said. She had a slight accent which he couldn't quite place–perhaps New York? "Can I come in and use your phone? My cell phone is dead and I'm way too tired to go down to the lobby."

Before he could answer, she walked passed him and entered the room.

'For real? Hmm–well, I may still have it in me,' he thought, as he watched her make her way toward the nightstand.

He closed the door and followed her into the room. She turned, still smiling–meeting his gaze. Something about her looked vaguely familiar. He cocked his head and squinted like he was trying to get a closer look.

"Do I know you?" he asked.

"Probably." She answered, pulling her other hand out of the pocket of her overcoat. It held a 45 caliber gun with silencer. Without hesitation, she shot him twice in the stomach.

Wilhelm looked down and watched as his blood poured out of two small holes. His hands went immediately to stop the bleeding.

"You! But why? It's too late!" he looked up incredulously.

"So what," she answered sharply. "You know why." The third shot got him right between the eyes. He died instantly.

The woman shook her head from side to side. "Clueless," she thought to herself.

She put the gun back in her pocket. Taking out a pair of thin surgical gloves, she carefully checked the pockets of his pants, jacket, and raincoat. Satisfied that nothing interested her there, she opened his briefcase, quickly rummaged through some papers, found what she was looking for, and snapped it shut. She picked up the briefcase, stepped over poor Wilhelm, cautiously avoiding anything red, and walked out of the room closing the door behind her.

Chapter 2

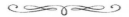

Like most towns on the fringes of suburbia, one quickly forgets what they look like two minutes after having driven through them. West Mendow was no exception. Close to the bedroom communities of Washington D.C., it's also safe to say that they could label it the doorway to the backwaters of Maryland. It did, however, have its moments. Twenty years earlier, it was on the brink of becoming the golden offspring of posh Potomac. Unfortunately, in the late nineties, the real estate bubble burst and the money that was pouring into the region quickly poured back out. Soon, West Mendow lapsed into the sleepy country town for which it seemed forever destined.

Danielle Mendow liked it that way. Fourth-generation blue blood, Danielle returned to West Mendow from Manhattan after 9/11 and being a "Mendow" gave her a certain cache in the community. For starters, it helped her succeed as the local branch manager of Capital Bank. Everyone loved her despite the research that showed bankers are the lowest head on the respectability totem pole. The pedigree and position did not hurt her a bit. She would always be the de facto mayor of West Mendow.

It was a very public romance. Residents stopped to greet her on the street or waved as they drove by. The police left her alone if she drove her Mercedes too fast down Main Street. Old Ned from "Old Ned's Deli and Bait shop" never let her pay for a cup of coffee. All this had a reason. She reciprocated their kindness. Danielle made sure they got the best banking service in the region., Business was business. She knew what it took to make it work.

Take Old Ned. This morning, just like every morning, she stopped at his shop so he could hand her a cup of coffee just so she could let him wink and say, 'on the house, babe.' This irked her to no end, but with his coffee shop right on the way to her branch (meanwhile, nobody should call any woman 'babe' unless they wanted their head bashed in) she felt obligated to stop in, smile graciously for the disgusting cup of coffee, and secretly wish that a house would fall on him. She hated old Ned. His coffee was repugnant.

But Old Ned was a customer of her branch, as were most of the businesses in West Mendow. Bank of America, SunTrust, and Capital One didn't have a prayer. Danielle owned West Mendow— figuratively and literally. Soon after she moved back from New York and took over the local Capital National Bank branch, the other banks started boarding up and rode their horses out of Dodge.

Compared to working at a New York bank, West Mendow banking was like an amateur hour for Danielle. The formula was simple. She laughed at every one's jokes as if they were being told by Jerry Seinfeld. She cried on demand at every sob story. She was everyone's best friend, got invited to every wedding, attended every funeral, and supported every non-profit including the most ridiculous ones. She approved everyone's loans (even the sketchy ones) and handed out tons of freebies and perks. She even got away with some very interesting interest rates that nobody needed to know about, but everybody did.

Eventually, her branch was no longer the West Mendow branch of Capital National, it was "Danielle's Bank". And it never lost a dime. As long as the branch kept growing and making money, management left her alone. Danielle loved it that way.

Danielle drove her red Mercedes C30 into the parking lot of her branch and pulled into her empty parking space right outside the front. It was always empty. Nobody dared park there knowing it was hers. Well, that was not totally true. There was also a sign on it that said 'branch manager' but that didn't stop certain people until a couple of towed cars put that little space grab to rest a few years ago. Town lesson learned.

It was a beautiful September morning. West Mendow was quiet, Fall was in the air, and 'TGIF'- it was Friday. She checked her make-up in the mirror on the visor and wiped the "joker smile" lipstick smudges that coffee cups make from her face. She smoothed out her natural colored eyeshadow, which highlighted her dark brown eyes. She ran her fingers through her wavy brown shoulder-length hair to give it that perfectly imperfect look. She saw a little gray, got freaky, and made a mental note to call Mimi next week to get rid of it.

Not bad for a forty-year-old, she thought. Despite the age and some signs of too much gravitational pull, she still congratulated herself for looking well preserved. She attributed this proudly to a smokeless, kid less, husbandless life and a small little tuck from Dr. Ulrich in Gstaad, Switzerland last winter.

Visor up. She opened the door and poured Old Ned's coffee into a nearby sewer like she did every day. Showtime. She could see the "all clear" signal (red plastic cup in front of teller window number one) through the all-glass doors, meaning all was well inside the branch. She unlocked the glass door of the branch and went inside.

The branch was a combination of glitz and more glitz. Marble floors, high-tech customer service stations, mood lighting, jazzy music, leather couches, glass coffee tables, glass-enclosed offices and conference rooms, a television showing cable news all day, computer stations for customers, and a coffee bar. The other branches in town looked like old museums compared to hers.

14

It was still early. The branch didn't open for another half hour. The noise of her high heels echoed on the floors as she walked through the empty platform. She headed towards the teller station before her and entered behind the counter through a side door. She continued walking while doing a quick scan of the cashier boxes, looking for anomalies. Reaching the other side, she opened the door into the kitchen that connected the front of the branch with the drive-thru.

Her head teller, Jen, was already in the back of the branch counting the drawers in the drive-thru.

Danielle started brewing a pot of dark roast espresso that could resurrect the dead. It was her little way of helping her staff get going in the morning.

"Anything going on?" she called out to Jen while counting out the scoops.

"One of my boys ate a crayon last night," she answered matter-of-factly.

"At least he didn't smoke it," Danielle answered. That happened once. She counted out the tenth scoop of coffee. "Anything good on the news?"

Jen kept a small TV in the drive-thru to pass the time during the lulls. She was obviously addicted to noise.

"Did you hear about that guy they found dead at the Willard?" Jen called out.

"No. How awful," Danielle replied evenly. Someone was always getting shot around Washington D.C. No big deal unless the killer was heading towards West Mendow giving Officer Joe, one of the town's three police officers, a reason to look serious and important.

"He got it twice in the stomach and once between the eyes." Jen reported in her 'I've seen every mob movie ever made' voice.

"Too bad." Danielle countered in her 'I've seen those same movies too' tone, plus I've lived in New York voice.

And on it went. Jen walked into the kitchen, plopped a pack of hundred-dollar bills on the counter and opened the refrigerator. Danielle marveled at how neat and attractive a mother of a pack of little kids could look at 7:30 a.m. while wearing the simple Capital Bank teller uniform of black slacks and a white, perfectly pressed tailored blouse. Her straight, dirty blonde hair was pulled into a tight ponytail that draped elegantly down her back. She didn't need make-up. Her facial features were naturally fine, reflecting the half Polish, half Norwegian lineage of her parents.

"He was German. He had just arrived yesterday from Munich," Jen said, turning her lanky 5'9" body towards the refrigerator, opening the door, and taking out a small juice box.

16

"Yes, that explains everything. Okay, so what?" Danielle answered, glaring impatiently at the coffee slowly dripping into the pot.

"He didn't have any luggage," Jen said, stabbing a tiny straw into the box and drawing a nice long sip.

"Let's state the obvious. Maybe whoever shot him, robbed him of his luggage," Danielle said, rolling her eyeballs. "Really Jen, it's too early. What's so special about this murder from all the others we hear about?"

Jen ignored that. "He was scheduled on today's flight back to Munich." She threw the juice box in the garbage.

"Well then, all signs point to terrorism," Danielle said, then laughed at her own poor joke. Not willing to wait, she swapped the coffeepot for a paper cup and watched eagerly as it filled.

Jen walked back into the drive-thru. "Oh, they're showing his passport picture again. He looked so nice. Like my dearly departed Uncle Phil." Jen whimpered.

Jen's Uncle Phil looked like a ghoul. Danielle couldn't imagine anyone else that unattractive. She had to see this. She walked into the drive-thru to take a glimpse at Uncle Phil's dead German twin.

Danielle focused on the screen. Her eyes widened. That man looked nothing like Uncle Phil. She knew that man. It was Bill Smith, her old colleague from Capital Bank International in New York. He wasn't German. He was from Bayside, Queens. Why did his picture have him tagged as Wilhelm Schmidt? Danielle looked harder. Yup. That was him. She never forgot a face. Someone killed Bill Smith at The Willard in downtown Washington D.C.

The newscaster went on to another story as she turned away from the screen. She walked back to the kitchen before Jen could read her face. A jumble of thoughts jumped into her head. None of them made sense. She knew Bill Smith. Why was he now a dead man named Wilhelm?

Chapter 3

Danielle snuck out of the kitchen and, deep in thought, walked into the main part of the branch, towards her desk in the far left corner overlooking the lobby. It was 8:45 a.m. There were fifteen minutes to go before the doors to the branch were unlocked. She sat down while her eyes rapidly surveyed the room. This position gave her the best view of her customer service officers. She deliberately chose this location so she could watch and hear them talk to her esteemed customers–and make sure they didn't piss them off, which customer service officers tend to do. She sat, pulling out the seat pillow hidden under her desk to give her petite frame a little more height. She thrived on being in the middle of things and for that reason left her other official glass-enclosed office empty. She felt like a goldfish in it, anyway.

By this time in the morning, she would be knee-deep in e-mails, but the news story about the murder shook her. Instead of turning on her computer, she picked up a pencil and started tapping it absent-mindedly on her wooden desk.

The first piece of the puzzle to solve was why on earth Bill Smith was calling himself Wilhelm Schmidt now? She gazed out the window, hoping some key clue would pop into her head.

The main street traffic was getting heavier. Everyone was getting on with the day except poor Bill Smith. Thoughts about Bill, then other colleagues, and then friends from her New York banking days, came flooding back. These were twenty-year-old memories. She hadn't gone there in ages. Life was too good today. Not that she wanted to think about the past.

It's just that she was another Danielle then - full of adrenaline and fire. She liked herself in those years, but she loved herself now. That's why she rarely went back. But it was fun-physically exhausting, mentally stimulating, and emotionally exhilarating. International banking was exciting and heart-pounding. But after six years of riding that wave, Danielle was drinking a little too much, smoking a lot, and was in denial. Her doctor warned her she was at heart attack levels. She didn't care. Who does at that age?

The end began when the first plane crashed into Tower Two at the World Trade Center on 9/11 and Capital International Bank's windows shattered a block away. Danielle knew that her life had just changed, and she made a pact with God. If she survived, she would clean up her act. She heard Bill Smith shouting over the screams and wails that everyone should evacuate immediately from the building, head towards the East River and try to get to mid-town. Danielle grabbed her ten-ton laptop, ran down the 21 floors of her office building, and sprinted like mad. The towers collapse shortly thereafter. It was unfathomable. She watched from

21st Street and Fifth Avenue as she struggled to keep up with the crowds running alongside her. When she finally reached her apartment in mid-town, her head felt like it would explode. Two weeks later, with Bill's blessing, she caught the bus home to West Mendow.

Meanwhile, Bill Smith had roped everyone together from his home in Bayside. By September 12, his back-up operation in Saddle Brook, New Jersey was up and running. Danielle continued working the bank relationships first out of 54th Street in New York and then out of her basement in West Mendow, Maryland. Other managers and personnel came online within days. Despite the devastation of the financial community in New York, Capital Bank International had minimal downtime thanks to the heroic efforts of Bill Smith.

Unfortunately, 9/11 not only brought terrorism home to the United States, but it brought terrorism to the Capital National Bank Board Room. Within six months, the board had worked themselves into a tizzy. Discussions revolved around weird fantasies that they would be the next terrorist target. Overtaken by hysteria, the paranoia vanished with relief after they had a unanimous vote to exit and sell off the international side of the bank.

Danielle helped them wind down the division, working remotely with Smith, who remained in Saddlebrook to shut down the operations. She worked diligently to transfer the remnants of the relationships to another bank in New York that was thrilled to get the nice new business she had worked her butt off to develop.

After a couple of slick political maneuvers only a New York hack could pull off, Danielle had the manager of the branch of Capital National in West Mendow kicked out so she could replace him. She turned her full focus locally and lost track of all her colleagues from those wild days in the city. Her blood pressure has been perfect ever since.

But something strange happened on the day they were to finally close the books. The auditors from headquarters in Washington D.C. discovered a $10 million gap. It looked like a duplicated payment from a SWIFT message of unknown origin that was payed twice on 9/11 out of a foreign exchange suspense account to a mining company that held an account with a small regional bank in Latvia. The entry was corrected, but only one payment was reversed. They overlooked the second entry. Because of the delay in investigating the second entry, the Latvian Bank assumed it was legitimate and gave the mining company a $10 Million credit. After months of trying to communicate with a bank whose employees could barely speak English, in a country whose financial sector was still unfamiliar with international payment protocol, the mining company had withdrawn the money, closed their account, and were never to be heard from again.

Nobody at headquarters knew what was going on, including Danielle. Apparently, Bill, in his all efficient manner, thought the issue would ultimately resolve itself like all the others and didn't make a big deal of it. But it didn't. Luckily for him, it didn't matter. The Board of Directors were so eager to sever all global ties, they agreed to write off the $10 Million, close the books and forget about it. For Bill and Danielle, two payment enthusiasts who prided themselves on how to move mountains and shift tides with finding lost money, this was an ugly disappointing ending.

The sound of a horn passing by the branch brought Danielle out of her trance. She turned on her computer and opened her Outlook. Finding it hard to concentrate on the mundane e-mails, she searched the local news site to see if there were any updates on the murder. Nothing.

A phone rang behind the teller line, then stopped. Jen must have picked it up. The ringing made her think of the last conversation she had with Bill.

She remembered how he picked up the phone on the first ring.

"Bill, its Danielle," she said, her voice trembling slightly knowing she was going to be giving him some bad news.

He seemed not to sense anything and replied, "Hey, little lady. How are those gents treating you on the plantation?" (Ever since she moved back home, he had this Scarlett O'Hara storyline going about her. It was weird. Most of the time she just ignored it)

"Yeh, listen. The $10 Million has hit Place's radar and Teddy said he's bringing it up to the Board during the meeting next week," she said getting the worse of the report over with quickly. "They are itching to close the books. What's going on? Did Bank of Latvia send the second one back? Do they get it was a duplicated payment, and it was a mistake?"

"They can't find the Mining Company. It just disappeared," he replied brusquely.

"Who's 'they' Bill? Who did you speak to? Did you hit everyone? Don't you think it sounds fishy? Is money just disappearing like that? Did you try to find the company yourself? I just don't believe their B.S. It smells. You just can't walk away with $10 Million in little Latvia of all places without raising all sorts of red flags!" she said, exasperated.

"Slow down. I did everything I could from here. The trail is cold. I called Hudd and told him the next step was to go over and crack some heads, but he told me to stand down. I don't get it either. They don't care so why should I?" She could hear the resignation in his voice but she would not let it go.

Gripping the phone a little harder, she asked, "You spoke to Teddy?" When that Bozo, Teddy Hudd, got the responsibility to wind down the international operation, she couldn't believe it. She

24

could only describe him as an incompetent dolt. Being roomies at Princeton with the Chairman seemed to be the stock that kept paying dividends for him. "What was his reasoning?"

With a sigh, he said, "He just wants to be done with it before he leaves on some cruise with his wife. He said he would recommend that the Board votes to write it off at the meeting next week."

"What!!!" Danielle shouted into the phone. "That's crazy. We could get it back. He doesn't know what he's talking about! Jerk!"

"I'm just the messenger here." He replied glumly.

Six months earlier she had a view of the Twin Towers. Danielle sat back in her chair and looked out over the nearby cornfields of West Mendow. The landscape was beautiful. The impressive mountain ranges of Maryland and West Virginia replaced the New York City skyline and the majestic Hudson River was supplanted by the meandering magnificence of the Potomac River but she still had the occasional twang for New York, especially when she talked to her old friends.

"Hey Danielle, are you still there? It's not like you to suddenly get so quiet," he said with a sarcastic laugh.

"Yeh, I'm still here," she answered softly. "Something's bothering me. Where's the money, Bill"

It was an innocent question. Money just doesn't get created one minute, then disappear the next without leaving some sort of footprint. In fact, the electronic age made it almost impossible to be untraceable. They both understood this. As seasoned veterans of the money transfer business, they knew there was always a money trail.

But the question touched a nerve, and Bill's reply was abrupt. "How the hell should I know. I just want this nightmare to end. Danielle, just give it a rest. We did all we could. If those guys want to eat it–so be it. Do you think it will haunt you? So what if billionaire John Place's bank loses $10 Million because of a blip on 9/11. Everyone lost something that day."

Danielle let out a little whimper. Frank's beautiful face appeared in her mind. She could still feel his touch on her cheeks and his lips on her mouth. Bill's last comment stung.

"Geez, I'm sorry," Bill said immediately. "That was uncalled for. I didn't mean... I know you lost Frank. I'm sure that still hurts like hell."

"That's all right. Forget about it. Let's move on. You're right. There are other things to worry about," Danielle replied, not wanting to open old wounds. They caught up on the last of the minor business issues, then bid each other farewell, not knowing that this would be the last conversation she would have with her old colleague from New York.

Because two weeks later, he disappeared.

Bill Smith. Wilhelm Schmidt. What happened there? Where did he go? What was he doing during those lost years and why crawl out of the woodwork now?

Danielle started staring at the screen on her computer as if the Oracle of Delphi would appear and give her all the answers. It remained dark. She got up from her desk to clear her mind and focus on business. She took a walk around the platform lobby to make sure desks were neat, there was no garbage on the floor, and the cubbies that held deposit and withdrawal slips were full. Her anxiety level started ratcheting down until she mistakenly looked up and saw Bill Smith's passport photo flashing again on the silent T.V. screen that hung in the lobby. The news story about the murder was being replayed. It felt like he was staring right at her. She froze. Could she reconcile the old Bill with the new Wilhelm? What did she really know about him?

When he wasn't traveling around the world, he seemed to live at the bank. He was there in the morning before everyone arrived and he was still there after everyone left. Mounds of paper always surrounded him. His phone was constantly ringing. He would call people "Pal" in that hard Queens accent, and Danielle would always tease him about it. Everyone at every bank in the world knew him or knew of him. Because of this network, he could resolve enormous problems with a few

27

phone calls. He knew payments like nobody's business. He ran a tight ship, had great audits, and understood operations, processes, regulations inside and out like he wrote the book. Everything she knew about banking, she learned from him.

The news story ended, and Danielle brought herself back to the moment. She returned to her desk. Shaking her head, she thought to herself why is that, to this day, she couldn't accept that he couldn't get those funds back.

The last question and his answer still echoed loudly in her mind. "Where's the money, Bill?"

Bill Smith. Wilhelm Schmidt. A banker's banker. Danielle worked with him for twelve years and knew nothing about him. He just did his job, did it well, and that's that.

"So why the disappearing act?" she whispered to the blank screen. Despite Bill's advice to move on, the answer to that question started haunting her again.

The shaking of glass doors unlocking jolted her. Her thoughts turned to her staff as they began arriving for work. She called out her "Good morning's" as they paraded to the kitchen to put their lunch and jackets away. She also reminded everyone to go get a cup of coffee and smiled to herself when she heard some muffled groans.

The teller line was getting busy and she knew within a few minutes someone would park at her desk to discuss some stupid problem. She laid her hands on her desk to steady her mind. Closing her eyes, she forced herself to refocus her thoughts on the day. With a shrug, she opened them, committed to giving up trying to solve this strange D.C. murder mystery of her old friend. She turned to her computer monitor and started plowing through her e-mails.

Chapter 4

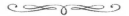

Danielle kept an ear to the news all weekend, hoping to hear more about the murder of Bill Smith a. k. a. Wilhelm Schmidt. All the updates concluded it was still one giant mystery. On Monday morning, Danielle was stepping out from the elevator onto the executive floor of the Capital National Bank headquarters in downtown Washington D. C. It was over a decade since they had summoned her there. Nothing had changed. There were a few modern touches like a flat-screen TV broadcasting Bloomberg and a Zen infinity fountain making that constant peeing noise. Other than that, at first glance, it still looked like George Washington's living room.

The Big Kahuna's office occupied most of the floor. Chairman Dr. John Place was the son of the founder of the bank, taking over when his father, Old Jack, passed away twenty-some years ago. He gripped the reins ever since.

"Over here," croaked a voice from around the corner. Danielle walked towards it, smoothing out her red Dolce and Gabbana suit she picked up during a "pond sprint" to Milan last summer. She was ecstatic that she finally got to wear it somewhere. She saw a mirror and stopped momentarily to check her dark brown hair - freshly cut under the unwritten Capital National Bank Executive Women's Hair Length Code. She gave herself a nod, took a deep breath, and straightening her posture, she continued walking.

The woman with the frog voice sat inside a green glass block capsule that seemed to double as a reception desk. Old Dolores Kagan held the record for the longest employment at Capital National Bank. She knew everyone and everyone's skeletons. Dr. Place considered her indispensable. Everyone else would have loved to dispense of her. Danielle wondered if the capsule protected the world from Kagan or Kagan from the world. It was probably bulletproof.

"Hello, Mrs. Kagan. It's been a long time. You look lovely as ever," Danielle said sweetly, although in reality she looked like a runner-up for the poster girl from Alien Fright Night. She wondered if they still made that eye shadow–what was it–slime green? She didn't want to look too long for fear she may turn to stone.

"Thank you, Danielle. It has been a long time– what–13 years?" She said with a raspy voice. Obviously, one too many cigarettes in her lifetime.

"How do you remember all these things?" Danielle smiled, knowing full well that Mrs. Kagan had the memory of an elephant. "I can't even remember what I had for breakfast!" She laughed, hoping she didn't sound too pretentious. It was politically important to make Dolores think you liked her.

"Well, that last meeting was a classic. I thought you were all going to kill each other," She scoffed, ignoring Danielle's attempts at endearing her. She tapped a hot pink fingernail to her temple and continued. "Let's see if I remember. What did you have to tell him? Oh yes, he would lose $10 Million that day? I heard him choking and screaming from here. It was so funny." Her face remained deadpanned.

Danielle cringed. It wasn't that funny then. She lost a lot of sleep during that time.

"Well, the past is the past," Dolores continued as her body swiveled back towards her computer. Weirdly, her head remained facing her, appearing disembodied. "I just hope it doesn't bite you in the ass," she added with a wink-her eyelid sticking together for a few seconds longer than normal.

Danielle tilted her head and stared back. "Hmm. What did she mean by that?" she thought.

"Just go take a seat. Dr. Place is on the phone at the moment. Rita will be out to get you as soon as he's finished," she said, flicking a bony wrist and dismissing her towards the direction of the lounge.

Her head finally followed her body and returned to her computer screen, becoming fully absorbed with what was on it. Danielle thought she was watching some kind of police show, but then again, it could have been secretly placed monitors in the executive bathrooms. Regardless, the word was she could do or watch whatever and whoever she wanted on her computer. Nobody would bother her. She was one dangerous old fox.

Danielle thanked her and quickly backed away.

A few Queen Anne chairs, couches, and a low wooden coffee table stacked with business magazines decorated the waiting area. A fake electric fireplace was up against one wall while the babbling brook fountain adorned the wall across. The chairs were uncomfortable, just like she felt. On top of it all, the trickling water was annoying her. She crossed and uncrossed her legs, causing her skirt to rise up her thighs. She adjusted her seating while pulling her skirt back down. She was having a hard time sitting still. Being there without knowing what to expect was making her fidgety. She blocked it out by replaying the events of last Friday.

Although technically the branch was closed, it was still busy at the 5:00 p.m. Phones continued to ring, people were waiting at the teller line, and Danielle's service officers were still working with customers. Danielle's Golden Rule was that they could not kick out any customers, so she waited patiently. An empty branch couldn't come soon enough, but it was Friday and payday-the branch's busiest day of the week. She was tired. All she wanted to do was kick back with a glass of Sancerre and watch a Tom Cruise movie on Netflix.

She packed away the papers on her desk and was shutting down her computer when Jen buzzed her on her intercom.

"Danielle. I have a Dolores Kagan holding on line two for you."

Danielle frowned. She only knew one Dolores Kagan, and she wasn't a good Dolores Kagan. She quickly reached for the phone, hoping it was just someone with the same name. Unfortunately, it was the bad Dolores Kagan calling to give her the surprising summons for an appearance down at Headquarters first thing Monday morning. Dolores barked she didn't know what the meeting was about, so she wasn't allowed to ask questions, but she had to be there. Shuddering, she hung up the phone. Danielle did not feel good about this meeting, however, when the chairman's office calls, you're either going to get promoted way up (not likely), fired (huh?), or arrested (uh oh).

"Destiny beckons," Jen said walking over to her.

"You listened too?" Danielle answered mocking shock.

"Of course," Jen smiled mischievously as she sat down in one of the customer chairs in front of her desk.

Danielle sighed. "So this means I need to add a major makeover to this weekend's horribly busy agenda," she said sarcastically, knowing full well there were no dates or events on the agenda. "Since I may walk the plank on Monday, it's still important to look "just so", wouldn't you say?" Danielle said jokingly.

"Mimi, pronto," Jen nodded towards the phone.

"Yes, to Mimi's, straightaway." Checking the time, Danielle called Mimi, who squeezed her in for "the works" at The Rejuvenation Spa the next morning. The branch had emptied of customers by then, so she announced to the employees who remained that she had an important meeting at the Chairman's office first thing on Monday and would most likely be late.

She left them to guess what it was all about. All eyes followed her adoringly as she sauntered out of the branch, wishing everyone a wonderful weekend. Masking her growing anxiety was becoming difficult. She hopped into her car and took the long way home, savoring the beautiful late Autumn afternoon. She drove slowly through the winding back roads, meandering this way and that trying to keep her mind off the meeting on Monday. She loved this part of the countryside where the suburban sprawl hadn't yet invaded. She also loved the notoriety of being the most famous branch manager on this side of the Potomac. But like the road she was navigating, life can take you to the same place in many ways. Her experience had taught her just when you think you're there, you may have to take a left.

Her window was open just a crack to let in the Maryland weather, which alternated from warm to cold every other week this time of year. This was the balmy week. Little breezes were coming from different directions, causing the branches of the maples and elms to put on a show for the distant mountains. The Fall smell of the wood-burning fireplaces from the surrounding farms permeated into the car. The White Oaks were changing color, and a few leaves were scenting the air as they wafted in the wind. As always, the elegance of the landscape whose fields were proudly farmed by four generations of Mendow's enamored her. As the last in the lineage, it was all hers now. But from very young, she never wanted to be a farmer herself. To keep the tradition going, she leased the land from afar for production to other farmers and businesses. What she found when she returned home devastated her. The land and buildings looked so neglected.

West Mendow was destitute when she came back from New York. In addition, her inheritance was in such financial disarray that it took her years to straighten out the family fortune. Resolving to do better, she put all her financial, management, and academic skills to work spending long hours with attorneys, farmers, builders, agriculturalists and the people of West Mendow themselves. She wanted to make the land profitable again. She wanted to restore West Mendow to its original glory. For all those interested in working with her, she provided the resources they needed and helped them along. The town became vibrant again, thanks to her. As she drove by the different homesteads, stables, and roadside businesses, she continued to be delighted with the development that was her brainchild.

But it wasn't just altruism that made her do it. Danielle made money. Lots of it. Beyond lots of it- for her and everyone her businesses touched. She loved the people of West Mendow, particularly those who respected the land and remained loyal to her family even in the lean years. Danielle made it clear that no one was to know the extent of the money she put into the town and the surrounding area, but everyone did. It was the town's worst kept secret. In due regard (and the fact that everyone else was making money too), nobody talked about it and that was that.

A creaky voice snapped Danielle out of her country drive reverie. It was that nightmarish noise of Dolores', croaking her one-liner that she must have repeated about 80,000 times in her life. She was back in the waiting area of the Chairman's office. "Dr. Place is on the phone at the moment. Take a seat. Rita will be out to get you shortly."

A male voice replied, "Dolores, has anyone told you how lovely you look today?" She could imagine Dolores giving him the finger.

The voice sounded vaguely familiar. She looked up to see her old colleague, Teddy Hudd, bounding over to her.

"Ah, Danielle Mendow. It's been a long time. You look terrific!" Teddy exclaimed as he sat down across from her. He cleared his throat like he hadn't spoken in a decade. He was tall, thin, and still boyishly handsome for his 64 years. Danielle always thought he was a jerk.

"So what brings you back into civilization?" he laughed, then raised his eyebrows like his own cleverness surprised him.

"I was told they will bring the International Department back and they're looking for me to manage it," Danielle replied poker-faced.

Teddy coughed like he had a hairball stuck in his throat. "No, that can't be so. I run whatever specks remain of that department and I have heard no such thing." He took out his blackberry and sent off a text.

"I was teasing you, Teddy." She answered, suppressing a smile. "I'm not sure why I'm here, but his majesty beckoned. So why are you here?"

"Oh," he paused, then let out a quick snort and chortled, "Ho, well, hmm" he continued with his Yale, Class of 1970 lockjaw laugh and throat clearing ritual. Quickly deflecting, he sat down across from her, leaned over and whispered,

"Listen, I know you'll never forget that it was me who walked you out the door in New York at the end but I think you did quite well for yourself. I hear you practically own half of Western Maryland. And we leave you alone out there to do whatever you damn please." He straightened up, satisfied that he brought the attention back to her.

"True," she admitted nonchalantly, checking her manicure. She knew she couldn't get a better deal than that. She sat back and looked down to straighten an imaginary wrinkle in her skirt. "Well, I'm still disappointed that this bank didn't have the patience to wait out the financial crisis so we could stay in the game. We would have been the only international homegrown bank in the region."

"You're preaching to the choir," he sat back, acknowledging wistfully.

Her cheeks redden as the memories came rushing back, "And I can't believe that the Board agreed to take that big hit at the end. We were so close to getting that money back and they pulled the plug! Kind of irks me that someone got away with an extra $10 million just like that." She said looking hard at him.

His face saddened as he leaned over to her again. His voice again, just above a whisper. "Chump change to the Place family dynasty, my dear. They've moved on. We don't talk about it anymore. You too. Danielle, old girl, you can't keep looking back." At which point, he looked back over his shoulder to see if Dolores was listening.

She wondered why he was so paranoid. She obviously hit an odd note by his reaction. She also wondered how he would react if she brought up Bill Smith and the murder at the Willard. Before she opened her mouth, he reached out and patted her on the knee.

"Really darling, it's okay to move on," he said like he was trying to rid her of a mental disorder.

Brushing his hand away, she said, "Yuck, Teddy. We don't say "darling" and we don't touch anymore. Look who's living in the past. There are laws against that. And, by the way, I don't own half of Western Maryland. Maybe one quarter." She snapped back. So much for going down memory lane with him.

He exhaled a quick laugh. "Okay, whatever you say," he replied, leaning back in his chair, the exuberance returning. Teddy looked down at his own fingernails and began picking at something on his right thumb.

"So are you still advising the Chairman on very important matters??" She smirked knowing that after they stripped him of the International Division he still held the title of senior executive vice president and advisor to the Chairman. In reality, however, he was just a glorified "Greeter of Important Customers and Prospects" for the bank.

What a dream job! He had the right look, an easy-going manner, the affected Yale accent, and dozens of dark blue, wide-pinstripe suits. The rumor was that he married very well, which gave him pedigree and vast knowledge on when to use the right forks and spoons during meals. It also didn't hurt that he and Place were roomies in college.

Before he could respond, a waft of Chanel No. 5 perfume floated by them. Both she and Teddy looked up to see the all–efficient and stunning Miss Rita Steele, personal assistant to the Chairman, standing there in an almost too tight black Armani skirt suit, beckoning them.

Teddy lit up light a Christmas Tree. Men.

"Miss Mendow, Mr. Hudd. Dr. Place is ready for you now. Please follow me," she said crisply as her dark hair and bangs glistened under the bright fluorescent lights. She turned, scurrying down the hallway, not bothering to check if Danielle and Teddy were in tow and keeping up.

Walking pass Mrs. Kagan's capsule, Teddy yelled out, "Catch anyone in the act yet, Dolores?"

She chortled back, "Only you, Mr. Hudd."

Teddy chuckled and kept trotting along behind Rita, making sure he didn't miss one second of her swinging derriere.

Rita Steele was a legend at Capital National Bank. Many employees felt between her and Dolores Kagan, the bank had all the staff it needed.

Unlike Dolores, Rita oozed beauty and class. She was about Danielle's height, but her figure was more sultry and curvaceous. She knew just how and where to tailor her designer suits, using that sex appeal to cause many a man to run into walls or fall down the stairs as she glided by. She was as cutthroat as a ninja, diabolical as a mafia kingpin, and brilliant as an MIT professor. Her meteoric rise started about ten years ago when she arrived at Capital National Bank as a junior analyst. Within a nanosecond, she was the Chairman's right-hand manager. She left no one intact on her ascent. She threw people off cliffs without second looks. She was both hated and revered. They called her the Hillary Clinton of the bank.

Danielle loved her. She was a big fan.

They continued marching down the longest hallway, passing bad museum replicas of colonial era paintings and furniture. Guessing that Rita would be all ears under that hair bob, she waited until she was a little out of range when she whispered to Teddy, "So you have no idea why you're here?"

Still staring straight ahead, Teddy shook his head no.

"We should have asked Dolores," she said in a

hushed tone. "She's like Santa. Knows if you've been bad or good." Danielle grinned, trying to lighten the moment.

"No, more like a cagey old bird," he murmured, then walked ahead of her to make his power entrance into Place's office before Danielle.

They had finally reached the double wooden doors marked "John Place, Chairman of the Board". Rita pulled them both open at once, creating a wind tunnel through the hallway.

"Ah, my old friends!" Dr. John Place stood up and waddled spritely around his enormous cherry wood desk. The desk was so big that by the time he reached the other side, he was out of breath. Despite gasping slightly for air, he showed sincere delight on his pudgy face when he saw his buddy, Teddy. He extended a chubby hand to Danielle and pumped it with enthusiasm. "Danielle, Teddy. Good to see you. Good to see you. Take a seat, take a seat," he said excitedly, pointing to two leather wing-backed chairs across from his desk.

Danielle hadn't seen him up close in a while. Despite his rotund body, he still carried himself with grace and energy. She always thought of him as the Hardy of the "Laurel and Hardy" duo with Teddy being his perfect foil, Laurel. Two very different guys, but loyal and inseparable.

He also had this habit of repeating everything twice like he had his own personal echo.

44

"Rita, Rita, bring the kids a coke with some ice." Place said, gesturing towards the bar.

Rita scowled at them while wiping a smudge where her deep red lipstick caked in the crease of her full lips. A shudder crawled up Danielle's spine. Danielle knew this request was obviously below her pay grade, but there was no refusing the boss. He continued. "I want you both to meet someone. This is special agent Peter Muckiss from the FBI." He pronounced his name like "mucus".

A light-haired man with a very prominent nose, who neither Danielle nor Teddy noticed before, turned from looking at the view of the U.S. Capitol Building to face them.

Danielle sat up straighter. It wasn't exactly the pat on the back she was expecting, but it was becoming a remarkable Monday morning.

Chapter 5

"It's pronounced Muck-iss with the emphasis on the 'iss'". Special Agent Peter explained patiently, probably having to clarify it at least one million times.

"Oh, sorry, sorry. What did I say?" asked Dr. Place apologetically as he plopped back into his desk chair, exhausted from having to go around his desk again.

"You said it like "mucus". He replied. Special Agent Peter stood tall, almost 6'3", with delicate skin and a well-built body. He wore a good custom-fitting dark suit, not too tight, not too loose, and well accessorized with a silver tie and cufflinks peeking out from his jacket sleeves. Altogether, he would have been a fine-looking package if one could ignore the nose- which one couldn't.

Danielle and Teddy looked at each other, trying to hold back a laugh.

"Muckiss, yes, Muckiss. I'll certainly remember that" Dr. Place said, knowing full well he will forget it in a millisecond.

"Yes, fascinating name. Is that French?" Teddy stealing a playful glance with Dr. Place.

Rita in the meantime had prepared a tray of glasses with Coca Cola, offered one to Special Agent Peter who refused it vehemently like it had rum in it, and placed two on a table between Teddy and Danielle. Danielle noticed she took her time bending over, allowing the gentlemen to admire her peekaboo cleavage for a few seconds.

"That settled that. Rita Steele was indeed full of herself," Danielle thought to herself. Her admiration of Rita hit a new high.

The boys had enough fun for the morning, Danielle surmised, and broke the spell. She turned towards Special Agent Peter.

"It's nice to meet you. Please call me Danielle."

"And none of this Mr. Hudd stuff. I'm Teddy. No formalities here," he said, waving an admonishing finger.

Special Agent Peter nodded. Pulling out a notebook, he started turning over pages and pages of handwritten notes until he got to a blank page. He looked up to see everyone staring at him.

"Okay, let's get this show on the road," asked Dr. Place as he put on his glasses. Teddy also took out a pair and put them on. This must signal let's get serious, Danielle thought to herself. She made a mental note to look into glasses, noticing everyone seemed to want to get to work once they put them on. Perhaps her staff could use some. She made herself more comfortable in her chair.

"Of course," replied Special Agent Peter. He cleared his throat. "I asked Dr. Place these questions last Friday, but he felt that the two of you may know more. That's why we called you in today. Was either of you aware of the murder of a German national at the Willard Hotel last Thursday evening?

Danielle remained motionless and composed, although her insides were exploding. This was the last thing she expected to hear. How did they already connect Bill to Capital Bank and then to her? Teddy also knew him, but had he made the connection? He didn't seem able to hide a certain discomfort and started fidgeting like he should have used the Men's Room before they got started.

Danielle was in a quandary. She couldn't deny not hearing about the murder. It was one of those stories that caught traction on the news because whoever did it managed not to leave one clue. Also, it wasn't a robbery. Nothing was taken, according to the press - at least, nothing obvious. Besides, anyone who didn't live in a cave was following this gruesome story because of its randomness.

Teddy piped up first. "Oh yes. Terrible tragedy," he said half-heartedly, looking down at his hands. Her eyes shifted to him for a second. She reminded herself that Teddy had an inexplicable distaste for anything German. He probably didn't think it was a terrible tragedy at all.

Everyone looked over at her. It was her turn to talk. "Yes, I heard some snippets about it," Danielle added dismissively. She didn't want to sound too ghoulish like she was listening to this story all weekend... even though she was.

Special Agent Peter continued. "The gentleman's name was Wilhelm Schmidt. If anything sounds familiar from now on, let me know. I won't go into too many details. They found him lying on the floor of his hotel room with three bullet wounds. He didn't have any luggage, but a bellhop said he thought he was carrying a briefcase when he checked in."

"Well, well. A briefcase. This was an additional fact even the public didn't know," Danielle thought. She couldn't wait to tell Jen.

Special Agent Peter continued. "If there was a briefcase, it was missing from the hotel room when they found the body. Everything else seemed intact. He was wearing a Rolex, a gold chain, and a ring on his right hand. They valued the jewelry alone at about $30,000. He still had about $2000 in cash and two credit cards in his wallet. So, the motive was not robbery.

"You're probably asking what is leading this investigation to Capital National Bank. We found a note in the breast pocket of Mr. Schmidt's raincoat.

It had an address, a time, and a date. 1400 K Street, Monday, Sept. 19th at 10:00 am."

He paused for effect. "That's this address. The headquarters of Capital National Bank!"

There was silence. The pause was one of those awkward ones.

"Bravo," Teddy cried out. "That's stellar detective work!"

Danielle loved the sarcasm. She looked down to hide a smile. Special Agent Peter was not amused.

"I'm not finished." He said stubbornly. "We're assuming that Schmidt had a meeting with someone in this building."

Despite Danielle's amusement with this gang, deep down she was getting uneasy. She realized eventually that they would connect the dots and figure out that Wilhelm Schmidt was really Bill Smith and there was more to this story. There was no way she wanted to be dragged into this nightmare. The last thing on Earth she wanted was to be is part of an investigation into Bill Smith.

All she could think about were all these Feds hanging around West Mendow ruining her perfectly planned West Mendow life. Even worse, she and Teddy Hudd may have to work together again to help solve the crime by figuring out what stupid Bill wanted with the bank again.

Her earlier momentary fantasy of "getting back to headquarters and playing the international game with the big boys" was stinking, and all she wanted to do was to return to her royal territory where she reigned and ruled in peace.

So she kept her mouth zipped, hoping not to draw attention to herself.

Teddy, fortunately, filled in the silence. "Well, he didn't have an appointment with me and Danielle's branch is way out in the sticks, so it wasn't with her. I'll ask around and get back to you." He quickly got up from his chair, buttoning his suit jacket. Danielle shook her head in agreement, followed his lead and rose.

"Wait, no, where are you going? There's more," Muckiss said, staring at them with narrowed eyes. Both Teddy and Danielle settled back quickly into their chairs.

During this time, Dr. Place became distracted and started playing what looked like Angry Birds on his I-Phone. Rita stood to the side against the bar on the far right of the room, arms crossed, still as stone.

Muckiss continued. "We did some background checks on Schmidt. We have a copy of his passport from The Willard. He comes from Munich. No wife, no kids. He works for a chocolate manufacturer called Joseph Franz Industries. They're mostly known for their chocolate shops called Park

Avenue Chocolatiers. I'm sure you've seen them. We have a few here in the D.C. area. They have about 75 in America–one or two in every state–and about one hundred all over the world."

Teddy and Danielle exchanged glances. He gave a little shrug. She crossed her eyebrows. Of course, they had both heard of Park Avenue Chocolatiers. The chain started popping up around ten years ago. It quickly became the premier Chocolatier vying for Godiva's number one gourmet chocolate spot. In fact, there was even a Park Avenue Chocolatier in the high-end shopping mall that they could access through the bank lobby. Was he trying to link the murder and the bank?

"I'm sorry, old boy. I'm still not connecting the dots," Teddy said, and took a quick look at his watch intimating that time was running out and was late for something much more important than trying to help solve poor Wilhelm's murder.

"Neither am I," said Danielle sweetly, while in her mind she was frantically trying to fit this all together.

"So there's no banking relationship with anyone or the company that you know of then?" asked a slightly frustrated Special Agent Peter.

"No, no," both Teddy and Danielle said simultaneously. She wondered if Dr. Place still associated her with the old international side of the bank, and that's why they called her into this meeting. She speculated that since she and Teddy were the only legacies remaining, maybe they could be of some help. Although they weren't adding much value to poor Special Agent Peter's investigation, it was certainly flattering being considered a "historian" for the bank. She felt this signaled the end of the meeting and quietly exhaled. She bent down to grab her purse, which she had placed on the floor next to her chairs, but before she reached it, she heard Muckiss give a little cough.

"There's one more thing," Special Agent Peter said as he reached inside his other breast pocket and pulled out a piece of paper. "We also found another address in a small pocket of his suit jacket." He looked down to read it a few seconds to build suspense. "30 Cooper Street, West Mendow, Maryland."

Silently freaking out, Danielle knew the party was over. She felt her cheeks get red. The room was getting hot.

Special Agent Peter looked up from his notes. Scanning the faces in the room, his eyes finally rested on Danielle. Dr. Place peered over his phone. Teddy straightened his back and turned. Rita, the human stone statue, uncrossed her arms, tilting her head slightly. They were all glaring at her.

"Does anyone know who's address that is?" taunted Special Agent Peter, keeping his eyes locked on Danielle.

Realizing she had to say something, she cleared her throat and said, "Yes, that's my branch address." It hit her at that moment that Special Agent Peter Muckiss knew all along where the conversation was leading. She made a mental note not to underestimate him.

Meanwhile, Teddy looked relieved, like his mistress' address was still a secret.

"So why don't you try a little harder to connect the dots," he replied in a most menacing tone.

If Bill Smith wasn't very dead at that moment, Danielle would have killed him herself. She felt like she was being sucked into a black hole. The guy's disappearance was a giant question mark over twenty years ago, and now the major clue to his murder just landed on her doorstep. She didn't need to connect the dots. She knew last Friday. Money and murder. Before he disappeared, he told her to drop it. But he brought it full circle by appearing again right in her backyard. What did he want? The jerk. Now he got himself killed, leaving her address as the only evidence - dumping this old nightmare back in her lap.

Her thoughts were to make a mad dash to the door, jump into her car, screech out of the parking lot and get on the next plane to Aruba. Unfortunately, real-life doesn't work that. She played it cool. Remembering the four "D's", she did what every senior banker in the hot seat would do in a situation like this - deflect, distract, deny, delay.

Starting with what she wanted them to think was obvious, Danielle stated calmly. "I'm sure you're thinking I know everything that goes on in my branch–which I should–but I don't. Maybe the guy was going to open a store in West Mendow and spoke to one of my service officers who convinced him to open an account with us. He may have simply been on his way to do the paperwork. I can easily check on that and settle this all quickly." Danielle knew that was a stupid explanation. Who would want to open a high-end Chocolate boutique in the middle of West Mendow where a night out at Phil's All You Can Eat Crab Cakes and Rib is considered fine dining?

At that point, Dr. Place joined the fun, hoping to move the meeting along. It was time to get rid of Special Agent Peter Muckiss, who was taking up way too much of his morning and ruining his chances to finish 18 holes before the cocktail hour. Danielle, who by that time was barely breathing, looked up to see him glaring at her.

"Danielle," he said with a slight growl in his voice, "can you please rack your brain and try to remember any relationships you had with any Germans or German companies. If you think of one or someone in your branch can remember something, call our friend here and let me know. This bank should not be in the middle of any international intrigue. We got out of the business a long time ago, just for this reason. No international messes. Just American messes." Getting off his chair, he repeated, "Only American messes."

"Here, here," Teddy echoed, causing Danielle to roll her eyes while letting out a quiet moan.

Addressing Dr. Place, she said with assurance, "I'll go back, ask around, and let you and the FBI know one way or the other." Inwardly she would rather do nothing of the sort but be lying on the white sand of Manchego Beach in Aruba for the next couple of weeks until this whole thing blew over. But that would look way too suspicious.

"Teddy, you do the same. Ask around downstairs. Maybe someone heard something and they don't know who to tell."

Teddy cringed. Danielle mused to herself that this new directive meant that he had to talk to the "regular folk". He may need therapy after this.

"Agent Muckiss," Dr. Place continued, standing with both hands leaning on his desk like he was all-business, "Are there any other details you want to share with us that could help jar the old grey matter around here or have you told us all you know so far."

"No, that's about it," replied Muckiss, snapping his notebook shut and putting it away. "We contacted the German police to look into Schmidt's background, but they still haven't gotten back to us."

"Okay, then. Okay, then. As soon as you hear anything more, you know where to find us. Rita, can you escort our friend here to the reception area?"

Rita walked over to the door, all eyes following her, as usual. Muckiss made his way over, but then in Colombo-style, he turned to Place and said.

"Oh–yes, I just remembered. I'm going to leave some pictures with you all in case it helps when you ask around."

They all mumbled their "fine, fine, good, good thinking, yes do that," comments while he gave out the extra photos. Rita then escorted him quickly from the room.

Dr. Place sat back down, took out a handkerchief, and wiped some sweat from his forehead and watched both of them as Danielle looked down at her hands and Teddy kept picking at an imaginary piece of lint on his blue wide-stripe trousers. Danielle wondered if everyone was thinking what she was thinking–how were they going to get out of this one? They all knew who Wilhelm Schmidt was. They didn't even have to look at the picture. Who was going to break down first and admit it? It was a long couple of minutes until Rita returned to the office.

"Mrs. Kagan is watching to make sure he leaves the building." She announced as she entered the room. "Congressional's holding your Tee Time."

"Good," replied Dr. Place, getting up once again.

"He was an interesting fellow," Teddy mumbled. "Bit of a slime."

Both Teddy and Dr. Place laughed like they were twelve years old.

"Mucus. Slime. Good one, Teddy. Good one." Dr. Place chortled, wiping a laugh tear away from his eye.

Shaking her head, Danielle wondered about their sanity.

"You know, I don't think that's the last of him," Danielle said, ignoring the joke and laughter as she got up to leave. "We seem to be his only lead". She pulled down at her hip-hugging skirt and buttoned her very tailored jacket. She caught Rita out of the corner of her eye watching her and gave her a tiny smile.

Rita remained expressionless.

The men stood. Dr. Place waddled around his desk to shake hands and bid Danielle farewell.

"By the way, how's the old homestead?" he asked.

"Doing well. Can't complain. Don't worry, your fees are still pouring in, keeping Mrs. Place in diamond and furs for yet another year," she said with a smile. Mendow Enterprises was one of Capital National's largest accounts.

"This whole incident is quite unfortunate. My apologies for not giving you a heads up. It was the way he wanted to play it. Can't argue with the FBI. Didn't want Mucus-geez what a name - to think we weren't taking him seriously."

"No, that's okay. I'm a big girl. I was just a bit blindsided by this whole scene. It was the last thing I expected this morning," she said truthfully.

On that note, Dr. Place announced he was going to run to the little boy's room and then he and Teddy could head off to Congressional for a break from all this hard work. They made a halfhearted invitation to Danielle to join them for lunch and a few holes, and of course, she graciously declined.

"More time with these guys?" she thought to herself. She'd rather be dredging the Potomac River in her bare feet.

Place ordered Rita to field all his calls and let Dolores explain to the masses he was out on important legislative business on "The Hill". Suppressing a smile, he added, "Hey Teddy, isn't the third hole on a hill?"

More raucous laughter from the frat boys ensued.

Danielle wondered how anything got done around here. It was only 10:00 am. It was a relief to know these guys distracted easily and that in a few moments they would hopefully forget this total mess. She headed for the door.

Rita followed her out. Together, they scurried silently towards Dolores' desk. The spaceship was empty when they arrived.

Turning to Rita she asked, "Can you say good-bye?"

"I'm right behind you." Dolores croaked, standing there in a "glow in the dark" turquoise polyester museum-quality pantsuit that hung loosely on her 4'6" frame. How did Danielle miss that! "Don't worry" she continued impassively. "I made sure he left the building. He gave me the dead guy's picture to show around."

"So, have we seen him before?" Rita asked warily.

"Nope" she snapped back.

Danielle felt relieved. If anyone from the bank could remember him, it would be Dolores with that elephant memory of hers. But nobody was talking.

"Good" replied Rita sharply.

Danielle and Rita turned towards the elevator.

"But then again, something tells me I do," Dolores intoned while gazing at the picture.

Both Rita and Danielle stopped dead and looked at each other. Danielle was just about to turn around to go back when Rita gently took her arm and guided her toward the elevator.

"It was nice seeing you, Miss. Mendow. Make sure you get your parking ticket validated at the Reception Desk in the lobby. Have a nice day".

The elevator doors opened and Rita gave her a subtle little push to get in. Danielle thought the last thing she saw before the doors closed was Rita mouthing the words, "…and don't come back."

Chapter 6

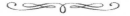

Nobody could make chocolate like Josef Franz. Legend had it that his recipe was so simple, yet so complicated, that anyone other than the creator could ever duplicate it. The ingredients, the order, and the mix were a trade secret worth millions. Supposedly, it was written only once and then locked in a vault in a bank in Switzerland, to which only Josef Franz had access.

Whenever Danielle went to headquarters, she would stop at Park Avenue Chocolatiers. They sandwiched the little shop between The Coach Store and Jimmy Choo's and part of the glamorous indoor Mall she had to pass through on her way to the underground parking garage.

While there, she would buy pounds of dainty little bonbons and beautifully designed chocolate bars that were as exquisite to look at as they were to eat. She would then show up at the branch with the pretty pink boxes wrapped in delicate lace, to which her staff would quickly fall all over themselves to grab at the contents. Jen would be at the center trying to control the chaos while stealing a few extras of everything for herself.

The ritual made Danielle the heroine of the day, while the extra sugar ingested during those afternoons always produced a peak in new business from her energized staff. Danielle knew what she was doing.

However, today, when she stepped through the door of the shop, her mind wasn't on how much chocolate she could load up on. Instead, she was trying to figure out the link between Bill Smith and Josef Franz. She thought a visit to the operation may provide some clues.

A soft chime followed as the door closed behind her. The intoxicating smell of sweet chocolate overcame her. Not a big candy lover herself, she couldn't help admiring the rows and rows of different shapes and sizes of chocolate that filled the glass cabinets. There were barrels of intricately decorated chocolate bars placed strategically throughout the floor. A step couldn't be taken without noticing something delicious.

The store was celebrating the fall with special Halloween and Thanksgiving-themed sweets, including a hot chocolate "to go" stand complete with marshmallows in a Josef Franz mug. Danielle started her study by giving the shop one overall grand scan. The style was very girlish - lighthearted and dainty. This was so not Bill Smith, who she rarely saw smile or even crack a joke. In fact, she never saw him eat anything other than greasy cheeseburgers and fries with an occasional knockwurst from a Sabrette cart. Why would he get involved in a business with which he couldn't identify? Maybe he knew working with some lightweight outfit like Josef Franz would throw everyone off his thieving trail? The connection was becoming the disconnect.

"Miss Mendow!" A young man wearing a crisp white tailored shirt and a pink bow tie cried out excitedly from behind the counter. They were forever excited to see her knowing that whenever she came, she always dropped a few "Benjamins".

Smiling back, she gave him a friendly but dismissive brief wave, embarrassed that she couldn't remember the cheerful boy's name. She turned away to scan the shop. Immediately, her eye caught a large framed wall-hanging with a banner that read, 'The Josef Franz Story–The man who changed chocolate forever." She walked over to inspect. A grainy black-and-white photo took up much of the poster. In it, a heavyset man who looked like he had eaten one too many chocolate bars stared joylessly into the camera. He stood, hands-on giant hips, blocking most of the view of a tiny store behind him. Danielle moved closer so she could read the caption. "Josef Franz in front of his first store in Munich, Germany circa 1928."

She read the rest of his history.

"Born 1898 in the small Bavarian town of Feldafing, Germany, Josef Franz began making chocolate with his mother at age 6. Passionate about the design of his chocolates and the flavor, his reputation spread quickly throughout the region. By the time he was sixteen years old, they nicknamed him "Das Kleine Chocolate Genie". They sent Josef to Le Cordon Bleu in Paris. He took the young cooking school by storm, upending the age-old tradition of chocolate-making. Upon graduation, he returned to Germany and settled in Munich, where a distant relative offered him an empty storefront in the heart of the city center.

Soon, Josef had a second store in Frankfurt, and a third in Vienna. He married Angela Parkauffnau, an up and coming young artist, who helped him create his now signature look of pink and white lace. In her honor, he renamed all the stores after her–Park Avenue Chocolatiers. Their son, Josef Jr. carried on the family business when his parents died tragically in a car accident on their way to a chocolate show in Brussels. Josef Jr. expanded the operation in Europe but it was his son, Josef Franz the third, who grew Park Avenue Chocolatiers into one of the most successful confectionery businesses in the world. Today, the franchise has over 225 shops in 32 countries and continues to expand as it makes chocolate lovers into loyal fans.

Danielle sighed in admiration for Josef Franz the third. She had a special place in her heart for wildly successful business people. The puzzle is coming together, she thought. Perhaps Josef Franz ran into Bill Smith somewhere, sometime right after 9/11, recruited him on the spot, showered him with tons of money, and handed him the keys to the international operations.

Would Bill bolt like that for money, she wondered? People do weird stuff when those Greenbacks are waved in front of them. After all, they tangled him up in a potential powder keg for losing $10 million dollars. Was that his ticket out? Hiding in the chocolate business? Did he even go as far as changing his name to Wilhelm Schmidt to cover his tracks? That's where the story gets murky. Will the FBI figure it all out? Still, what did it have to do with her?

The door chime rang softly in the background, signaling another customer had walked in. Danielle turned. It surprised her to see Rita Steele, whose figure looked like it never saw a piece of chocolate in its life, stroll up to the counter.

"Miss Steele!" the young man announced in the same excited voice he used with Danielle. "Today's my lucky day!" he exclaimed gleefully.

"Hello, Cove," Rita replied in her cool, deadpanned voice. Cove? Yes, Cove. That was it. Danielle pressed her lips together and wrinkled her nose, remembering he had one of those weird nature names.

As if she heard that, Rita stiffened like a cat who sensed a mouse behind her. She turned and stared directly at her.

"Danielle. I thought you were on your way." She said speaking to her like it was past her bedtime.

"I'm just picking up some chocolates for the staff," Danielle replied, joining her at the counter. "Cove," she coughed out, "can you box up the usual?"

"Right away, Miss Mendow" he answered, his eyes shifting to Rita for a split second. Danielle noticed Rita giving him a subtle nod before he disappeared in the back.

Danielle raised an eyebrow towards her and said in a low-pitched, polite voice. "That was an interesting meeting upstairs."

A look of annoyance passed over her features. "Waste of everybody's time," She replied, glancing sideways towards Danielle. "That FBI agent was overly melodramatic. I think he watches too much CSI."

Just about to voice her concurrence, Danielle felt her cell phone vibrate through her Louis Vuitton handbag. She unzipped it, reached in to turn it off, but noticed it was an incoming call from Jen. Looking at her watch, she feigned a moan, "Ah, the life of a branch manager. Excuse me, I've got to take this. I think it's overdraft approval time."

"A girl's gotta do what she's gotta do. Nice bag." Rita said with a wink and turned away.

While the young counter man furiously loaded big pink boxes full of chocolates and Rita browsed around, Danielle returned to the far corner of the shop to complete business with Jen.

"Pay it, Pay it, Pay it..." Danielle repeated about ten times. Jen was reading all the checks for clearing that were overdrawing their customers' accounts. Since Danielle knew most of her customers, she approved them all - feeling confident that their overdrafts would be covered. "So what else is happening there?" she asked when Jen finished with the list.

"Nothing exciting. The usual. But what happened to you? We're all dying! Why did they call you in?" Jen said eagerly.

Danielle wanted to give her the lo-down, but preferred doing it in private. "It's a long story. I'll call you from the car in a few minutes. As soon as he fills the boxes, I'll be hitting the road."

"The Boxes! Oh, You're at Park Avenue Chocolates! Everyone was hoping you'd remember."

"Of course!" Danielle replied, letting out a short laugh. "You know, I'd never let you all down. See you soon." She was just about to push the call ended button when she heard Jen say, 'Wait.' Danielle put the phone back to her ear. "What's up?" she asked, furrowing her eyebrows.

"Yeh, sorry. I'm in the back and I forgot all about this. There's one more thing. There's some guy that wants to speak with you and he said he would not leave until he saw you today."

"What does he want? Can't anybody else help him?" Danielle asked. Ugh, one of "those", she thought to herself. She was hoping to take a momentary diversion through Coach and Jimmy Choo's on her way out, but if she couldn't shake this guy, she'd have to go straight back to the branch.

"I don't know. He said he only wanted to speak to you. We told him you would not be back for a while if at all, but he wouldn't leave. He said if you called in to let you know."

"Do I know him?" Danielle asked with a slight annoyance in her voice.

"I've never seen the guy before. He's very insistent, but in a nice way. In fact, he's kind of cute. You know, Tom Cruise-like Mission Impossible 2."

"He looks like Tom Cruise? Seriously?" Danielle replied, raising her voice in disbelief. Jen knew how to get her back quickly. "Well, I'll be there in a flash. Tell him to wait." Chuckling to herself, she put the phone back in her handbag. When she looked up, she saw Rita glaring at her wild-eyed.

"What's up?" Danielle asked, returning her stare while wondering how Rita could hold such a peculiar expression.

Rita quickly looked away. "Nothing. I just remembered I have to be somewhere in a few minutes and haven't placed my order. Cove, Cove, look here. Can you put together the usual for Dr. Place? He's having a luncheon tomorrow and wanted something special for his guests."

Before Cove could answer, Rita exploded out of the shop as evidenced by the sound of a frantic door chime enveloping the room. Peering through the window, Danielle watched as she practically sprinted down the Mall's still empty corridor–still hearing her heels clacking intensely on the marble floor until she vanished around a corner.

Cove and Danielle exchanged glances and shrugged. Shaking his head, he said, "That lady's a walking Tsunami." Catching his breath like he was completely exhausted, he continued. "Okay, Miss Mendow, I'm almost done here. I just need to put the boxes in some shopping bags and you can be on your way."

Still thinking about Rita, Danielle marveled at how people in high places could get away with acting so strange. This morning's meeting was a case in point. Meanwhile, she paid a giddy and demonstrably overjoyed Cove, who now made his quota so early in the morning, and added a $20.00 tip for the strenuous work he just performed. Although the mystery of Bill Smith wasn't solved after her visit to Park Avenue Chocolatiers, a gut feeling was telling her she may have gotten a little closer.

Chapter 7

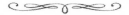

Danielle sped out of the Capital National parking garage using the K Street exit. She couldn't wait to get out of Washington D.C. and back to her bucolic West Mendow. She tried every side street to get to the George Washington Memorial Parkway quickly, but the traffic was not cooperating and unusually heavy for mid-morning. It frustrated her. There was so much to think about, but she had to focus on them to avoid hitting some idiot on a scooter or running into a sleepy bus driver. Luckily, as soon as she was off the Parkway and on to the Beltway, the road opened and she floored it to make up for the lost time.

She lowered her window and unleashed the sunroof. The cool fall air filled the car, replacing the trapped city heat from this morning. The bright sun blinded her momentarily, reminding her to put on her Prada sunglasses. The office drama of the day deserved some mindless karaoke, so she popped a "Best of Motown" CD in her console and tried to ignore how agitated she was.

The soft coo of Diana Ross singing "Some Day, we'll be together" brought her thoughts back to Bill Smith. She supposed there was a reason he left Germany and resurfaced. But why now? What was he doing during the last decade? The old-timers from Capital Bank New York still brought it up at alumnae gatherings. It was still a story for the ages–even today. After a few drinks, someone would inevitably start the mystery questions and conspiracy theories. It would go on and on. "Anyone hear from Bill? "Whatever happened to Bill? I heard there was a Bill spotting in Tanzania?" And so on. In the end, they all agreed he must have either been hit by a truck or was sitting on an island somewhere sipping margaritas and quietly managing people's offshore accounts.

"Now, this all could be a coincidence" she thought as Gladys Knight was hearing it through the Grapevine. "Bill could have been in town to catch up with some old friends and just the met wrong psycho in the lobby." But it was the name change that still bothered her. When was the FBI going to catch on?

The more she thought about it, the more troubled she felt. "Where's the money, Bill? I bet you knew where it went all along–you old coot," she muttered to herself.

"And why were you dragging my branch into this?" she asked the steering wheel. "Were you reaching out to me?"

Easing on to River Road exit from I-495, she leaned on the Mercedes' pedal with a little more gas, enjoying the circular ramp with some good old six-cylinder traction. Checking her rearview and side-view mirrors for cops, she cranked up Diana Ross singing "Ain't no Mountain High Enough" hit the gas a little harder and started up the long single lane road that would take her home. It was clear sailing up ahead as she drove towards the sleepy center of Potomac. Gorgeous mansions graced both sides of the road, and she loved how each one was a marvel in its architectural originality. Politicians, titans of industry, and celebrities have addresses in Potomac and it's not unusual to be in the local hardware store with astronauts, cabinet members or NBA stars buying paint or plumbing parts. The quiet elegance of this part of the drive calmed her down, and she turned off the music to commune with her favorite and more comfortable surroundings.

All would have been well if that black Ford SUV behind her would disappear.

Danielle had half an eye on that car since the George Washington Memorial Parkway. It never left her tail. Not a paranoid person, she was, nonetheless, highly sensitized about events since the morning meeting. Little things seemed significant.

Once passed the speed cameras, she hit the max. Not that it bothered her. She enjoyed giving the Benz some exercise. But the strong wind from the open windows created a deafening wind tunnel in the car. Her carefully coifed hair of the morning was blowing all over her face, making it hard for her to see. It wasn't worth it. She closed the windows while monitoring the rearview mirror.

The Ford kept up. It was about two car lengths behind her. She tried to get a look at the driver through the darkly tinted windows, but couldn't see anything. The car was creeping her out.

Danielle had reached the point where River Road became less populated with homes and thick with trees. Here, the lanes get narrower, more winding and hilly. It's a race car driver's dream when it's empty, but when there's a tailgater it's nerve-wracking.

She tried to keep her eyes on the road ahead. She sped up. The Ford SUV stayed right with her. She slowed. The Ford slowed down with her. She put more pressure on the gas. The black Ford was right behind her.

"This is insane!" she thought, as she gripped the steering wheel tighter to keep control of the car. The Ford didn't let up. She was finding it hard to concentrate on the road. She punched her Bluetooth.

"Capital National Bank, West Mendow Branch. Have you considered refinancing your home today? This is Eddie. How may I help you?"

Eddie sounded like he had too much of her coffee and a handful of Prozac that morning. Danielle didn't expect that anyone would refinance their house after hearing that and made a note to have Eddie reprogrammed to sound like he was in his right mind. Meanwhile, she needed to speak to Jen.

"Eddie, its Danielle. Is Jen around? I need her right away." She said with urgency, keeping one eye on the Ford.

"Sure! Everyone can't wait to hear about..." Eddie said eagerly.

Danielle took a deep breath to restrain herself from making a tasteless comment, then said sharply, "Eddie, no time for talking. I need Jen now!"

"Okay, okay. Hold on, let me find her." He put her on hold where she had to listen to a hideous viral loop of the innumerable glorious reasons to bank with Capital National. The universe could have been swallowed into a black hole by the time Jen picked up with her usual "Yo" greeting.

"Eddie needs rehab," Danielle said, her eyes darting back and forth from her rearview mirror to the road ahead.

"You called to tell me that?" Jen answered. "It's kinda busy here. Can we discuss Eddie another time?"

"No, listen. I'm on River Road, about five miles from the West Mendow. I'm doing 65 mph in a 50 mph zone and there's a big black Ford that's been on my butt since Virginia. I think it's following me," Danielle said breathlessly.

Silence.

"Jen, you still there? I said I think I'm being followed," Danielle repeated slower and louder to make sure Jen heard her better this time.

Jen let out a burst of laughter. "Are you serious?"

"Yes, I'm serious" Danielle shouted into her dashboard.

"Okay, calm down. Is it like a good following you? Like George Clooney in a convertible? Or is it like a bad following you like Larry the Cable Guy in a pickup?" Jen asked with a hint of amusement in her voice.

"You're not taking me seriously. It looks like some kind of government car." She said nervously.

"Why would a government car be following you?" Jen asked. Danielle could just see her suppressing a smile.

"It's a long story." She answered wearily.

"Okay, I'm busting a gut to hear it, but I really have to go unless you want me to embarrass myself and call the cops for you or something."

Danielle glanced in the rearview mirror. The black Ford was weaving frantically behind her.

"Can you just stay on the phone with me? The car is acting strangely now. Its flashing its brights."

"And how many years have you been driving? It sounds like the car behind you is doing everything it can to pass you up. Are you road hogging again?" Jen asked with a note of annoyance.

Closing her eyes for a split second, Danielle admonished herself. Of course! That's what it is! What was I thinking? "Okay, I'm an idiot," she said peevishly.

"No comment. Gotta go," Jen blurted, and the line went dead.

Danielle slowed down, put on her right side blinker, and drove on the shoulder. Without skipping a beat, the Ford sped passed her and disappeared around a turn.

"I'm losing it," Danielle thought to herself. Although the Ford disappeared and the driver was obviously some jerk, her heart continued to race as she pulled out on to the road. The loud booming ringtone of the Bluetooth startled her. It was Jen again. She punched the "ok" button to answer.

"Yo, is everything okay?" It was Jen, back on the line.

"Just as you said. It's gone." She said sheepishly while staring at the road. Nothing else looked suspicious.

"Do you still think someone was following you?" Jen asked like she was talking to one of her kids.

"Okay. Stop patronizing me. I know you think I'm crazy, but it been a strange morning." She said with a nervous laugh. "Can you hold down the fort till tomorrow? My head's about to explode. I'm going to head home. I'll bring the chocolates tomorrow. I'm going to stop by Sheila's and pick up a double tuna salad sandwich."

"Whoa. A double tuna. Hey, you are really shaken up," Jen laughed.

"That's an understatement," thought Danielle. An old colleague shows up dead in D.C. The FBI drags her into it, which is not a good sign. That Muckiss character makes a dramatic show of finding her address on Smith's dead body. Then he grills her about it in front of her Chairman while that twit, her arch-enemy, Teddy Hudd, is just sitting there gloating in her embarrassment. Rita Steele, her idol, who she's never witnessed out of control, becomes totally unhinged in a chocolate shop. A black Ford with intimidating tinted windows and beef with her driving was perilously stalking her brand new C30 on the way home. And she didn't want to stop and think about that crazy bat, Dolores, who sends shivers down her spine when she hears that croak she calls an excuse for a voice.

"As I said, it's a long story. Hard to describe," she murmured.

"Hey, if you're not coming in, what do you want me to do with that cutey who's been waiting for you all morning?" Danielle had completely forgotten about him. As she began thinking of excuses, Jen suddenly announced she was off the hook. As they were speaking, she could see the guy holding a cell phone to his ear while rushing to his car, getting in and driving off.

"Too bad. You would have liked this one. Just your type," She said giggling. "Oh, not to change the subject, but you got a box from Zappos' and some other stuff this morning. I'll send Eddie to your house with your mail. He needs some air."

The mention of Zappos' made her feel better. "Those must be the red shoes we ordered a few weeks ago," said Danielle wistfully. Her other title was the self-ordained Closet Queen of Impulsive Mail-Order.

"Yeh, those shoes. I think so." Jen replied.

"Okay, good. I'm feeling better already," she confessed.

"I thought that would do it," Jen answered cheerfully. "We're done." The phone disconnected.

Danielle's anxieties eased a bit. To further calm herself, she kept her mind tuned to silly thoughts about where in West Mendow she could possibly ever wear a pair of three-inch BCBGMaxMara red snakeskin open-toe ankle strap shoes. Her heartbeat slowed, and she breathed easier as she drove a steady 45 miles per hour until she reached Cooper Street.

Sheila's Café was at the end of town on the main drag. Slowing down to a crawl to obey the 25 mph speed limit, Danielle, who rarely noticed these days, cheerfully soaked in the familiarity of Cooper Street with its dated little strip malls, restaurants, and two-story office buildings. She passed Old Ned who was turning off the hose on the side of his Deli probably getting more water to make his disgusting coffee. A little further down, she saw Mimi standing outside her "spa" smoking a cigarette and picking tobacco leaves off her tongue. Such a class act. She passed two local farmers eating a hot dog while filling up at Pedro's Petrol and Auto Body's Shop. For the zillionth time, she told herself how good it was to be home.

Her shoulders loosened. She was back in the world she built and knew would protect her.

Stopping at the only red light in town, she watched a man in a dark suit and sunglasses walking in front of her car to cross the street. The morning jitters came back for a millisecond until she realized it was just Henry Grimaldi, the owner of Grimaldi's Funeral Home. He gave her his signature spooky smile as he strolled by without a care in this world. She shuddered and quickly took off when the light turned green.

Located in a cute little white Victorian house, Sheila's Cafe was probably a showpiece in its day. It was just about to collapse when her old classmate and former West Mendow High School all-star wrestler, Sheila Duvette, bought it and approached Danielle with a business plan to turn it into a sandwich place by day and bar by night. It was a big hit with the out of towners who were passing through and looking to stop for a bite at a place that was "country quaint".

Danielle parked out front, walked into the little restaurant greeting everyone like she owned the town, which she did, and ordered, knowing exactly what the doctor would have prescribed. She caught up with some local gossip with Sheila while grabbing a giant bag of potato chips and a diet coke. She handed a twenty-dollar bill to the cashier, told him to keep the change, then headed home. The double tuna was talking to her and telling her to 'eat me now' so she didn't want to waste time contemplating the universe while meandering the back roads. This time around, she took the shortest route. Left, two miles, right two miles, and left on her street, Beatrice Lane. She always got a kick out of seeing her street sign. According to the alternate family lore, someone named Beatrice Lane after her great aunt Beatrice, who was allegedly conceived somewhere in the cornfields.

She turned right into her driveway- which in another town would have been zoned a small street. Beautiful old oak trees lined either side. Magnolias and Pines joined the party behind them.

Beyond them was a gently sloping hill covered with a well-tended lawn. Crabapples and dogwoods sprang up randomly everywhere to break the monotonous greens.

The driveway curved into a full circle in front of a magnificent 6500 square foot estate that was hidden behind the half miles of trees. In the middle of the circle stood a 12-foot replica of Shubin's marble statue of Catherine the Great in the guise of Minerva. The statue appeared to be rising from the depths of the ocean, but in reality, it was a white stone pond that, with the sun's reflection, gave Catherine an eerie glow.

Catherine the Great had been guarding this house from the time some paper rich tech guy bought it from a Saudi prince in the early nineties. But soon after purchase, the tech bubble burst and the market crashed. The house laid untouched and empty for a few years, resplendent in its gauche Middle Eastern Oil decor coupled with the bizarre taste of the dot.com ex-millionaire. Danielle had bought it for a song when she moved down from New York to West Mendow. They signed the deal while the tech guy was busy kissing her feet, having just been spared his fingernails being removed by a loan shark from Baltimore.

The three-story European villa-style home was high enough on the hill so that each of its fifty windows had stunning views of the fields and mountains that surrounded her 10-acre property. She was always in awe of what she could afford to own after moving from a 650 square foot one-bedroom in mid-town Manhattan.

She exhaled deeply as soon as she stopped the car in front of the house. She was at the finish line. She reached over, grabbed her lunch and trotted inside. The coolness of the marble entry quickly overpowered her as the anxiety and sweat that had drenched her from the emotional morning dissipated. Her only thought now was taking that first bite of her sandwich.

Chapter 8

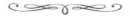

Peace, at last, she thought to herself as she threw her car keys and handbag down on the marble center hall. The clatter shattered the stillness of the massive foyer.

"Who there?" a voice yelled from the kitchen. Danielle turned to see her housekeeper, Eleni, emerge from the kitchen with a rolling pin raised above her head. Dressed in her usual all-black peasant skirt and blouse, she looked more frightening than any hoodlum lurking in a dark back alley.

"Put the rolling pin down Eleni. It's just me." Danielle answered calmly. Holding her lunch bag closer so Eleni wouldn't see it, she quickly walked passed her and went into the kitchen.

With nostrils flaring, Eleni stared as Danielle walked by her. In her broken English, she asked, "Oh, why you home now? Why you no at work, hon?"

Danielle didn't answer. Eleni followed her into her newly remodeled French country kitchen. Danielle caught her continuing to glare as she unloaded the bag on the white marble countertop.

"Ah! What is that?" Eleni shouted while staring

at the wrapped sandwich like it was rat poison.

"Tuna salad," replied Danielle sighing, waiting for the bomb to drop.

With hands-on-hips and the rolling pin dangling by her side, Eleni started her usual rant. For a woman in her seventies, she had the lungs and energy of a teenager. Her voice could make volcanoes erupt. "You hungry? You tell me. Why you eat garbage? I make you excellent food like roasted chicken, potatoes with lemon, spanakopita, moussaka. Those foods make good blood," Eleni admonished, bringing up the rolling pin and waving it at her while she talked.

"That's okay. I like Tuna salad," Danielle said lightly unwrapping her sandwich. She learned a long time ago not to react to Eleni's usual melodramatic tirades or it will never end. Greeks always like to have the last word, and so does she. Hopping on to a white leather-backed counter stool, she made herself comfortable and took a big bite, letting out a satisfied groan. "Better than drugs," she thought to herself.

In a dismissive wave, Eleni turned her back on her, checked to make sure her long gray braid was still in place around her head, and walked over to the farmer's sink where she stood there pouting, Danielle took another bite. It was so good. She watched Eleni continue to stand there, hands-on-hips like she was posing for the next cover of "Insulted Housekeeper Magazine."

The doorbell chimed Beethoven's Fifth, and she remembered that although it was less than half an hour since she last spoke to the branch, it was probably the "always eager to please the boss" Eddie dropping off her mail and the shoes. What a suck-up.

"Eleni, can you get the door?" Danielle said while struggling to open the giant bag of potato chips. She couldn't wait for that first taste of salt and grease.

Eleni skulked off. Danielle took another bite of her sandwich and stuffed a few potato chips in her mouth for added flavor. She sat chewing and snorting like a starving horse. She was in tuna salad heaven.

She heard a deep voice behind her. It was definitely not Eddie's whose voice was more in Tabernacle Land than planet Earth. She looked towards the kitchen door. Following a still petulant Eleni was a guy in a sweaty Georgetown Hoyas' T-shirt and black gym shorts. She looked around him, hoping to see Eddie with her shoes, but nobody was there. Eleni retreated to her spot by the sink and kept herself busy with some plant growing out of a paper cup.

"Ah, so this is the famous Danielle Mendow," he stared with a dumb smile.

Danielle kept chewing but managed to ask who he was without dropping food out of her mouth.

"Rake Harris. I just bought the house down the street. I was out for a run and saw you turn into your driveway. Thought I'd do the neighborly thing and drop in to introduce myself to the legend of West Mendow," he replied.

Tilting her head, she asked herself how she missed him. No mortgage? She always knows who's moving in and who's moving out. Must have been an all-cash deal. This was intriguing. Danielle did a quick analysis of her new neighbor. He was cute in a rumpled sort of way. Without the sweat and the day-old growth on his face, he could be almost good looking. There was a playful glint in eyes that seemed slightly Asian, but his olive-colored skin showed Mediterranean roots. He seemed like an outdoorsy kind of guy, weathered, and from the sharp muscle tones of his body, it looked like he did more than plant azaleas.

Another awestruck fan. Game on, she mused to herself.

Before she could say anything, Eleni turned to Rake and yelled across the expansive kitchen, "You eat? I make keftedes. Greek meatballs. Danielle doesn't like keftedes. Nobody eats them. She like to eat garbage."

"So why do you make them?" asked Rake falling into the Greek grandmother's food trap.

"Yes, the million-dollar question," Danielle said drolly rolling her eyes.

Rake declined respectfully. Eleni watched the two of them and announced in her broken English that she had to go iron something. She gave a not-so-discreet nod of approval to Danielle as she left the kitchen.

Danielle was sure he saw that. He seemed the type that missed nothing.

"Interesting lady. Related?" Rake asked.

"No, she's not. Just old-school and a pain in the butt. I let her live here because she drives her sons and daughter-in-laws crazy. They felt that one of them was going to one day "accidentally" push her into the Potomac. Thought I would spare the rescuers."

"Oh? Well, that's kind of you." Rake answered.

Good come back, thought Danielle. She sat up straighter. This was getting interesting.

"Not totally altruistic. She also keeps an expert eye on the house. Great with a rolling pin. They say she killed a man back in Crete with one. On top of that, she also uses it to roll out a mean filo dough," she said mischievously.

"A Renaissance woman. I knew I liked her," he said with a laugh.

He certainly was charming, she thought "So, what made you buy a place in West Mendow?" she asked, losing interest in her lunch and swiveling around to give him her full attention.

"Just retired. Change of pace from the D.C. chaos," he replied while running his hand through his curly salt and pepper hair.

"Ah, one of those D.C. guys who came out here to wash off the smell of city life, get healthy and plant a few tomatoes."

"Something like that." He said looking around. "Nice kitchen."

"Thanks. Just had it remodeled. The irony is that I hate to cook, and Eleni uses only one frying pan and one burner. Maybe one day, I'll read the instructions and figure out what all this stuff is that the designer insisted I put in for resale, even though I don't plan on going anywhere."

"Can't help you there. Can barely boil water. I do my best with a corkscrew," Rake replied, scratching his head like he was just as confused.

Rake went straight for the punch. She wondered if she should take that literally or figuratively. Danielle laughed a little longer and louder than usual, then realized she sounded like a giddy schoolgirl. She pulled herself back together.

"So, you bought Jeb Kreuger's old farm?" Sucker. He's been trying to unload that white elephant for years, she recalled.

"Hey - I'm not that crazy. I'm on the other side of you."

That threw her for a loop. And he paid cash? The house on the other side was on the market recently for close to three million dollars and just as big as hers. It was previously owned by a trust fund baby who used it as a secret love nest. One night his father caught him there drinking and carousing. The next morning, he was back in Daddy's basement and the house had a for sale sign in front.

Mr. Harris was becoming more appealing by the second.

"That's quite a house," she said, then dropped the bomb. "Your family must love it." Code word - 'You better not be married?'.

The dopey smile came back. He got it. They locked gazes. Unconsciously, she stopped breathing while waiting for the answer. Her heart started pounding a little faster and she couldn't control it. She hoped he couldn't hear it. He didn't answer right away. She wondered if that was deliberate, to keep her in suspense.

His head leaned to one side as he continued to stare at her as if he had to think about it. He finally replied with just the slightest smirk.

"No, it's just little ol' me and my dog Spike" he finally answered.

He had a disconcerting way of looking at her,

menacing and bemused at the same time. It kept her off balance while simultaneously electrifying her. She felt her cheeks getting hot. Uncrossing her legs, she hopped off her stool and smoothly pivoted towards the freezer pretending she needed ice. The last thing she wanted him to see was her blush.

"You know, my kitchen looks like it needs a facelift and since you already went through it, do you want to come by and give me a few pointers? Maybe I can hire that designer of yours and we can take appliance lessons together."

She smiled to herself. The icemaker plopped ice in her glass. He was grinning boyishly as she turned to respond. She started heating up again. She thought her ice was going to melt right there and then.

"Sure," she said a little too quickly.

"How about tonight? I can make some pasta and open a nice Merlot I picked up at a vineyard in Virginia the other day."

She opened her mouth to say 'yes', but before a sound came out she snapped it shut like a crocodile that just caught its prey. She wasn't sure. Would she seem desperate if she accepted right away? Wasn't she super busy doing nothing? Shouldn't she wait a few days to build suspense and excitement?

"Well?" he prompted, raising his eyebrows.

Before her brain could catch up with her mouth, she blurted, 'why not' hoping she didn't look too eager. Underneath it all, it thrilled her to be asked on a date. There weren't too many eligible prospects in West Mendow, and fortunately Rake seemed to land nicely in that category.

"Great!" he said with a broad smile. "Come by at 7. Hey–and I'm a casual guy. Nothing fancy, as you can probably tell," he said looking down at his shorts.

She followed his eyes in that direction for a second, felt her cheeks get warm again, then quickly looked away, pretending to be in search of something. "Can I bring anything? Keftedes?" She said with a laugh.

"No, just your pretty smile. Oh–and you can leave that glob of mayonnaise that's hanging off your chin at home." He turned around and strolled out.

Danielle ran to the mudroom off the kitchen where she knew there was a full-length mirror. She was horrified. Not only was there a huge blob of mayonnaise on her face, but her silk Chanel blouse was full of potato chip crumbs. Maybe that nod of approval from Eleni was really a sign to clean up. She could never understand that lady. No wonder her daughter-in-laws rued the day she landed in this country.

Despite her slovenliness, Rake still found something to like about her so the full picture couldn't have been all that bad. She made her way back to the kitchen, reminded herself she had to squeeze into a pair of Ralph Lauren jeans tonight, and wrapped up the rest of her sinful sandwich.

"There are other ways to manage stress than pigging out on a tuna sandwich" she chided herself. She set off, dashing out of the kitchen towards the marble foyer which led to the winding staircase. She was heading for her bedroom where she could change into some gym clothes. She resolved to put the morning's events out of her mind and focus on a hopefully enchanting evening with her new neighbor.

On her way through the expansive foyer, she noticed a large box with some mail on the round mahogany table which adorned the middle.

Eddie must have dropped off her shoes and the other mail while she was talking to Rake, she thought to herself. She walked over to the table to take the box of shoes upstairs and noticed that one piece of mail was a large 8 X 12 envelope with no return address marked private and confidential.

The handwriting was small, and the postmark was from D.C. It was very light and bulged a little on the bottom.

"Hmm. What's this?" she thought and started opening it. Out dropped a blue and silver flash drive, the size of a BIC cigarette lighter. "That's it?" she thought, turning it around in her hand. She peered inside the envelope for anything else. All she could see was a small white piece of paper folded in half. It was a note. She pulled it out and read it.

"Danny, you would know what to do with this. Take care, Bill."

She took another look at the flash drive. The morning panic returned as she read the note again. Her hand went to her mouth as she drew in a breath. It's not every day someone gets a message from the dead.

Chapter 9

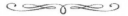

A loud trill exploded from the red leather Coach handbag that she had thrown on the hall table earlier. It scared the hell out of her for a second until she realized it was just her cuckoo parrot ringtone from her cell phone. Danielle was in no mood to answer it, so she continued to let it shriek while she tried to concentrate on the note. She read it several times, still confused. It was impossible. Why now? The screeching seemed to get louder, distracting her. She reached into her bag, fumbling for the phone to see who was bothering her at this very critical moment. She snorted when she looked at the caller I.D. Her eyes rolled. Who else, of course, but Jen.

"What?" she answered gruffly, not bothering with all the greeting pleasantries.

"Oh, okay. One of those afternoons." Jen replied lightly. "Let me guess, you are with the man of your dreams and I'm interrupting a juicy moment?"

"No, on the first and later on the second," Danielle answered, taking a deep breath while calmly turning the flash drive around and around in her hand. Jen didn't deserve the antagonism. Bill did, for dragging her into some tangled plot - but he was dead.

"Well, I just wanted to let you know that even though I thought you were nuts this afternoon, I kept an eye out for a black SUV with D.C. plates and there happens to be one sitting in our parking lot. Okay, see ya!" she blurted and hung up.

Danielle, of course, called her right back.

"I knew that would get your attention," Jen said. Danielle could just picture her smirking.

"Is anyone in the car?" Danielle asked, forgetting about the flash drive.

"Not that I can see. The windows are tinted."

"Can you get the plate number?" Danielle asked, her heart pounding.

"Done. You underestimate me." Jen deadpanned.

"Good. Keep an eye out for the driver. I'm jumping in the car right now. I need to see it for myself."

Danielle threw the flash drive in her purse and ran for the door. As she maneuvered into the driver's seat, she saw Eleni yelling something in a frenzy from the doorway about her tuna sandwich and meatballs.

"No time, no time" she yelled back waving off the hysterics. She put the car in drive, pressed hard on the gas pedal, and sped down the long driveway. She made a left at Beatrice Lane heading for the branch barely missing Rake Harris who was jogging home.

To make doubly sure she hadn't knocked him off the road, she glanced back in her rearview mirror. It relieved her to see he was still upright. But that's not all she saw. Along the run, he had also taken his T-shirt off displaying a well-toned chest that gleamed brightly in the afternoon sun. "Man, o' man" she muttered to herself, staring a few seconds too many and driving right passed the turn to Cooper Street. She swore it was the sun's glare, not the six-pack abs that blinded her.

"Well, that was embarrassing," she thought to herself as she realized she lost a minute or two during that bit of maneuvering. "Now he must really think I'm an idiot." She smiled to herself remembering the mayonnaise. Although she could fill Yankee Stadium with her ego, she never took herself too seriously especially with getting a man. If it happened, it happened…, as long as she wanted it to.

But back to business. Danielle cleared her mind so she could focus on driving. Her eyes kept shifting from the road to the speedometer so she could be sure she was driving just under 35 miles per hour–the silly town speed limit. The last thing she needed after blowing the turn was getting stopped by her nemesis, Officer Joe, the jerk who could smell her speeding from miles away. Now that was a classic love-hate relationship. He loved her and she hated him. It was a long story dating back to a misunderstanding in High School. The trouble was that he had a single-minded memory like an elephant savant and just couldn't let go. Not that she didn't take advantage of it occasionally which to her amusement just grated on Sally Kingsley's nerves–the foolish girl from Spanish class that he eventually married. She shook the random thoughts of Sally and Joe from her mind as it was distracting her from the task at hand–discovering why the menacing black SUV ended up in her parking lot in West Mendow.

She reached Cooper Street, took a right and within minutes was pulling into her parking lot hoping to see the Black Ford SUV. There was no sign of the car.

She pounded her fists on the steering wheel in frustration. "Damn" she cried out to nobody. "It took me only seven minutes to get here!" She gripped the top of the wheel and laid her forehead on her hands pressing her eyes closed.

It was only 2:00 pm and Danielle felt an entire week had passed since this morning. The ghost of Bill Smith kept getting closer and closer. Agent Muckiss would find out in a day or two that Wilhelm Schmidt was really an ex-Capital National banker, Bill Smith. Once that happened, he was going to ask questions about him that she was sure would eventually lead to his rather abrupt departure. Then, if there's an iota of a brain in his head, he would start asking former colleagues (she being one of them) about him and the missing money and her alleged role in it will come forth.

A knock on her driver's side window startled her. She looked up to see Jen's goofy face staring intently at her.

"Are you alright?" she asked, mouthing the words.

Danielle rolled down the window. "I drove here like I was competing in Le Mans to see who was in that car. What happened to it?" she asked accusingly like it was Jen's fault that the Ford SUV disappeared. She continued glaring at her as if she should have blocked the driveway so it couldn't escape.

Jen studied her curiously like it was the first time she had ever met her. A puzzled look came over her face. Speaking slowly and evenly she said, "I don't know. It was here one minute then gone the next. And no, I didn't see anybody. And no, we don't have cameras outside the building much to everyone's surprise and shock."

Danielle understood Jen was mocking her and was speaking to her like she had processing problems. She took a deep breath. "At least you have the plates. You do have the plates, right?"

"Yes, I said I had the plates," Jen rolled her eyeballs.

Although Danielle had no idea what to do with

"the plates" information, this one piece of the puzzle somehow calmed her. She turned off the engine and opened the door to get out.

"You're coming in? Are you sure? Maybe you should go home and rest. The branch is dead. You won't have anything to do. We can call you if we need you, but I don't think we'll need you today. No, probably not. We're good. We're good. Fully staffed." Jen said cheerfully and all too quickly.

She thinks I'm cracking up, Danielle thought to herself. On the other hand, the offer sounded good. After all, she had to get ready for her big dinner with Rake and there was a lot of prep in the beauty column to be checked off. Then she remembered the flash drive.

"Actually, I've got something to show you." She said reaching over to grab her purse.

Jen stepped back. "Is it dead or alive?"

"Don't be silly," Danielle playfully scolded, getting out of her car.

Jen looked her up and down as they walked towards the door. "Don't take this wrong, but you look a bit of a mess." She said pointing to a stain on her blouse. She then reached over to brush off some crumbs stuck in her suit. "And there's goo on your face." Jen continued pointing to her own chin.

Danielle started wiping it off. "My hair? Is that okay?"

Without skipping a beat, Jen asked, "Uh, was it caught in a tower fan oscillating on high?"

"Funny," Danielle answered through a tight mouth and squinting eyes.

"You may want to fix yourself up before you go in," Jen said as politely as she could, trying not to set her off.

"No, I'm good," Danielle answered, buttoning her jacket and running her hand through her hair. "Better?" she asked, looking hopefully at Jen.

"Um. Just walk quickly and wave like the Queen when we get in and head for the drive-through. Nobody will notice. We'll lock ourselves in and you can show me what you've got. I'll go first."

Danielle entered the branch a few seconds later expecting a barrage of questions about the morning, but her staff was very busy either surfing the net or yapping on the phone. Nobody even noticed her. Any other day she would have been highly insulted. Today, she was relieved just to reach the other end of the branch without turning heads. She passed behind the tellers, who were occupied proofing or away from their stations. She entered the kitchen, which was unusually empty, then opened the door to the drive-through. Jen was waiting for her and closed the door as soon as she walked in.

Wearing her best Mommy face, Jen patted the

high chair next to her, signaling for Danielle to sit.

The Drive-Through teller room was in the back of the branch. It held a long bar height desk cluttered with papers, tickets, pens, check separators, and bowls of candy. The tellers sat on high stools while servicing customers through a large window with tubes and sliding drawers that faced out on two pretty Victorian homes. Three drive-through lanes separated the bank from this charming old neighborhood of West Mendow. Danielle was proud of the view. It took quite a bit of money to improve aesthetics. When she first became the manager of the branch, the homes in this part of town were dilapidated and ready to be condemned. Her Mendow Foundation bought the eyesores and renovated them to ensure the branch was surrounded by an attractive area. She wanted her customers to have something pleasant to look at while they were doing their bank business. Of course, the Foundation also rents them out, bringing in a nice chunk of change from the young professional families that like to live close to town. After all, business is business.

Jen spun around in her chair to face her. "Insanity does not become you," she began. "I will not allow you to escape this room until you tell me what is going on in that twisted little brain of yours today. And be fast. I have to balance and get to a little league game before my eight-year-old calls social services and asks to be adopted."

Danielle lowered her eyes.

"Are you silently praying for some customers to come through so you could delay starting the story?" Jen asked with nostrils flaring.

But this was one of those rare occasions where there wasn't a soul around. The only action outside seemed to be a couple of squirrels scampering up a nearby oak tree. They both watched as some light paper danced by, twirling with the fall breezes.

The warm afternoon sun suddenly peeked out from behind a passing cloud, brightening the little area where Jen spent most of her day. This was Jen's home away from home. Danielle knew Jen loved this private enclave because in a few hours she would be in the middle of a circus at home. To Danielle, this area felt like she was in jail. She looked around and shivered. The room was claustrophobic.

"How can you stay in this place so long?" she asked.

"I like it back here. You like it out there. You are changing the subject." Jen responded even-toned.

"You're a mind reader," Danielle answered, tapping her head with her index finger. They worked together for many years.

"Enough stalling. Start spilling the beans."

Danielle took a deep breath. "Well, I've always described my days in New York as if they were the best times of my life... and they were... to a point." She stared out the window. "But, it ended badly."

"I know, I know. 9/11 drove you out. It was horrible. Blah, Blah. You and the rest of the world."

"Do you want to hear the story or do you want to make stupid comments to an empty drive-through?" Danielle shot back.

"Sooorrrry," Jen said. "Go on."

"Well, remember that guy who was killed in D.C. on Friday that you said reminded you of your Uncle Phil?"

"He was your boyfriend?" Jen said incredulously.

"Ew. No." Danielle replied, scrunching her face like she was smelling rotten fish. "He was a colleague at Capital Bank in New York."

"Oh. So he worked at the bank. Wow. Like, so what?"

She preceded by telling her how he had moved the operation out of New York right after 9/11 but in the process misplaced $10 Million dollars. Then, before he could find it, the Chairman ordered him to shut the place down.

Jen's mouth fell open. Here was a woman who wouldn't let anyone go home unless they were balanced to the penny. "What happened to him?" she asked.

"He disappeared. 'Poof'! The next time I heard about him, he was lying dead on the floor in a room at the Willard Hotel with two bullet holes in his stomach."

"Man o' man," Jen said softly, nodding her head back and forth while Danielle nodded her head up and down. A customer drove up to make a deposit. Neither of them noticed until she got their attention by lightly tapping on her horn. They both jumped.

While Jen took care of the lady, Danielle replayed the morning in her mind. When she was with Capital Bank International, it wasn't the General Manager who would come to D.C. to meet with senior management but Bill Smith. He would visit, shake some hands, and give some reports. If so, how on Earth could she be the only one who remembers him? She was sure Teddy Hudd knew him as well as John Place. Even Dolores, who forgets nothing, was going to recognize him if she hasn't already. So why was everyone playing dumb... like her?

The woman drove off. Jen swiveled back around to face Danielle. "Go on," she said, giving her full attention again. Before Danielle could speak, Jen added, "So you think he took the money?"

"Well, that didn't take you long. It looked kind of obvious to me, but I'm not sure," she answered truthfully. "Nobody really dug into it."

"Come on. You tell the story like you think he did it. If it wasn't him, who else could it have been?"

"I don't know. Something just never smelled right with the timing of the events."

"Why?" she asked, grabbing a Snickers bar and unwrapping it.

"Because It's just too obvious," Danielle answered.

Jen threw her hands up in an over-exaggerated gesture of exasperation.

"No, hear me out. On September 11, the payment systems of all the banks in New York were in a downward spiral. You remember, they shut down. Only a few banks managed to get them back up and operating after the Twin Towers collapsed. There was a lot of confusion and meltdowns, to say the least, that day. One of the best-kept secrets of the financial district was that when the dust settled, some big banks were completely out of balance. The public still doesn't know the extent of the damage but let's put it this way, the entire system was teetering off a cliff for a few days. And you just can't shut off the payment system like the stock market. You've got to keep going. It took weeks for the banking system to straighten everything out, but there were rumors that during that time people were taking advantage of the chaos."

Jen swallowed. "I've been with the bank since high school–before 9/11 but I never really knew the full story of what happened at Capital Bank that day. Were we one of the good guys or did we blow it too?"

Danielle answered. "We were high-fiving each other for days because Bill had the off-site fired up and running like a space station within hours. He reported that we could account for every dollar."

"But that wasn't true, right? Money was missing. When did they find this out?"

Danielle looked out the drive-thru window as if she was watching a movie replaying the past. "Bill was out on one of his many business trips and Compliance sent a team to do a surprise audit, which is standard in the business. They couldn't balance the Foreign Exchange General Ledger account–there were one too many $10 Million debits to credits. They tore the place inside out, looking for all the instructions to match up. After a week they realized one was a duplicate payment."

"Whoa! A duplicate payment? How do you duplicate a $10-Million-dollar payment?" Jen replied excitedly.

"It happens more often than you would think," Danielle said, turning to her. "Don't forget, there are over $100 trillion dollars that fly around the world every day. That day, the heart of the financial system was imploding. Anything was possible."

Danielle returned her gaze to the window, hoping the quiet view would help her remember every detail. Jen watched her, absorbed by the new information.

She continued. "Here's where it becomes a little complicated, so try to follow me. The duplicate was made to a small new trading partner in Munich– Der Rhiner Bank, with further credit to some mining company. Now, the original instruction came from one of our oldest correspondents– National City Bank in Dublin. It looked good, but it was a straight foreign exchange transaction without further credit. The second instruction from National City Bank in Dublin looked good as well, so we paid little attention to it, so they moved on. The auditors weren't really experts in payments, so it wasn't a surprise that they were struggling with this. It wasn't until one of them whose mother worked in one of the German Banks and knew the lingo from stories around the kitchen table who finally spotted the problem."

"Our hero?" Jen asked.

"Well, he opened a can of worms. He went back to the second instruction and discovered that the second instruction that they thought was good really wasn't. It looked like a duplicate, but it really wasn't."

"How so?" She asked, trying to keep up with the technicalities of the payment system. Jen was confused. "The Dublin Bank would have been out the money twice and would have contacted us right away. After all, a ten-million-dollar hole would have hardly gone unnoticed even during that time."

Holding up her hand to stop her going further, Danielle said, "You would think, right? But that's where the circumstances of the day come in."

"The plot thickens?" Jen asked.

"Like concrete," Danielle responded. "So here's where the next mess happens. While investigating, everyone was focusing on the reference field and the mining company, but nobody looked at the debit account number. One digit was off, changing the instruction completely. So instead of hitting the National Bank of Dublin, it hit a very underutilized Foreign Exchange General ledger account. Mind you, now, it took weeks for the auditors to get to this point. It was almost like someone set up the maze to stall the ultimate discovery."

Puzzled, Jen asked, "But doesn't the system track to see if it made any changes on a payment like a repair to an account number before it's sent out? You could see that, right?"

"Yes, there's always a paper trail," Danielle concurred, "but that's how this one came in through the SWIFT payment system. It dumbfounded us. The auditors went nuts. Bill flew back immediately from wherever he was and tore the system apart with the tech guys to find the glitch."

"Why didn't you just get the Mining Company to pay you back in the meantime," Jen asked.

"Because the Mining Company folded shop and 'poof', again, walked off with the dough," Danielle responded looking to see what Jen's reaction would be to that crazy part of the story.

"The Dublin Bank was whole," Jen asked again in disbelief.

"Yup," Danielle answered.

"And nobody could find the Mining Company," Jen repeated.

"Disappeared like a ghost," Danielle stated.

"And Bill? Mr. Perfect Banker. What did he have to say about this?" Jen added cynically.

"He couldn't believe it. Supposedly, he was getting obsessed with it. In the end, the General Manager told him to give it up because Senior Management was shutting the entire New York operation down and walking away from International. We were still operating from the off-site. He spent the next few months winding down the impressive operation that he built, selling the clients off–at least the bits that were left–and packing the place up. Then, suddenly, he vanished. Gone. Never to be heard from again."

Taking a moment to digest, Jen finally declared, "That's some story."

"Yeh–I know. Not the brightest highlight of my career. I didn't want to believe that the money was gone, but everyone kept telling me to forget about it… a consequence of the times… and all that."

Jen gaped at her. "After all these years, I can't believe I never heard that story from you."

"What's to tell? It's over and history. But now, the ghost returns and I'm really creeped out. Why was he looking for me?"

Jen tilted her head, not understanding. "What do you mean by that?"

Danielle then replayed the meeting at Place's office with Hudd, Rita, and the FBI guy, Muckiss. She mentioned how funny it was that Place kept calling him Mucous just to give the story a little kick. But when she got to the part about finding the branch address on Bill's dead body, Jen winced.

"Oh, I see your point. And the SUV that was following you… the one that may have ended up in our parking lot–may have had something to do with all of this so now you're freaking you out?" Jen asked, trying to put the pieces together.

"No. I think I just freaked out. The black SUV just gave me a good reason. It looked… sinister," Danielle answered, squinting her eyes and pressing her lips tight.

"Hm. Okay. Whatever. Let's forget about the SUV. Let's get back to you and Bill so we can figure out why he had our address in his pocket and why this is making you so nervous." Jen said enthusiastically, reverting to her CSI persona.

"Hey! This is almost as fun as when West Mendow had to fire the Meter Maid Man after they caught him embezzling from the parking meters. A man with too many coins in his pocket all the time. Just didn't fit. Remember that?" Jen's eyes shined as she reached for a yellow legal pad and pencil to take notes.

"So you think he took the money back then," she continued staring intently at Danielle. "You, in the meantime, buried the memory while you were building your empire. Now, some sort of guilt is surfacing because you think you should have been more diligent in getting the money back."

Danielle made a phony eureka face. "You know, I never thought about it that way." Jen nodded her head like she just solved "Pi". Danielle continued in a serious tone. "But no, I really don't give two cents about Capital Bank and its ten-million-dollar loss. I think someone murdered Bill because he knew something." She paused for effect. "It's a matter of time before the FBI pieces it together–

maybe two days. The German police will start filling in the holes–okay three days because Muckiss has to get involved and once that happens, the trail will lead to me."

Jen stopped writing. She looked up, wide-eyed. "How's that?"

"Okay–hang on to your seat. Only two people had access to the Communications Room in our Disaster Recovery procedures–Bill and me. He trusted no one else to put the bank in front of their personal life. Remember, I was the only one who didn't have a family to take care of or anything to do except being a single hot chick in New York during the woo woo days. So, in a disaster, he thought I was the only one who would keep my head on straight and do what I had to do. My only job before running out was to go in and cancel the SWIFT keys, turn the Communication Channels off, and alert the off-site to gear up."

"And you did that, right?" Silence. Jen continued. "You didn't" Silence. Jen stopped talking.

"As soon as we were told to evacuate, I put the Disaster Recovery Plan in place. I tried to get into the SWIFT room, but my key card wasn't working. I looked everywhere for Bill but couldn't find him. The building shook, and the alarms were blaring. I could hear people screaming in the hallways and the stairwells. Even though we weren't in the twin towers, there was still so much panic because we could see what was happening outside. Lower Manhattan started smoking up and the entire area was going dark. I had to abandon the plan and run. I thought the building was going to collapse at any minute."

Danielle's eyes started watering at the memory of that horrific day. She stopped talking, knowing that with the next sentence her voice was going to crack. Jen saw she was struggling to keep it together and remained quiet. Quickly composing herself, Danielle took a deep breath and went on. "Anyhow, when we finally regrouped, I asked Bill, off the record, what happened to my key card and whether he got into the room to do what had to be done. The question stunned him at first because he thought I had followed the plan. I told him that was impossible because I couldn't even open the door. It baffled him. He said my name showed up all over the reports that I did. Everything went perfectly!"

"So what did he do?" Jen said with amazement.

"He said 'not to worry'. Things were going so haywire that day that there must have been some sort of system problem, and the automatic back-up system must have kicked in to cancel the keys and get everything going. He said he would look into it."

"And did he?" Jen asked, putting the blank legal pad and pencil down.

Danielle was wringing her hands. "Who knows? I never heard about it again until…"

Jen finished the sentence. "… the ten million dollars went missing."

"And that's why we always chalked it up to a systems problem." Danielle said, adding the last piece of the puzzle.

Jen continued her interrogation. "What happened to the SWIFT keys?"

Inhaling, Danielle said, "According to Bill, the back-up system canceled them immediately. SWIFT reassigned new ones within 24 hours, and that was that. They're systems' generated and quite complicated. After all, nobody really knows how to manually work the algorithms so that part didn't faze us."

"Or so you thought," Jen added.

"Or so we thought, Sherlock, "Danielle laughed nervously.

"You think Bill took the money, but you couldn't come right out and say it because your fingerprints were all over it?"

Nodding, Danielle answered, "Touché, Madam. Your powers of deduction always amaze me."

"The official report makes no mention about it because Bill credited the automatic backup feature of our payment software for kicking in and saving the day," Danielle stated.

"So the truth is buried with him," Jen said.

"Perhaps," Danielle commented.

"Oh. Now I see. So even though he's dead, you're afraid he could have still thrown you under the bus to deflect suspicion–to what–his corpse? Come on, Danielle, if it hasn't happened after all these years, why would it happen now. And if it came up now, you're covered. The back-up system kicked in, putting the disaster recovery plan in motion. You said yourself, 'it went perfectly'," Jen explained, not missing a beat.

Danielle could trust Jen to put a Band-Aid on a wound, kiss the boo-boo, and try to make it feel better. But this gash was going to need a tourniquet. "You know, you're good. But not that good, she said with a smile. "You didn't ask me one important question."

"Yeh, what's that?" Jen replied.

"Whether the payment software had an automatic back-up system," Danielle answered.

Jen snapped her head as she raised her eyebrows in surprise. "Well, did it.?"

"No," Danielle answered simply.

120

Chapter 10

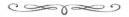

A cloud passed over the sun, darkening the drive-through while Danielle continued her story. Jen remained silent, captivated by the tangled events. Daniele admitted she had always felt Bill Smith was slicker than a used car salesman. Nobody doubted his extensive knowledge about payments, but they never questioned his reports. Senior management at headquarters always took his word as gospel, never doubting that Bill could deceive them. The way he talked about payments made their heads rattle. They never bothered to learn the business, and Bill enabled them. Danielle knew better. She was one of the few payment experts and part of an elite club that grew up in the payment business and witnessed the evolution from paper telexes to electronic blips on a screen. So when Bill said there was a back-up payment system, they didn't question whether or not it was true.

Jen gasped, putting her hand to her mouth. "So there was a cover-up!"

Danielle nodded. She was just about to say, 'See, I told you there more to the story' but as she raised her finger to make the point, they heard a polite honking outside the drive-thru window. Startled by the unexpected distraction, they both turned simultaneously to look. A dark-haired, well-put-together woman with big Prada sunglasses and a Chanel shade of pink and red lipstick smiled and waved at them through her car window.

"Hi Jen!" she said cheerfully.

"Hello Mrs. Edwards, "Jen replied, matching her chirpiness.

"Sorry to interrupt such a serious-looking discussion, but I was wondering if you could cash this check for me. There's a spectacular sale at Niemen's and I don't want to lose a second!"

While waiting for Jen to process the check, Danielle gazed at the sleek white Volvo S80 decorating her drive-thru and fantasized about trading places with this elegant woman right now. She could hear the car's speakers playing what sounded like Gladys Knight, not wanting to say goodbye to some no-good lover. This brought back memories of her own losses on that fateful day of September 11th in New York. Flashbacks of the nightmare were returning. Years later, she could still smell the smoke from the twin towers. Although Capital Bank was a few blocks away from Ground Zero, everything around them was going haywire. She could still see the thousands of dust-laden people confused and disoriented, trying to make their way home. They forced people to evacuate their offices from miles around and scatter. The most nerve-wracking part was tracking down friends in or near the towers. She lost several that day, including the love of her life in Tower Two that morning. It took years to get over that loss, and she still had dreams of what could have been with Frank Giuseppe. Maybe that's why she was still single. Nobody could live up to him.

Shaking, she got up from her stool and began looking for something to distract her thoughts. The air in the drive-thru was stifling - as if someone had just turned off the ventilation. Her breathing got heavier and her neck was sweating.

"You're turning red," Jen whispered to her as she counted the cash for a second time, then placed it in the metal chamber that slid out to the driver's window.

Danielle reached up and touched her cheeks. They felt hot. It was hard to hide the feelings of that awful day. She tried to lighten up. "I'm just picturing those racks at Niemen's, marked down shoes galore, slashed price tags in Chanel, discounted Elie Tahari. You know me. I'm just a little ol' addict getting anxious about my next bargain fix."

Jen gave her a sideways glance while Mrs. Edwards grabbed the money and smashed it into her handbag, trusting Jen's perfect check cashing skills. Thanking Jen profusely, she shouted, "You're the best", then shifted into drive, and blasted off.

"So?" Danielle intoned as she watched her roar off the branch lot. With eyebrows raised, she turned to Jen and asked, "Who was that interesting creature?"

"Victoria Edwards? Oh, she's the new vicar's wife. She's something else. They're renting Betty Potter's cottage down the street until they buy a place." She paused. "They came from New York." She whispered like it was some sort of terminal disease.

"Fascinating," Danielle said, tapping her fingers on the counter. "Remind me to take her to lunch. It could be a new mortgage there. And of course some other interesting tidbits. It's always good to be friends with the vicar's wife."

"Okay, well, forget that. One-track mind. Looks like you're feeling better so let's get back to the story, shall we?" Jen said impatiently as she patted a nearby stool for Danielle to hop on once again.

"Are you following it so far?" Danielle asked, while wiggling into a more comfortable position. "It's getting kind of technical. I could go back and explain it a little more..."

"No, no. Your point here is that since there was no automatic back-up system, someone had to enter the communications room and turn all the knobs and switches manually. Whoever did it, and I'm sure it wasn't you..." Jen grinned.

"Are you kidding?" Danielle answered with mock horror.

"… it wasn't you, but somehow someone got hold of your key card and ran off with more than just the 'How-To Manual'. At least, that's how I would have done it," Jen said, blowing on her fingernails.

"Impressive. You have quite a criminal mind. Sometimes you scare me." Danielle said. "But to your point. Who could resist the temptation of doing something very profitable during all that chaos?" I wasted this poor girl in this one-horse town, Danielle thought. Here she was, stuck working in the branch of a small bank when, with a mind like hers, she could have been anything. But that's what happens when you marry your high school sweetheart and start having kids quicker than light can travel. On the other hand, Danielle was very lucky to have her stuck in this place. Plucked out of the teller pool, Danielle groomed her into her alter-ego–a pillar of common sense, integrity, perseverance, and spunk. While Danielle's forte is bringing in business, she is also impulsive and uncontrolled. Jen keeps it together for her - stepping in and taking over- with Danielle's blessing.

"Well?" Jen asked, tipping her own head to the side, mimicking her while meeting Danielle's eyes.

"Yes, okay. After mulling over all the possibilities, that's exactly what I think happened," Danielle said conclusively.

Jen stared at her for a few seconds. "Nah. It

sounds too simple. I think you did it," she blurted waving her away. "It explains why you're so rich!"

There was a slight pause, then they both started laughing. When a problem was driving her mad, Danielle loved how Jen could reduce it to something they could joke about. High Maintenance meets the Big Easy. The perfect couple.

During this laughing binge, a car pulled into the rarely used third and farthest drive-thru. Because of the giant cement pillar holding up the roof, whatever car uses that station is completely hidden. Giggling and shaking her head, Jen sent out an empty canister through the tube by rote. The vacuum quickly sucked the canister landing with a "thunk" They could hear the driver taking the canister out and filling it with a transaction.

While calming down, Jen tried to close the subject with a slim chance that for once Danielle, the Drama Queen, would focus on something other than herself. She tried to convince her that the old story of the banking fiasco of 9/11 was so over that even Bill Smith's death seemed anti-climactic at this point. Despite how beautifully her own conspiracy theory fit, she argued that the murder was most likely just a coincidence–wrong place, wrong time - or someone settling an old score. But Danielle wouldn't buy it. She kept pressing that by having her branch address on him, it implicated her somehow in the case.

They agreed to disagree, and Jen changed the subject. Soon the sucking noise started, signaling that the canister was on in the tube on its way back. Jen unscrewed the lid while she brought Danielle up to speed about some customer service issues that Eddie was blowing royally. Giving Danielle 100% of her attention, she pulled out a plain white envelope. She turned it around and saw it was addressed to Danielle. "Oh, it's for you," and held it out for her to take.

Danielle looked at the envelope like it was carrying the Ebola virus. It was another white envelope for the second time in the day. She ran to the drive-thru window, desperately looking for the car that sent it through, but the driveway was empty.

"Come on, take it. What's wrong?" Jen asked, extending her arm further for Danielle to take it.

Danielle turned towards Jen, brows furrowed, as she eyed the envelope. Why would she be getting a note through the Drive-thru today of all days, she thought to herself? Something didn't feel right.

"Stop it, Danielle. You're freaking me out. It's probably just a note from a customer," Jen said dismissively.

"No. I don't get notes from a customer through the drive-thru. No, it's not right. You open it. I don't want to," Danielle replied nervously, waving her finger while backing away.

"You DO get notes from the drive-thru but you never pay attention to your notes so I just take care of them," Jen said with annoyance.

"Oh yeah, that's right. Guilty as charged" she replied, laughing nervously while assessing her manicure and hoping that the note would go away. An awkward silence ensued.

Rolling her eyes and muttering "what a baby," under her breath, Jen slid her fingers through the side opening of the envelope and pulled out a piece of paper.

Looking puzzled, Jen asked, "So, what is this about a flash drive?"

Visibly shaken, Danielle gazed wide-eyed up at Jen. Whoever it was, had already driven off so she didn't have a clue. Her anxiety turned to anger when she realized in that split second she may have missed catching the person who, she was even more convinced now, was stalking her.

"Give me that," she said sharply and grabbed the note out of Jen's hand.

There were four words written with a pencil in big letters, all in caps. 'WHERE'S THE FLASH DRIVE?' The handwriting differed from the one on Bill's note from the afternoon. But unlike Bill's, this message went right to the point. Danielle thought quickly. Two people now knew about the flash drive. One was dead, and the other was tracking her. In the meantime, she felt vindicated. She was indeed being followed on the way home. She wasn't crazy. There was something to worry about. The flash drive meant something, and someone is trying to scare the pants off her to get it. And it wasn't the FBI. There's another player.

What could possibly be on that flash drive? She couldn't waste any more time not knowing. She had to go to download it immediately. She had to go.

Danielle looked at Jen. Jen looked concerned. "Um,"

"Yes, the flash drive. Uh, I downloaded some pictures of West Mendow the other day and promised them to a reporter from 'Maryland Today' Magazine for an article she was writing about me and well, I must have forgotten all about it with everything that was going on and there must be some sort of deadline she's working with and so I have to go now... gotta run." Danielle blurted.

Danielle grabbed her handbag, unlocked the door, and was just about to step out into the kitchen area.

"Danielle, That's the fishiest story I've heard from you yet today and you've been full of them." Jen called after her.

"I'm ignoring that," Danielle replied, not skipping a beat. She was just about to walk out then remembered to ask one more thing, "You wouldn't have noticed what kind of car that person who dropped off the note was driving, did you?"

"No. Goodbye. Too much weirdness for one day. You need to give me a break. Hey! Weren't you going to show me something?" Jen yelled after her.

Pretending not to hear that last line, Danielle snuck out of the branch through the kitchen door - a gigantic policy "no-no" at the bank. All branch bankers learn on their first day of training that you enter through the front door and leave the branch through the front door. Bankers sneaking out a back door have been known to be bopped on the head now and then–the muggers hoping to grab bags of cash or sneak into rob the place. But Danielle took the risk, thinking that if she was being watched, they were watching for her out front. Her stomach had a few butterflies breaking policy, but she had to change her routine. She was playing a new game with higher stakes. There was no room for error or miscalculation. Not noticing the car in the drive-thru was a big mistake.

Convinced the coast was clear, she snuck around the front looking for anything suspicious, including a black SUV Ford. Everything seemed normal. She jumped in her car and sped off, keeping her eye on the rearview mirror. She drove around West Mendow's downtown a few times, which took all of about five minutes, not really sure what on earth she was accomplishing with all this clandestine behavior, but it made her feel like she was back in control. She was trolling for something evil and sinister to stand out, but everything looked boring as usual. She was feeling stupid. It was time to head home.

Chapter 11

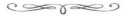

The cell phone in her handbag pinged - alerting her to a new e-mail message. Keeping her eyes on the road, she deftly unzipped the new Coach purse she bought on her latest shopping spree at Saks and dipped her hand in to mute it. Instead, her fingers touched the small flash drive, reminding her that this little gadget was the start of all her troubles. Grabbing on to it, she pulled it out and rubbed the blue and silver device between her thumb and forefinger, wondering what secrets it held. She grew unsettled, realizing that she deliberately kept it from Jen. Admittedly, she didn't altogether understand her own actions. Her gut told her she somehow owed Bill Smith a moment alone. Perhaps there was something on there that he wanted only her to know. Did he want to protect her from something or someone that she trusted today? Did he want her to do something with it that wasn't legitimate? Finally, why was someone chasing her all over Maryland for it?

Then the unthinkable crossed her mind. Was Bill Smith murdered over this? The uneasiness she felt a moment ago seethed into anger. If that's the case, she thought, gripping the steering wheel tighter, why did he pass this hot potato on to her?

This is the part in the movie that someone would

scream out, "Stop fooling around and go see what's on the @##$$% flash drive. Please put us out of our misery!!!" But as she was hurtling towards that very notion, she spotted Rake Harris again–this time sprinting back towards his driveway. His strong muscular back was bathed in sweat. His broad shoulders remained straight as his arms kicked back and forth in a show of determination. His hair, curly in her kitchen, was now plastered to his head looking like the carved stone hair on the bust of Greek sculpture.

"What's up with this guy? Doesn't he have anything else to do except flaunt those Adonis pecs all around town?" thought Danielle. She made her turn on Beatrice Lane, catching a last glimpse of his well-toned hamstrings. She wondered if he was really jogging all that time and if so, where he got all that energy. He certainly had a lot of endurance. She looked forward to putting that to good use. Pleasantly alarmed where her mind was going, she forgot all about the flash drive and the nonsense that was going on at Capital Bank and kept thinking about Rake and all that stamina. Her mind started drifting. Was he the one that would finally try to tame her? His presence seemed to calm and excite her at the same time. Has she just met her match?

"Really? Oh, snap out of it, Danielle," she said to herself. "You haven't had a boyfriend that checked off all the boxes since the Dawn of Man. You're just reading too much into him without even getting to know him." Furthermore, it was an accepted fact that handsome men with good teeth, a full head of hair, no belly, and could afford the right address didn't come around that often in West Mendow. With her luck, he was probably exactly what his name was–A Rake. And what kind of stupid name was that? Sighing, she drove up to the front door and, not surprisingly, was overcome by the loneliness of her immense but empty home.

The black-and-white marble foyer glistened as the light of the late afternoon sun met the amber shades of the stained glass windows adorning the entrance. Still feeling uneasy, Danielle scoped the place upon entering, looking for anything out of the ordinary. All appeared in order.

"Eeez you?!?" Eleni, the human security system, yelled out from the kitchen. She quickly affirmed that it was indeed the mistress of the house before she was attacked by a butcher knife. 'Kala'(good) she heard as she ran upstairs to her master bedroom suite.

The flash drive was drilling a dent in her hand as she looked feverishly for one of her laptops. Searching under pillows, magazines, and books, she stopped short in front of the large mirror over her gold-gilded dresser and took a second to check herself out. It was worse than she thought. The crisp, well-put-together Danielle of this morning was the disastrous train wreck Jen was trying to describe her as this afternoon. Flash drive or no flash drive, she could not go out on the first date she's had in eons looking like she did.

A major overhaul makeover was about to begin.

She looked around the room, laying out the master plan. Some would say that this room could be a house in itself. When she bought it from the dot.com guy who bought it from Prince Weezee, or whatever his name was, she decided not to change a thing. Well, there was one thing. She took the mirrors off the ceiling. After all, there was nothing more shocking than seeing yourself at this stage of the game waking up in the morning. Well, not true. She did two things. The 360-degree mirrors in the bathroom were removed as well, sparing herself that glimpse of horror as she stepped out of the shower room or small marble-encased pool that substituted for the Jacuzzi. After that, literally, everything else remained the same just so she could watch the stupefied faces of her guests when she gave a house tour. Who else could boast of a gold gilded headboard with a matching gold quilted bedspread (which she had laundered immediately upon purchasing, of course.), layers of silk window treatments, assorted dressers, desks, chairs, end tables, chests, lamps, and oriental rugs with enough shine to power a small city. The furnishings and electronics alone could fill five normal bedrooms. It was quite a collection for a tiny little prince with terrible taste.

The lavishness reached into the colossal bathroom. Along with the enormous tub and shower, animal-themed sinks, fixtures, vanities, lights that could illuminate a football stadium, his and her toilet rooms (okay–the only really good idea), walk-in linen closets (really, how much company did the little prince need that could warrant so many towels and body lotion), adorned the room. It took Danielle days to figure out how to turn the shower on. Meanwhile, she had to use another of her half dozen less complicated bathrooms until she found some poor victim from the fixture company who agreed to come to West Mendow to give her lessons.

It was all so tacky. She loved it. Save tasteful for the next life.

The flash drive could wait. A greater emergency needed immediate attention. Kicking off her shoes, she walked over to her dresser, opened the top drawer and hid the thumb drive under some lingerie. The suit she put on so carefully this morning was ripped off, as she wondered where she was going to start- hair, body, face, feet, nails. It was endless. Looking in the mirror, she realized she needed time - lots of time. The body survey was not concluding well. While trying to fluff her limp hair, she glanced desperately at the clock. They were meeting in two hours! Would it be enough time?

Here Rake was jogging all day like a maniac, burning millions of calories, and firming up for tonight while all she was doing was driving around mostly and eating tuna sandwiches with potato chips. She looked down and couldn't see her toes. Alarmed, she had to accept the fact that the protruding belly was payment for her indulgences.

There was nothing she could do about that now. She would just avoid turning sideways. Time to move on to dousing in her signature, unforgettable jasmine and vanilla scent.

She hurried into the bathroom and ran the tub, watching the water vomit out of the mouth of a gold trout. As it was filling, she walked to her closet, which was about the same size as her studio in Manhattan over a decade ago. She strategized her look for the evening.

"Not too casual. Not too formal, okay? Let's eliminate dresses and skirts. One wall eliminated three to go." Did she go through the slacks, jeans? No. Black. Always safe. Don't play it safe? Red? Really? Back to Black. Tight? Yes, by all means, this isn't Yoga. Two walls to go. The Blouse. Cleavage showing? For sure. Tight? Haven't worked out in a week, risky. Black? Too "black widow" may get suspicious. White? No, that's the server look? No way. Red, Fire, Hot, TV Anchorwoman. She smiled. Could help with the interrogation. Shoes next, impractical and sexy, The Danielle Trademark.

After all the hoola boola, she chose a black pair of Ralph Lauren jeans that made her butt look "just so" and a gray silk shirt that said "casual, elegant evening"–no more, no less. She couldn't guess what Rake would look like. He could go either way by realizing he was on a date and get all cleaned up or thinking he was going to hang out with his new pal, the neighbor, not noticing that she was also a knockout.

"Your bath is hot and ready, your Highness," said a mechanical voice from the bathroom. When she first moved in and heard that little voice, it amazed her that the little prince thought of everything money could buy. Even his bathtub was set to announce when it was full and at the right temperature. She was so impressed by that innovation, that she never got around to turning it off. Secretly, she enjoyed being called "your Highness" in the privacy of her bathroom.

As she sank deep into a watery bliss, she thanked Little Prince Weezeeweezee for being an expert on bathing. Within seconds, her mind held only thoughts about how safe she was feeling at that moment.

Chapter 12

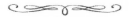

The black SUV slowed down, then stopped as it passed in front of the Mendow estate. The driver rolled down the window for a better view, then let out a breath in frustration. Thick trees hid most of the house. A ridiculous monument of some lady that looked like the Statue of Liberty obscured the rest, including the front door. Although Danielle's car was last seen going up to her driveway, it was impossible to tell where she was at the moment.

The driver's finger tapped on the steering wheel. After slithering around town following her, it was obvious that there were only two places that the flash drive could be–the bank or the house. A plan was forming when the Bluetooth started ringing.

"Where are you?" asked the voice on the other end of the phone.

The driver snapped back, "I am doing what you should have been doing. Going after that other flash drive."

A slight late September breeze caused some prematurely dried leaves to fall off a nearby tree and land on the windshield. It was close to 5:00 p.m. The driver knew the rush hour would bring out a few more cars than usual. The black SUV was a standout in this one-horse town. The driver did not want to attract attention in the event Mendow started asking around town whether anyone had seen a strange car driving around.

"So what are you going to do?" asked the voice on the phone.

"The less you know, the better." The driver replied curtly, turning on the windshield wipers.

"Don't hurt her. She didn't ask for this. Smith was a dick for getting her back involved. You've stirred the pot too much already."

The driver clutched the steering wheel. "I'm doing this for the both of us, you idiot! Do you think I like this?"

The voice started chuckling. "Yes, I do"

The driver smiled. "Alright, just a little. She'll only be getting what she deserves if she doesn't cough up that damn flash drive."

"You scare me sometimes." The voice responded after a brief pause.

"That's what makes us a great team. You dare, I scare." The driver said. "I've got to go. I need to pick up a few things."

The driver hung up before the person on the other end said goodbye. The driver took a long last look at the direction of the house. Crickets and frogs competing for the "Noisiest Pest Award" were piercing the quiet of the woods surrounding the car. Another breeze blew by, this time throwing leaves in the driver's face. The driver quickly rolled up the window and started the car while muttering about how unbelievable it was that anyone wanted to live out in the boondocks with all these thick trees and creepy noises. The car was put in gear, then sped off.

Chapter 13

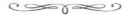

The daylight had faded. Danielle's eyes adjusted slowly to the darkness. Dusk had taken over, bringing a sense of gloominess. She watched as the last of the lingering light from the skylight over the bathtub played one last song on the bathwater. The vanilla from her favorite Chanel bath soap was taking its final bow. It was the curtain call. As much as her body wanted to stay in the temperature-controlled water, it was time to leave the stage and return to the real world.

Deliberately leaving the lights off, she wrapped herself tightly in the embrace of a gigantic, fluffy white towel while staying true to her pledge to avoid all mirrors. Pausing, she watched water slither down the drain, taking the day's drama with it. "Good riddance," she thought to herself as she walked purposely into her bedroom. The only care she had now was how she was going to squeeze herself into those size four jeans. She eyed them suspiciously as they lay ready for war on her bed. Of course, all the fault lies with Eleni, who always shrinks her clothes. Well, at least that's what they laugh together over while Danielle walks around like Frankenstein for twenty minutes to loosen them up.

She was approaching the final battle–in position

on her back, stomach sucked in as far as it would go, her breath still, teeth grinding, careful not to pull too hard on the belt loops, her fingers, on one hand, masterly grabbing the zipper while simultaneously the other is trying to button the waist and then with one final burst of strength, the zipper's in place, the jeans are buttoned, and she's free to exhale–just a bit.

She performs the safe "Get up" move she learned in Yoga which is recommended for people who don't want to fall over from vertigo after doing an eternity of weird yoga stretches on the mat. Over time and with much stuffing, she also learned it works well for women who just rammed the lower half of their body into too-tight jeans made for 18-year-old girls with no hips.

After buttoning up her shirt, she gave herself a thumbs up in the mirror, took a squat to stretch out her pants, and headed quickly for the make-up and hair mirror to try to roll back time with the tricks she learned from her personal make-up artist, Stefan. Satisfied from the neck up, she stood up and stood back, approving her front view, grimaced at her side view, then headed for the door. She tip-toed downstairs carrying her shoes, hoping to be super-silent so as not to rouse the house beast - the perpetually nosy Eleni.

As she pulled out of the driveway, she imagined St. Catherine giving her a "You Go Girl" which brought a wicked smile to her face. She was planning on having a lot of fun tonight with her new handsome and single neighbor. Bill Smith and the mystery flash drive will just have to wait until morning.

The ride took all of two minutes after turning left on Beatrice Lane. She made a quick turn into his driveway. It was just as long as hers and after a few bends - she was at his front doors. Although it appeared about as large as her house, Rake bought the "country farmhouse" model–complete with dark wooden beams, white planked siding, and a pole to hitch her Mercedes to in case it wanted to gallop away. It was not one of her favorite designs. In fact, Danielle thought here was another one of those houses that fell into the "White Elephant" category.

She did her final make-up check, pronounced herself "not bad for a broad in her forties" as always, flipped up her hair, and opened the car door. Her Manolo Blahnik's led the way, touching down gingerly, barely missing one of Spike's poop presents, no doubt a warning to the new woman who may take away his BFF. "It's going to be me or the dog," she said to herself, which could be a tough choice for a guy like Rake. She knew she was jumping ahead of herself, already strategizing the type of poison that works best on animals. Was she really thinking that way? Yes.

She rang the doorbell. It was precisely 7:00 pm.

The house looked unusually dark for company. She heard Spike barking from some far off room, but that was the only sound except for the crickets coming from the house. The silence amidst the dusk and the rising moon gave the gigantic fake farmhouse an eerie sense of unreality.

Danielle slowly stepped back from the door. Something just didn't seem right. Leaves rustling from a slight breeze made her feel like there was someone, something around, but she couldn't see anything out of the ordinary.

Spike continued barking his head off. The silk shirt Danielle was wearing became too light for the chilly evening, giving her goosebumps. She began rubbing her arms to warm up.

"Okay, enough of this." She thought as she made her way back to the car, keeping her eyes down to avoid stepping on any of Spike's booby traps. She reached out to open the door when a hand grabbed hers. She froze.

"Hey. Where are you going?"

She looked up to see Rake staring at her at once concerned and confused.

"You're not running away from me. I haven't even made a pass at you yet!" His head tilted to one side as his eyes locked onto hers.

The touch of his hand sent a bolt of electricity through her, catching her completely off guard. The fear she felt a minute ago evaporated. Now, all she could feel was a relief. His appearance made her speechless. Even more uncharacteristic of her, she couldn't think of a good comeback line. All that came out of her mouth was "Um".

"Um?" he repeated, raising his eyebrows and giving her a mischievous grin. "That's it?'

How can he make her feel like such a dork when he's around? She needed to get a grip.

"Yes, "um", as in where were you? Your dog sounds like he's trying to break the Guinness Book of World Records for relentless barking. Your house is pitch black. Frankly, it looked like you forgot we were getting together tonight! And I'm cold. Either you invite me in or I'll be warming up in my car on my way home." Okay, a little girlie, she thought, but at least her vocals started working again. Maybe her brain will come next.

"Testy, testy. Let's go. Can I warm you up on the way in?" Before she could cleverly protest, he wrapped his big arm around her and practically carried her inside. Their bodies touched. Right away she knew that they both fit well together in each other's curves. She closed her eyes, inhaling his scent. He smelled like fresh pine and cinnamon. Combined with her Vanilla and Honey Spritz, they made an excellent room spray.

Rake whisked her through the front doors. Propping her up then making sure she was steady on her Manolo Blahnik's, he turned away to switch on the lights. Looking around, she was surprised but not surprised to see a barely furnished house. Whatever furniture that was there looked like it belonged somewhere else, not in a faux farmhouse. She stared into the enormous living room straight ahead. A black leather couch sitting on a red rug faced a beautiful built in fireplace that had a tremendous 50-inch flat screen television set perched on top of it. Men and their wide screens, she mused. In an interesting touch of creative design, two boxes from Home Depot acted as the coffee table. The Dining Room to the left had a glass table with four black leather chairs. She assumed the room on the right was some sort of office, but it was filled with boxes which hid most of the doorway so she couldn't see much. It was someone's 650 square foot apartment plopped into a 4500 square foot McMansion. She didn't even bother going through her mental Rolodex for an interior designer. This was hopeless.

She looked around for Rake who had disappeared, presumably to silence Spike, who by this time must have exploded because the house was suddenly silent.

"I let him out. Geez, that dog could drive you nuts when he has to go." Rake said as he walked back into the hall from one of the many doors. "Feeling better? You were pretty jumpy out there."

This was the first time she got to see him in the light this evening. He really cleaned up well. A shower, a shave, a fresh white cotton tailored shirt, a pair of tight blue jeans, and loafers with no socks made her quickly forget how annoyed and creeped out she was outside. Was this guy really her neighbor? How lucky could a girl get? He put one hand in his pocket, relaxed his body on the other hip and with a tilt of his head, gave her that crooked grin which turned her into jelly earlier that afternoon.

"So, why did you leave me out there thinking I've been stood up?" she said, looking away so he wouldn't catch her leering.

He held up a bottle of wine with this other hand. "I realized I didn't have any good wines being a beer guy, and you looked like a Sancerre kind of gal so I ran out to pick up a few bottles not thinking you would be so punctual. I was putting the car away when you drove up."

"It's polite to be punctual," she said playfully. Was she really thinking of leaving a few minutes ago? This guy was hot, and she hadn't been on an interesting date since W. was president. "And its thoughtful of you to ply me with my favorite wine." She countered, taking a step back.

Amused, he answered, "I could think of nothing else."

"It happens." She teased, enjoying the banter. "By the way, your house is lovely. What do they call this style... mid-century minimalist bachelor pad?"

"I could use a new piece here and there." He said laughing. "Come on, all this fun is making me hungry. Would you like to escort me to the kitchen and keep me company while I boil the water? You can help by opening the jar of Ragu."

It looked like she was going to need that bottle of wine right away. He held out his hand to show her the way.

"Have I mentioned how amazing you look tonight, Danielle?" he said, his head rigid while his eyes gave her an MRI exam.

She stopped. Again, he made her speechless. Electricity shot through her a second time that evening. The comment was just so inappropriate and ill-timed. Couldn't he have waited a bit like after a glass of wine? On the other hand, she found his candidness so refreshing. He had no filter. It was attractive, in a way. A man who says and does whatever he wants whenever he wants. Other women may find that irritating. Danielle thought it brought him into her league.

So she gave it right back to him. "I know."

She patted his face and started walking - swinging her bum a little more than usual. He ain't seen nothing yet, she thought to herself and opened the door ahead.

"Closet" he warned.

"I know that," she said, quickly closing the door.

They both laughed. He took her hand and led her towards the kitchen.

Everything about him turned her on. His smell, his humor, his looks, his clothes. Okay, he could use some help in the home décor area, but his goofy domestic style just made him more endearing. He walked like he could hold a beer while reading a copy of The Republic. It was such an appealing mix. She started picturing what he would look like in the morning–his hair all tousled, his beard peeking through his smooth pale skin, staring at her with a lazy smile while he was sipping a roasted Asian blend made by a French filtered press.

He turned on the lights. She gasped. His state-of-the art - $200,000 gourmet kitchen looked like a scene from Twister. Every inch of the counter was full of stuff–pots, glasses, plates, food, more boxes. And there was Spike, right in the middle of it all on the standing on the island, tail wagging like a propeller. If Eleni could see this now, Rake and his dog would be begging for a Cyanide pill.

He glanced over to see her reaction. "I'm glad you're not bolting for the door right now. I'm still unpacking. I'm not too good with this stuff," he said while picking up some loose newspapers off the floor.

"The idea never crossed my mind". She replied, still staring incredulously at Spike. Meanwhile, she was trying to remember which restaurants were open late on Monday night.

"Ever since we moved here, he's had a thing for that island. He just loves to jump on it and cause havoc."

"Go figure." There was that Chinese place...they're always open.

"Off Spike. Get off!" Rake said, walking towards the dog, sternly pointing a finger at the back door. Spike stayed, barked a bit more, tried to bite off Rake's finger while giving a little dance.

"I don't think he takes you too seriously" Danielle smiled. They could always go back to my house for leftovers, she thought.

"Okay, that's enough." Rake walked up to Spike, heaved him off the counter and carried him at arm's length towards the back door. He kicked it open with his foot and threw the dog out, slamming the door quickly behind him.

"My hero," Danielle said, batting her eyelids. Her mind was still spinning. Maybe we can just drink a lot of wine and find some potato chips. I'm up for that. Some TV, a little snuggling...

Rake ran his fingers through his hair and looked around. "So..." he sighed, taking a deep breath.
"Why don't we just start by looking for a corkscrew," he said, opening drawers and rummaging through clutter.

That nice glass of Sancerre was feeling like a pipe dream at the moment, she thought to herself as she watched him opening cabinets and drawers, digging around. In the meantime, the phone in her Louis Vuitton shoulder bag started vibrating. Danielle reached in to turn it off, taking her sights off Rake for a few seconds who was rummaging around some inside a closet while mumbling to himself. Before flipping the switch to "off", she instinctively glanced at the screen, curious to see who would call her at this hour.

"Hmm," she said to nobody as she read the caller ID. She looked up at Rake who was now staring at the front of the refrigerator dumbfounded, scratching his head like he was trying to solve the mystery of the universe. "I have to take this. Its business," she said walking away - glad to be focusing her attention on something other than the awkward mess around her.

Her eyes widened as she listened to the voice on the other end.

"Holy shit!" she said, ending the call and staring at her phone. "No, no! It's not happening!"

"You okay?" Rake called out, snapping out of his hunting stupor. Moving quickly towards her arms outstretched, he asked: "What's wrong?"

Looking up at him, she shouted, "I'm burning!" Her mind started racing in a million directions.

Rake grabbed her shoulders and drew her towards him. "Yes, yes. You are hot and amazing, I told you that already."

"No, I'm on fire!" she said louder.

Rake's face lit up. "Oh, baby. I was hoping for this," and he closed in for a kiss.

"What are you doing?" Danielle said angrily, pushing him away. "I've got to go." She turned around and ran out of the kitchen.

Rake sprinted after her and caught up just as she reached the front door. He reached out, grabbed her arm and turned her around, preventing her from grabbing the door handle. Closing his eyes for a second like he had to reach into his brain, he took a deep breath to calm himself then said, "Hey, I'm sorry! I guess I was getting the wrong signals. I never do that on the first date. I... I... was overwhelmed. Wait!"

Danielle didn't think for a minute that Rake Harris wouldn't try to steal a kiss from her on the first date, and she was secretly looking forward to it. But sadly, she didn't have time for this at the moment. However, she felt a little sorry for his battered ego and stopped for a few seconds to explain.

"Rake, you got to let go. It's not you. I've got to leave right now. I have an emergency. It's me. I mean, my branch. It's burning. It's on fire!" her voice wavered as she was trying to keep calm.

For a split second, she thought she saw a sense of relief on his face. But it quickly changed to surprise rather than concern.

"So you aren't upset that I tried to kiss you?" he said sheepishly.

Danielle paused, thinking that men could have the world crash in on them and they can only think of one thing.

"Not at all." She said silently cursing the timing of the latest disaster. Gently prying Rake's hand from her arm, she pressed her lips, shrugged her shoulders then opened the door and ran as fast as her Manolo Blahnik's would take her.

Chapter 14

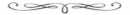

Danielle could see the tips of the blazes as soon as she made the left on Cooper Street. The smoke looked like thick ropes being pulled by a force from the heavens. The streets were devoid of traffic as most cars had pulled over to watch the show like it was the fireworks on the fourth of July. The traffic lights were thankfully green as she hit the gas and sped towards the branch.

Fire Chief Green had broken the news to her on the phone while she was driving. It was bad which wasn't good. The fire started all at once–like a major gas pipe circling the branch had blown up. Nothing was salvageable. He assured her that if everyone was in the bank when it happened, they would have instantly burned to ashes. He proclaimed it was a miracle the tragedy struck when the branch had closed and didn't believe anyone nearby was hurt.

That wasn't what her gut was telling her. The secret conspiracy theorist was saying the timing was deliberate because nobody was really meant to get hurt. It was just a message. Someone was giving her a very expensive, yet not fatal, signal that she couldn't ignore. Is the lunatic who is looking for the flash drive an arsonist and Bill's murderer? It fit–at least in her current unhinged mind. The flash drive obviously had some clues to this mayhem, and she ignored it to put on a pair of hot pants and strut her stuff around some strange guy who moved in down the street. Well, feminism hasn't gone far for her. She was disappointed in herself. She was losing it, just like she lost the branch.

Taking a deep breath and closing her eyes for a few seconds, she told herself to pull it together, stop playing Honey West, that sexy sixties private investigator she used to watch on TV in reruns and get back to the immediate emergency which was saving her business. When she opened her eyes, her vision was blurred by the swelling yellow and orange fireball. Just as she thought it would consume the town of West Mendow, a group of fire trucks surrounded the raging blaze and began dousing it with enough water to turn Cooper Street into Cooper River.

With shoulders slumped, she bemoaned that everything she built was ruined. How on earth was her business going to be up and running by tomorrow morning?

The bright lights of the fire trucks and police cars up ahead were blocking the branch. Driving on, she slowed down as she approached the melee. The smoke from the flames permeated the car. A police officer walked out from the sidewalk and held up his arm, stopping her from getting closer. The glare from the inferno blinded her, almost causing her to run him over. She slammed on her brakes as he jumped out of the way. She brought down her window, cringing at the acrid smell of the burning bank.

"Joe. It's me. Danielle," she called out, recognizing the young police officer. "I didn't see you. I need to get over there. Can you let me go by?"

"Hey Danielle, sorry about your branch. Can you pull over and walk from here? We're trying to keep cars as far away as we can in case things get out of control," he said, squinting through the driver's side window.

"No problem," she answered, eager to get closer to the action. Then she remembered her ridiculous date shoes, which she was planning to kick off at Rake's as soon as possible. Annoyed, because they were already hurting her feet and she didn't even walk anywhere, she dutifully pulled over and got out of the car.

"Thanks, Danielle" young officer Joe replied.

"Happy to comply," she growled, thinking how much she hated Manolo Blahnik's after 9 pm. "How's the family? Did Emily start first grade this year?" Always polite. Always the town banker, despite the unfortunate circumstances that brought them both out at this time of night. She knew the young police officer very well. His parents grew up with her and when Joe Jr. followed in his father's footsteps and joined the West Mendow police force, she approved his student loan, then the mortgage

161

for his house, and recently his home equity loan for the family room extension. He owed.

Joe began describing how amazing little Emily danced at her last ballet recital and how Miss Sonia said she could be the next Margot Fonteyn, but Danielle couldn't care less. Miss Sonia called everyone a budding Margot Fonteyn to keep them coming to her ballet school. She had already tuned out, her attention captivated by the giant clouds of smoke ascending less than 100 yards away.

"That's great, Joe. Chip Off the Old Block," she said walking away cutting him off as he started describing some sort of Bumble Bee dance.

She spotted Jen, Eddie, and a few others from her staff up ahead gazing silently at the fiery site.

The staff must have sensed that Danielle had arrived. They turned and watched as the surrounding bystanders parted to let her through. The crowd whispered, pointed and stared as she tried not to hobble and keep her head up. Her crew started walking over, meeting her halfway - anxious and despondent.

"Any news?" one of them asked.

Danielle shook her head, staring into the flames. "Holy Moly," she said, as she watched the firefighters continue to douse the branch with water. "This is unbelievable. What a catastrophe."

While the rest of the staff stood by absorbed by all the action, Jen eyed Danielle suspiciously.

"What are you trying to say?" Danielle asked, meeting her gaze.

"I didn't say anything," Jen replied guardedly.

"Well then, don't look at me that way," she admonished.

"What way?" Jen answered.

"You know," Danielle replied.

"No." Jen snapped.

"Okay, stop it, you two." Eddie piped in. "I just want to know… has anybody thought about what we are going to do tomorrow morning?"

Typically, the hand-wringer and perennially overwrought, Eddie was, for once, the only one making sense. Danielle hadn't been thinking straight since she arrived and had her first look at the destruction. Besides the immediate disaster, other thoughts were also creeping through her mind which, not surprisingly, Jen had sensed. Does this have anything to do with the events of the day? Is this the ultimate message?

Before tackling that, Danielle had to put her house in order. She kicked into gear.

"Good question," she shouted, making sure

everyone could hear her above the fracas. "Okay Eddie, tell the rest of the service staff to show up tomorrow morning in the Rocktown Regional Office where I know they have some extra desks. They can be a few minutes late since they probably need to reorganize their mornings. Jen, tell the part-time tellers they can stay home until further notice, but tell the full-time tellers to go help the tellers and customer service officers in the branch. First thing in the morning, I want everyone to call every customer to tell them we'll be operating from there until we hear otherwise. I'll call the regional manager, Suzanne, with the plan and let her know we are going to be using her branch and offices. I'll ask her to run the customer database that we can use for phone numbers. We'll wait for permanent instructions from head office, but that's what we're going to do for now. Any questions?"

Everyone stood sober and silent, nodding their heads, trying to digest the new reality. The beauty of modern banking technology is that anyone can work out of any branch in the network at any time since all customer data was stored in one central location. This applies to customers as well. The inconvenience for the people of West Mendow is that they now lost their local town branch and they have to go to Rocktown, which is about ten minutes out of their way to do their banking. Will they do that? Who knows? Although Capital National has the latest banking technology available and tech-savvy customers never have to venture into a branch again, Danielle knows her market. The people of West Mendow still like to walk into their local branch, talk to their banker, and have a relationship with the person they've entrusted their money to. This took Danielle years to build. She was now watching it all go down in one night. Will it be wiped out permanently? Who knows what the powers that be in head office will decide to do about West Mendow tomorrow. It may be bye-bye time.

While she was answering a few questions here and there, Chief Green walked up behind her.

"Sorry about your branch." He said leaning his 6'7" frame over her.

Danielle looked up, startled. "Oh!" The guy just appeared out of nowhere. "Chief, how did this happen?" she cried, still shocked as she stared into his handsome, ageless face.

Chief Green had been Chief Green since Danielle was born, or something like that. He helped her family build West Mendow and was very supportive when Danielle returned and brought it back to life. Chief Green lived and breathed fire. If fire was a woman, Chief Green would have married it.

"Not a clue," he answered. "We'll probably know more in the morning." He turned and strolled towards the glowing blaze, vanishing like a shadow into the night.

"Like a moth to light," said Eddie, watching him disappear.

"Well, that was helpful," Jen said. "I'm going home. I'll go make my calls. This is too depressing. Do you want me to pick you up tomorrow and we can go to Rocktown together?"

"No. I'll be fine, Mommy," Danielle answered. "You don't have to worry about me."

"I never do," Jen said with a laugh, walking away.

The light from the fire continued to radiate the autumn night. People drifted away like embers, slowly extinguishing into the darkness. The remaining onlookers stared at the flames talking quietly to one another, some laughing, some sipping at something in true West Mendow tradition, others smoking as if there wasn't enough poison in the air. They looked like guests at a bonfire, mesmerized by the unexpected show, banking the scene (pardon the pun) to rehash at the watering and gas holes in the next few weeks.

The firefighters busied themselves doing their best to snuff what was left of the smoldering piles of metal, wood and burned brick of the exterior. The roof had caved in earlier, adding to the bubbling mess like a layer of chocolate syrup on top of melting chocolate ice cream. The staff, one by one, dissipated. Danielle bravely stayed for a few more minutes like a captain going down with her ship, but after a while, she couldn't take the smell anymore, became depressed and wanted to leave. She realized there was nothing left to do but wait for the damage report in the morning. She started tearing as she slowly walked alone back to her car. At first, she thought it was from the smoke, but soon realized she was feeling the overwhelming events of the day.

The destruction of her branch finally broke her. She spent years building her professional reputation, and it was suddenly crashing all around her. The people in the head office didn't trust her. Her best friend, Jen, doubted her sanity. She couldn't even kick-start a normal relationship with the desperate bachelor next door who probably thought she was nuts. Yup. Most likely that was over too. She convinced herself that If he really cared, he would have followed her to the fire, held her hand, and whispered to her, telling her it was going to be alright.

On the other hand, she didn't know him that well, and all signs were pointing to the fact that he was a big jerk. Imagine, making a pass at her within minutes of her arrival. What a cad.

What was wrong with her? She wondered if this is what it felt like to hit bottom. Yes, there was always the personal empire she built in and around West Mendow, but it was never enough. Yes, it was great inheriting a bunch of great, fertile land which handily turned into an agricultural jackpot. But there was more to prove. She wanted to conquer the business world and make it on her own in a man's world. 9/11 kicked her off the ladder. Since then, she was slowly climbing back up until Bill Smith's ghost shoved her off again.

She sat inside her car for a while, watching the fire slowly smolder. Officer Joe discreetly kept people away from her, assuming, and rightly so, she was too distraught to talk. Her cell phone was vibrating, buzzing, and beeping incessantly. The news was getting out, and she knew a million people wanted to talk to her. However, she only had to speak to one–Suzanne–her regional director–to advise her of the contingency plan in motion. She needed to get that call out of the way pronto so she could focus on her own misery and what to do about it. She called, spoke business for only a few minutes, while Suzanne muttered a few "hang in there's" and said goodbye.

The fire was almost out and the final stragglers had slipped into the shadows. Joe drove off waving goodbye. The silence of a typical evening in downtown West Mendow was returning. Danielle put her seat back and closed her eyes. Her phone went off again, signaling a text. Thinking it may be Suzanne with a last-minute thought, she looked at the screen. The number was unrecognizable, but the text message was short and to the point.

"I want the flash drive. See what I can do? Next time, it won't be as subtle."

She sat up with a bolt. She couldn't believe what she was seeing! She looked outside the car, searching for someone who may be using a phone. It was too dark to see anything. She realized she was alone in that part of the street and what was left of the action was happening over 50 feet away. Feeling vulnerable and off-guard, she made sure she locked her doors. She threw the phone on the passenger seat, started her car, put it in drive, and took off.

Speeding down Cooper Street, Danielle's mind raced as fast. "Not as subtle?" she thought. What is this person going to do next? Release an atomic bomb? Could the deranged maniac be targeting her house next?

Her phone signaled another text. She gasped.

She was not one for texting and driving, but now she was nervous that somebody may be following her. She reached over for the phone.

"I know u have it."

Checking her rearview mirror, she kept driving.

Another message. "You can't escape, Danny."

She slammed on the brakes. There were only two people that called her Danny. One was killed last week in a hotel downtown by three bullets, and the other one she would have loved to kill herself if he hadn't been in One World Trade when it collapsed. It couldn't be.

A police siren blasted through the silence of the night, and the inside of the car lit up like a microwave oven. Danielle looked to the right to see Young Officer Joe driving up beside her. He flapped his arms up and down, which she assumed meant 'roll down your window'.

Joe was normally a numnut, but tonight his timing was brilliant. She quickly did what she was told. She hoped the texter was watching.

"Hey Danielle, you know there's no texting and driving this town," he said with a wink and a smile.

"Ha, ha Joe." She answered in her best pseudo-laugh.

"Actually–I was just checking to make sure you're okay. You had a weird look on your face and you were driving pretty fast."

Regaining some composure, Danielle thought this was very opportune. "No, No, I'm fine. Thanks for asking. But can you do me a great big favor? I have so much on my mind right now that I forgot to give something to Chief Green before I left the scene. Can you give him this flash drive? It's the blueprint of the branch and the surrounding property. He may need it for the inspectors' tomorrow."

"Yes, of course!" Joe answered, excited to be an important participant delivering vital information in Chief Green's investigation.

Danielle reached into her glove compartment and pulled out an old flash drive she kept in her car for the times she needed to double-check names, phone numbers, and statistics when she did her property rounds. As she made the hand-off to Young Officer Joe, she leaned very far out the window and waved the gadget around making sure everyone within a 50-mile radius could see it. He stretched his arm out trying to grab for the target a couple of times but Danielle kept pulling it away at the last second so anybody watching would get the point– "Flash Drive to Joe". She finally allowed him to latch on to it. They both pulled on it for a few more seconds until Danielle let go. Officer Joe fell back to his seat, curiously eyeing the little prize.

"Thanks," Danielle said, sitting back in her seat while picturing the other precious flash drive in her underwear drawer.

"No problem," Joe replied, slipping the flash drive into his breast pocket and giving it a pat like it was a good little boy. "I'll make sure I give it to him first thing in the morning."

He never questioned why on earth Danielle would have blueprints of her branch on a flash drive in her glove compartment, as if people do that all the time. Of course, Danielle counted on that. "Regards to the family! And send me a picture of little Emily in her Tutu so I can keep it on my desk!" Danielle yelled out as she put her window up.

Before Joe could say "Will Do", she put the car in drive and took off again.

The phone was silent. If the texter was watching, she hoped the diversion would shut down the stalking, at least until tomorrow. Meanwhile, she realized she was putting off the inevitable. She had to look at that flash drive that was back in her dresser. Someone shot Bill Smith over it. Her branch was burned down because of it (obviously no coincidence) and it ruined her dinner date–jerk or no jerk! And the icing on the cake? She hated being called Danny. Did the texter know that?

Danielle kept checking her mirrors, looking to see if anyone was following her, but the roads were quiet. West Mendow was lapsing back to boredom despite the most exciting event that just happened since that time a small plane landed in someone's cornfield and killed a deer. After all, it was after 10 pm and it was time to hunker down in another true West Mendow tradition.

But Danielle couldn't rest. She needed answers.

Chapter 15

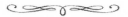

As she drove farther and farther from the smoldering wreckage of her professional life, Danielle's thoughts went from her own miserable circumstances to what could be happening at home. "Eleni's at home alone," she said out loud, horrified at the thought that whoever was after her created the fire to distract her while they were ransacking her home. "No," she said under her breath, trying to convince herself. That plan would be too extreme, too risky. But maybe not. Someone who may have already murdered someone could be that deranged when sending a message. She checked the rearview mirror for the hundredth time.

Shivering with these crazy thoughts, she drove faster down Beatrice Lane towards her house. A light between the thick row of trees surrounding her property caught her eye. Instinctively, she slammed hard on the brakes and glanced around, hoping it was just an animal to avoid hitting and not someone lurking in the woods. She made sure her doors were locked and her cell phone nearby in case it was the arsonist. It could also be Rake out training for his imaginary triathlon. She didn't want to hit him either. It would mean losing out on another potential boyfriend. A damaged car, no boyfriend. She hated when that happened: Could this dreadful day just end?

Nothing stirred while the car idled. She sat, listening to the silence of the forest. Her breaths were quick and the beating of her heart went up a notch. "Calm down!" she told herself. Her nerves were on edge. Was this all in her imagination? As she took her foot off the brake, a silver fox trotted out from the woods, turned, gave her a wearied look, and continued crossing the road. It was that fox, Danielle thought, a bit relieved. Danielle always hated that fox. It lived somewhere very close to her driveway, scaring the heck out of her at all hours. How many times had she tried to run it over?

With her heartbeats settling back to normal, she checked the rearview mirror for the one hundredth and one time, just to make sure, before she made the left into her driveway. As she approached the entrance to her home, she thought she saw St. Catherine give her the thumbs up-a gesture she does mostly when Danielle makes it to the door without incident after a few too many cocktails. So far, so good.

The house was dark just as she left it. The front door was still locked. Nobody tried to break in-at least from there. She inserted her key and walked into the marble hallway. Her heels broke the silence of the house and she bent down to take them off. She reached for the light switch, but before she could turn it on, the house suddenly brightened.

"Who there?" a voice called out from somewhere. "Eh? Eh? Who izzz?"

"Ah, the human alarm system," Danielle thought to herself, satisfied that Eleni just earned another bonus.

She sighed, trying to relieve some of the stress of the evening, "It's me, Eleni"

Eleni came out from the shadows. She stood in her traditional black skirt and blouse–her long grey hair loose around her shoulders. "You have bad date with Reek? You home too early."

Danielle noticed she was holding a rolling pin in her left hand and a long carving knife in her right. "Um, are you, cooking something?"

"No. Why you ask?" she replied quickly.

"Well, you know. What's in your hands." She pointed, wondering if Eleni had just killed an intruder.

"I get ready for bed," Eleni replied shrugging her shoulders like it was an idiotic remark and everyone carries these tools to bed with them.

"I thought maybe you heard something that maybe scared you? You know, like a noise outside or something?" Danielle said casually, hoping Eleni couldn't detect the actual concern.

"Noise? No noise." Eleni replied. Sniffing, she

continued. "You smell like smoke. You try to cook at Reek's house? I told you never cook. You don't cook good. Reek get sick?"

Danielle gave Eleni her fake laugh, "Ha, ha. No, no. I didn't cook. We had an emergency at the bank. It caught on fire. I had to leave Rake's house as soon as I got there and go watch my lovely branch burn to the ground." Saying it out loud drove the enormity of the event home. A wave of sadness overtook her.

"Oh. 'Ise Matiamesni'". Eleni answered, shaking her head and wagging her finger at her. After all these years of having Eleni in her house, Danielle knew what that meant. She had been given the evil eye by some mystery person out in the stratosphere. That was terrible in Eleni's book.

"What?" Danielle said, rolling her eyes bracing herself for Eleni's lecture about the Evil Eye, its symptoms and cures.

"Yes, you have the Evil Eye. I teach you that, you remember? I start prayers to make bad luck go away," she said while fishing around for her Evil Eye Dispersing tools in her pockets.

"Right, the Evil Eye." Here we go. Danielle took a quick look around. Everything other than Eleni, of course, appeared normal. Reminding herself that downloading that flash drive was vital, she made a run for the stairs. Her escape had to be swift before Eleni could suck her in further with this insane conversation. Climbing two steps at a time, she yelled back, "I'm good! No need to summon anyone from the other side!" She reached the landing in marathon time and took a quick peek down to see Eleni's dark figure shaking her head, pulling something colorful out of her pocket then spitting at some invisible spirit.

The flash drive was just where she left it. Danielle grabbed it from her underwear drawer, thankful there were no perverts that beat her to it. She was dying to look at it at that moment, but one laptop was downstairs and her other one was in the trunk of her car. She had to get out of there. The last thing she wanted to do was have Eleni standing over her shoulder, reciting some mumbo jumbo while spitting away evil spirits and distracting her.

Maybe she could go to Rake's house? No. Talk about distractions. There was no way she could focus on technology while that hunk of manhood was nearby. There was only one person left.

Carefully sitting on the edge of her bed hence she slides off the slippery Gold Brocade Bedspread the Prince's father gifted her at the closing of the deal (remember, she made sure it was dry cleaned–twice!) she picked up the phone on her black lacquered nightstand and called the only person who would listen to her at this time of night.

"Don't you ever rest?" Jen asked without bothering to say hello.

"I hope we're still on speaking terms because I'm ready to finish the story," Danielle replied, trying to pique Jen's interest.

"Seriously? And I'm ready for bed. Bobby's ready for the nuthouse after watching the kids all night. All we want to do is crawl under the covers and pretend we're in a dark mine that just collapsed with no way in and no way out."

"That's strange, Jen. When did you think that one up?" Danielle said sarcastically.

"Go to bed. If you thought today was bad, tomorrow's going to be like an erupting volcano."

"This can't wait," Danielle pleaded.

"What's wrong now?" Jen sighed. Danielle could hear Bobby in the background whispering for Jen to hang up on her. "Is there another big black car following you? Did your house burn down too?"

She paused. "I'm getting these weird texts."

"Danielle!" Jen yelled.

"I know, I know. It sounds so stupid. But whoever's texting me wants the flash drive," Danielle replied, agitated.

"So, what's on it? What is this big deal about this flash drive? I'm tired of hearing about it. You acted like a lunatic this afternoon with that note that came through the drive-thru. And that story about the reporter–well, that one had B.S. sprinkled all over it." Danielle could hear Bobby groaning in the background.

"Okay, okay. But I had to think fast, and my brain is on overload. It's all too much now..." she said, straining her voice and pretending to sound tormented. She was hoping to use the ploy to gain Jen's sympathy.

While Danielle listened to Bobby use some inappropriate language and tug at the phone, she remembered that while driving home, she saw the light on at Sheila's Café. Sheila would allow a few late-night winos to stay and drink on occasional nights, and with the big fire, she probably couldn't get rid of them. Danielle was hungry and could go for a strong glass of something to calm her down. Plus, she could use Sheila's illegal Saturday poker night back room to set up a laptop and make a few more calls while she was trying to think about her next moves.

"I need you to meet me at Sheila's," Danielle stated.

"What? That's random. Look, Bobby's had it and went to sleep on the couch. I have the bed all to myself and that's a rare treat. I want to enjoy it. We have a big day tomorrow, Danielle. I need my rest," Jen begged.

"No. I need to see what's on that flash drive and

I need you to be there." She sensed she was losing this one.

"Why don't you come to my house. I really don't want to get dressed again. We can do it here, "Jen implored.

Danielle took some deep breaths for a dramatic pause. "Jen, I don't want to put you or your family in any danger. I'm not paranoid, but I know there's someone out there making a lot of trouble for me. We've got to figure this out. Plus, I'm hungry and you never have anything for adults to eat at your house. Please?" she pleaded.

Danielle knew that Jen loved a good whodunit. She hoped that the secret of the flash drive and solving the mysterious case of her temporary insanity might be just enough to get her out of her pajamas.

Jen broke. "You will pester me all night until I break, right?"

Danielle relaxed. The argument was turning the corner in her favor. "No, I'll be with you till we figure this out."

"You know. If the black SUV doesn't get you, Bobby will," Jen said.

"I am truly grateful. Tell him I'll put another of your kids through college," Danielle replied.

"You said that 14 kids ago." She gave out a low groan. "I'll be there in twenty minutes. Tell Sheila to make a pot of coffee. This is going to be a long night"

"Thanks, Jen. Be careful! Oh and bring your laptop!" Danielle said, smiling to herself in victory.

The phone went silent on the other end. Staring at it for a second, she thought about how she tortures that girl. Jen was in that tiny circle of friends that she could count on and vice versa.

Quickly changing into a more comfortable pair of jeans and a sweater, Danielle quietly descended the stairs and tiptoed her way to the front door, hoping she wouldn't trigger Eleni. Gingerly twisting the doorknob, she slipped through and made a beeline for her car. She checked her handbag three times to make sure that the flash drive was there and reprimanded herself each time for being so obsessive compulsive. Satisfied that all was well; she put her car into drive. Her stomach clenched at the sudden sight of Eleni staring at her from the door–a vision in black except for the long knife at her side, brightly reflecting the moonlight. Others would say she didn't look happy, but then again, Danielle knew it was Eleni's normal face. Conflicted, she stopped the car.

"I'm off to Sheila's for an hour. I have a meeting," she yelled through the window feeling guilty about sneaking off.

Stalwart and without a word, Eleni waved her off with the knife. Permission granted. Relieved and grateful that she had Eleni guarding the homestead, Danielle sped down the driveway and raced back to town.

Chapter 16

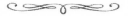

It was almost 11:00 pm when she turned into Sheila's back parking lot. Straining her neck, Danielle took a wistful look but could barely see the smoke from the last vestiges of her ruined bank on the other side of town. She shook off the sight, grabbed her handbag, got out of her car, popped the trunk open, and pulled out a laptop.

The parking lot was conveniently located behind the restaurant which was perfect for hiding her car. She never considered that the bright red color which tonight was shining like a beacon under the full fall moon would at some point be a liability, screaming her location to the world. Her sudden stealth status required some changes from now on and she made a mental note to look for a more modest car. How depressing, she thought. But if her new bizarre pastime was going to be devoted to sneaking around looking for murderers and such, something black, low key, and of course, elegant would make more sense.

As she mulled that over, she opened the back door to the Café and entered through the kitchen. Sheila was baking pies.

"Mmm, that smells so good. "she said, inhaling the mix of apples, cinnamon, and butter.

"Oh, Danielle! What a surprise! I heard about your branch from Old Ned, who stopped in for a beer a few minutes ago. Too bad the fire didn't spread to that dump of a place he still calls a coffee shop," she said laughing. "Anyhow, sorry. What a bummer."

Sheila was rolling out some dough, her flabby upper arms jiggling like jello on a stick as she pushed and pulled the rolling pin. She had flour all over her apron, the floor, the walls...everywhere. The place looked like there had just been a flour fight.

"Yeh, bummer," Danielle answered as she eyed the bowl of sugar-soaked, gooey apples.

"You want a slice? I'm just taking a few out of the oven right now. I made some fresh tuna salad too." Sheila asked, pushing a wisp of grey blonde hair out of her face and wiping her hands on her jeans.

With all the drama of the day, Danielle hadn't had a bite since lunch. The aromas were getting to her. Danielle's stomach started consuming her brain and without hesitation, she agreed to eat all sorts of evil calories.

"Yes, yes, and yes, but first things first," she said, walking over to the refrigerator where she knew Sheila kept her secret stash of Sancerre–her favorite Sauvignon Blanc - and poured herself a generous glass. She took a "Sailor's Sip" and told Sheila she was going to the backroom to make some phone calls and do a few emails.

"Jen's meeting me here too, and she's on her way. Don't let anyone know we're here, okay? I'm not ready to talk to anyone yet," she added.

"Okay, mum's the word. Did the Chief figure out what happened yet?" Sheila asked cheerfully while cutting off a chunk of dough and stuffing it in her mouth.

"Not yet." She answered, eyeing Sheila and wondering how much crust went into her pies or into her mouth. "I'm off."

"Okay," Sheila sang out and resumed rolling out what was left of the dough.

On her way out to the hallway, she heard Sheila say to herself, "I can't imagine what would set up a blaze like that so fast. It was like a bomb hit it!"

Maybe it did, thought Danielle.

The house was cut like a cross. The front door led to a hallway connecting the front of the house to the back. All the public rooms were in the front. The back rooms faced the parking lot. Old black and white photos of what the house had looked like in the late early 1900s lined the wall. Decades later, the house looked about the same. The original paint on the white wooden clapboard that wrapped around the outside walls continued to hang on desperately. Shutters could have been straighter and doors better fitted, but it just wouldn't be Sheila's. West Mendow didn't like change, and Sheila's was one of the last hold-outs to a primal, simpler time. The pub continued to smell of lingering generations of beer from decades of trapped air that couldn't escape from the windows that were painted shut forever.

The floors warmly embraced her footsteps as Danielle made her way to the farthest room. The vibe of this deliberately dumpy establishment kept it warm and friendly. Totally unprofitable, Danielle was still proud she was preserving a bit of West Mendow history by maintaining this landmark.

The back room where they would meet held a beat-up old oak rectangular table and six wooden chairs. Danielle imagined this was once an old guest room for weary travelers stopping in for a meal on their way to or from the Capital. There was a working fireplace at the far end that wasn't working that night or ever since she owned the place. The walls had some old prints scattered on them showing scenes of West Mendow when horses were the only transportation and three or four buildings made up most of the downtown. A beautiful reproduction of the countryside overlooking the Potomac River hung over the fireplace with a placard that read, "Mendow Farm 1890". Danielle had the original in her home.

This had always been their secret meeting room when she and Jen had to conspire off-site about something and wanted a quick bite. Many successful and devious plans were launched from here away from the big ears at the bank. They considered this their home away from home - a place to go where noisy kids and annoying housekeepers couldn't ambush them. The excitement and challenge of the next hours were igniting her adrenalin. Her heart began to beat a little faster. With a smile, she set her glass of Sancerre on the table and unpacked her laptop.

Jen arrived five minutes later, marching in like a bloodthirsty zombie ready to rip her apart. Without speaking, she took off her overcoat, threw it haphazardly over a chair, and sat down. Her appearance, confirmed she had one foot in bed before she called because her normally perfectly executed blond hair was up in a messy ponytail and she was still in her pink pajamas.

The two made quite a rumpled pair. Danielle appeared to be barely hanging on to her once immaculate big date night look and Jen, who looked like she called it a night over an hour ago.

Danielle had already set up her laptop and was fishing around in her handbag for the flash drive. Trying to lighten the mood, she started, what she thought, was a funny story about a call she made earlier to Eleni to tell her to keep the doors locked and call the police if anything outside or inside looked suspicious.

Laughing, she continued the story. "Eleni said she would kill anyone who came into the house with her bare hands like she did to a bear that tried to attack her in the mountains of Crete when she was a young girl."

Jen stared at her for a few seconds, blinked, yawned, looked away, then opened her laptop.

"She said she killed a bear, Jen! What a piece of work!" Danielle said, bobbing her head around to try to catch Jen's eyes again.

"Maybe we should alert the military and have her sent to Afghanistan to conquer Isis once and for all," Jen replied curtly, staring at her laptop while it was powering up.

"Funny," Danielle said under her breath. "Ha, Ha."

Sheila quietly brought in some pie, sandwiches, and a cup of coffee for Jen. She discreetly left the room, leaving a light dusting of flour in her wake like a little fairy.

Jen got up and closed the door. She sat down next to Danielle, who returned to her vast handbag in search of the flash drive. Jen remained silent.

"Ah, success!" Danielle said to herself, pulling it out of her bag with relief. She held it up to the light like she wanted to read what was inside without plugging it in.
"Give me that thing," Jen said sharply, snatching it away from her. "Before we see what's in it, tell me again where it came from."

Danielle realized she never finished the story. She took another gulp of her wine and a giant bite of apple pie then began explaining to Jen how she came home, found the envelope, and read the cryptic note from Bill Smith which made her jump out of her skin.

"So let me get this straight," Jen said while forking a piece of apple pie in her mouth. "This guy who got shot three times at the Willard last Thursday has time to mail you a flash drive but didn't bother to write anything more that would give you a clue as to what this is all about. Okay—was there a return address on the envelope?"

"No," she answered vigorously, shaking her head.

Swallowing another bite, Jen asked, "Was it even mailed or hand-delivered?"

Danielle thought back to that afternoon and tried to picture the envelope. It was a large manila 8 X 12. There was a postmark and a stamp, but in her panic, her mind didn't register it.

"You remember. It came to the bank and Eddie brought it to my house with the shoes. I know it was mailed from somewhere, but I didn't pay attention at the time," Danielle said with her eyes closed, hoping she could picture it. "Eleni must have thrown the envelope away because I never saw it again. You know, I didn't think to look for it

189

either. I guess that was kind of stupid," she said, wrinkling her nose and reaching for her wineglass.

"You're off your game, girl," Jen replied, straightening up and planting her butt firmly in her chair. She appeared more energized either from the challenge of deciphering the mystery flash drive or from the overly sweet pie. "Okay, we'll deal with that later. Let's see what's on this baby."

Danielle felt like she was wilting as the tension was slowly vanishing. Her partner in crime was on board. This should get a lot more fun.

Jen powered up the laptop and plugged in the flash drive. "It's probably a bunch of photos from his last vacation to Bali. 'Hey, thanks for helping me embezzle the money.' 'Here's how big my stomach got and how much hair I lost in the last ten years.'" Jen rambled on and on as she keyed in her password and located the drives.

Laughing quietly, Danielle leaned over and focused on the screen. The day's events could be leading up to this moment. She stared in silence, waiting for the first hint of what the murder and today's disasters were all about.

Columns of numbers burst on to the screen. They both jumped back as if the numbers were going to spray all over their faces. Giggling at their simultaneous reaction, they pulled in closer for a better look.

"What the hell is this?" Jen leaning in even further to get a better look.

"Scroll down. Let's see if there's an end to this," instructed Danielle as she scooted her chair close to Jen.

Jen hit the down arrow button. The numbers went on forever.

They looked at each other and shrugged. Sitting back, Danielle took another sip of her wine and Jen reached out for the coffee, gulping down half a cup. They looked back at the screen, hoping the break would help them see clearly.

"Okay, so he sent me a flash drive with a bunch of numbers and said I would know what to do with this," Danielle said with irritation.

"Did Bill think that you were a cryptographer in another life?" Jen asked.

"No, Miss Smarty Pajama Pants. Once a banker, always a banker." Danielle replied, staring at the screen.

"And you were just professionally acquainted?" Jen asked, squinting like there was more to the story.

"Of course! What are you implying?" Danielle responded, wrinkling her nose. "Ewww."

"Nothing, nothing. Just ruling stuff out like poker probabilities or lottery sequences. Gambling stuff," Jen smirked, turning back to the screen.

Leaning back in her chair, Danielle said, "I will not ask how you know those things, but who knows with that guy. Maybe all those business trips he used to go on were only to the slot machines in Vegas."

Jen turned to Danielle. "What business trips?"

"He was on the road a lot. I always thought that was a bit bizarre for an Operations Manager but the General Manager in New York seemed okay with it and Capital International was always running perfectly," she explained.

"Who was the General Manager?" Jen asked, rubbing her right temple.

Danielle took her eyes off the screen. "Jeremy Weebly. He's the president of NOBA Bank now."

"NOBA? Never heard of that one," Jen frowned.

"Northern Bank of Annapolis. We have lunch now and then. At one point, he asked me to buy the bank and put him out of his misery." Danielle said offhandedly.

"Why didn't you? You always wanted a bank." Jen answered coolly.

Head tilted, Danielle answered like she was talking to a child. "Optics, of course"

"Yes, optics, the first thing that came to my mind..." Jen said, nodding then rolling her eyeballs.

"Not the bank that I want, okay? Too small." Shaking her head, Danielle continued. "Anyhow, forget Jeremy. He was always a bit disconnected about what was happening around him. He couldn't stand New York and jumped ship right after 9/11 taking the first offer he could get. We can write him off. Too squeamish. Minor league."

"You know, it's those squeamish, unassuming ones..." Jen said wickedly.

"Trust me. Let's just move on." Danielle squinted as she started looking passed Jen and began staring at the reproduction over the fireplace. Jen turned to see what she was looking at. The room was dimly lit by the screen of the laptop. The wind had shifted downward toward Sheila's and the smell of the fireplace in the main pub started seeping through the walls of the old house. A faint noise from the television could be heard interfering with the occasional laugh or the clink of a glass coming from the pub room.

This was a safe haven for some of the old-timers who had no one to go home to or someone they didn't want to go home to. Sheila kept the place open as long as she could stay awake, and even

193

then she sometimes left and had the last person lock up. It was just that kind of place, and West Mendow was that kind of town until maybe tonight.

Jen looked back at Danielle, who was still staring at the print on the wall. "What's so fascinating about that painting tonight. You've seen it a million times." Jen asked.

"It's talking to me," Danielle answered, still looking at it. "But I don't know what it's saying."

With her mouth open, Jen stared at Danielle. "I'm worrying about you for about the hundredth time today. I remember a Twilight Zone episode about a man who stared at a painting too long and then became part of the painting. Is the old farm sucking you in?"

Danielle remained silent.

"It's saying to 'stay out of it, right?'" Jen said. "Hey, I'll play. Let's just get to the end of where this was going sometime tonight. We have a big day tomorrow. You know, we have to come out of the ashes." Jen sighed.

Danielle remained quiet.

With her voice getting quieter and more deliberate, Jen continued with resignation, "Okay, its saying 'stay out' because you're going to get lost." She stopped. There was no reaction. Nothing She went on. "It's saying, 'stay out' because we won't be able to see you behind the trees."

"Yes, that's it!" Danielle cried out, coming out of her trance and slapping her hand on the table. "You're right!" You won't be able to see me because you're looking at the forest!" Grabbing Jen by the shoulders, she shook her maniacally, eyes gleaming. She let go and stared at the screen. "We need to see the trees. Break the numbers down. Bill was a banker. We are bankers. What do bankers do? Move money! Jen, the trees. We have to look at the trees.!"

Both ladies started breathing heavier. They looked at each other, eyes blazing. There was a slight pause. Seconds later, Jen announced excitedly, "I have a thought!" She looked at the screen and pointed.

"A thought! Wonderful! I'm so proud of you! I knew you could do it! What, what is it?" Danielle said, turning to see where her finger was pointing.

Jen rolled her eyes. "Ha, ha. Okay. Cut the drama. Look. It seems to be a spreadsheet without columns or punctuation. The first six numbers are dates."

"Yes. They do all look like dates. Okay, what are the rest of the numbers.?" Danielle said, shifting closer to the screen.

"Okay, a universal rule in banking is that all account numbers have seven digits, correct. And all account numbers assigned to bank members of the American Bankers Association can be written with seven digits, right? Well, look at this line. "051505" could be May 15, 2005."

"Yes, I see. Keep going," Danielle encouraged.

"The next seven numbers are probably an account number of City Savings because the second set of seven numbers are City Savings ABA number…. I know them all," Jen said, proudly turning to Danielle and pointing a thumb towards her chest.

"Such a genius. And you do recognize the next set of seven numbers," Danielle said, leaning closer.

"Geez. Those are Capital National Bank account numbers. And they all start with 062. Oh, my! That's our branch!" she said, sitting up in astonishment.

They turned to each other–mouths open–like they were just struck by lightning. They looked back at the screen to confirm it. They both nodded in unison. "What the hell?" Jen said under her breath.

There was a final set of numbers that were either four or five digits. Jen ran her finger down the column, reading some numbers out loud. "I bet these are dollar amounts." She whispered.

Danielle sat silently as her mind tried to absorb what she was seeing. Jen continued to toggle through page after page of numbers with dates ranging from 2012 to 2019. Seventeen years of account numbers, ABA account numbers, and dollar volumes passed right before their eyes.

"Amazing," Jen said. "We're looking at millions of dollars in transactions coming into and out of our branch on a daily basis."

"Geez, where's all this originating and how was it being swept out?" Danielle said incredulously.

They both paused. Danielle turned to face Jen. "And why the hell didn't we know about it?"

"Well, ladies," chimed a male voice, "It sounds like you've been laundering a good deal of money from your little outpost for years."

Jen and Danielle looked up, startled. Rake Harris was leaning in the doorway. Besides an immediate mistrust of him activated by this sneaky entrance, she took two seconds to admire how great he looked standing there in his tight-butt jeans, cowboy boots, white tailored Ralph Lauren cotton shirt and navy blue blazer. His hair was a bit wind-blown and a light evening shadow was dusting his face.

But she froze when she noticed that hidden underneath his jacket was a gun holster. She braced herself for the worse.

Jen didn't flinch. "Who the hell are you?" she asked defiantly.

He straightened up and took a step into the room. He moved his hand towards his back.

Danielle grabbed the edge of the table and pushed it with all her might at him. She caught him right in the groin. He doubled over, fell and curled in a fetal position.

"Danielle, what are you doing? You could have chopped him in half!" Jen cried out as she shot out her chair.

They both heard a rifle unlock and turned to see Sheila point two barrels at Rake's head.

"I saw this guy sneaking around the back and next thing you know, he's in here listening to you two through the door. If he wasn't so darn good-looking, I would have blown his head off."

Rake moaned and turned over on his back.

"Keep your hands where I could see them, cowboy," Sheila responded totally unsympathetic to the fact that he was obviously doubled over in pain.

"Keep that heater on him, girl, until we find out what he's doing here," Danielle said as she marched over and stared down at his writhing body. "Rake, what on earth are you doing here?" Danielle asked angrily. Another interesting prospect turned out to be some weirdo stalker, she thought to herself.

"Put the rifle down, Sheila" Rake winced, still trying to catch his breath. "I wasn't planning on shooting anyone."

"Then what were you reaching for back there, Tic Tacs?" Danielle asked.

"My Badge," he winced.

The ladies all looked at one another, perplexed. Sheila lowered her rifle.

"Keep calm. I'm going to reach into my back pocket," Rake said. Leaning up slightly, he did as he said and brought out a little folded wallet. He flipped it open with his thumb and held it up high enough so they could see it.

"Rake Harris, FBI," he said as his eyes closed and his head hit the floor.

Chapter 17

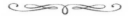

The three ladies stood together transfixed on Rake. Silently, Sheila wondered if she was going to be arrested for pointing a loaded firearm at a federal agent. Jen questioned herself on whether she could get tossed in the brink for bad sarcasm. Danielle was mortified because in a panic she almost cut her neighbor and evolving, but still mysterious suitor, in half.

"Can one of you ladies give me a hand?" Rake winced putting his badge away and reaching up, hoping someone would grab on to him.

Nobody moved. Rake collapsed back down.

"Hey, what's all the ruckus in here?" someone shouted from the hallway. A wobbly old man appeared in the doorway. He swayed here and there and finally focused on Rake, who was still splattered on the floor.

"Hey man, what are you doing down there?" He asked, blinking like he couldn't believe what he was seeing. He then noticed Sheila holding the rifle on her side and the table out of place.

"Trying to catch a mouse, Fred. Go back to the bar and call your wife to pick you up. I think you had a little too much to drink." Sheila answered, waving him away.

In the few seconds that Fred the Drunk had captured everyone's attention, Danielle spotted the computer on the floor next to Jen, caught her eye, and signaled to take out the flash drive.

"Oh, okay," Fred answered squinting at Rake. "Must have been some moose."

"Mouse, Fred, mouse. There are no moose in West Mendow." Sheila answered, laying her rifle against a wall. She took him by the shoulders and turned him around. She then gave him a little push to get him started out the door. He walked towards a broom closet.

"Wrong way!" Sheila called out to him, pointing her finger down the hall that led back to the bar. "Geez, he must have gone through a whole keg tonight. Marybeth is going to kill him," she said while turning her attention back to Rake, who was slowly getting up on his own. He took a deep breath while holding on to his groin and looked at all three of them. Everyone looked at each other in embarrassment. Sheila was just about to say something when Rake cut her off.

"Don't talk," he said, holding up his hand. "Don't you have something in the oven?" he asked politely, giving her a way out.
"Uh," she said, appearing momentarily confused. "Yes, yes, I do. I should go check on it"

She turned to Danielle and Jen. "Are you going to be okay?"

Jen and Danielle both nodded in the affirmative. Watching Sheila, Danielle started playing nervously with her earlobe. She turned to Jen, lifted her chin, and opened her eyes wider in her best Gloria Swanson impression. She hoped Jen was catching her message. Jen coughed. Mission accomplished. Danielle thanked Sheila for all her help. Sheila opened her mouth slightly like she was about to say something, then quickly changed her mind. She turned towards the door, slung her rifle over her shoulder, gave one more quizzical glance back, and left the room.

Danielle held that maniacal expression for a few more seconds. Jen coughed again, hoping Danielle would relax her face. Rake tilted his head, watching the two of them with amusement.

Jenn rolled her eyes and reached for her coat. "I gotta go too. Big day tomorrow. Turning to Danielle, she asked, "Are you going to be alright?"

"She'll be fine." Rake answered before Danielle could open her mouth.

Danielle shot him a nasty look. "I can speak for myself, Mr. Party Crasher." Turning back to Jen she asked, "Yes, I'll be fine. We're good, right?" she asked, playing nervously again with her earlobe.

"Yes, we're good, Danielle." She answered, patting her pocket then pulling out her keys. "See ya tomorrow."

Rake watched Jen leave, then moved closer to Danielle, who was picking up her laptop from the floor.

"Shoot." She said placing it on the table. The screen had broken off halfway from the keyboard and all the lights were out.

"Dead?" Rake asked, staring at the pile of metal.

"Like a stiff in a morgue." She said feigning sadness. Secretly she was pleased it broke. The flash drive, however, survived and was safely tucked away in Jen's pocket. Not wanting to let Rake know how happy this made her, she punched a few keys feigning frustration and prayed the old horse wouldn't boot up.

She then fumbled around with the screen. For a few seconds, she pretended to try and stick it back on just to drive her fake disappointment home. Finally, she proclaimed that it was hopeless.

"Do you want me to try?" Rake asked, moving closer.

"No, we have plenty at the branch. It's not mine anyhow. It's Jen's. She'll be a little pissed in the morning but now she's going to get a brand new one. I'll send it off to the Technology Department to see if they can salvage anything, "she answered, taking a step back as he closed in on her personal space. Their eyes met. A million thoughts about him raced through her mind, but they always led back to the same question. 'Who the heck was this guy?'. She felt her face flush. She glanced away. All her bravado vanished, and suddenly she was tired. She needed a hug, and this guy fit the bill in his mysterious way. But she would not let him know it until she had some answers. She was losing steam and his aura seemed to be wearing her down. 'I am not a quitter. I can do this. No man is going to get the better of me unless I want him to,' she thought.

She took a deep breath. The words came to her like she was thinking about them all night–which, in truth, she was. "I don't know who you are. Why you're here, and what the hell happened to my life today but I'm tired and I want to go home. But, before I do, can you answer one question for me?" she seethed.

He was so close to her now, she could feel his body heat. "So you want to know why I'm here, right?" he said quietly. She felt his breath on her lips. Not finding the words, she paused for a few seconds, inhaling and exhaling heavily, heart racing, pondering her response while staring into his eyes.

The silence allowed her to regain her composure. "No", she answered matter-of-factly, putting her hand on his chest and giving him a little push away. "I really don't care" although secretly she did - she just wanted to throw him off base with her answer. Plus, that little move gave her a chance to feel his pecs, which were impressively solid and left her with an inward thrill. Outwardly, however, she needed to keep the upper hand for the next few minutes until she could get the heck out of there and sort things out.

Rake was rattled. "Oh!" he replied, moving back further.

"All I want to know is, well, when are you going to leave me alone!" On that note, she grabbed the broken laptop and her handbag and walked passed him to the door.

To her surprise, he followed her like a puppy.

"Don't you have any pride?" she called over her shoulder as she continued walking. He kept a couple of feet behind her as she made her way down the hall to the kitchen. Sheila was there, taking more pies out of the oven while Danielle and Rake paraded by.

"You need help, honey?" she shouted as they marched past her.

"No" they both shouted back in unison and in single file, they exited through the back door.

Danielle could see the smoke of the branch in the distance as she marched towards her car–a reminder of how spectacularly she lost control of the entire day. The air had turned chilly and most of the homes in the neighborhood had darkened as it was now close to midnight. The reverie from Sheila's front room was quietly fading into the night. Rake was still on her heels.

"Danielle," he said, grabbing her arm and swinging her around. "I'm worried about you."

"How can you be worried about me already? We just met this afternoon when you invited yourself into my home. I ran out of your house even before we could enchant each other with the usual barrage of stupid questions boys and girls ask when they first meet. Then you barge into a work meeting where my head teller and I are reviewing some private information, accuse me of money laundering, make it very clear to show me you're wearing a gun holster–and by the way, I assume there's a gun somewhere on your body–then the icing on the cake, no less, flash an FBI badge. Really Rake, I've had enough of you today." She said with false annoyance.

She poked her index finger in his chest. "Now please let me go before I scream that you're molesting me." She jerked her arm out of his grasp.

Rake looked down. "Gee, I never looked at it that way. I guess I don't think too straight when I'm around you."

His humility disarmed her. She smiled to herself as she watched him kick at a pebble. He ran his hand through his hair–an endearing habit she noticed about him when he seemed confused. The angry girl was neutralizing. This was awkward. She stopped staring at him, hoping he would stop acting so pathetic. She saw Sheila watching from her kitchen window. She held up her rifle like an umbrella in one hand while her other played hand "thumbs up/thumbs down". Danielle slowly shook her head no. Sheila gave her a big thumbs up, pumped her rifle higher like a victorious soldier and disappeared from view.

Danielle didn't know what to think of Rake at this point. A handsome single FBI agent with mountainous pecs living next door would have been exciting any other day. But today, with all this going on, the timing was suspicious. She had nothing to worry about. After all, she was just an innocent bystander caught in someone else's game. A victim of circumstances. By the time they connected the dots–which could be another 10 years - they would see that.

"What the hell." She said out loud. She put both hands on Rake's face, drew him down to her, and planted a big, long, sloppy kiss right smack on his mouth. He responded quickly. He grabbed her around the waist and pressed her in tightly. Their bodies fit so right together. It felt great.

Before he could say anything, she pulled back, turned around, and hurried towards her car, swinging her rear-end in Rita Steele's style. She got out her keys, jumped in, and took off.

When she looked back through her rearview mirror, Rake was still standing in the same place, rubbing his face and watching her curiously as she drove away. She couldn't help noticing the goofy smile that had grown from ear to ear.

"Nobody can out-surprise me, Rake Harris," she said, pleased with herself. This was the best she had felt all day.

She turned into her driveway. Up ahead, the statue of St. Catherine was glowing from top to bottom as the full moon and the thousands of dollars spent in floodlights lit her up from all over. She looked grand and satisfied, like she just won a battle and was ready to walk on and win the war. But the roller coaster of emotions was hitting bottom again when she saw a police car parked outside of her front door. Were the surprises of the day ever going to end? Maybe after all that happened, she should have expected this.

But as she drove closer, she realized it was just Officer Joe who, upon seeing her drive-in, got out of his car and started walking in her direction. As she drove closer, she lost sight of him in the shadows for a moment and almost ran him over. He jumped quickly out of the way into the light. One day she swore she was going to get him.

"Hey Danielle!" he said cheerfully as she rolled down her car window.

She looked at him warily. "What's going on Joe? Did Eleni call you?" she asked while 99% sure Eleni would first take matters into her own hands and then call an ambulance–before she would call the police.

"No, no," Joe said jovially waving his hand around. "I was driving by and saw someone I didn't recognize standing at the foot of your driveway. Since it was so late, it looked suspicious, so I stopped to see who it was."

Danielle was busy turning off the engine and rummaging in her bag for the house keys–half-listening when Joe's comments suddenly registered in her mind.

"How long ago was this?" Danielle, she looked up with additional concern.

"Oh, just now–maybe five minutes ago," Joe answered, checking his watch then putting it to his ear to make sure it was working.

"Male or female?" Danielle responded quickly.

"Ah…Female," he answered.

"Did she say what she was doing here?" Danielle asked, trying not to sound alarmed.

"She told me she was from the newspaper. I think she said the County Times. She wanted to ask you some questions about the fire," he replied.

That's peculiar, Danielle thought. She wasn't nervous a stranger knew where she lived–after all, the entire town made such a fuss when she bought the Prince's little hideaway–but it was late–very late -to file a story about a local fire. Then again, she wasn't answering her phone to unknown numbers, so any reporter trying to get a quote from the manager of the bank that burned to a cinder for the morning papers had to hunt her down. Okay, sounds legit, she thought. She would let it pass. And she was too drained to begin another chapter of hysteria tonight.

"So what happened to her?" Danielle asked more calmly.

"Don't worry, Danielle. I've always got your back. I shooed her away," Joe said, waving his hand again like he was swatting a fly.

"Thanks for that. I'm really too tired to talk to one more person." Danielle said, hoping Joe would get the hint and shoo himself away too.

He took a step back from her car, then stood there for a few more seconds–perhaps waiting for an order, but Danielle was lost in thought.

"Joe, before you go, did the woman leave a card?"

"No," Joe answered, furrowing his eyebrows like the question required a lot of thought.

What reporter doesn't leave a business card? "Did she have a car?" Danielle asked, feeling the butterflies again about this shadowy figure.

"You know, I don't remember. As soon as she moved out of the way, I drove up here. I don't know how she left. She was a real hottie though," he chuckled.

"Okay, well that's nice," This guy is useless, she thought. It was a miracle he passed the police exam.

Exhausted, she didn't have the strength to worry about one more thing. Lois Lane went poof in the night. But there was a slight permanent crack in her armor after this long and crazy day, and as much as she tried to shrug off even this minor incident, it was just one more thing to shake her up and set off her nerves.

Joe must have sensed that in her. "I'll stand here until you get inside, okay?" he said. "Just give me the all-clear signal and I'll be on my way."

Worn out, Danielle got out of her car. Joe stepped aside, letting her pass–always facing her like she was royalty. True to his word, he was still there when she entered the house and turned on the alarm. She waved at him through the side window and mouthed the words "thank you". Joe walked to his police car taking a last look around, got in and drove off.

As much as she poked fun at him, she knew deep down that he would take a bullet for her–he was that kind of guy. As he made his way down the driveway, she felt a sense of isolation and fear. Joe's departure was her last protection- well, legal protection (who knew what she would have to cover up if Eleni went to town on someone).

It was way past midnight. Danielle slowly and quietly made her way to her bedroom so she wouldn't wake Eleni, the sleeping beast. Her feet became heavier and heavier as she reached the top of the landing. The French doors to her bedroom felt like iron weights as she pulled them open. Once inside, the stress of the day hit her all at once. She could hardly unbutton her blouse to take it off. Her feet were so swollen it took every ounce of energy to peel off her shoes, which she swore had shrunk. Removing her pants felt like she had loosened a giant harness (which it kind of was…) and in two seconds she was in her pink flannel pajamas, under the covers - make-up be damned.

Right before she closed her eyes, she remembered to turn off her cell phone. No more calls, texts, or messages from anyone–were going to be allowed through. She was fried. She reached over to her nightstand and just as her thumb reached the switch, a text popped up. She couldn't help it. Her curiosity was getting the best of her. Did she have a shred of energy left? She closed her eyes tightly. "No, don't do it," said a squeaky little voice in her head. "You'll be sorry!" Another deeper voice responded, "But it could be Jen. You can't miss a text from Jen."

She brought the phone closer. Her eyes opened just a crack. She just wanted to see who it was from.

"What?" She couldn't believe what she was seeing. It was a message from Dolores Kagan, of all people. It surprised Danielle that the woman even knew what a cell phone was. She had to read it. Within a split second, however, her amusement turned to horror.

"I just recognized the picture the FBI guy gave me. It was your old friend Bill Smith. You knew that all along. What are you hiding?"

Danielle let out a moan and fell back on her pillow. "The gig is up. I'm screwed," she said to the invisible jury on the ceiling.

Chapter 18

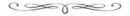

Dolores Kagan knew she was a pain in the butt to everyone at Capital National Bank. She was the first to admit that she spent the last 45 years refining skills that would annoy and grate on people's nerves, like eavesdropping on private conversations and reminding people how late they arrived at the bank that morning. As the longest and possibly the oldest (although she would never admit to that) employee, Dolores could frighten the fearless and demoralize the most driven with one snarky comment or vicious stare.

She had such an irritating personality that even her own dearly departed mother wouldn't respond when she went to visit her at the nursing home - many times pretending to be in a coma or near death.

So when Dolores finished texting everyone who came to see Dr. Place that morning, she poured herself a large congratulatory Johnny Walker and sunk into her big red velvet cushiony reading chair to relax and watch the cars drive up and down Connecticut Avenue from her 12th-floor window.

The Scotch was smooth and doing its job. The traffic got lighter as time passed. The few cars going in and out of the city became a little blurry–their headlights merging into the taillights of the cars and busses ahead of them. As the night wore on, she could still hear the occasional squeaky brakes as cars stopped for lights. Doors continued to open and close as people finished parking and headed back to their apartments from a late night of work or partying. Dolores loved Washington D.C. and she loved her job just for this reason. She watched people all day and all evening. At the office, he helped them dig their graves and then kick them into it. At home, she schemed how to make everyone as miserable as her. And who was going to blame the little old lady in the Chairman's office? She was an institution. She was the bank. She was the game.

Tonight, she was just where she wanted to be–sitting in her favorite big old chair plotting the next twist of her own reality show–wondering how far she had to take it before she got to the best part and could watch as somebody snapped.

She looked around the formal living room for inspiration. The one lamp she had turned on made her dark, heavy furniture look bigger and formless. Gloating to herself in satisfaction, she was pleased that her apartment looked the same as it did 30 years ago. Even the few people who had made it inside recently marveled at how she stopped time. She toasted herself with another congratulatory gulp of her miracle juice.

Putting her head back and closing her eyes, her body relaxed even further. She was just where she wanted to be after hearing the news today. Dolores didn't like change. In fact, she didn't like much of anything. That's why when anyone got too close to changing the status quo, it was time to step in and take them out. Everything was just fine until poor Bill Smith went and got himself shot up at the Willard. Something was going to come down, but she didn't know what. That's why she didn't want to be the first to say anything when she saw the photo that FBI guy with the unfortunate name gave her. She had recognized Smith instantly. What she couldn't understand was why nobody else did. And if they did, why didn't they just say so. What were they covering up?

Her eyes remained closed as she swirled the remaining Scotch and ice in her glass. She kept thinking that at least Teddy would know who he was. They used to have lunch together every other month when he would come down from New York to D.C.

Sitting up just a bit so as not to disturb her "up-do" beehive for too long, (After all, she was taught that flat hair just like panty lines are to be avoided like children on an airplane), she took a deep breath. Her thoughts were coming quicker now as the alcohol relaxed her. Dr. Place was another one, she thought. Although Bill was two senior managers removed, Place met with Smith a month before he disappeared and that man never forgets a face–especially if that face is telling him the bank just lost $10 million.

She also couldn't help notice that Rita quickly shut her up when she went to tell her that she recognized the man in the photo. Rita knew too.

And that Coco Chanel wannabe was obviously hiding something. When she walked out of that Chairman's office this morning, her face looked as red as her suit.

Dolores opened her eyes, looked at her glass and said, "What the hell," before finishing off the rest of her drink. She laid the empty glass on top of a doily on the side table and glimpsed at her cell phone to see if anyone responded to her texts. She thought to text them all with the same message, letting them know that she knew and taunting them about the FBI guy was a stroke of genius. But her cell phone was quiet. There were no messages. Disappointed for just a second, she shook the thought and cackled, "They'll start squealing soon."

The beloved Cuckoo Clock that she picked up in Hamburg on a teen tour over 50 years ago perched on top of her gas fireplace struck 12 midnight. Dolores grabbed the sides of her chair and slowly hoisted herself up, simultaneously feeling the effects of a tumbler of Scotch and her 70 plus years. She made her way to her bedroom, stopping only to blow a kiss to her signed autograph of Frank Sinatra–the only man she ever loved.

She continued her night-time ritual by setting up her clothes for the morning, organizing her make-up and hair tools, wrapping her hair, and slathering half a jar of Ponds on her face. Next, she opened a new giant-sized bottle of Jergens–having used up the old one yesterday–and creamed up her arms and legs. Finally, she put on a fresh pair of lavender-scented flannel pajamas and crawled under the covers, pleased that she had the resolve to keep herself so well-preserved.

The Scotch had made her drowsy, but before she dozed off, she hatched one more scheme for the morning to heighten the tension about Bill. She was going to start the day by calling the FBI agent and telling him she thought she knew who it was in the photo. She would add that she is also sure the others would have recognized him by now, and to know more, he should call them right away. Delighted to move the game, she easily fell asleep looking forward to the terror she was going to wreak on her victims in the next few days.

Her alarm went off at 6:00 am in terrible cacophony with the Cuckoo Clock. Dolores struggled to hoist herself out of bed - her old lady body not cooperating as fast as her stinging brain and headed for the bathroom. She had a delightful sleep, dreaming about boiling pots and sharp objects, but she had to admit the head was still a little cloudy from the alcohol. She was looking forward to her daily cold shower and a cup of hot coffee to clear out the cobwebs.

She looked in the mirror, a little frightened by what she saw, but got over it quickly when she remembered what a glorious day it was going to be.

She tucked the "up-do" into the giant green plastic shower cap that she bought at Woolworth's 25 years ago that was still doing the trick (they don't make them as they used to) and got into the shower. She sang all three verses of "Fly Me To The Moon" while she soaped up and rinsed off. The splashing water that was falling on her head helped her keep time and, in her mind, stay on key. The quilted red fabric shower curtain that matched her bedspread kept the sound in - mercifully sparing her neighbors from the concert.

Clear headed and refreshed, Dolores pulled the heavy shower curtain aside and stepped out of the tub. As she brought her foot down, she noticed her bottle of body lotion had spilled all over the floor, covering every tile. Something didn't register right. She tried to stop her foot from landing, but her brain was working faster than her body. Before she could stop herself, her foot landed, and in a split second, she lost her balance. She tried grabbing on to something, but everything was covered with body lotion and she couldn't hold on.

The last sounds she heard before everything went forever black was the crack of the head against the sink, a door slamming, and one final "Cuckoo" from that damn clock.

Chapter 19

Less than twelve hours earlier a horrific fire destroyed their place of work but the resilient employees of the West Mendow branch dragged themselves into Rocktown City Regional Branch located ten miles south on Rocktown Turnpike. By 7:30 a.m., there were thirty Capital National Bank people stuffed in the glass enclosed conference room off the lobby. Muffins, bagels and boxes of coffee, courtesy of West Mendow's finest and most popular bakery, which coincidently was owned by Mendow Enterprises, covered the oval conference table.

Rocktown dated back to the 1700's boasting many famous travelers using it as a stopover before the final 22-mile trek into Washington, D.C. Some hundred-year-old buildings still existed here and there but mostly strip malls and middle income homes overran the city, popping up in the 1950s as the farmlands were being sold off. The city had a major boom when the Red Transit Line that went directly into downtown Washington D.C. was built in the 1970s and it hasn't stopped growing since. The town has a major road running through it, which continues to attract commercial business and brings a lot of traffic through the area. For a banker, its business heaven.

Regional Director, Suzanne Matson, was in charge but she sat peacefully in the corner texting on her cell-phone while Danielle and Jen stood at the other end running the show. Flying by the seat of their pants, they worked out where everyone was going to sit and who would do what, when.

Everyone transfixed their attention on the two ladies who spoke quickly and with authority. They agreed earlier that Jen would put her head teller duties on hold and help Danielle with the questions and service issues from West Mendow customers. They directed Eddie to do Jen's legwork to free up Danielle to pursue "bigger picture" issues such as making sure the branch is rebuilt and secretly getting to the bottom of the hoopla around the flash drive.

Danielle ended by giving an impassioned pep talk. Suzanne kept nodding her bleached blonde head, looking up occasionally, pretending she was listening and cared. She knew Danielle would naturally take charge, which was quite all right in her books because she had more important things on her mind like snagging a new husband.

After some vigorous applause, Danielle wiped a fake tear, gave an "aw shucks" wave, then looked around for a place to sit so she could catch her breath. Jen took over filling in some important minutia about teller stuff, which caused Danielle to instantly tune out. It was the first time all morning she had a second to put her thoughts together since she dragged herself out of bed following a short and restless sleep. She spotted a seat next to Suzanne and made her way to the back of the room.

Enamored by the legendary Danielle Mendow, the Rocktown branch employees couldn't keep their eyes off her as she squeezed by the people standing and sitting. To no avail, Jen made all sorts of noises to keep their attention.

Putting on her most humbled look, Danielle made some eye contact and mouthed a few "thank-you's" towards a few people. She knew they were thinking it was going to be quite a treat working with the wildly successful West Mendow branch and their celebrated branch manager. Conversely, she was sure her team was wondering how they were going to get on with the notorious boneheads from the Rocktown Regional.

Delighted by the dynamics, Danielle thought this would be a lesson in fortitude for her staff despite the road that got them there. Then, thinking about the road, the sight of her burned down branch flashed before her–a sight she could hardly turn away from as she drove by it earlier this morning.

One of the nice-looking young tellers from Rocktown Regional jumped up and offered her his seat before she made it to the back wall next to Suzanne. Danielle made a show of gratitude for his chivalrous behavior and took a mental note to poach that suck up from Suzanne. There was a special place in Danielle's heart for people who adulated her.

Finally reaching the end of the conference room, she sank into the chair. Her autopilot was disengaging as the caffeine that kept her going so far was quickly dissipating. Her head fell back against the wall and started filling with the memories from yesterday's crazy, unbelievable events.

Her eyelids felt like magnets were pulling them shut. The image of the rubble heap that was once her branch wouldn't go away. When she drove by this morning, it looked one hundred times worse from the night before - a heaping pile of burned junk. Some facilities people from head office had already arrived and were standing around drinking coffee and speaking with Chief Green, who was shaking his head as if mourning a corpse. A few other suits were milling about as well, kicking at the large fireproof vault in the middle of the rubble - the only part of the branch left standing. There weren't any safe deposit boxes to worry about - her branch had none (the first time she was grateful for that) so she didn't have to worry about that liability. In terms of the cash, Jen said there was only about $23,000 in the vault, which looked like they could recover it–a minor consolation. Whatever. It was not their problem this morning.

Meanwhile, last night's quick contingency plan was going well. Thanks to Eddie, who, much to her surprise, dug deep and found enough wits for once to get them all out of their momentary stupor, they were all ready for today's opening.

It was nearing 9:00 a.m. when the doors to the branch were to be unlocked. Danielle opened her eyes and gave Jen the neck slashing signal to wind it up and throw everyone out. They needed some private time together before all hell broke loose on the platform. Jen nodded acknowledging the order and asked for some last questions which, not surprisingly, were about lunch schedules. After addressing this important issue, everyone started filing out.

The conference room emptied. Danielle turned to Suzanne who was concentrating on applying red lip liner to an already overly outlined pair of, not to subtly, botoxed lips. She looked up and saw Danielle staring at her.

"I have a meeting outside the bank this morning." Suzanne offered with a wink.

Amused, Danielle cleared a slight tickle in her throat, "Right. Well, good luck." Suzanne's chronic off site "meetings", were a godsend to Danielle. Although technically her boss, her hands-off style kept her out of Danielle's hair. Coming up from the ranks, Suzanne knew her job well and was a straight-shooter. There was a mutual admiration between the ladies. Danielle made Suzanne shine, and Suzanne let Danielle do what she wanted. It was a perfect arrangement. A few "dates" thrown to Suzanne also helped now and then, but they never spoke about that part.

"I've got to run," she said, unbuttoning the top

two buttons of her shirt. "Oh, I forgot to give this to you," reaching into her briefcase. She handed Danielle a print-out of accounts. "It's your top twenty customers by income to the bank. I thought you would want to call these guys first."

"Good idea, thanks!" Danielle said, taking the report from Suzanne. "I haven't seen my accounts by income for ages–I just look at deposits. Let's see, number one–Mendow Enterprises LLC. Wow! I make this much money for them? They should pay me more. Number two–Mendow Land Holdings, LLC. Okay, not a surprise. And number three, well, look at this, Mendow Distributors LLC. And there's Mendow Golf and Recreation LLC. I can't believe that's showing up. I always thought it was such a dud. Shows how much I know about golf."

"I guess you will call yourself four times," Suzanne said with a laugh as she struggled to get up in her two size too-tight pencil skirt.

Wide-eyed and very impressed with herself, Danielle kept staring at her own numbers. "Doesn't anybody else make money for this branch?" she said as she flipped the report to the next page. Let's see who's rounding up number five. Oh! Who's this? Joseph Franz Chocolatiers? The chocolate shop in the lobby at headquarters? Are you sure this is my customer?"

"Let me see that," Suzanne said as she put on her suit jacket. She played accordion with the package for a few seconds, obviously in need of reading glasses but no doubt too vain to admit it. She finally got it in focus, read it, and handed it back to Danielle.

"Yes, it's yours," she said. "It's coded to your branch. You probably never noticed because their income is all in fees and you look at deposits."

"No, sometimes I do a fee review." Danielle said, staring at the report. "But this one never comes up. And we've had the account for how long?" she asked, searching for the date on the page.

"I noticed at least fourteen years according to the report." Suzanne said, shrugging her shoulders. "Let me see that again." She took the report back from Danielle, did some more arm exercises, and took another look at it.

"Wait. Oh, now I know why you haven't seen it. This account is in your branch but its relationship is managed by that twit from head office–Teddy Hudd."

"You're kidding!" Danielle said, grabbing the package back from Suzanne. She looked for the relationship management code. The number she saw was obviously not hers.

Suzanne's cell phone started ringing. She looked to see who it was, broke out in a wide grin while she announced she had to take it, grabbed her enormous Michael Kors handbag, and hurried out of the conference room while mouthing a two-edged, "Toodle loo! Have fun!".

Who says "toodle loo" anymore, Danielle thought to herself as she watched Suzanne through the glass wall striding quickly towards the branch exit. Halting suddenly like she was just electrocuted, she rummaged through her bag for a hairbrush and began moving again. Her handbag - no doubt full of a drawer of cosmetics–slipped off her other shoulder as she straightened out that size ten orange suit she was wearing on her size 14 body. Finally, giving one last pump to her dyed too many times hair, she just made it out as the glass door closed giving her a little "toodle loo" pat on the butt on the way out. Danielle knew she wouldn't be seeing her any time soon, which was just fine. She now had the run of the place.

Jen sauntered back in as soon as she saw Suzanne leave and grabbed a seat at the conference room table. "That lady is one piece of work," Jen said as she took Danielle's spare laptop out of her briefcase and booted it up. "What was up with that orange suit?"

"Probably looking to get squeezed." Danielle said laughing. Jen continued watching the screen. "Get it? Orange? Squeezed?"

"Yeh, got it the first time." Jen said, rolling her eyes and pulling the flash drive out from her bra. She inserted it into the computer.

"Well, I thought it was funny." Danielle said soberly, moving into the chair next to Jen.

Just like a rerun of the night before, they patiently stared at the screen, watching the column of numbers appear.

"Let's remember what we're looking at." Danielle said. "The first set of numbers is the date. The second set are random account numbers that we assume are accounts at other banks. The third set represents the ABA number, which tells us at what bank these accounts are held. The third set is Capital Bank account numbers and the fourth set are dollar amounts."

"That's right. That still makes sense from what I see." Jen said as she was moving up and down the columns with the arrows on the keyboard.

Pointing to the screen, Danielle said, "Good. Go back to the beginning. Write the first five account numbers down and ask Eddie to look them up. Let's see if we can make any sense out of this."

Jen copied the numbers and left the conference room. Danielle continued to stare at the screen. She guided the pointer to the beginning of the columns. Row 1, Column 1: 020102. February 1, 2002. Looking out at Rocktown Pike from the floor to ceiling conference room window, Danielle tried to understand the significance of that date. Why does the record start there?

It was six months after 9/11. She was home in West Mendow by then, doing her best to keep her customers at Capital Bank International. Bill Smith was allegedly still making heroic attempts to locate the lost $10 million dollars while the Board was deciding to shut the whole operation down.

Car doors slamming in the giant parking lot in front of the building occasionally interrupted the silence in the conference room. Customers were arriving and making their way into the sizable platform lobby. Rocktown Regional was a pumped up version of her branch with a bigger footprint and a second floor that housed management and lending officers. Because of its location on a major thoroughfare in a much bigger and busier commercial area, the high-volume branch made hers look like the lazy teenage son. She always thought the bigger the branch, the bigger the problems, and was happy in her quiet mini-kingdom in West Mendow. But paradise was possibly lost last night and shuddered at the idea of a change in the game. She had to make sure that didn't happen. There was so much to figure out.

"Okay. Eddie's checked out the account numbers," Jen announced as she returned to the conference room. She sat down next to Danielle and pulled her chair in towards the conference table. Turning towards Danielle, she asked, "What's wrong? Do you see any black SUV's out there?"

"Funny– "Ghost of Joan Rivers". What did you find?" Danielle asked, shifting her attention back to the screen.

"Well, not much," she said while reading from a piece of notepaper. "The first number is the account number of the chocolate shop in the lobby of our headquarter building in D.C."

"Chocolate shop? How bizarre." Danielle said, bewildered. "Suzanne's income report shows a chocolate company coded to our branch that is managed by the twit, Teddy Hudd. Hmm. From what I can see of these dollar amounts, it looks like a busy little shop that makes a lot of money with tons of customers. I wonder if it does some wholesale business because when I was in there yesterday, there were only two customers–Rita Steele and me. In fact, now that I think about it, nobody's ever in there when I go." Danielle continued while scanning the screen.

"Interesting. Well, before you retire that thought," Jen said, "the next account number is a sub-account number for another chocolate shop in Manhattan on 5th Avenue near Rockefeller Center."

"Chi, chi," responded Danielle. "And I assume the third account number is a sub account number of a shop on Rodeo Drive in Los Angeles, the fourth on LaSalle in Chicago, and the fifth in Palm Beach, Florida."

"West Palm" Jen corrected her.

"Ah, yes," Danielle said, pursing her lips and wrinkling her nose. She continued in a bad British accent. "Going for the nouveau riche snowbirds."

"And how did you deduce all that?" Jen asked with a sniff.

"Elementary, Dr. Watson. If I were going to open a chain of high end chocolate shops, that's where I would start. You go where the money is." Danielle answered matter-of-factly- her eyes glued to the screen.

"But what would that have to do with you and Bill Smith?" Jen asked, returning to a soberer tone.

Before Danielle could answer, Jen gently closed the laptop and turned toward Danielle. With brow crossed and pursed lips she said in her most mommiest voice, "You know, we're both avoiding the elephant in the room."

"Last night?" she answered, avoiding eye contact.

"Look at me, Danielle. Yes, last night." Jen replied with concern.

Danielle turned and nodded. "I know," she said with a touch of disappointment in her voice. Sheila was out of her mind with that rifle."

Jen groaned. "That's not where I was going. You know she loves pointing that thing around. She thinks she's Annie Oakley. This is not about Sheila. It's you! You were out of your mind all day! And what was up with that guy!"

"Oh, him?" Danielle said, feeling her face get warm. "I don't know. He's an enigma. He moved in next door and I didn't even notice, which I can't believe, barged into my house yesterday looking like this pathetic slob, all sweaty while I was trying to enjoy my chips and tuna salad sandwich. He wouldn't leave until I agreed to go over to his house for dinner. So, I got all excited–maybe because I hadn't had a date since the Ice Age and got all dolled up, but when I got to his house, he asked me to cook. Before I could think of a way to get him to eat out, I got a call about the branch, and made a bee-line for the door. I thought that would be the end of him for the night until he hunted me down at Sheila's only to flash an FBI badge at me. Does anything sound wrong with that?" she asked oozing sarcasm deliberately leaving out the conversation and poor judgement in Sheila's parking lot which ended with that impulsive kiss. Looking back on it, she realized how embarrassed she was.

Danielle was gazing at the ceiling. Jenn took a deep breath. Waving her hand at the laptop she said, "Just so we could rule out this weird thought I'm having and move on, do you think this guy is connected to any of this?"

The suggestion stunned Danielle. Why didn't she think of that? She thought through the possibilities. Was she so grateful to have a guy pay some attention to her that she couldn't see through his motives? Was he a plant? Was he deliberately trying to get close because of this whole Bill Smith mystery? Why would some hot guy rent a gigantic mansion in the middle of nowhere by himself and act like it's the only place he wanted to be? How did he manipulate her so easily? Was she so susceptible?

"Well?" Jen prodded.

Avoiding Jen's gaze, she answered, "I know you love conspiracies and would suspect your own mother if it made a good story, but I don't think Rake Harris is involved with any of this." The response was blurted out so quickly she didn't even believe it herself.

Even Jen sounded skeptical. "Come on, Danielle. It's just too coincidental. There's a connection. It's obvious to me. I don't understand why you can't see it. How often does an FBI agent move into a mansion that just happens to be next door to you?"

"And of course, your next question is 'why would he show any interest in me', right?" Danielle said. Twisting her mouth, she tried to appear visibly hurt but inwardly she was also wondering.

"Okay, sorry. Let's drop it." Jen said quickly, realizing that she may have hit a nerve. She opened the laptop again, and they both turned their attention in unison to the screen.

While Jen was busy taking down some more numbers, Danielle kept thinking about Rake. Jen's suspicions were nagging at her and deep down her instincts started sending off sparks, signaling her handsome new neighbor may not be a lucky coincidence after all. But so far there wasn't anything substantial she could put her finger on. He seemed pretty normal in a West Mendow kind of way. She was probably overthinking him and should take him just for what he said he was - a nice guy who did like her and just wanted to move out to a quiet suburb to escape the city. She turned all of her attention again to the screen and blanked out the events of the last 24 hours as they were just frustrating her and leading to a lot of depressing dead ends.

"I'm just going to do a few more because I'm sure they are all chocolate shops somewhere in the U.S." Jen said, talking and scribbling at the same time. "For some reason, they are all coded to us. On the surface, this entire business seems harmless. So, do you think they killed your friend Bill Smith over this? Again, this sounds like he just could have been in the wrong place at the wrong time. Maybe Bill was working for the Chocolate company and there were some service problems he couldn't sort and he wanted us to help him, that's all, case closed. Bad luck for Bill. All very innocent."

"Innocent? How so?" Danielle asked.

235

Jen looked up. "I don't know. Come on, let's just play it out. You know, like when we try to figure out whether a transaction's real or a fraud."

Danielle looked at her. With a deep sigh, she said, "I hate this game but I know you'll bug me, until we do it so let's go for it and get it over with. You name it, I'll come up with a simple explanation. Let's see if we can close this thing up"

"Why did the branch catch on fire yesterday of all days?" Jen said quickly.

Not missing a beat, Danielle replied evenly, "The branch burned down on its own. It was a time bomb. I was complaining to facilities for years that we needed to get it professionally inspected and brought up to code."

"So you don't think it was arson." Jen replied, pushing her chair away from the conference table.

"Probably not." Danielle answered more confidently than she felt. "Next?" she continued leaning back and crossing her legs to face Jen.

Pausing for a second to think, Jen suddenly sat up and reminded her about the messages about the flash drive on her cell phone. "Admit those were very direct," she said, nodding.

"No. I got that one. Probably some assistant with bad English who needed the flash drive back to do some work with it. Whoever it was, knew Bill sent it to me and couldn't explain what it was all about

236

because he was dead," saying the last four words slower and more deliberately.

The dramatic delivery didn't seem to affect Jen, who shrugged and said, "Stretch, but I'll go with it. New one. How about the FBI guy from the Chairman's office?"

"Just doing his job." Danielle answered dispiritedly.

"But why FBI? Why not just local police?" Jen asked, bringing both hands up and flapping them around like she was trying to catch an invisible answer.

"The Willard always calls in the FBI because of its high profile and location near the White House." Danielle answered.

"You know that for a fact?" Jen asked, impressed.

"No, I just made it up, but it sounds plausible, doesn't it?" Danielle said, mustering up a mischievous grin.

Narrowing her eyes, Jen hissed, "And Rake?"

"I think we answered that." Shifting in her seat, Danielle realized she replied a little too quickly. She turned her face away from Jen so she wouldn't see her smile to herself. The nagging feeling about Rake disappeared when her tired mind started bouncing between the "embarrassing" kiss and that warm, well-toned chest which for a second brushed against her own. 'I'll take care of Rake even if he is a secret agent", Danielle said, turning back to Jen. She started thinking about how she was going to get to the bottom and out of the middle of this mess. Working and being at the branch all day would not let her think about it–it would be too distracting. She needed retail therapy.

Jen started to say something, but Danielle raised her hand signaling to stop. "You know, I don't have any patience for banking today and I'm really tired of all this. You're right. All of this is explainable. We should just forget it. I'm taking a break. Why don't we just take care of our customers today? Don't we have a client at the Rocktown Mall that I can pay a personal visit to?"

Jen had so many other tasks to take care of and was actually relieved that they didn't have to work on this further. Danielle didn't seem interested anymore and by announcing she wanted to go to the mall, she thought Danielle could be over her madness all together and become her old self again. Evil theories notwithstanding, nothing was leading to anything sinister. There seemed to be an innocent answer for everything.

"Fine by me." Jen said, tearing up her notes.

Sighing, Danielle thought about the text she received from Dolores that had stolen a couple of more hours of good sleep from her. She wondered what was up with the old bag. She never mentioned it to Jen as Dolores was part of the old-timers group–a player of Mount Olympus proportions and out of Jen's league so far. Danielle would take care of Dolores. Then she could use it as a lesson for Jen for future take downs. But another time, not today. First, off to Nordstrom to clear her head and start thinking about what may happen when Agent Muckiss discovers Wilhelm Schmidt is Bill Smith and very much a part of Capital National's financial history.

"Yes, I surrender," Danielle said to the laptop and reached out to close it. As the screen was disappearing, she noticed Jen had gone a few pages ahead to more recent years while she was jotting down her numbers. The latest ones showed the dollar amounts were getting bigger and bigger. The frequencies of the transfers were also increasing. Danielle had analyzed a lot of cash businesses in her day, and this one's cash transfers seemed very odd for a chain of chocolate shops.

Popping the laptop all the way open again, Danielle scrolled up and down comparing the numbers - 2003, 2004, 2005... and so on. As time went on, more account numbers were being added and hundreds of thousands were moving into the main account. The build - up of transactions was steady. The amounts were so gradual and consistent, that if she wasn't looking for a pattern of odd transactions, the unusual dollar increases in the chocolate business could easily be swallowed by the normal growth of a healthy branch like the West Mendow branch.

239

Danielle sat up straighter and pulled her chair in closer to the conference table. Her eyes lit with excitement. The tiredness in her body quickly vanished. This was getting very interesting. She turned to Jen who was sitting there watching her curiously.

"You're not on your way to Nordstrom," Jen said drolly.

Ignoring her last comment, Danielle returned to staring at the screen and after a few seconds asked, "Jen, best guess. How much money do you think a chocolate shop makes in a week?"

Getting up from her seat, "I don't know, planning on buying one?" Jen said with exasperation. She took a position behind Danielle's chair and leaned over her shoulder to get a closer look at whatever caught Danielle's attention.

"Look closer. Are you noticing something?" Danielle asked.

"Pretty darn lucrative for a chocolate shop. There's way too much...." Her speech slowed down as she continued and her eyes lit up as she continued, "... money going in and out especially as the years go on."

They both took a breath, exchanged a knowing look, smiled at each other, and returned to scrutinize the spreadsheet on the laptop.

After a few minutes of scrolling and changing tabs, Danielle turned to Jen. "Are you thinking what I'm thinking?"

With her voice barely audible, Jen gave a quick look around the room and said, "Damn straight. The whole thing smells. We've got a money launderer in our branch. Your FBI friend was right last night, but now we know who it is-Joseph Franz Chocolatiers."

"The chocolate shop in the lobby. And Teddy Hudd is in on it because all the fees are going to his profit center in International. What a scam!" Danielle whispered.

They both sat quietly, thinking. Danielle had a million questions. Why her branch? What did Bill Smith have to do with this? How did that old lizard, Teddy Hudd, get involved and why? Did this have anything to do with the missing $10 million? What did the FBI know? Did Muckiss get wind of this scheme somehow and he's trying to connect the dots? Finally, why are all the dots connecting to her?

Chapter 20

They listened mindlessly to a Barry Manilow instrumental loop that could be heard through the glass doors of the conference room. Enthralled, Danielle watched as Jen tugged and played with a sweater ball hanging off her vest. After a few minutes, Danielle shuddered and broke from her trance. She sighed loudly to catch Jen's attention.

Jen stopped picking at her sweater and looked over at her wide-eyed friend. "Okay. So what do we do now?"

Exhaling like she just ran a marathon, Danielle said, "I don't know. I've never ridden in this rodeo before". Jen slowly shook her head in agreement.

The door to the conference room swung open, startling them both. Eddie poked his head through announcing that the beer guy, Marty Strueber, wanted to cash a $3500.00 check immediately and someone's approval was required for an override.

"I'll go," Jen intoned, rising from her seat like an arthritic walrus. "Geez, our daily pest from West Mendow found us already. Eddie, did you tell him?"

"Not me, man. He's got a homing device." Laughed Eddie disappearing back into the lobby.

Before Jen left the conference room to follow, she pointed her finger at Danielle and said, "Don't move. I'll be right back."

"Ay, ay, Captain," Danielle replied, waving her off. "Where am I going to go? This is much more exciting than a sale at Nordstrom's," she said to an empty conference room.

The cell phone in Danielle's suit jacket suddenly interrupted the silence. She saw her house number on the caller I.D. She hoped it was Eleni and not Chief Green standing in her kitchen calling to inform her that her house was burning down.

Warily, she answered it.

"Your next-door neighbor, beautiful man, was here and want to say something. I give him your number." She said in her "lovely" broken English. Well, well. So Rake couldn't stay away from her kitchen. Hopefully, he wasn't there just for the meatballs.

Within minutes, her cell phone went off again. This time he heard a smooth, deep voice.

"Hey lady!" He said playfully.

She melted. She couldn't hear anything else but his breathing. She couldn't think of anything else but that electrifying kiss from last night. Everything seemed trivial at this moment except the fact that Rake called her.

"Hey yourself" Danielle cooed. She couldn't believe that just moments ago she was obsessing over whether he could be involved in all this bank drama. She just would not believe it. Instead, she had to have him. He was going to be her boyfriend whether or not he wanted it. And he'll want it. Feeling a little warm, she unbuttoned her silk blouse to let in some air.

"So, what are you wearing?" he asked nonchalantly.

Not seeing that one coming, she looked down subconsciously as if she saw her black Armani pantsuit for the first time that morning. Was this a trick question? There must be a good reason he's asking. She pictured Eleni standing beside him, frowning. She wondered if she should warn him to back away and be careful. His next line could catch him a rolling pin in the head.

"Um, why do you want to know?" Danielle replied hesitantly.

"Because," Rake answered, drawing the word out slowly to ratchet up some suspense. "You seemed a little stressed last night," he said with a little chuckle, "and my surprise appearance sent you over the cliff in more ways than one... I liked that."

Danielle felt her face get red as he was speaking. He obviously would not let her forget the train wreck from last night.

"So I thought a nice ride up to Sugarloaf Mountain right before lunch would give you a much-needed break. Maybe we can start over again? You know, actions speak louder than words."

"Okay," she said too quickly. Did he catch the eagerness in her voice?

She heard a slight laugh. Yes–he caught the eagerness in her voice. "But what does that have to do with what I'm wearing?"

"Just tell me. You'll see." He teased.

Still believing the question odd, she gave him what he wanted. "I'm wearing a black pantsuit, my signature red blouse, and some kickin' Manolo Blahnik heels." She expected to hear a growl.

Instead, he simply replied, "Good. Hope those pants aren't too tight." and hung up after he said he'd see her shortly.

Did he notice her pants were a little tight last night? What did he mean by that? She looked at the clock hanging on the colorless walls. It was getting close to 10:00 a.m. She didn't have time to be insulted and perplexed. It was inventory time.

Taking out her compact, she checked her hair and make-up. Nothing looked good enough. Sighing, she examined her nails and felt nauseous. What happened? Did they go through a blender between last night and this morning? She didn't even want to think about her toes. At least she shaved her legs or she thought she did–after all, it was quite early when she woke up and her brains were on automatic and who knows what she really did. So, she took a quick peek and shuddered. The package would just have to do. Or did it? She could just focus on the exterior and pray that if something happens, it would be in the dark.

Putting her brain into fourth gear, she checked off some major work she could easily fix. Followed by a quick calculation that would baffle even Einstein, she figured probable repairs plus transportation time, which included the 40 minutes it would take Rake to get from her house in West Mendow to the branch in Rocktown she could manage some improvement. In the meantime, she direly needed a place for a quick hair and nail restoration. She got up, went to the window overlooking the main road and scoured the landscape. She spotted exactly what she was looking for, almost across the street from the branch. Thank goodness, May Bell's Beauty Bar was waiting for her just a few steps away.

Stuffing the flash drive in her pants pocket, she thought for a moment about what she should do about Jen's laptop. Opening the door to the conference room, she looked across the platform for Jen. The staff was swamped with customers at the teller window and Jen was running back and forth trying to move the lines along. Danielle took the laptop for safekeeping and work on some theories while her toenails were drying.

Unable to catch her attention to say goodbye, Danielle walked out of the bank unnoticed. It was faster to walk to May Bell's, so she left her car in the parking lot and headed for the crossing light right next to the branch.

Although the briefcase was fairly light with just the laptop and some reports, the flash drive in her pocket weighed heavily. She was mad at herself. How could she not notice what was going on right in her own branch? Did Teddy the Twit know or was he just as clueless? Was someone pulling the wool over his eyes as well?

The day was warming up as autumn in Maryland likes to do. Slipping off her suit jacket, Danielle felt the heat of the rising sun hugging her shoulders. Despite the stressful morning, Danielle was letting the thoughts of the next hours change her mood. After all, what could be better than a little TLC from a quick spa treatment and a long lazy afternoon with her hunk of a neighbor?

The noise of the busy branch behind her and the increasing traffic of the four-lane highway ahead contrasted the peace of her little empire in West Mendow. Although being the big fish in a small pond wasn't all bad, she did sometimes miss the excitement and challenge of a big city. The street cacophony was like a drug that she was once addicted to and could easily get hooked on again. It was what she loved about New York and Washington D.C. But was she willing to give up all that she built in West Mendow to go back to that crazy world? On the other hand, was this it? She always said "no" when she asked herself that question. But what would compel her to leave the security of her current persona and make another dramatic move yet again?

The light turned red, and the cars screeched to a halt to let her cross. "No, stop thinking this way," she thought to herself. "Rocktown Pike branch is too much work. Why start all over again. I've got the best of both worlds. A nice desk, a prominent position in the community, a loyal staff, and the freedom to do what I want. No wonder Suzanne doesn't stick around. She would have to talk to customers all day. I hate that. Bummer. Look what it did to me the last time. I ended up with a lot of wasted years and nothing. Even now, someone's taking advantage. Laundering money through my branch? If I ever want to be in the big leagues again, I will be in complete control."

The self-cross-examination ended. By this time, she was across the street and staring at May Bell's dumpy storefront. Last week, she wouldn't be caught dead there. Today, she had no choice. Walking towards it with slight trepidation, she noticed the writing on the window was weather-worn. From afar, it looked like it read May Bell's Beauty Ba but getting closer she could see the "r" under a bunch of dirt. She took a deep breath and reached for the doorknob.

Bells tinkled as she walked in. She wondered if that was deliberate. May's Bells? May Bells? Mary Bell's? Clever name, but the place didn't live up to it. Simply outfitted, the salon was empty except for four rapidly yapping young ladies on the left sitting behind nail stations against a washed-out pink wall. The right had four empty hair stations and an unmanned reception desk with an old phone, an even older cash register, and a manual appointment book empty of any markings. It didn't seem the kind of place someone would come to blow a lot of money.

Even with the noise of the little bells, the animated conversations continued as if she wasn't there. Time was a-wasting, and Danielle was confused about what to do. Not used to being ignored, Danielle was just about to say something nasty, when a middle-aged woman emerged from a door in the back. Stout, with a brown Cleopatra hair-do and round tortoise-shell glasses, she gave one loud clap, bringing everyone, including Danielle, to attention. "A Customer! Shame!" she said sharply to the noisy girls, while marching towards the front of the shop. The girls stopped gaggling immediately and lowered their heads as she passed by.

"Whoa", she said, grabbing Danielle's hands and inspecting them. She then messed up her hair while leading her to a chair. "Obviously, the works!" She announced. "Honey, you came to the right place. May Bell is going to fix you right up."

Danielle caught a quick glance at herself in a nearby mirror. She felt haggard but didn't think she looked that horrible. Nonetheless, she put herself into May Bell's hands and sank gratefully into the nearest chair. Admittedly, she was a tad skeptical about what May Bell and her little crew could do in such a short time, but she didn't have another option. "I've got half an hour" she directed, turning toward the mirror.

"Hey. This isn't Mission Impossible." She said laughing. "Whatcha got? Hot Date?" May Bell asked.

Leaning back, Danielle smiled mischievously thinking about the next few hours and said, "You better believe it. Do what you can. I'll pay."

"Let's go girls!" May Bell said, snapping her fingers. Danielle braced herself. They swarmed around her like Dorothy's preparatory scene before meeting the Wizard of Oz. They wrapped her in a black salon poncho and began fawning and fussing over her. Fluff ups here, blowouts there, a few plucks, feet rubs, neck massage spritzes, nail polish... all that was missing was one of them whitening her teeth. Danielle was feeling human again.

After a while, their attention seemed to get divided between her and the window. Every minute or so, one or two of the girls would walk up to the big picture window and peek out. May Bell noticed as well.

"How come you keep getting up? What's going on out there?" May Bell shouted, looking up for a second as she finished up the topcoat of Danielle's touched up manicure.

251

"Big excitement at the bank across the street. Police everywhere. It looks like it may have been robbed." One girl said, straining her head to get a better look.

"What?" Danielle asked bolting from her chair, not waiting for an answer. She ran in paper flip flops to the window, her black poncho billowing behind her. Alarm bells rang in her head when she saw the scene across the street. Two police cars were parked in the front with lights flashing. Cars were driving into the lot and being waved to leave by two officers near the front door. The traffic on the Pike was slowing with drivers rubbernecking hoping to see somebody else's tragedy.

Since the police were already out of their cars, Danielle knew it wasn't a robbery unless Jen shot the bandits (which wouldn't be all that surprising, but that's for another story). "What the hell is going on there?" she said to herself. She was having problems processing the situation since it could be so many things at this point considering the events of yesterday. Was it related or just a coincidence? She shrugged. Whatever it was, she didn't care. All she wanted to do was spend the day with Rake.

The cell phone in her jacket pocket vibrated, announcing she had just received a text. She wanted to reach for it, hoping whoever it was would clue her in, but she didn't want to ruin her manicure. She let it go.

A motorcycle drove into the parking lot of the branch, catching her attention. Danielle watched with interest as a man with a strong build and tight leather pants climbed off. As soon as he removed his helmet, her eyes widened. It was Rake. "Well, well..." she thought to herself. Licking her lips, she watched as he straightened his hair and looked around curiously at the police cars. A collective "oooh" came from the rest of the girls who had joined her at the window.

'Hands off, ladies, he's mine,' she thought to herself as she glared back at the cooing chorus of the stylists. Turning back to Rake for a better look, she felt pleased with herself that she could still attract such a gorgeous stud. Without thinking about her manicure now, she carelessly pulled off her poncho to get ready to leave, forgetting she was still drying everywhere.

"Hey, what are you doing?" May Bell said sharply coming up behind her holding a giant hairbrush. "Your toes aren't ready yet, let alone your nails."

"I know, I know. But you see that hunk over there? That's the one. I don't want him running away because he can't find me. We were supposed to meet at the bank. I have to go."

She took one look at Rake and said, "Wow! That's a fine leading man. I see your point. For Pete's sake! Girls! Keep working! We'll have you outta here in two minutes, all dolled up."

They pushed her back into the chair and swarmed on her like moths to light. After they finished, they brought out the industrial blowers for the fastest drying times recorded. Fans blew so much cold air all over her hands and feet that she swore every bit of moisture had evaporated from the salon to the Potomac. Before she knew it, the girls were congratulating themselves, and Danielle was relieved to be pulling out her charge card.

Not even looking at the bill, she paid, thanked the girls and started walking towards the tinkling door. She took a last look through the window, hoping to spot Rake waiting outside for her, but didn't see him in the parking lot. Noticing her disappointment, one girl mentioned he went into the branch and hadn't come out. Since her nails were dry, she reached for her phone to let him know she would be there in a few minutes. Her screen lit up with the missed text. It was from Jen.

"Wherever u r, don't come back. They r looking for you. Would not say y. Smells BAD!"

That text came ten minutes ago and no messages since. She couldn't understand why they would look for her, of all people? And what was up with the 'smells bad' comment? Were those police cars related to her?

"Smells bad? Looking for me?" she said out loud, forgetting she had an audience behind her. It was imperative that she find out what was going on in that branch.

Looking up, she saw May Bell watching her while pretending to read a People Magazine behind the cash register of the reception station. Danielle wondered if she heard her reaction. Did the tone in her voice and the terror in her face after seeing that text make May Bell suspicious of her? Obviously, yes. Why would Jen do that?

Danielle tilted her head coyishly and smiled showing way too many teeth and said calmly, "You all did a terrific job and I know you're very busy and I hate to interrupt. But can you do me a great big favor? It seems that hunk of a man we were all so hot about..."

"You were hot, honey. I got my man. We just wanted to pull you together so he wouldn't run the other way when he saw you. You walked in here and needed some major work. You looked like you had a dreadful night. You looked like roadkill." She said seriously.

"Okay, okay," Danielle responded with all the patience she had. This one would obviously not be running for office anytime soon. "... and I thank you for all the hard work."

"A few more hours would have helped," May Bell said, staring at her.

This lady was relentless, Danielle thought to stare back. What can you say to that?
"Just kidding," May Bell shouted, breaking out in hysterical laughter. "Hey–you should have seen

your face! You look amazing. That guy's gonna lose his socks when he sees you!" She continued guffawing while Danielle stood there confused and not sure whether May Bell was sane enough to ask for a favor.

She looked around at the other girls to see if they looked like they could help, but after assessing the landscape, Danielle quickly realized she may be on her own. Giving it one more shot, she fixed her eyes back on May Bell. She was just about to speak when May Bell, wiping a laugh tear with the back of her hand, said, "Okay... enough of that, what do you want?"

A line from Pink Floyd came to Danielle's mind, "The lunatic is in my head." Everything that was happening in these last couple of days was all a test. Would she pass if she could stay nice? What's going to happen if she hits the limit? This one was getting close.

Sweetly, she said, "I'm supposed to meet Mr. Wonderful, who, by the way, doesn't carry a cell phone, at the branch. But with all the police action, I'm not sure they'll let me in. You know, I'm just a nobody. If possible, can you walk over ..."

"Hold on there. If they won't let you in, why would they let me in... What if there's a robber in there?"

"There's no robber. The police wouldn't have gone in. It's something else. I don't know. Just tell them you're a business customer and point to the salon and tell them you need change. They'll be cool with that." Danielle was pretty sure they would turn her around and give her the boot, but at least she could get closer a look at the situation. "See if you can find out what's happening. Police love to talk." And she could tell in the few minutes they had together that May Bell was persistent enough to get some good intel. "Ask to speak to Jen. She's the head teller. Tell her I'm here. Tell her I need a sign."

"Alright," she said skeptically. "If you say so. And how about if I should see that Harley guy. Should I tell him you're here?"

"Of course! Tell him I'll be there in a few minutes, but Jen comes first." Danielle answered enthusiastically. Although she couldn't wait to strap her hands across his hard chest and ride off into the sunset with him, she felt she needed to hear first from Jen.

May Bell seemed to understand her instructions. "Hey, I had a cat named Jen." She said brightly.

"That's fascinating!" Danielle groaned softly. To distract May Bell from starting a boring cat story, she quickly reached into her handbag, careful not to ruin her manicure, and pulled out a $50 bill. "Thanks for doing this." She said handing it to May Bell.

"Aw, you didn't have to". May Bell said taking the money. She got up and slid the bill in the back pocket of her snug denims. She came around the reception desk and started towards the door. "You really like this guy, don't you?"

Her answer came out hesitantly. "It's complicated."

"Whatever you say. But you sure seem to be working really hard on trying to get him." She replied and walked out the door.

The girls in the shop stood at the window like little cubs watching Mamma bear go out for food. May Bell crossed the busy road at the light and headed towards the entrance of the branch. She gave an admiring look at Rake's motorcycle as she marched by and passed the police cars that were parked near the doors. The officers were no longer guarding the entrance and Danielle could just barely see them through the glass windows in the lobby talking amongst themselves. Straightening her shoulders and pulling herself up, May Bell took a deep breath and disappeared inside.

"Atta girl." Danielle thought to herself. "Hopefully, we'll start getting some answers"

The Beauty Bar was still devoid of customers, and Danielle felt sorry for the girls who seemed to have nothing to do but stare out the window with her or read magazines. She wondered how this place was profitable. Ever the banker, she made a mental note. "No small business loans for May Bell's Beauty Bar from Capital National Bank", thought Danielle. On the other hand, she knew these places made a ton of money–especially cash–which brought her back to thinking about the newly discovered money laundering operation running out of her branch.

The minutes ticked by. Her thoughts were interrupted by one of the girls with an obvious toe-fetish who asked to check her pedicure for the umpteenth time to see if her toenails had dried. This reminded Danielle that she should be getting close to leaving.

But May Bell still hadn't emerged from the branch. Danielle wondered if they arrested her for telling cat stories. There should be a law. Whatever was keeping her, they all continued to watch for Mamma Bear. The girls started fidgeting like they needed feeding. Even Danielle thought this entire scheme was taking too long, adding to the sense of apprehension.

May Bell finally rushed out the doors of the branch, looking nervous. Her eyes were darting around the parking lot and her shoulders were hunched over. The girls jumped when they saw May Bell trip down a tiny step then quickly righted herself, avoiding a collision with the cement.

"She's okay." One of the girls said relieved. They returned to their nail and hair stations like they were going to get flooded with customers. Danielle turned back to watch May Bell. Something wasn't right. She was half-way across the parking lot when suddenly she stopped and turned back like someone was calling her from inside the branch and froze in place. Rake appeared at the door. May Bell pointed to the salon. He looked across the street and nodded in her direction while he walked to his motorcycle.

Danielle smiled to herself, looking forward to their meeting and wondering how she was going to stay on that bike with her tight Armani slacks and Manolo pumps. (So this was what he meant when he asked about her outfit. He wanted to know if she was Biker Chick. How appropriate!) She always fantasized about being a biker girl in a road movie, and now she could play it out. She watched dreamily as he kicked on the motor and revved the engine twice. He put the bike into gear and slowly made his way across the parking lot to the light.

At the same time, the two police officers in the branch came out and went to their cars.

Danielle guessed the drama was over as she watched them open the doors of their black and white cars. May Bell stood like a statue in the middle of the parking lot, apparently lost in all the confusion. As they were getting in, Danielle caught a flustered Jen charging out of the branch while opening a huge Capital Bank umbrella.

Danielle's insides exploded! Between her and Jen, an open umbrella meant only one thing. "Danger, Run!"

Thinking about her rendezvous with Rake and watching him on that motorcycle made her forget all about the ominous text and Jen's earlier warning. But here it was again. She had to get out of there. The "Drop and Run" code they put in place for extreme emergencies was in play.

Rake was pulling into the Salon parking lot. At this moment, she should have been swooning and sighing, but there was no time for that now. She needed an escape plan. It didn't matter that this whole thing may not be about Rake. This was the only sign they swore they would never question.

Frantic that she only had about ten seconds left, she looked for the closest girl and asked if there was a second door out the back.

"I thought that was the guy we did all the work on you for." the young girl answered, looking past Danielle and out the window towards Rake. She rose from her station.

"I just got a text from his wife. He didn't tell me the jerk was married!" she answered without skipping a beat.

"Men are pigs," announced her big-nosed co-worker getting up from her station, who punctuated that statement by spitting into the carpet. Grabbing Danielle's arm, she pulled her quickly to the back of the shop. "The storage room has a gigantic window. You'll make it. Everyone escapes from there. We'll try to stall him."

"You girls seem to be pros at this," Danielle said with remorse as the girl opened the door to the bathroom.

"You think you're the first lady we've helped escape from some sleazy guy?" the girl said with a wink as she gave her a little push into the darkroom. The other girl joined and shoved her Manolo's into her hands. They wrapped her briefcase strap around her, then draped her handbag over her shoulder. Danielle reached nervously into her bag (to hell with saving the manicure) and quickly pulled out a one hundred bill. She shoved it into the hand of the big-nose girl who nodded in acknowledgment, then motioned her to be quiet. The door closed silently. Danielle heard the tinkling of the bells signaling that Rake just arrived.

Her eyes quickly adjusted to the unlit room. She could hear the girls outside "ooohing" and "aaahing" over Rake and could imagine that they were busy removing his jacket to his protests and playing with his face to sidetrack him. She made her way over to the window, praying that it opened easily. Relieved that it glided up smoothly, she lifted herself over the window ledge and reached the cement pavement on the other side, fully intact. She brought the window back down to cover her tracks, took a step back, and looked around to see where she was.

Struck by the decaying smell of garbage, Danielle realized she was in the back alley of the strip mall that not only held May Bell's misnomer of a Beauty Bar, but a Chinese Restaurant, Dry Cleaners, and Florist. The co-mingling of the smells was toxic. Danielle needed to come up with phase two of the Great Escape before the aromas killed her.

The plan had to include a hide-out so she could disappear and think. But first things first. Across the alley was a one-story white cement structure that looked like the back of a small office complex. That was the good news. The bad news was there were no doors so she couldn't go hide inside. She was blocked. She couldn't go to the left because she would run smack into Rake and his motorcycle, as she was sure that he had disentangled himself by now to go look for her. She couldn't go to the right because the alley was too long and Rake would see her running away in her paper flip flops when he turned the corner. Her heart started pounding when she realized in those few seconds she would be trapped.

"This better be good, Jen." Danielle said to herself, wondering what on Earth made Jen give her the "Run, Don't Stop" sign.

She heard a faint rumbling of the bells and May Bell's voice yelling at the girls to let Rake go. There was some muffled conversation and Danielle heard the bells again "This is it!" she thought to herself. "He's coming!"

She looked around desperately for a quick out, calculating whether she had the chops to sprint to

263

the end of the strip mall in 10 seconds or less. She looked at her bare feet and the paper that was separating them from the rough pavement. She took a second to mourn for the demise of her perfectly good pedicure but quickly gathered her brains, realizing her indecision about how to get out of there was taking up too much time. She heard Rake kick start his bike and rev up the engine. Did May Bell give away her position, or is she sending him on a wild goose chase?

The engine grew louder and nearer. "So much for the wild good chase." She thought. "That May Bell. Fifty dollars doesn't buy you anything anymore. Especially loyalty. I'm doomed."

Rake would round the corner in seconds and there she would be–standing on ill-fitting paper flip flops, in the middle of a garbage dump, clutching her briefcase with smudged nails, perspiring, and looking guilty about something that was still a mystery to her. So much for a relationship with him.

She closed her eyes, waiting for the ax to fall when she felt a tap on her shoulder. She spun around and was looking down at a little old Chinese man with gray hair, millions of wrinkles, wearing a white apron.

"Kim from next door called. You hide in kitchen closet. Come. Bad man won't find you." He pulled her into the back door of Fung Kwon's Chinese Take-out before she could even open her mouth to say thank you.

The closet was full of boxes of vegetables and a few busy non-human tenants (mental note to staff while working in Rocktown Branch–don't order takeout from Fung Kwon's). While waiting in the heart of darkness, she found a little bench and assessed her situation. First, she needed to send the girls' next door (excluding May Bell the Traitor) something to thank them for their help. She didn't know why she had to get away from Rake and was certainly disappointed at the missed opportunity to spend some time with him, but she would have to leave that for later. She could hear his motorcycle going up and down the alley a few times and then fade away as he gave up looking for her. It was sad to think that whatever chance they had to get to know one another was now probably over. Why would he ever want to speak with her again? It was back once more to the dorks of West Mendow.

The smells from the restaurant permeated through the pantry. Lunch time was approaching. She could hear the phone ringing as people were calling to place their orders. A pair of feet stopped outside the pantry door. A soft knock followed.

"Lady, lady. Bad man gone. Do you want to come out now?"

"No. Lady, lady loves her new hang-out," she thought to herself. Be nice. Remember, it's a test. She didn't waste a second opening the door and bolting out.

She stopped for a moment to thank the little Chinese man who saved her and planted another hundred in his palm. He just smiled and reciprocated with a takeout menu. She made a bee-line for the door. She poked her head out to make sure the alley was empty. Satisfied, she checked her pedicure, threw her paper flip flops into a nearby garbage bin, and put on her black pumps. Hoping nobody was looking, she did a little dance to shake off any last remaining free-loading little creature friends that may be clinging on her Armani suit. Finally, with some fresh lipstick and a light touch of powder, she walked with renewed dignity towards the end of the alley–away from May Bell's, away from the smelly Chinese Takeout and discovered an ATM outside the Florist where she promptly withdrew $500.

Coming around the strip mall, she saw the Capital National Bank across the street had quieted down. The police cars had disappeared. Sadly, Rake was nowhere in sight. He had obviously given up on her. It looked like business as usual.

Danielle was alone and confused. What had just happened? An hour ago, she was getting ready for a hot date and a chance for the best looking boyfriend this side of Esquire Magazine. Now, there was nobody. She desperately wanted to call Jen, but she still didn't know what was going on inside the branch and didn't want to chance getting Jen in trouble.

She also wanted her car, but she didn't want to risk being seen at the branch. As she stood there, she noticed conga lines of busses passing by. What if her exit strategy involved one of those buses? Danielle hadn't taken a bus since her days in New York. She wouldn't even know how much or how to pay if she ever got on one. She nixed that thought. She then remembered a Metro station nearby. But she would have to walk there. She was definitely not up for that.

Then it hit her. They could be watching out for her. And here she was, standing in plain sight! Doing a quick 360-degree scan, she backed into a shadowed crevice in the wall. Suddenly, she felt something vibrating on her body. Danielle jumped letting out a loud screech immediately thinking it was one of her wannabe pals from the Chinese Take-out pantry and started patting herself down. Feeling the cell phone in her pocket, she closed her eyes and let out a sigh of relief. It was vibrating incessantly. Reaching in, she grabbed it, pulled it out and checked the caller I.D.

It was Jen. Relieved, she was just about to answer it when she had a paranoid thought. Maybe it wasn't Jen. Maybe, Jen had her phone confiscated, and it was a police officer. Or worse, maybe it was Rake pretending to be Jen.

Her phone vibrated and vibrated as she stared at it. It finally stopped. She took a deep breath, thankful that the danger was forestalled. She was just about to put the phone away when it started vibrating again–but this time it was alerting her to a text. She started dreading these text messages after last night's with Dolores and this afternoon's with Jen's and half of her didn't want to look. But the other half thought that was being idiotic, so she brought the screen closer.

"Boobeyhead. It's really me. Answer the stupid phone."

Her shoulders dropped, and the stiffness in her back eased. Relief. Only Jen got away with calling her "Boobeyhead". As she stared at the screen, Jen called again.

"Jen, this better be good," she said agitatedly. "I am across the street with a ruined pedicure, bugs possibly crawling this moment into my underwear, and smelling like Pork Lo Mein. What was going on in there? Why did you give me the signal of all signals?"

"Dolores Kagan is dead," Jen whispered.

"What?!" It took a moment to register, but then she saw the connection. Dolores sent her a text message last night essentially accusing her of knowing about what happened to Bill Smith or even intimating, she may have even murdered him. And if that was the case, the police probably thought she knew something about something. That batty old lady was dragging her into this even further. And where did that get her at the end? Jen remained silent.

Danielle inhaled deeply while she wondered what bomb was going to drop next.

"Hey, are you still there?" Jen said softly.

"Why are you whispering?" Danielle asked, bringing the phone closer to her ear. "Are they still there?"

"Yes. There are three cops waiting for you to come back. I'm talking from the bathroom."

"Oh," Danielle said, surprised since she didn't see the cars. Poking her head out from the shadows, she looked up and down the Pike but saw nothing suspicious that looked like a police car or that black SUV. She wondered if they were hiding around the back of the branch in the drive-thru waiting to pounce. After all, she saw that ruse used a few times working with the cops on stings.

"Are you looking for the cops? I told them to park in the back. We can monitor them through the drive-thru window if they decide to make a move. What are you going to do?" Jen asked nervously.

Danielle nodded her head. She and Jen must have been separated at birth, or they've been working together too long. They thought alike and finished each other's thoughts. But for this, she had to think for herself since Jen didn't have the full picture. She paused for a second to gather her thoughts. The next steps were crucial. "First," she said, trying to sound casual, "I don't know what the big deal is. You know and I do that after I left Sheila's, I went straight home, got in my pajamas and was snuggled up in my little bed for the rest of the night freaking out that my happy, boring, insignificant life just exploded. So how could I possibly have gotten involved in anything that had to do with that crazy nut job other than that I ran into her yesterday morning at headquarters?"

"Well, Rake told me off the record...."

Now her blood was boiling. "Rake? My Rake? You're talking to Rake?" So, it somehow involves him. She felt her face turn red. But how? Is this why he was coming to see her? Was Rake playing her? Oh boy, she hated being played.

"Jen, what happened to Dolores?" Danielle asked nervously.

"Rake said that while Dolores was in the shower, someone entered her apartment–you know–a la Psycho..."

"Geez. She was stabbed to death? Bad ending..." Danielle cringed, remembering that awful scene from the movie.

"No. Actually, whoever it was, took a giant bottle of body lotion and doused her bathroom floor with it. As soon as she stepped out of the tub, she slipped and cracked her head on the bathroom sink. Quite brilliant." Jen replied calmly.

"Yes. brilliant." Danielle was impressed.

270

"Agree. But don't admit that to anyone." Jen answered coolly.

"Of course not," Danielle said indignantly as she watched the traffic on Rocktown Pike get heavier as noon was approaching. "Why would you think I would go around saying that?"

"I hate to tell you this, but the lobby surveillance camera caught a short, dark-haired woman entering and leaving the building at that time through the basement laundry room exit."

"What!?!" Danielle yelled into the phone. "Do they think that was me? That's crazy!"

"Yeh, I know. But something else was weird. In Dolores' last seconds, she outlined a big "M" in the body lotion on the floor next to her," Jen explained further.

"What's the "M" for?" she asked, not getting the connection.

"Really? Mendow, Danielle. Danielle Mendow. That's what they think! They found her cell phone. It had some cryptic message to you about something she thought you did. They want to talk to you about Bill Smith again!" Jen answered, trying to keep her voice down.

"There's no way this is happening!" Danielle was pacing mindlessly in her little hidden corner. Her voice was getting louder and louder. She was attracting attention from people around that part of the mall. "No, no. it can't be! I had nothing to do with any of this!"

"Stop, Danielle. I know." Jen implored. "Look, I've got to go. I've been pretending to poop long enough in here, and they're going to get suspicious. You still have my laptop?"

"Yes," Danielle said, a little calmer.

"Money?"

"I'm okay." She said while trying to remember what she started with that morning.

"Then go find a place to get lost and figure something out."

"Tell me about Rake, Jen. What is he all about? Why is he involved?" Danielle pleaded.

"I don't have time, Danielle. All I can tell you is I think he's a good guy."

"Is that it? You don't want to help me anymore?" she said, her voice cracking.

"Danielle, you don't need my help. You need to get out of here and get your head straight. I don't have the energy to figure out what's going on with you or those transactions. But you gotta get on this fast, girl, because you just stepped in some quicksand and you're sinking."

This new attitude from Jen was confusing. "I thought you were my friend?"

"I am. But whatever this is all about is above my pay grade. I gotta go."

The line disconnected. Danielle tried calling back, but it seemed Jen had enough and turned off her phone altogether. Danielle stared incredulously across the street at the branch. Jen deserted her. Without Jen, she had to admit she was lost. She looked around and saw another bus crawling down Rocktown Pike. It was heading east towards Washington D.C.–its last destination showing as Union Station. Perfect. It stopped about 20 feet from her and opened its doors to let out a rider. Without thinking, she ran to it as fast as her Manolo's would take her and just made it before the driver closed the doors. She didn't have a Metro card or exact fare, so she handed it to the driver, telling him to keep the change.

The bus was crowded, and she spotted a seat towards the back. She made her way down the aisle, hoping not to attract too much attention with her Armani Suit, Chanel Bag, Manolo's and a visibly upset face that was just slapped with a murder charge. Sitting down, she put her briefcase on her lap and her handbag on top, hugging it like a long-lost son. Her head leaned towards the window. Her eyelids got heavy. The stress of the last two days was catching up to her.

Before her eyes completely closed, she heard Jen's voice repeat in her head. "You just stepped in some quicksand and you're sinking fast." What an understatement.

Chapter 21

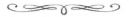

The bus jolted. Gripped by a sudden fear, Danielle's eyes quickly shot open. Out of her now new habit, she looked around for anyone that looked suspicious. From her amateur perspective, she concluded everything looked fine. The constant rumbling of the tires, the smell of the diesel fuel permeating from the back, and her own exhaustion quickly put her back in a trance-like state. Soon, her breathing slowed and the panic that kept her so hyped up to this point started to slowly melt.

The bus headed southeast, opposite the afternoon sun, but it was still strong and fell heavily upon her. As it rambled along, Danielle had plenty of time to think. Nothing made sense anymore. The week before she was the Queen of West Mendow, the perfect banker, the successful businesswoman, the model cougar, the girl who had everything! This week she was wanted for money laundering and the murders of Bill Smith and Dolores Kagan. To add insult to injury, she was also friendless. Nobody could have convinced her in a million years that this would ever happen to her. It now replaced every hope she ever had of her picture on the cover of Forbes. Now her thoughts were about her picture being in every post office on the ten most wanted list.

Startled by that last thought, her eyes popped open. She sat up like an electric prod poked her. There's going to be a manhunt, she thought. Every police officer from here to the moon is going to be looking for her. This is really serious. "Think, Danielle, think," she said to herself.

Reaching into her handbag, she pulled out her cell phone to see if there was anything more about Bill or Dolores on her news websites. The second before she hit the WTOP News app, a wild thought struck her. What if they could trace her movements through Google maps or another app? All those espionage thrillers she reads always mention that there are chips in cell phones that are used to track the people holding them.

Deciding not to chance it, she slid the bus window open, and without giving it two seconds of thought, tossed her phone out the window and into the heavy traffic on Rocktown Pike. Leaning back, she breathed a sigh of relief, hoping she just avoided disaster. She imagined hearing a crunch and seeing her phone flattened like a pancake in the middle of the road. The image thrilled her.

"How liberating is that? I am now officially disconnected." She thought to herself, smiling. She caught the reflection of the new Danielle in the bus window. A few mascara smudges notwithstanding, she was pleased to see that her spa treatment was holding up, including the nice buff of her hair. Hah, if Rake could see her now. Her eyes gleamed, and she was smiling from ear to ear.

Happy that her escape plan was working, she also noticed behind her reflection, a few passengers staring at her as if she belonged in an insane asylum. Was it the perfume she was wearing? Ode de Chicken with Broccoli? She didn't care. Nobody, good or evil, could haunt her now. She was phone, voice-mail, text, and email free!

The bus made a few stops along the Pike, dropping off and picking up all sorts of people–day laborers, mothers with baby carriages, men and women in suits and dresses. She was just one of the 'anonymous' now. How humbling. Deep down, she was getting excited about this new chapter in her life. Here she was, in the middle of the day ambling towards Union Station with a bunch of strangers and Danielle Mendow, the wanted woman, felt kind of safe. No, very safe. For her, it was a brilliant cover. Nobody would suspect that she knew how to take the bus.

Relaxing back again, she contemplated her plight. The bus rolled by the Beltway exit, the National Institute of Health, a Hospital and some apartment buildings. They drove through a section of small homes and office complexes. At this point, the Pike turned into Wisconsin Avenue, crossing over into Bethesda.

The city of Bethesda was a sharp contrast to West Mendow. Highly educated, the population was way over 50,000, almost twice the size and three times as wealthy per capita than Danielle's home town. Danielle used to describe Bethesda as

West Mendow "super-sized". Bethesda was a great place to live, work, and eat, but it was also over-priced and bloated.

Since Danielle's lifestyle was all about over-priced stuff and bloat, she would occasionally stop in Bethesda on her way home from a meeting downtown and spend some time keeping the high-priced boutiques on Woodmont and Bethesda Avenues in business. Exhausted but exhilarated, she would then grab some escargot and a glass of Sancerre at the bar of her favorite French restaurant, Monsieur Herré Babi, in the city's heart. But today, she was someone else–a fugitive from justice–a master criminal in the eyes of the law. Someone who could kill two people, launder millions of dollars, and escape right under the eyes of the law! What a crazy turn of events. Will they ever be convinced from this point forward that she was really just an incidental character in this global scandal?

Realizing the irony, Danielle shook her head to block the panic from starting up again. Mumbling to herself, she said angrily, "I have done nothing wrong and yet I'm running away like I did! What is wrong with me?"

Just then the bus stopped and opened its doors. A few people who were sitting in front of her, gave her a parting glance, nodded and scuttled out the back door. The portly bus driver wrapped his giant arms around the enormous steering wheel, ready to close the doors. But he didn't move. Instead, he seemed to be distracted by something on his left. Holding her breath, Danielle looked. She hoped it wasn't about her. Why wouldn't she think that? After all, it's been all about her for the last two days and some would argue all her life. She tried to look closer. Something was happening. Seconds later, Danielle noticed a police car siding up to his window. The young, dark-haired officer sitting in the passenger seat stuck his arm out and motioned for the bus driver's attention. Danielle craned her neck to get a better view. The bus driver slid open his window and turned his balding head to talk to the police officer. Since she was sitting so far back, she couldn't hear the conversation. Not wanting to risk being around if they were asking about a runaway banker, she quickly thought about her options. She realized she was a sitting duck standing out like an advertisement for Armani instead of someone who couldn't afford a car. Making a split-second decision, she held up her briefcase to cover her face and slipped out the back door just as the bus driver turned to scan the remaining passengers.

Fortunately, this bus stop had a shelter that Danielle hid behind as the bus closed its doors and the bus ambled away. The police car followed behind the bus and Danielle anxiously watched them disappear down Wisconsin Avenue. Still a little shaky, she ran into the closest store. By some Divine Intervention, it was a thrift store.

"My first lucky break of the day," Danielle muttered, looking around perusing her surroundings. The front of the store had shelves and tables full of glassware, knick-knacks, toys, games, pillows, and many other useless items that people would actually still buy. There were broken chairs, tables, couches, and lamps chaotically placed throughout. Bad oil paintings, old posters, and framed pictures of old creepy people lined the walls. A hand-painted sign on an archway with a door made from hanging beads led to a "Fashion Boutique".

Moving away from the front window, Danielle was intrigued, of course, by the "Fashion Boutique". She began snaking her way through the aisles. A few patrons stopped to look at her when she walked by, but quickly lost interest and returned to the shelves and tables like vultures scavenging carcasses.

If the back of the store was anything like the front, she couldn't imagine anything fashionable from this decade, even this century, worth getting excited about, but at least she could hide out in there for a few minutes until the coast was clear. The beads cackled as she pushed them aside. She stepped through into a not surprising den of old men's and women's clothing hung and scattered on shelves and baskets.

"So what do we have here?" asked a male voice coming from behind a rack in the corner. Danielle tried to see through the hanging dresses, but they were packed too tightly.

"Are you talking to me?" Danielle answered.

"Is there anyone else in the room?" the voice replied. Danielle looked around and didn't see anyone. Expecting Robert De Niro's psycho taxi driver, Travis Bickly, to come out of hiding, Danielle moved slowly back towards the archway. She was almost there when a short, rotund figure emerged from between the dresses. With his hands on his broad hips and black square-framed glasses falling to the tip of his nose, he let out a merry little chuckle. "I just crack myself up," he said, smiling. His expression quickly took on a quizzical look when he saw his customer backing out. "Hey! Where are you going?" he asked.

Stopping, she said a silent 'thank you' that the voice and subsequent jolly jelly man that followed it seemed harmless enough. With his pants barely making it around his Humpty Dumpty stomach and a white short-sleeved shirt that could have been substituted as a tent on a camping trip, the guy looked more like a middle-aged version of her Uncle Fred Mendow rather than a nutcase.

"You scared me," Danielle said laughing putting her hand to her chest feigning a heart attack.

"Is it my haircut?" the man replied, laughing with her. "The barber down the street always ruins my hair and gives me such a freakish look. Is that it?"

"You mean you're not bald?" Danielle said in

mock horror as the memory of the close call on the bus a few minutes earlier started fading away.

"Oh my God!" he squealed, putting both hands on his head. "This time he went too far!"

They both laughed and Danielle felt instantly at ease. His name tag said "Bobby". She was just about to ask him about the inventory when suddenly he became very serious. She noticed he was staring at her feet like a cat waiting to pounce on its next meal.

Before she could get too self-conscious, he blurted, "Those aren't real Manolo's, are they?"

Danielle looked down. "Oh, my shoes? Well, yes, they are," she answered cautiously.

"Ooohhh. What will it take to have those? I know at least three women who would sleep with me for those." he said salaciously.

This was getting weird again, Danielle thought to herself. When was the last time this guy looked in the mirror? It would take more than a pair of Manolo's...On the other hand, she realized that she needed to shed her look. Wearing an Armani suit and $600 Manolo's were definite attention grabbers, and this was the last thing she needed as a girl on the run. If this guy had to have her shoes to get laid, maybe she could make a deal.

Remembering she needed to keep all the money she had for a genuine emergency, she said abruptly, "I'll trade you!" causing Bobby to jump.

"Oh!" he said as his hands moved down to her feet like the wicked witch going for Dorothy's ruby slippers.

"Hold on there. Not just yet" Danielle replied, taking a small step back. "First, show me what shoes you have in a 6 ½ or 7."

Bobby jiggled his way towards a shelf of old shoes. Following behind him, Danielle's stomach turned as she imagined the stinky feet that wore them. Nothing else in the world repulsed her as much as wearing someone else's shoes. It was unthinkable. She scanned the rows of pumps, t-straps, and Maryjane's that would have hit her garbage can years ago. It was panic time.

Bobby saw the look of horror on her face and said nodding his fat head sympathetically, "It happens to many people. Listen, I've got a pair of new, never been worn, pair of sneakers in a size 7 in the back. I was saving them for a special swap. I think a pair of Manolo's falls into that category. Let me go get them."

"That sounds great," Danielle replied, relieved. Looking forlornly at her feet, she kissed her $600.00 Limited Edition Love Print pumps goodbye, then watched as Bobby wobbled towards another rack and disappeared behind it. She looked down again. Oh well, she thought to herself, they were uncomfortable anyhow. They were a runway look, not a run-away look. She sighed and looked around further. When all this was over, she would just have to buy another pair.

Would this ever be over? The thought of this nightmare never-ending made her anxious. She took a deep breath and scanned the rest of the inventory while trying to shake off the fear. Sneakers meant "athletics" and "casual" which were never her thing. However, desperate circumstances required a major compromise. To get out of the area unnoticed, she would reluctantly accept the dreaded dress down. A slight chill ran through her body as she had a fleeting thought that this disguise may be permanent. That can never happen! What an ordeal! There had to be a way out of this mess, but first things first.

"Everything in the bins is clean. Don't worry!" Bobby boomed from behind the rack. Danielle saw a big box of trousers in a corner. Rummaging through it, she found a pair of size 4 Old Navy Khakis that looked almost brand new. Knowing she could squeeze into anything with enough aerobics, Danielle walked over to a rack with jackets. There she found a surprisingly nice GAP denim jacket.

While holding it up for inspection, she heard Bobby come out from the rack behind her. Admiring her choice, she turned around to find him holding up a pink pair of Adidas and a T-shirt with a yellow smiley face to complete the look.

Danielle put on her best fake "pleased" face. "Wow! Nice choice! You're saving me a trip to The Urban Outdoor Store. Isn't it just like a man to call you at the last minute for a hike on the Potomac!" she said. She wondered if the story sounded plausible enough for the change in clothes or whether Bobby was cleverer than he looked. After all, he managed to get a pair of $600.00 Manolo's for a $20 used outfit.

"There's a changing room behind that curtain," he said, redirecting his gaze downwards towards his prize.

He handed her the sneakers and a T-shirt. Within minutes, she successfully pulled up the zipper on the pants, stuffed her size 7 feet in a pair of sneakers she wouldn't have been caught dead in last week, and buttoned the denim jackets so Mr. Smiley Face wouldn't see the light of day.

The Armani suit she wore was tucked into her briefcase, and she made sure to double-check that the flash drive was still in her handbag.

"Well, well," Bobby said, wiping some sweat off his forehead. "I see you can pull off the nature girl look too!"

"Really?" Danielle replied, giving herself a second look in the narrow mirror hanging outside the dressing room. Ugh, she thought to herself as she glanced away from her reflection.

The tone in his voice betrayed the truth, but Danielle didn't care. She was happy to get out of her uncomfortable suit and shoes. The new, old clothes brought her back to her teenage years when she would jump on a horse and ride for hours in the back of the woods of West Mendow. Those days were so much simpler and happier. "Why did I have to complicate my life," she thought to herself. Maybe the events of the past couple of days were a wake-up call. Maybe this is all leading to some kind of epiphany!

The Thrift Shop was suffocating her. Bobby was holding out his stubby, sweaty hands for her shoes.

"I know it's not much of a trade, but I will treasure them," he said apologetically. She held them out, and he gently took them from her hands. Holding the shoes close to his chest and petting them like a miniature poodle, he continued. "I know I'm getting the better deal here. Heck, I priced these the other day on E-Bay. I'll give you three hundred bucks for them if you throw in the Gucci handbag…"

This guy was some operator, thought Danielle. But she could use the money, and she had no desire to allow the FBI to track her if she uses her ATM. She had to play.

"Three hundred bucks for both? This handbag alone is worth another zero." She paused for effect then said, "Four hundred dollars and you have a deal."

"Wicked lady" Bobby shouted with glee. "Okay!". He reached in his pocket, pulled out a wad of cash, and peeled off four one hundred-dollar bills. Danielle's eyes widened. She made a mental note to revisit Bobby again and have him open an account with her.

"The clothes are on me." Pointing behind her, he said, "Oh. And take that backpack for the briefcase and the stuff from the handbag. You should be happy I'm taking the Gucci away. It's not a good complement to the outfit."

Danielle rolled her eyes. The guy knew how to rub salt in the wound. She picked up the backpack. Fortunately, it was neutral enough and did not have a Barbie face on it. She stuffed everything in while asking for directions to the Bethesda Metro.

"Okay, I'm off!" she said enthusiastically and thanked him while walking quickly towards the door. "Come again!" he shouted after her. She looked back to wave, but he had already disappeared behind the racks taking her shoes with him.

A CVS drug store was up ahead and Danielle stopped in to pick up some provisions and find some compliments to her new disguise. She found a Nationals Baseball Cap, a pair of cheap but trendy Foster Grants, and a bottle of Dasani. She asked a young clerk to help her pick out a no-contract cell phone and show her how to set it up, which he was pleased to do. Everything was paid for in cash since she had seen enough detective shows to know that credit cards could be traced.

All she wanted to do was disappear. The more she changed her appearance, the better she felt. Her walk became lighter and quicker. At the Metro Station, she spotted two police officers near the escalators checking out the riders. Were they looking for her? She wasn't even fazed. She just walked right past them and even stayed on the same escalator step as it made its way slowly down towards the station.

When she reached the bottom, she walked over to a garbage can, pulled out her Armani Suit from the backpack, and threw it away. "I've molted," she said to herself. "It's time to grow another skin."

Chapter 22

Perched on his motorcycle behind the Capital National Bank branch in Rocktown, Rake Harris watched Danielle stumble clumsily onto a public bus heading towards Union Station. Nice move, he thought to himself, admiring her great escape. Could have been a little more graceful, but it probably wasn't easy running in those weird little shoes. Women and their shoes, he thought to himself.

Taking out his cell phone, he quickly shot off a text reporting her movements to Muckiss, who responded immediately that it was okay to back off. He and his team would pick up her trail from there.

Knowing better than to interfere in someone's case, he got on his bike and slid on to Rocktown Pike towards home. His feelings were mixed. The good news was that he accomplished his mission for the Bureau. The bad news was that Danielle Mendow was suspected of two murders and being pursued by the local police and the FBI. That's pressure. However, he knew in his heart that if there was anyone that could pull off an escape and disappear, he was convinced that it was her. But that wasn't what was bothering him. His heart already missed her.

Traffic was getting heavy this time in the afternoon, preventing him from burning some serious rubber but giving him a long stretch to replay the events of the last few weeks and get his head straight.

It all started three weeks ago when his old buddy, Peter Muckiss, called to ask him to monitor a woman named Danielle Mendow. He remembered that meeting well. Rake Harris felt recharged. He was a year into his early, unfair, "had no choice", forced retirement bestowed upon him by his ex-boss and nemesis, Bob Murphy. He quickly discovered that retirement did not become him. The idea of spending the rest of his life in first gear after twenty-five years of driving in fourth gear was becoming more distasteful by the second. So he stayed in shape, hoping that Bob Murphy would get hit by a truck and he could return.

Muckiss's phone call didn't come soon enough.

The assignment seemed simple, in fact, a bit beneath him, but he was okay with that. It was a start. He was happy to do anything not to have to play another boring round of golf with the other retired special agents of his class at the Bureau. He didn't even like golf but his pals didn't like running five miles a day either, hence the compromise if he wanted some sort of social life.

The next day, Muckiss shared the file on Danielle at their meeting in a Starbucks in downtown Bethesda. The assignment intrigued

Rake the second Muckiss handed it to him. He didn't expect to be handed a bonus. Here was a smart, successful and most importantly, hot little lady. Keeping an eye on her would definitely be more interesting and challenging than he first imagined.

The light ahead turned red. He noticed that the woman in the car on his right was smiling at him. Normally, he would do a little flirty thing like rev his engine, but today he was more interested in trying to decipher this enigmatic assignment. Something wasn't sitting right with him. Although he was sure that Danielle could take care of herself, (he had the bruise on his backside to prove it) he believed he had to protect others from her. She was like a Twister–strong and powerful but also destructive if anything gets in her path.

Businesswoman and banker. And that was just the start. The light turned green. Back to the meeting. The thick dossier Muckiss handed him was fascinating. It took him a while to read through it as Muckiss watched. The only remaining member of the Mendow clan, at 21, she inherited thousands of acres of prime underdeveloped southwest Maryland property bordering Sugarloaf Mountain and the Potomac River. But Danielle wasn't interested in spending her life on the farm. After graduating first in her class from Columbia Business School, she stayed in New York to conquer Wall Street.

The dream, however, turned into somewhat of a

bust. Ironically, Danielle was not very good at making money for the large investment banks but was a genius at moving it around the globe. Many banks tried to recruit her, but she joined Capital International Bank, the international arm of Capital National after a chance meeting at a Christmas party with banking legend, Bill Smith. Smith was then the operations manager at CIB. Bill immediately began grooming his new protégé so that eventually she could free him to move up the corporate ladder. But shortly after 9/11, Smith disappeared along with $10 Million from the bank. The international division shut down a few months afterward.

With employment prospects at a historic low–especially in New York–the greatest little money mover this side of the Atlantic had her wings clipped and she returned to West Mendow licking her wounds, knowing there was nowhere else to go. The bank cut her some slack and assigned her a hokey little branch to manage in her hometown miles from the action in D.C. Anybody else would have been thoroughly humiliated, crawled under a rock, and, most likely, thrown in the towel taking the easy way out by selling off the land little by little and living off the proceeds. But that wasn't this girl. Within a few years, she made a fortune turning unused land into thriving farms and starting distribution and recreation businesses. At the same time, her branch grew- becoming a resource for loans and investment to the locals. What was once a sleepy little hamlet was now one of Maryland's most important regional economies.

Muckiss sipped on his coffee. Rake noticed out of the corner of his eye, he was being watched with great interest as he followed this enthralling woman's career. The more he read, the more he was hooked. He closed the file and gave it a playful tap.

"Just your type, right?" Muckiss said with his signature sniff. "She's cute, feisty, and highly intelligent. Easy..." he continued pausing for emphasis, "not to let out of your sight."

"Glad you clarified that last comment, buddy." Rake said, glaring. "You've been driving me nuts since the Academy. I'm not looking to get fixed up for the hundredth time by you. Once was enough. I enjoy being single. I'm sure when the right one comes along, I'll know it and... well, if this is why you asked me to do this..."

"Rake, I gave up on you years ago. Nobody seems to be good enough since Angela, God rest her soul. Just take the case and stop the showboating. Let's just move on. I have another meeting in an hour downtown, so we've got to hurry this along. Any questions?" Muckiss asked, moving the file closer to Rake.

Starbucks started filling up as the lunch hour approached. Still holding on to the photograph, "Okay" Rake said tersely, pulling his chair closer to the small table they were sitting at near the window overlooking Wisconsin Avenue.

Running his fingers through his hair while still staring at the picture, Rake asked, "Peter, did they ever suspect her of taking the money?"

"Looks fishy, right?" Muckiss inhaled. "To be honest, we really don't know. The FBI was not asked to be involved with that investigation. Remember, Capital National Bank is privately held by John Place and he never complained. Apparently, they kept the investigation in-house and didn't bother reporting it at the time. Bill Smith mentioned something about missing money when he contacted us a few weeks ago. He said that what he knew would blow the lid wide open on an international money laundering operation involving the bank. We heard something was blowing in the wind at Capital National, but we could never get close enough to uncover anything."

"And Smith wanted to spill the beans suddenly?" Rake said, looking up.

"He said he documented every little bit, but he would not give us anything until he met with us personally. He said he didn't feel safe. We were okay with that because we didn't know what the hell he was talking about at the time." He sheepishly scratched his upper earlobe, then took another sip of coffee.

Allowing that last statement to sink into his brain, Rake waited a minute before replying. "This is some story." he finally said with a sigh. He closed the file and handed it back to Muckiss. "So what did you do with a whopper like that?"

"I went in to see Bob Murphy," Muckiss replied, slipping the file into this briefcase.

Rake shuddered as he remembered their mutual boss. "That guy is such a jerk. He wouldn't know how to do an investigation if he had the playbook in front of him written in large print! Can't wait to hear what that genius had to say," Rake said rolling his eyes, knowing it would be the worse option.

"He made me call John Place–against my better judgment, I might add"

Rake cringed. Muckiss was an excellent agent, but he played too much by the book. Unlike Rake, he actually listened to his boss and did what he was told.

"That must have been nasty," Rake said, wondering how much damage that did to the case. "What did you say to him?" he asked, watching Muckiss bite into a Biscotti.

"Well," he said chewing and talking simultaneously, "he asked the head of their international department, Teddy Hudd, who remembered knowing about the missing money and reminded him they wrote it off and shut down the international operation immediately after that. He remembered hearing that his Operations Manager had disappeared but heard later on that a hungry lion killed him while on a safari in Kenya. I'm not joking. It amazed him to hear that he was still alive, made a big showing of being relieved or something like that, then asked why all the curiosity over a decade later."

"You didn't go into the whole thing about the money laundering, did you? I mean, how wouldn't you know he wasn't the ringleader or involved in some way," Rake said, eyeing the Biscotti and regretting he didn't order one.

"No, no, no. I told him that Bill Smith sounded unstable and crazy, accusing the entire planet of theft. We were just doing our due diligence and following up since Smith made an official complaint."

"And he believed that?" Rake said, catching Muckiss's eyes smiling.

"Who knows? John Place is such a royal nut job on his own. Did you ever meet the guy? Too much money. Screwed up his head."

The problem with Muckiss, Rake remembered, was that he had an irrational disdain for rich people and always assumed they were guilty about something until proven innocent. It was probably why he wanted Rake to keep an eye on Danielle

Mendow. He assumed she was obviously a major player in some conspiracy.

"When are you meeting up with Bill Smith?" Rake asked, changing the subject away from the beleaguered John Place.

"He's flying in from Munich two weeks from this Thursday and we're meeting the next day, Friday a.m., at my office. I already assumed you were going to say 'yes' to help me out, so we rented you the place next door to Mendow's house, which was conveniently empty. Lots of white elephants up there at the moment. Just take a couple of suitcases. It's furnished. Oh–and it's pet-friendly so you can bring your pooch, Spike, for company."

"And you just want me to keep an eye on her. I still don't understand why. How is she involved?" he asked, rubbing his temples.

"Oh. I didn't mention that? Bill Smith asked us to. He said something about trying not to drag her into this, but it may come to that. Whatever. She could be in on it–maybe even the mastermind - or an innocent bystander. Who knows, but she may lead us somewhere or nowhere if you get my drift," he answered as he took back his file.

"Not really, but I guess you have to cover your ass." Rake muttered.

"That's what it's all about in the swamp. Oh, and it's your call if you want to make any contact,"

Muckiss said with a wink. He took out a Blackberry from his right suit jacket pocket and handed it to Rake. "Send me a report via text every morning on this secure phone. You know–the usual routine stuff. Who's going in and out of her house. Where she goes–who she sees. But contact me immediately with anything out of the ordinary. Here's the address."

Rising, Muckiss' chair made a squeaky noise on the grey slate floor, causing some nearby heads to turn. He ate the last of the biscotti, then began patting his pockets like he was looking for his car keys. He beamed and said, "Welcome back. Sorry, this isn't the big CSI case you'd prefer, but Murphy wouldn't approve anything else. One day you're going to tell me what happened between the two of you."

"Not likely," Rake answered with a grin. "Better we keep a few stories behind closed doors."

"Gotcha," Muckiss said, picking up a newspaper from a nearby table. "Enjoy West Mendow. I know it's right up there with Antarctica in terms of excitement but hey–it's better than sitting around waiting for your hair to fall out." He tapped him playfully on the head with the folded newspaper, then put it under his arm while weaving around tables and making his way towards the door.

"Yeh, hah, hah," Rake said to himself as he watched Muckiss walkout. He brought his coffee up to his mouth and realized he hadn't drunk a drop of it and it was now cold.

Thus began the dance with Danielle Mendow. Three weeks later he was watching her board a bus heading downtown and out of sight. Muckiss asked him to let her go. Like that was so easy.

Chapter 23

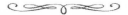

Rake replayed the Starbucks conversation over and over as he carefully weaved his bike through the traffic on Rocktown Pike towards West Mendow. He realized Muckiss did not have a good feeling about Danielle. He was sure that the veteran FBI agent and former colleague probably suspected Danielle was in cahoots at some point with Bill Smith. It was certainly a plausible theory. After all, the rags to riches story from her dossier was a bit unbelievable without some shot of major capital from somewhere. But they paid Muckiss to be skeptical. He never met Danielle. Rake did. Rake knew how to read women. Muckiss didn't. There was nothing in her character that made him question her integrity. Danielle was pure hard grit–sharp, quick, and feisty. She seemed to enjoy the challenge of working for what she got. He couldn't believe she would risk committing a crime to do it.

At least, that's what her sidekick, Jen, made him think earlier during that strange conversation they had in the bank vault. Jen - another piece of work. She was like a Mini-Danielle when she opened her mouth–exasperating but fascinating. It was uncanny.

His motorcycle veered towards the left median as he became more absorbed with his thoughts on

Danielle. A car honking from behind disturbed his musings. Speeding up, he headed back towards the middle of the lane and refocused on arriving in West Mendow in one piece. But the tedious Rocktown Pike with its strip malls, nondescript office buildings, and ill-timed traffic lights didn't keep his attention for long. He still couldn't shake off the memories of this morning.

He rehashed last night's events. Electrified by that kiss, Rake realized he needed to keep close to Danielle at all times - closer than what Muckiss advised. It was wrong. It got personal. Muckiss would be pissed, but screw him. Although he didn't know Danielle for very long, Rake had a gut feeling. Something rattled her these last couple of days and she was in it up to her eyeballs. It was frustrating that he hadn't yet figured it out. He just knew she was in the middle of something out of her control. She could be in danger.

Up half of the night worrying about her, he felt like such a dolt, when Muckiss called and told him they identified the victim at the Willard as Bill Smith–an ex-colleague of Danielle's from New York. Then he dropped the second bombshell about Dolores Kagan. The Feds were connecting her to that murder as well. He wanted to warn her that a posse was coming and hear her side of the story. But she wasn't answering her cell phone. He ran to the shower and was in his leathers in minutes. The sun was barely up when he rode up her driveway. Her car wasn't in the driveway, and he was afraid he didn't catch her before she left for work.

Panicking, he sought help from her housekeeper, who in another life must have been a defensive linebacker for the Redskins. He had a hell of a time getting any information from her about Danielle's whereabouts, but she finally gave in when he agreed to drive her to Church on Sunday morning.

Back on his bike, he called again from the road. He almost ran into a tree when she actually picked up, explained where she was, and agreed to spend the day with him. If she was involved in anything untoward, he couldn't tell from her voice. In fact, she sounded quite normal–even flirty. Excited about being with her, he couldn't reach her fast enough. "Come on, come on" he kept repeating as he hit every red light in the county.

It was going to be sunny and warm–the perfect Fall day for a bike ride with the prettiest lady on this side of the Potomac River. To hell with Muckiss and his cynicism. He could already feel Miss Mendow's arms wrapped around his chest, holding on for dear life as they made their way west into the sunset.

The bank was a few miles from where he crossed into Rocktown. As he neared, he heard sirens and saw the flashing red lights.

The commotion seemed to come from the bank. The police cars alarmed him but he tried to keep his cool. He couldn't tell what was going on so he revved the engine and picked up speed. Was the branch robbed? Did someone get hurt? Or, was it the unimaginable? The Feds got there before he did.

Within seconds he was in the parking lot. He tried to figure out what was happening. In one move, he slid off the bike while slamming down the kickstand. He needed to get into the branch quickly and look for Danielle. While running towards the branch, he reached into his beat-up black leather jacket and pulled out his old badge.

He slowed down when he reached the door so as not to draw too much attention to himself. Flashing his badge at the police officer standing inside the door, he mumbled some nonsense about a federal investigation and money laundering hoping it was somehow unrelated to why they were there. Fortunately, the officer didn't look at his identification or check out his biker outfit or care about his semi-plausible story. He just gave a slight nod, said 'okay' and turned his attention to the action in the lobby. Rake wondered if he would have gotten the same reaction by simply telling him he was there to make a deposit.

Scanning the room, he saw Jen behind the teller line watching worriedly as three police officers were flashing a picture asking if anyone had seen "this woman". Rake strode over to her nonchalantly, like he sees this all the time. They locked eyes. Jen's widened. At that moment, she confirmed his worst fear. The police were looking for Danielle.

The employees obviously knew the woman in the picture. She was their boss or colleague. However, they all kept nodding in the negative like they had amnesia.

With arms crossed, Rake held his breath as he leaned against the teller counter, watching as the police finished their questioning. After conferring with what appeared to be a senior employee- they opened doors, looked under desks, and disappeared into offices continuing their search. One was let behind the teller counter and entered the employee kitchen, which led to the drive-through. So far, Danielle vanished successfully.

Rake let out a long breath. "Her staff is very loyal," he said quietly to Jen as they watched the frustrated police officer go through the kitchen door.

She stood stiff as a mannequin as she turned her attention to him. A plastic smile lined her face, but her eyes were red and her smooth blonde hair was falling out all over the place from her ponytail. The white shirt under her uniform vest was a bit rumpled and hanging out. She looked exhausted.

"My worry meter is hitting the max. They said something about Danielle and two murders as if I knew how Danielle was connected to the Bill Smith guy and a woman from the bank named Dolores Kagan," she asked, masking her concern. The stiff smile remained as she continued. "I'm glad you're here, but I don't know whether that's good. At the least, I hope you can give me some answers."

He watched her chest rise and fall like she wanted to say more. He could hear her deep breaths and felt her anxiety as she continued looking at him. Her words and body language were in obvious opposition.

"We're on the same team, Jen," he answered calmly.

"Oh? That's not what she thought! You looked like a torpedo hit you last night - she got you on your ass so fast." she said a bit too loudly. Jen's tone attracted the attention of the staff, who by this time were back at their stations pretending to work. It also prompted one police officer to make his way over to where they were standing.

Rake stiffened.

"Everything alright over here?" the young officer said as he approached. "Oh, you're the FBI guy. So, why are you here again?"

"Just closing the loop on last night's fire at the West Mendow branch. There was cash in the vault and we need to get a confirmation of the amount from Mrs. DeMatteo here who is still the official head teller of the West Mendow branch. It seems to be a very small discrepancy that we need to understand for a federal investigation so we could record it for the audit."

"Okay. Is it something we should be worried about for this investigation?" the young officer asked, frowning.

Jen turned away while Rake responded professionally. "No, I don't think so. Just routine stuff. Don't even know why we crossed paths. I'll be out in a minute. Sorry to have interrupted whatever you were doing."

After a quick nod, the officer turned towards Jen. "We're going to need to stay awhile in case Mendow returns. I need to move the police cars so we don't impede your business."

"Oh. Okay. You can park them around the back." Jen answered. The officer thanked her, leered noticeably for a split second, then returned to his partner.

They were setting a trap, Rake thought as he watched the officers confer with one another. Rake looked at Jen, who had kept a straight face throughout that brief confrontation. It upset him that her outburst caught the attention of the young officer and everyone else within a ten-mile radius. He guessed Danielle didn't tell her how the evening really ended.

He ran his fingers through his hair and twisted his neck to release some tension. "Please try not to attract any more attention, okay Jen? I could get in trouble for making up stupid shit like that."

"Alright, alright." She said, keeping her eyes on the young officer as they huddled with each other.

"Is there someplace quiet where we can talk?" Rake asked.

She turned her attention back to Rake. "We can go into the Safe Deposit room. Go tell one of the customer service reps over there that you want to see a box. They'll take you in and I'll meet you there."

Rake did what he was told, and within a few minutes, he was in a small room surrounded by hundreds of little silver boxes with locks and numbers on them. A customer service rep began to unlock one when Jen walked in and shooed him out.

"We only have a few minutes until someone thinks we're doing something suspicious in here," Jen said leaning up against a wall of silver, hand on hip.

Rake watched her deliberately, maintaining an awkward silence.

The silence made her uneasy. Jen shifted a bit. She couldn't hold it in and threw the first grenade. "You know, she didn't let me know she was leaving and now I'm trying to get her on her cell phone and she won't answer."

The revelation surprised him, but he didn't let it show. Behind the facade, he was stunned. A million questions flooded his brain. Did he misjudge her? Was she indeed involved in the money laundering scheme? Maybe she was an accomplice in the original theft? Did she know more about the murders than she let on? Was she unraveling? Was it she who burned down the branch? Is she really on the run? He shook off the thoughts. They were talking about his beautiful Danielle; the woman he was having the hots for–not some sinister conspirator. He just didn't want to believe it.

They were locked in a momentary stare down. Rake wondered how much he could trust Jen, while Jen wondered when Rake would finally spill the beans and confess why he was addicted to Danielle.

Rake broke. "Okay, off the record. Tell me what you know."

"What? No, you tell me" Jen said pointing her finger in Rake's face then turning it to herself.

This went on for a few rounds until Jen had had enough. "I'm out of here."

Rake grabbed her by the arm as she headed for the door. "Look, this is a sensitive case so I'll disclose what I can." He reached into his back pocket and pulled out his badge. "Take this, for now, let's pretend that I'm not an FBI agent but someone who is trying to protect our friend."

Warily, she took the badge and said, "You know that sounds weird considering you just met her yesterday, she blew you off at dinner, then almost crippled you a few hours later."

"Points well taken but, let's just say, besides all that, I'm, well..." he looked away in search of the right word. Then, returning his attention back to Jen, he said, "intrigued." Well, that was an understatement, he thought to himself.

Furrowing her brow, Jen half believed him, knowing how Danielle could turn people into fanatics. "To keep this story going, I'll give you the benefit of the doubt. Go on."

Breaking no laws, he told her as much as he could legitimately right up to Dolores' murder and the strange message the victim left in the body cream. He didn't say Danielle was officially a suspect or even a person of interest, but focused more on her need to be protected. He was here to help her get out of this mess.

Jen listened, mesmerized, taking in every detail. She gasped and said a few 'I knew it's' throughout the saga. After he finished, she stared silently at him. Rake could see her digesting and recalibrating the information. After a minute or so, she broke into a wide grin and said she suspected it all along.

"What do you mean? Is Danielle involved in any of this?" he asked feeling the pit in his stomach.

"Well, let's put it this way, Danielle could probably handle anything from a business standpoint–heck, she lived through 9/11. Do you think a fire at her branch and a couple of random murders could match witnessing 2000 people killed while the twin towers were collapsing right in front of her? Nothing much rattles her anymore." Jen said emphatically.

Rake lowered his eyes to hide his confusion. He stared at the gray rug while trying to make sense of what Jen just said. He couldn't. He had a fleeting thought that Danielle could be insane. But he shook his head. He felt bad as he went in that direction and erased it from his mind, for now.

Jen continued. "Are you listening? I know little about you, but for some reason, you've gotten under her skin. I've never seen it happen before. She's just not thinking straight anymore. Oh, and she's not insane."

He shot up like a rocket. How did she know what he was thinking? And she figured out he had a crush on her? Geez. He must be acting like he was seventeen years old again and just found out the head cheerleader liked him. Jen laughed at his reaction. "Hey, don't worry about it. Danielle has a unique power over men which demeans them in her eyes. You, on the other hand, may not know it but have the same kind of power to throw it right back at her. You've knocked her off her game. This is creeping her out, and she's not sure how to react."

Looking down at his feet again, Rake said something, but Jen cut him off. "Hey, don't get all cocky about it. Something else is stirring her up. When Danielle saw the news report on that guy who was murdered at the Willard, she kind of fell apart. It was so out of character. I've known her for a long time. She is not like this."

He looked up and tilted his head. "Like what?" asked Rake.

Jen let out a breath while waving her arms to make a point. "Like this! Attacking you! Knocking you over. Sneaking around the branch. Telling me things about her past I didn't know. Freaking out over nothing. Imagining stuff like people following her and being tailed by black cars. So, thank you for filling in the gaps. I thought she was losing it! So let's go." Jen stepped around him and made her way towards the door.

"Wait. What do you mean by gaps?" Rake asked, blocking her way. "Are we missing something? Jen, did Danielle tell you something that could help us?"

Rake noticed she was tightening the grip on his badge. She turned to face him.

"I don't know if I should answer you as 'Rake the FBI Agent' or 'Rake the Friend'. She answered, taking a step back.

"I can't tell you unless you're honest with me. I've got to do what's right, Jen," Rake replied.

She crossed her arms and slowly tilted her head back and forth, assessing him.

"Jen? What's going on here?" Rake asked, hands on hips. The tension was building. He didn't know which way she was going to go. He assumed she was weighing her options. He knew she knew something. It could go both ways like her boss. Either she was in it up to her eyeballs or she was an inadvertent victim.

Jen took a deep breath, gave a big exhale, and let her long arms dangle to her sides. "Okay, I give up. You look like a good guy and truly gaga over Danielle so hold on to your hat. Maybe we can figure this out together." She began repeating the story Danielle related in the Drive-thru from yesterday. Rake noted she was careful in making sure they perceived Danielle more as a hapless bystander. And Bill Smith was the mastermind. The story fell in line with what he knew from the file, but Jen was connecting some dots for him. All along, he wondered why Danielle was a suspect to begin with. Now he knew. She confirmed that a stolen identification tag was used to unlock the SWIFT communications room. This explained why she was associated with the scandal. It was her I.D tag. Jen then told him how Danielle went out of her way trying to find the money, but Bill kept telling her to stand down. Then he mysteriously disappeared and Capital National wrote off the loss. The timing of the events was very suspicious, but he still couldn't understand her irrational behavior. Why didn't Danielle just tell the truth?

"Let's look at this again." Rake said. "She says she's innocent, but she's still freaking out. You say nothing could ever ruffle her feathers, but this has really gotten to her. I'm not getting it."

"I know. Neither am I. To be honest with you, I'm believing she's not an innocent bystander in this whole thing." Jen said matter of fact.

"Whoa," he cried as his head jerked back. His hands came up in a stop position. He took a step back like he needed to see a bigger picture.

"Um, that didn't come out right," Jen smiled, covering her mouth. "Before you put an arrest warrant out for her, let me explain. I think she feels responsible for everything–the missing money, Bill's disappearance, his resurrection, and finally the illegal money laundering that was happening right under her nose. It seems Bill had been protecting her for years, and now he's dead. The lid has blown off, and she's going to have to explain all these criminal activities, cover-ups, and bloopers if we're ever going to find Bill's killer. How could a brilliant banker and businesswoman who suddenly becomes a multi-millionaire allow all that to happen without being the mastermind?"

"I'm not following. So you think she did it?" Rake asked.

"Of course not, but she believes everyone will think she did. And because of that slip up in the SWIFT room, which, by the way, up to this day, nobody explained, she got the ball rolling. You know, you could say she set the con in motion and just sat back and watched it play out. In the end, it worked. She got exactly what she wanted."

"But she did nothing deliberately." Rake replied, shaking his head.

"Or so she claims," Jen responded.

There was a pause. Rake was baffled. He thought Jen was her friend.

"I just sowed the seed of doubt, right?" Jen laughed. "Well, that's how Danielle feels. Who's going to believe her?"

"But the FBI knows that Bill Smith was going to talk. I presume he was here to show us that flash drive and tell us about an international money laundering scheme going on at the bank." Rake stopped. He was getting Jen's point. Bill Smith was killed before he could implicate anybody and that somebody could have been Danielle. Why would he send her the flash drive? Maybe he blackmailed her and the threat to call the FBI had gone too far because he actually did. In fact, the pieces were fitting nicely into that theory.

"Don't," Jen said.

Startled from his thoughts, Rake answered,

"Don't what?"

"Don't think that way. But you see what I'm getting at? Jen answered.

Feeling guilty that his thoughts were actually going in that direction, he shook himself slightly to change course. "You're a good friend, Jen," he said.

"I know. She drives me crazy, but I love her." Someone started knocking on the door, asking to come in. They turned to check that the door was closed and locked. "Hold on!" Jen shouted. "Give us another minute! We're still counting."

Rake's shoulders drooped. "So, what do you think her next step is?

"I think she's going to disappear if she hasn't done so already."

"What?" He shouted. He realized his voice was too loud and lowered it. "She can't do that!" he protested, twisting his body and running his hand through his hair nervously. "Why would she do that?"

Jen could understand why Danielle found him so appealing. He had these endearing little gestures which betrayed his professional facade. "Because I'm going to tell her to."

"You can't do that! She's... she's... very much a part of this investigation! We... um... need her to be here. It's my job to keep her around! I'm.. I'm...

going to get into a heap of trouble if I let her out of my sight," he pleaded.

Amused, Jen said, "Look, Rake, it's not about you. I know how Danielle works. She's got to disappear so she could regroup. She's not thinking straight, and the only person who could help her now is herself. Let her go. She'll come back. She's got too much at stake."

Calmer, he said, "No. You will not do that"

"Yes, I am. You won't know, so you do what you have to do. Protect her, but don't get in her way. Now, I have to get back to work." Jen started toward the vault door.

"Jen, you're not thinking. We still don't know who was in that SUV and what they would do to get that flash drive. You may put her in real danger." he said as she reached the door.

Pausing as she put her hand on the door latch, she turned and said, "Look. Whoever is after her, knows where she lives and where she works. If it's business as usual, they'll find her. I know you want to help her Rake–we all do–but unless you're willing to lock her away for no reason, you know that if she sticks around here, she's bait."

Wincing, he knew she was right, but damn if he was going to take the fall for it. Deciding to play it Jen's way, for now, he followed right behind her as she left the vault. They both stopped when they saw a pair of police officers listening to a heavy Asian woman in too-tight jeans who was yammering on and gesturing nervously to something outside the window. Jen and Rake looked to where she was pointing and noticed it was toward a day salon. They looked at each other and snuck closer to the threesome, hoping to eavesdrop on the conversation.

She was at the end of her tirade because all they got was "….and she gave me $50 bucks to find out what was going on in here! When you guys showed up, she seemed to get awfully nervous... like she robbed the bank or something... you know what I mean? I bet she won't even stay long enough for her nails to dry. What a waste"

"It's Mendow. Let's go" one officer said, putting away his notebook.

Although Rake's instincts were screaming 'Don't Interfere!', his emotions were stronger. He looked at Jen and mouthed, 'stall'.

The spectacle of the two police officers and the salon lady had caught everyone's attention, including the few customers that were in the bank. There wasn't much movement going around, and Jen had to think fast. Rake had maybe three minutes to get over there and do the right thing without having the police officers believe he was involved in any of this.

Rake watched as Jen she did the only thing that

could be done in those few seconds. He knew it was sophomoric, but it worked. As the officers made their way to the door, Jen started running towards them as if she had to tell them something and slipped right in front of them, blocking their way. Clutching her leg, she started moaning. It was just enough time to let Rake slip out the door and head towards his bike.

Everyone circled over her, including the two police officers and the woman from the salon. She gave it her best academy award performance, complaining about the pain. Somebody suggested they call an ambulance, but she refused as she struggled to get up on her feet. She kept grabbing the officers for help hoping to buy a few more minutes but they pushed her on to the staff and with apologies; they declared they had an emergency and had to go.

As everyone continued to grab at her to help her up, she looked out the double glass doors of the branch and could see that Rake had reached the bike and was putting it in gear. Meanwhile, the police officers were making their way to the car while the Salon lady started walking towards the traffic light to cross the Pike and return to her salon.

This was all happening faster than she liked. She brushed everyone off as she reassured them she was fine. She hurried to the coat rack by the doors where Capital Bank umbrellas were kept to help customers go to their cars during rainstorms. She grabbed one, ran out the door and opened it. She held it high over her head as if she wanted lightning to strike it.

Rake was on his bike waiting at the light and turned back to see what was happening. The police were in the car with their lights flashing and the driver was on the radio. They had not backed out yet, but knew they were going to any second. When he saw Jen holding the umbrella, he knew instinctively that he was witnessing some sort of signal between her and Danielle that he would figure out about soon enough.

He didn't think the police connected him as complicit in their search for Danielle, but he didn't want to chance it. As soon as the light changed, he crossed Rocktown Pike and hid his motorcycle behind a laundry truck on the other side of the strip mall. He took his leather jacket off and put on a baseball cap and sunglasses he had in his seat. By the time the police from the branch got in their cars, the light changed again. The police were still waiting at the light when Rake sauntered into the salon behind May Bell who had just walked in. He had two minutes at the most.

Two young girls, one he couldn't help notice, with an enormous nose, surrounded him, lunging at his nails and brushing his hair. May Bell turned to see what was going on and began swatting them away. Sullen-faced, they returned to their stations.

"Can I help you?" May Bell asked, looking him up and down with a gleam in her eye. Fortunately, she did not recognize him from the branch.

He looked around and quickly realized Danielle wasn't there. Relieved, he said, "Um, no. I thought this was the laundromat. My mistake"

He heard some giggles on the way out and someone yelled out, "Cad!" As the door closed behind him, he heard May Bell asking about the lady who was here before. One girl giggled and answered that she ran out the back and disappeared.

Good. She flew the coup; he thought. He passed in front of the salon and saw the police car drive into the parking lot in the window's reflection. He bowed his head lower and picked up the pace back to his bike. His cell phone vibrated in his pocket. Although he didn't recognize the number, he answered it, giving him more of a reason to keep his face busy. It was Jen.

"Don't talk. There's no time. I keep a spare key to Danielle's car in case she asks me to run an errand really quick. I'm giving it to Eddy. He's going to drive it up the Pike to pick up lunch but I'm going to call the number on the card the police left with me pretending I don't know that and tell them I saw Danielle pull out of the parking lot. That should buy her some time to slip further away somewhere."

"She's not here." Rake said, sneaking a peek at the police officers entering the salon.

"I know. Don't ask. I'm just telling you what's about to happen so you don't go crazy and make a scene."

Jen disconnected. Within seconds, Eddy was in Danielle's Mercedes and pulling out of the parking lot. Just like Jen predicted, the police officers that were still in the branch came running out, spotted it and jumped in their cars to follow.

He had to hand it to Jen. She must have watched a lot of cops and robbers on TV to think that up in a few minutes. He got on his bike and took a couple of spins around the strip mall to make sure all looked normal. There was no Black SUV's lurking around, no other police, and thankfully, no Danielle.

Rake rode back to the branch and parked behind a corner to keep a look-out and make sure there wasn't further trouble in the branch or from the strip mall. As his heart slowed down to normal, he thought about the two ladies. Jen and Danielle were totally in sync with each other to where they actually made plans in the event of dangerous situations. Scratching his head in disbelief and chuckling to himself, he wondered what on earth would possess them to develop such elaborate signals and fallback procedures.

Suddenly, he realized, and he sobered up. Why, somebody who knew that at some point, the truth may catch up to them!

Did he make a mistake letting Danielle go? Before he could answer that, he saw her peering around the corner of the other end of the strip mall. He sat upon his bike for a better look. She seemed scared and tired. Her clothes were disheveled. She clenched her briefcase and handbag like they were life vests. He felt sorry for her. A second ago, he wanted to have her arrested. Now he wanted to put his bike in gear, race over to her, put her in his arms and tell her everything was okay.

But he and Muckiss had had a long game going on, and he didn't want to ruin it for his friend. He had meddled enough. Earlier, Jen convinced him Danielle Mendow was a survivor. If anyone was going to come out right in all of this, it was going to be her. He didn't have to help her–at least, not now.

He watched as she pulled out her cell phone and assumed she was calling Jen. The call ended quickly, at which point she looked visibly upset. She put the phone back in her jacket pocket and looked around. A bus was pulling up at the stop to let off a passenger. He could see her checking the direction on the top of the windshield. From his hiding place, he could see it read, "Towards Union Station". He watched her stumble quickly towards it and before you could say, "Sayonara" she staggered through the door.

The bus slowly disappeared down Rocktown Pike. What a morning, he thought to himself as he kicked his bike into first gear.

Chapter 24

The traffic on the Rocktown Pike lightened as Rake got closer to West Mendow. With very few drivers on the road, Rake kicked his bike into top gear and continued to travel West following the lazily moving sun. The glare and the dry dust in the air were blinding. Even with his sun visor over his eyes, Rake had to squint the rest of the way home to make sure he wasn't passing through any red lights. The thick leather jacket he wore was too hot for the Indian Summer afternoon. He was itchy and sweaty. Although he knew he looked smoking hot in it, he couldn't wait to get home and rip it off. It disappointed him he didn't get a chance to show off his riding prowess and all to Danielle, but he was content knowing she made a remarkable escape that could rival the magic of the Great Houdini.

The exit to West Mendow Road finally came up. Easing on to it, he drove through the center of the little town, then slowed down when he came to Danielle's branch. It was still smoldering. He paid his respects, then headed home, passing by Sheila's Luncheonette. He smiled, remembering the night before. The sensation of that perfect kiss came back. He closed his eyes for a second to enjoy it and when he opened them he had to make a jerky swerve, to avoid mowing down an old lady trying to cross the street.

The West Mendow High School seemed to be letting out for a late lunch, so he cut through a few back roads to avoid the lunatic seniors who seem to forget all the speeding and parking laws they learned in Driver's Ed. He finally got to his street, slowed down in front of Danielle's home to make sure everything looked okay, which it did, and finally reached his own.

Danielle's home. He suddenly felt a sadness for her. A week earlier, she was at the top of her game. Today, she was on the run. What was supposed to be a fluff assignment for him was now becoming personal. At that moment, he vowed he would do all he could to help Danielle get out of this mess.

His garish house loomed ahead. It felt empty and lonely even before he got there. He turned up his driveway and parked his bike by the front doors. He kicked down the stand and took off his helmet. His shoulders slumped as he watched his orally fixated dog, Spike, blocking the entrance while busily chomping on an old tennis ball. 'Man's best friend' barely acknowledged him.

"That must be some delicious ball," Rake called out. The sandy-haired mutt looked up and with the ball stuffed in his big mouth, ran off to the back of the house, obviously giving Rake the message that he will not be sharing.

The silence of the house was eerie as he walked through the door, hearing only his own footsteps. He hurried across the marble foyer, tearing off his jacket and flinging it on the two-story banister. He wondered what it would feel like to have someone he adored greet him again one day with a big kiss and a beer. Well, at least he could solve one problem.

He marched with a purpose into the kitchen towards the refrigerator. On his way, he looked around dreaming what it would be like to have a clean kitchen, dinner simmering on the stove, and his favorite Bee Gees music playing in the background. Alright, maybe not Bee Gees–after all, that's an acquired taste nobody needed to know about right away. He would keep that to himself and not inflict it on anyone else until the ink was dry.

He opened the refrigerator door, ran his hand through his helmet-matted hair, and sighed as he studied the contents. 'It be nice if one day it would be stacked with healthy food, some gourmet left-overs, chilled fruit, and better beer?' he commiserated to nobody. Shaking his head, he became concerned about all these unsettling thoughts of domesticity. What was getting into him? Could it be some sort of invisible gamma rays emitted from the manicured lawns in the suburbs that cause people to think about stuff like this? A wave of depression was overcoming him. He was doomed. Before he started thinking about window treatments, he grabbed a can of Budweiser and slammed the door shut, hoping to shut down the vision. The can of beer was halfway drunk, scorching his throat as he made his way to the living room.

"Dammit," he said to no one, plopping on the oversized brown leather couch. He grabbed the remote to turn on the giant fifty-two-inch television hanging over the fireplace.

The D.C. news was playing, and it was broadcasting outside of the Capital National Bank headquarters with an update of the Bill Smith murder right at that moment.

Rake sat up and fumbled with the overly complicated remote to find the volume.

"… they identified the body this morning as that of Bill Smith, who was traveling under the alias, Wilhelm Schmidt. Last heard, Smith was an employee of Capital Bank International, the New York branch of our very own Capital National Bank. He disappeared over a decade ago and had been assumed dead when word came back a lion attacked him on an African safari."

The camera then panned to a woman sitting behind the desk back at the studio. "Laurie, tell us more about Bill Smith."

The attractive blonde with the microphone standing outside continued. "Thank you, Debra. There have been no further leads in the murder of the mysterious man who went by the name Wilhelm Schmidt. Why did he change his name?

Why did he lead people to believe he was dead? What was the purpose of his visit to Washington D.C. and why now? The FBI is trying to track down his family, but meanwhile, former friends and colleagues are stunned at the news. Teddy Hudd, the Senior Executive Vice President of the International Division had this to say."

The camera cut away to Hudd's office–a traditional banker's office with walls full of extensively carved dark wooden shelves, a desk that must have cost as much as the mortgages the bank had foreclosed on, and carpeting worthy of Versailles. Hudd sat on a large leather chair framed with oak in a seating area across the room. The attractive blonde interviewer sat across from him.

His whole appearance reeked of a bank, Rake thought to himself remembering those guys sitting across from him while he tore through their excuses for bank fraud and corruption. He loved watching them go from pompous jerks to sweating dwarfs when the judges sentenced them for ripping off the little guys who trusted their life savings to them.

"So, Mr. Hudd," the interviewer began. "What can you tell us about your former colleague?

Hudd coughed and sputtered for a few seconds before he spoke. "Well, he was a brilliant banker and a loyal employee. Together, we got our operation through the worse of 9/11. We kept going when most banks in lower Manhattan experienced some serious operational problems."

"How do you explain his disappearance?" The interviewer continued.

Hudd laughed pretentiously. "It wasn't a disappearance at first. We all thought Bill needed a vacation after six months of working twenty-four/ seven, and the Chairman told him to take some time off. Poor Bill. He reluctantly agreed and the next thing we heard he was gone forever!".

Looking down at his hands, he fidgeted in his seat, then uncrossed one leg and cross the other.

"Mr. Hudd," the interviewer said, raising her voice a notch to retrieve his attention, "It wasn't long after that, your Chairman closed the International Division. What do you do now?"

Eyes shifting, Hudd squirmed again. "I am the special advisor to the Chairman."

Rake thought he saw a hint of a smile on the interviewer's face. And who said gorgeous blondes didn't have a wicked sense of humor? It looks like she had his number.

"Moving on, Mr. Hudd. It's been rumored that the International Division lost a lot of money during that time and that Bill Smith and his staff tried to recover it but were shut down before they could trace it."

Hudd was stone-face. Rake leaned in closer to the television waiting to catch every word and nuance of the response.

"We had some minor losses like everyone else but nothing to write home about." He answered without skipping a beat.

The interviewer was relentless. "Ten million dollars' worth?"

Again the pretentious laugh. "Now, where did you hear that?" Hudd responded. "No, no, no. Lop off a few zeroes maybe, and we're in the ballpark."

Rake's gut told him the guy was hiding something and was dying to hear more, but the interviewer didn't seem to catch it and moved on. "Who do you think killed Bill Smith?"

Oddly enough, Hudd seemed prepared for this question. "I think you may be trying to make this more than it is. I'm leaning towards a random robbery of an innocent tourist."

"But nothing was taken. His passport was still in his pocket. His wallet was intact and full of money. His co-workers in Munich claim he was truly beloved, a great, generous guy all around. The only clue is a video of a dark-haired woman entering the elevator with him then leaving the hotel 15 minutes later."

The camera moved in for a close-up of Hudd's face full of insincere remorse. "It's very sad." He said, nodding his head back and forth. "You're not even safe in a five-star hotel next door to the White House."

Rake rolled his eyes. "What a goofball."

The camera then cut back to the interviewer standing in front of the Capital National Bank Building. She continued, "The video that was mentioned during the interview with Mr. Hudd is being studied at the moment by the FBI. However, D.C. News has just obtained a copy."

Rake quickly pressed the DVR button to "record". He watched intently. The first screenshot showed a busy Willard lobby. The date of the recording was September 17, 8:30 pm. A man with a trench coat, briefcase, and small suitcase was walking towards the elevator. A dark-haired woman rose from one of the lobby chairs and followed him into the elevator. Her black raincoat fit snugly against her body and an ample bosom was peeking through like she was naked underneath or wearing a very provocative dress. She kept one hand in her pocket. The door had almost closed on her when a hand that essentially signed Smith's death warrant came out and held it open to let her in.

Fifteen minutes later, the woman stepped out of the same elevator looking exactly like she did earlier, hand in pocket. She strolled out the door, catching a few discreet stares from some middle-aged men milling about whose wives were obviously not around or looking elsewhere.

The camera is back with the interviewer who asked that anyone who recognized the woman in the raincoat call the D.C. police hotline. She promised more updates as they come available.

Rake turned the news off and pressed the DVR to view the video again. The image of the woman in the black rain coat was unsettling. From a distance, she looked like Danielle–the dark hair, petite body with just the right amount of curves, and a kick-ass pair of shoes. But an oversized pair of aviator sunglasses masked her face. He also would have noticed if Danielle was that well-endowed.

Fumbling with the remote again, Rake discovered how to zoom in on parts of the screen. He tried to find a clear shot of her face but couldn't. He then had some fun zooming in and out on our bosom but gave that up when he started feeling like a twelve-year-old watching his first dirty movie while his parents were out.

He gave Peter Muckiss a call. Peter picked up on the first ring. "Did you see that D.C. News piece?" Rake asked without saying hello.

"Yeh. That Hudd's a piece of work. If that video didn't exist, I would put him as our number one suspect."

"Really? How so?" Rake replied, walking back to the kitchen to grab another cold beer from the fridge.

"Just to be put away for being such a major jerk," Muckiss replied with a laugh.

"I hear you." Rake laughed with a snort. "You wonder how guys like that get to where they are." Rake said while popping the tab with one hand.

There was a pause before Peter spoke again. "Rake, I've got some bad news."

Rake's hand stopped before he put the Budweiser to his lips. "What," he said with trepidation.

"Your girl has flown. Disappeared. We had her in our sights up until Bethesda. She was on the bus and we were tracking her with her cell phone until she threw it out the window. We got a police car to track the bus right away, but it got too close. She must have seen it at a light and got spooked when the bus driver recognized the officer and leaned out his window to say hello."

"Geez Peter. Really? You couldn't keep an eye on a middle-aged woman on a bus?" Rake said angrily.

"Hey, she's a wily one, remember? Look. I've got all my guys combing the area. I'm sure she'll show up somewhere. But it doesn't bode well for her. She running, Rake. It's the first sign of guilt."

"Get off of it, Peter. You know she's not capable of murder," Rake said with annoyance.

"How do you know that?" he countered. "Does she have an alibi for the 17th? How about this morning while Kagan was being murdered?"

Rake thought Muckiss was losing it. "Okay, if you think she's some kind of Black Widow, what would her motive be?" he asked sarcastically.

"She stole the money, of course! How could she have built that fortune without a lot of seed money? It fits Rake. You're denying it because she's got you snagged in her little web."

"I'm not snagged in anyone's web!" Rake said with indignation, even though he knew he was. "That was not her in that video. Did you see the boobs on that woman?"

"You can always prop those up."

Rake chuckled at the thought that Muckiss was the expert at those sorts of things, then got serious again. "You're barking up the wrong tree, Peter."

"Murphy wants me to bring her in and throw the book at her. The Kagan mess hasn't come out yet and once it does, he's going to have the press all over that too. He needs to show a perp. He thinks Mendow went for Smith because she found out somehow that he was ready to talk."

"And Kagan? What did she have to do with this?"

"We hear Kagan had the memory of an elephant. Her cell phone showed she was texting all the old-timers, including your girlfriend, that she knew who killed Smith. Why she did that, who knows. She was a weird bird. Maybe she wanted to do our

335

job and draw out the killer for us."

"Sick" Rake commented.

"We got her in the building on camera, Rake. As much as you don't want to believe it, it's her," Muckiss said.

"You don't know that," Rake replied quickly.

"Murphy's gunning for someone fast. It's going to be her," Muckiss insisted.

Murphy, Rake thought. Here we go again with that buffoon. He's always looking to prop himself up stepping on everyone in his way.

Rake was pacing all over the place while Peter was still talking about how they were tracking Danielle but he wasn't listening. All he could think about was how he was going to prove that the woman in both tapes was someone else - not Danielle.

Interrupting Peter's monologue, he asked, "I know this is unorthodox, but can you email me the tape from Kagan's building?"

"Still not convinced? Okay, but you didn't get it from me. Hey, I don't want to put your girl away as much as you do, buddy. But if she's guilty, she is guilty, and you can't change that. Let me know if you come up with anything."

Rake hated that Muckiss kept calling Danielle his girlfriend–like he could sense something–but he would not get into any arguments that may piss him off yet, so he just played it out with him. Instead, he asked if he could keep Murphy off his back for a few days until he could find the actual killer.

"You probably have about 24 hours before the dragon breathes fire, but I'll see what I can do. Maybe I'll throw him a bone about someone else, like Hudd, to set him off in another direction for a few hours," Muckiss said with a snort.

"Thanks." Rake said, taking the last gulp of his beer and tossing the can towards the garbage pail. Already full, the can fell off the top of the pail and rolled back to his feet. Rake took a deep breath, blocking a curse that wanted to shoot from his mouth. Meanwhile, Peter started shuffling some papers on the other end of the phone like he was looking for something.

"Hey, did you get wind of any money laundering going on out there?" Peter snapped.

In his need to protect Danielle, Rake had forgotten about what he overheard last night at Sheila's and what Jen confirmed this afternoon. In fact, it seemed like THE KISS had made his brain scrambled eggs with some of the most incriminating information that directly related to Danielle. But not to make himself look like an incompetent idiot in case Peter was well aware of the money transfers, he said, "I was just going to bring that up."

"Go on" Muckiss replied as if he was waiting for this all along.

"Last night, I followed Mendow to a place called Sheila's. She and her head teller were in a back room huddled over a laptop trying to decipher some sort of data. After a few minutes, they realized they were looking at a history of money transfers that neither seemed to be aware were going through their branch." He left out that afternoon's conversation with Jen since it was told to him in confidence and there didn't seem to be anything new.

However, Rake was embarrassed to say what really happened next which was the reason he didn't get more information. Instead, he just explained that they saw him spying on them, shut the computer, and made some sort of excuse about it being late and having to go.

"So you're saying that they were acting like they just discovered it?"

"Yeh" Rake said, in the kitchen now pacing back and forth running his free hand, as usual, through his hair. "I was hoping to get more out of her today but as you said, she went up in smoke."

"Okay, so what were they looking at? Where did they get the information from all of a sudden?" Muckiss asked, voicing surprise.

Rake realized that Muckiss didn't know about the flash drive. From what he gathered after Jen confessed, only she, Danielle, himself, and some mystery person knew it existed.

"Should we bring in the head teller and see if she'll talk?" Muckiss said, breaking the Rake's train of thought.

"I don't think we need to water board her yet." Rake replied irritably.

"Murder and money laundering. This case is getting bigger and better by the minute. Maybe bigger than me. Murphy's gonna love this. It's going to get lots of attention. But we need to get this solved right. I don't want him to be calling for the electric chair for the dynamic duo–our only suspects so far - and then get a pie thrown in our face"

"You're right. So don't pull the head teller into this yet, okay. Just help me out. You find Danielle and let me know where she is. She's the key, not the killer."

"Okay, but I'm bugging the head teller and Mendow's phones. Cameras everywhere. I'm putting everything on it. Gotta go. I'll be in touch." Muckiss hung up without waiting to hear any argument.

Rake stared with annoyance at his now silent phone. He needed to clear his head and think of his next move. He bolted from the kitchen, peeling off the rest of his clothes and leaving them where they dropped. Within seconds, he was in a pair of shorts and a t-shirt. He threw on his sneakers and was out the door sprinting down his driveway, quickly picking up speed. Where is that girl, he asked himself as he panted and sweated towards her house? He needed answers, and there was one person who knew more about her than anyone else on this planet. He just hoped he could get through to the other crazy old broad in this story. Twenty-four hours were going to fly by quickly.

Chapter 25

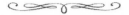

It was a little after 4 p.m. when Danielle's bus pulled into the venerable Union Station in downtown Washington D.C. Making sure nobody was waiting for her, Danielle first popped her head out the door, then seeing the coast was clear of blue uniforms, quickly disembarked. She stepped right in line with the other passengers who were heading towards the main terminal. The steep escalators brought her swiftly into the grand station itself where she looked around trying to get her bearings, then moved before she was trampled. Although it was just after rush-hour it was still crowded. Danielle found herself caught in an undertow of people being unconsciously led towards the front exit.

Through the hustle and bustle, she glimpsed herself in one of the many little shop windows lining the perimeter. She wasn't sure what to make of the look. On the one hand, she blended in well with the tourists, but on the other, she felt like she was having an out-of-body experience.

Would she ever be part of her old world again, she wondered? Her fists clenched. Of course, she thought to herself, hoisting her drooping backpack back on her shoulders. She just had to figure out what on Earth happened in the last couple of days that brought her from the top of the world to wearing a pair of used sneakers and carrying a couple of bills in her wallet? She didn't even want to think about how matted her hair must be under that baseball cap!

The skylights from the arched ceiling in the Great Hall caught her eye, and she looked up to admire the classical architecture. The few times she walked through Union Station lately, she was always in a rush to get to an appointment. Today, she did not know where to go. Confident of her guise, she took a few minutes to wander around and appreciate her surroundings. However, the effort was short-lived. A texting millennial zombie bumped into her, almost knocking the knapsack off her back again. What a jerk, she thought to herself. Here the guy is, in a suit and tie, acting all important, and he didn't even apologize for hitting another human being. Shaking her head as she muttered her disgust, she lifted the shoulder strap of the slippery backpack again to straighten it out. Suddenly, she stopped walking. Geez, she thought to herself. I'm carrying the answer to my horrible predicament all along!

That shifting burden on her back was the key. She needed to get into that laptop and flash drive again. In the escape's kerfuffle, she wasn't focused on it and to be honest; she forgot all about it. The anonymity of Union Station would be a great place to hide while taking another look at it. She quietly thanked the Zombie, who reminded her she was invisible. Now all she needed was a quiet place right here to decipher Bill Smith's message to her. She looked around the great hall for somewhere to concentrate.

Her breath quickened as the excitement built. The banker's code was complicated, but she was up for it. Dates, numbers, and account numbers were her life's work. There was a story to tell, and she had to put the plot together. She backtracked towards the food court where she would find a table and sit behind her screen, blending in like every other disconnected human these days.

She followed the smell of grilled hamburgers and barbecue. On her way, she noticed a Harley Davidson store and paused. A picture of Rake straddling that motorcycle in his tight black denims, cowboy boots, and black leather jacket flashed through her mind. The second she thought of him, her heart started racing. She still didn't get him and didn't get herself being so into him. Was he a good guy or a bad guy? She so wanted him to be a bad good guy. She looked down and smiled at the embarrassing thought. Was it getting hot in Union Station? She unbuttoned her jacket.

She continued towards West Hall while replaying that delicious scene of him riding towards her as she watched him through the window of May Bell's "salon" for human trafficking. For a split second, she was thrilled he was headed her way. She could just picture the two of them riding through the Shenandoah Valley with her arms around his chest and her legs parallel to his.

Then Jen ruined the fantasy with that stupid umbrella! Danielle sighed. So close now so far.

She was dying to get into that laptop, but the food stores were teeming with people who were eating like a famine was imminent. Every table was full. Lines were wrapped around corners. People were noisy and sloppy. Danielle shuddered. I can't sit here, she thought to herself. I may be in sneakers and jeans on the outside, but it's not who I am on the inside. I'm no Styrofoam girl. The flash drive will have to wait.

She turned towards the exit again.

Danielle realized that once out the door, she really had no clue about where to go or hide. In fact, she recognized there may even be police cars out there patrolling the streets in search of her. Forget the police cars, she further surmised. How about the cameras? She read enough Washington D.C. mystery thrillers to suppose there are cameras in Union Station too. What if they recognize her even with the baseball cap? What if...what if? Her pace quickened as she kept her head low. She was getting paranoid.

There was a little corner behind a colonnade right by the exit that Danielle spotted. She squeezed into it to think. She decided there was only one solution. Pulling out her CVS phone, she punched in the number of the only person she knew that would pull her out of this mess with no questions asked.

A police officer was strolling by and Danielle sank deeper into the crevice. Come on, she said to herself as the phone kept ringing. The call was picked up after the tenth ring. "Stranglers Point Inn," announced the voice on the other end. The familiar tone was female, husky, and unpleasant. Danielle breathed a sigh of relief.

"Willa, it's me, Danielle," she whispered while poking her head out to make sure the police officer had walked away.

"Danielle? What? I can barely hear you. Sounds like you're in the middle of Union Station!"

Danielle looked at her phone, wondering for a second how she knew that, but realized it was probably just a figure of speech. She shook off the coincidence and continued.

"It's a long story," she answered a little louder, "and all I can say right now is I'm a long way from West Mendow."

"Okay" Willa answered matter-of-factly." I've known you for a long time. Nothing surprises me. Are you in some kind of trouble?"

Danielle looked at her phone again. The woman was a seer! "I'll tell you what's going on when I see you. No questions yet, okay? I need you and

"Catherine the Great" to come and pick me up right now. You're still flying her, right?"

There was a long pause on the other end of the phone. Danielle got nervous, wondering if Willa couldn't pull through for her. She was just about to beg when Willa started talking.

"I was just double-checking. You know, there's a storm brewing over the Chesapeake moving up from the Atlantic. If you can be at the Severn Inn outside of Annapolis in an hour, we may beat it."

With that news, her muscles loosened up a bit and Danielle felt genuine relief for the first time that day. She knew she could count on Willa. Now, the trick would be how to make a one-and-a-half-hour road trip from Union Station across the Severn River in northern Maryland in under an hour.

"Okay–not a problem. I'm almost around the corner. Hold on a minute." Danielle answered quickly so that Willa couldn't change her mind. She had to move. Checking first to make sure the coast was clear, Danielle bolted for the exit and was outside the doors of Union Station. She eyed a taxi line about 100 yards away. With a little over $600 left in her wallet, she wondered if it would be enough to get one of those drivers to break the speed limit (and probably a few other traffic laws) to get her up there. She would soon find out. "Still with me?" she said into the phone. "I'll meet you on the beach next to the Inn."

Willa inhaled. "Just hope we can turn that sucker around before the winds blow up.".

"We'll be fine," Danielle answered confidently, as if she knew everything about aeronautics and weather.

The next hour was going to be stressful. She needed some serious provisions to get her through the trip. Knowing Willa was going to save her, the nervousness dissipated. She took the risk and ran back inside for a Diet Coke and a bag of Potato Chips. She moved quickly while covering more of her face with her hat and collar. She was feeling on the mend. She could just taste the salt on her tongue. She made it through West Hall again, looking for just a snack stand and avoiding anyone wearing a uniform. She rounded a corner and noticed a jumbo TV on a far wall hanging over some tables and chairs. People were looking up, mesmerized with what was playing. She walked closer. She put her hand to her mouth. It horrified her. Staring at her from the screen was a giant Teddy Hudd sputtering something to a reporter. Before she could figure out what was going on, the screen changed to a video of a woman in a raincoat in the lobby of what she assumed was the Willard Hotel. The woman was seen entering rather than leaving.

Danielle's horror turned to understanding. She could see why there was a question about her involvement. The woman had some resemblance to her–except for those boobs! Well, she thought, she should be so lucky! Nonetheless, it wasn't her, but she and the woman in the video were probably the only ones certain about it.

She backed away, not wanting to look anymore, tripped on a table leg, and knocked over a chair. She reached down to put it back upright.

People nearby turned to see from where the noise came. As she rose with the chair, she saw everyone around staring at her. Fear struck, and she started thinking irrationally. What if someone sees the resemblance between her and the woman in the grainy video? She realized she was being a stupid idiot when, within seconds, everyone lost interest in the klutz that just collided with a chair. The eating and doing whatever continued. Danielle cursed herself. She was acting weird again. She needed to get a grip.

The clock was ticking. She had to get out of there, but she was famished and needed something to eat. Also, a good greasy meal always calmed her down. She was beyond Potato Chips.

Straightening up, she went to the nearest food counter, which to her delight, was a McDonalds. There was no line thanks to Divine Intervention who even got the clerk to step it up after she told her she was in a real rush to catch the AMTRAK. Within seconds she was paying for a Diet Coke, fries, and a 'what the heck', double hamburger all wrapped and ready to go.

The transaction was fast, and like a linebacker, she was dodging out the door and running to the taxi stand. Miraculously, it had no line either.

Two for two, she thought to herself, looking up and thanking the heavens.

The late autumn afternoon was warmer than usual, and a strong wind was blowing the skirts and jackets of the professionals as they rushed in and out of the station doors. Feeling the heavy air and the darkening of the sky, Danielle's little knowledge of flying weather told her she was in for a rough ride tonight. She took a deep breath to calm down. She had to get through this. She approached the first car and tapped on the passenger side window.

The driver rolled it down. "I need to get to Annapolis in under an hour." She said sweetly.

"No." he answered abruptly, closed his window, and drove off.

Relieved because his car smelled like cheap cologne, she watched him speed around the circle, then turned her attention to the next yellow cab. The heavyset driver rolled down his window.

Using another tactic, she asked, "How much would it cost to take me to Annapolis?"

"Uch" he answered roughly.

"I didn't get that. Was that a price? Just give me a price." Danielle replied, trying not to sound too annoyed. She looked up and saw a police officer walking towards her. She knew he was just coming over to keep things moving, but she didn't want to take any chances.

"Come on. Just say a number! She said sharply looking back at the driver. "Please!"

"Um. Okay. $100."

Not bad, she thought. "I'll give you $200 but we have to get there fast." She looked to see how close the police officer was getting.

The driver caught her checking and said, "$300."

"Deal" she replied, tearing the door open and sliding in face down.

The driver gave a quick wave to the officer as he pulled out. "You good back there?" he asked as Danielle lifted her head.

"Yes, I'm good now." She answered as she turned and watched Union Station become the size of a souvenir.

Chapter 26

The situation made his muscles tight. A run to Danielle's would loosen him up and let him think better. Rake dashed up the long circular stairway to his bedroom, taking the stairs two by two, not breaking a sweat. He looked down from the top landing for a second, still amazed by the square footage of this faux farmhouse which felt like the size of the high school he attended in Westfield, New Jersey. The utility bills, let alone the rent, was probably costing the taxpayers a new bridge to nowhere somewhere. The rent alone was just another example of government waste. He hated that.

He stripped off his shirt and did a quick bicep flex admiring himself in the bathroom mirror. Not bad for a retired old goat. Sadly, he had nobody to impress. Then he reminded himself that was yesterday morning. Today he did–Danielle. She would love him for his middle age muscles (and his brains, of course).

"Damn that they lost her," he said angrily. He stretched his arms overhead admiring his tight, lean abdomen. He remembered feeling kicked in the gut when Muckiss told him she was missing and a suspect no less! What a bunch of buffoons! He couldn't believe he was once part of that keystone cop brigade. If only he could follow her himself. Everyone knew he was a skilled agent. He would have been on her like a hound on a fox. It was just that egomaniac Bob Murphy's fault believing he was always after his job. Why still be competitive? He didn't even work there anymore.

Turning sideways, he gave himself a nod of approval. He leaned in closer to the mirror to examine his teeth. "Who cares," he growled. "Murphy can take his little brain and blow it up. I've got a great pension, a comfortable life, a dog who loves me, and some good years ahead of me." Straightening up, his face went blank. Deep down he knew something was missing, and he felt it every minute lately. He cleared his head. He had to find her.

He entered the massive bedroom and walked towards the only piece of furniture besides the bed and a nightstand. The FBI Staging Department must have run out of money for the second floor when they were preparing the house for him because this room was close to empty. He opened a few drawers of the dresser that looked like they made it out of cardboard in search of a pair of running shorts. After digging around for a few seconds he realized he hadn't done laundry in eons and everything must be ripe for a cleaning.

With hands-on-hips, he scanned the sparsely furnished room hoping for an idea. Clothes, socks, and shoes were piled all over the floor. He kicked at a few mounds and was glad that nothing crawled out. Determined, he finally located a pair of gym shorts. Shaking them furiously to air them out, he deemed them passable and put them on.

Next, he pulled out the least disgusting smelling rumpled T-shirt which unfortunately had a picture of a young Sylvester Stallone as Rambo on the back. Hoping nobody would see him wearing it, he slipped it over his head.

He didn't want his nose to get anywhere near his running shoes and kept a safe distance while lacing them up.

Remembering last night, he was glad he didn't offer Danielle a tour of his house. He couldn't imagine what she would've thought when he showed her the bedroom. If the fire hadn't caused her to split, he was sure this sight would have given her a reason. Under his breath, he vowed to clean it up soon. Then he chortled, "Not," and grunted.

Danielle. Her brown silky hair reminded him of those glamorous starlets of the forties. The way she looked at him with those big brown eyes kept him captured in her magical spell. The tight little body he hoped to fully embrace one day made him regularly catch his breath. He hoped that kiss last night was real and not just a game she liked to play with men. Tease them, then drop them. Didn't she do that same thing to him this morning? Tease and drop. What was she running from and why? Instinct told him the attraction was mutual but he couldn't quite figure out the motive for the zaniness. Although he didn't know her that well, and there was always some drama underway the few times they met, but from what he heard, she didn't have that kind of reputation. She was as solid as they come. This all started with the murder of Bill Smith. Is his ghost coming back to haunt her? Did some past guilt make her snap as Jen suspects?

He ran down the stairs and tried to excite Spike to come with him. "Come on, boy. Let's go for a run" Spike had other things in mind though. After giving him the 'no comprendo' look, he trotted off and laid down under the stairs in his favorite napping spot.

"You are the laziest dog on the planet," he called after him as he bolted out the door.

He sprinted down his driveway. Reaching the end, he stood panting and jogging. Going right would take him towards the cornfields of West Mendow and away from her house. Preparing for the mad dash, he continued to jog in place for a few seconds breathing in the dry fall air and feeling the blood rush through his body, heating his muscles. They hired him to monitor her. He was being paid. She split big time, but could she have possibly doubled back and come home? He darted off to the left.

The oxygen seared through his nose causing his eyes to water as he pushed harder and harder in the warmth of the late autumn afternoon. Raw energy made him run like he was sprinting towards a finish line. What would he do if she was there? Certainly not hand her over to the Feds. Maybe he would grab her, throw her on his bike, ride off into the sunset, and never look back. Would she come? He knew he would have a lot more fun with the unpredictable Miss Mendow than anyone else he knew. But first, he had to get her out of this mess - and fast -before anyone else got hold of her.

Danielle's house loomed ahead. The statue of Catherine the Great caught the sun and her head glowed through a halo of light. Distracted by the bizarre statue, he almost missed seeing the black SUV parked outside the front door as he overran past the house missing the driveway.

"Shoot," he said as he screeched to a halt. Bending over, he tried to catch his breath while watching a few beads of sweat drip into the asphalt.

A black SUV. The head teller, Jen, had mentioned something about Danielle and a black SUV during that weird secret meeting in the bank vault. But he was having a senior moment and couldn't remember the issue. He inhaled deeply and jogged slowly up her long drive keeping an eye on the surroundings.

The late-model Ford Explorer appeared empty as he slowly approached it. With hands forming a visor over his eyes to block the light, he peered into the windows as best he could. The black tint, however, prevented him from seeing much. The little that he managed to make out, seemed ordinary enough. A bottle of water in the cup holder, a raincoat in the back seat. He turned and looked towards the house. It stood dark and lifeless like nobody was at home. The countless windows were shuttered and closed. A chill ran through his body. It was almost like the house was in mourning for its missing owner.

Suddenly, screams, like a flock of terrified bats, pierced the air. The terrifying clamor came from behind the house. Rake's head jerked towards the noise and watched as two bodies rounded the corner of the house and barreled towards him.

It took him a few seconds to process the scene. At first, he thought it was Danielle being chased by a mad gargoyle, but as they got closer, he realized it was another woman in a black suit trying to run away from Eleni.

"Fee-Ye!, Fee-Ye!, (Go away! Go away!)" Eleni shouted, waving a rolling pin at the woman.

Spotting him, the stranger picked up speed and raced in his direction. Amazingly, the old lady kept up - stride by stride. Rake couldn't help smiling at the strange spectacle.

"Help me, help me" yelled the brown-haired lady breathlessly–her high heels causing her to stumble in the soft ground as she ran. The tight black skirt kept her long legs from going too fast and in her clumsiness, the white tails of her tailored blouse had escaped the confines of her belt. She tried valiantly to keep her black jacket from slipping off her shoulders which gave the overall effect of watching a giant bird trying to fly away from an extinct species that wanted to eat her. Whoever it was, Rake thought it was a damn funny sight, and he bit the inside of his lip to prevent himself from laughing out loud.

Eleni continued to scream out in her high pitched Greek as she got closer to the woman. As she ran, her hair bun spun out longer and longer, and as it unraveled, it flopped wildly behind her - the extinct species resembling an alligator with a long tail. She went through a myriad of facial contortions, from pain to anger, then surprise when she saw Rake, but with her short feeble-looking stubby legs which protruded from her billowing black skirt, she never missed a step. Rake put little money on the stranger and started walking cautiously towards her.

The stranger finally cleared the great lawn and reached him. He held out his arms, and she fell into them exhausted like she just finished a marathon. Eleni was in his face a few seconds later. The woman whimpered and slid behind him to hide, her arms still keeping a tight vise around his chest.

"Eleni, put that thing down. You're going to hurt someone." Rake demanded trying to sound serious.

"Who is this person? Why she go snooping around Danielle's house?" Eleni answered, trying

357

to get around Rake who kept blocking the stranger.

"Cut it out, Eleni! Gimme that thing before you hurt someone," he said wrestling the rolling pin from her and tossing it away. He then grabbed her by the shoulders trying to keep her from attacking the woman stuck to his back. He gripped her tightly, but it was like trying to hold on to Mike Tyson. "You know, if Danielle ever fired you, they could use a woman of your talents in Homeland Securty," he said trying to lighten up the situation.

She scowled then took some deep breaths. He felt her shoulders relax, so he released her.

"Okay, you can let go now." Rake said over his shoulders to the woman behind him while keeping an eye on Eleni. "She's disarmed."

The woman remained pressed to his back a bit too long.

"Mmm, I'm beginning to enjoy this," she cooed into his right ear and hugging him harder.

Rake began tugging at her arms until he broke free from her grasp. He quickly backed away and went and stood by Eleni.

"Watchoo doing here?" snapped Eleni to the disheveled woman.

"I'll take care of this, Eleni," Rake said to her, putting his arm out to cover her mouth. He turned to the stranger.

"I hope Eleni didn't shake you up too much but, indeed, what are you doing here?" he asked politely, eyeing her with curiosity.

"I just say that!" Eleni said pushing his hand away and rolling her eyes.

"Um, yes. I know you did." Rake answered, keeping his eye on Eleni's prey. "But I don't think this woman is dangerous, right?" The woman vigorously nodded. "Okay, see? You don't have to attack her like that so calm down!"

"Thank you," replied the stranger giving Rake a coquettish smile. "I'm fine now." The smile faded as she glanced over at Eleni who was giving her the stink eye. "I'm Rita Steele," she said her stare alternating between both of them as if they instantly should recognize that name.

"I don't care if you Maria Callas. Why you snooping around Danielle's house!" Eleni said taking a step forward and wagging a finger at her.

Rita took a step back trying to keep some distance between her and the old lady.

"Eleni. Cut it out. Let me handle this." Rake said stepping between the two ladies. "Rita, to give Eleni some justification for her behavior, you obviously scared her. Now, you don't look like the threatening type but she's not used to people sneaking around on her private property."

Rita shrugged and looked down remorsefully.

Rake softened. "Okay, Rita. So why are you here?"

Behind him, he heard Eleni say "yeh" but ignored her.

"This might look suspicious to you, but I'm just trying to find Danielle," Rita said brushing her hair back out of her face. She gave a little laugh, smoothed out her blouse, and fixed her jacket. Standing straighter, she continued, "I'm the Chairman's assistant. Mr. Place has been trying to reach her all day. I've called everywhere and nobody seems to know where she is so he asked me to come out and try to find her."

Eleni's eyes widened. "You work for bank? You work with Danielle?"

Rake looked at Eleni. "See?" he said holding out his hands. "Now don't you think you overreacted?" he continued slowly making sure she understood. "The Chairman of the bank is concerned about your boss and sent his assistant around to look for her and you almost clobbered her!"

Before he could turn and apologize to Rita, he overheard Eleni as, "So why you break window in back door and sneak in? You think Danielle is dead inside? Why you don't just ask me now?"

This stopped Rake in his tracks. He looked back at Eleni who had her lips pursed, hands-on-hips, and eyes targeted on Rita ready to shoot daggers.

Did she break a window? Now that was interesting, Rake thought. He looked at her for an explanation.

Without missing a beat, Rita said, "I guess I was knocking too hard. I knew she had a housekeeper. I was just trying too hard to find out if you were around," she said defensively.

He detected an Ivy League school with a slight New York accent. And she was smart. She went for the housekeeper. Why didn't he think of that, he wondered? Eleni would have to know how to reach Danielle. Maybe all he has to do is ask. Rita was one step ahead of him. "So where is she?" Rita asked, cutting into his thoughts.

"How I know. She goes to work. That's all I know." Eleni answered. She stooped down and pulled out a weed from a crack in the asphalt. "Ooh. Dinner," she said, looking at her prize and then quickly hiding it away under the folds of her skirt. Eleni straightened up and stood defiant.

Rake looked dejected. Rita's shoulders drooped. "Has she called?" Rita asked.

"No call, no written letter, no say goodbye. She goes to work. Maybe don't come back for a week. Maybe in Paris for shopping. Its Danielle."

Rake and Rita looked at each other, then back at Eleni.

Waving a finger at him, Eleni said, "Reek, you put lady back in car and make sure she go home now. I go inside and clean up mess."

"No, wait!" Rita cried out, making a move to follow her. The sudden weight on one foot caused a loosened spike in the heel of her left shoe to completely break off. Losing her balance, she fell sideways on the brick driveway. Rake reach out to grab her, but it was too late.

"Whoa," he said, watching her helplessly as she hit the asphalt. Her left wrist broke her fall, but her right hand slammed the pavement seconds later as she bounced on her derriere.

The fall stunned her to silence.

"Are you okay?" Rake asked while bending down to help her up.

"My ankle!" she cried as he tried lifting her by the arm.

Eleni threw up her hands, snorting.

"Oh, okay," as he gently let go. "Can you try to get up on one foot?" he asked with concern.

Her face was taut with pain as she reached out and rubbed her right foot. "I don't know," she cried.

"Eleni, help me get her inside. We need to put some ice on this ankle before it swells," he said, kneeling down and trying to see what was wrong with her foot.

Eleni moved towards the front door mumbling, "I bring ice. She stay outside."

"Please, it hurts so much everywhere. I just need to sit on something soft for a few minutes," Rita implored.

"Ha! That's why you need cushion on bum like fat Greek ladies!" Eleni turned to Rake. "Okay, okay. Bring her in. No want Danielle to be sued. Everybody wants her money." Eleni reached under the mass of folds in her skirt and took a key out of another mysterious pocket, walked to the front door, and closed it behind her.

Rake and Rita stared after her. "Alright, let's get you inside." After several attempts at trying to get her all the way up, Rake realized he would have to lift her and carry her into the house.

"You can't be more than 98 pounds," he grunted as he hoisted her up. She giggled at the sarcasm, grabbed him around the neck and for a split second their eyes locked. Rake quickly looked away and focused on getting her quickly inside.

"Thank you," she purred into his ear, "You're so strong and have perfect timing."

Eleni had left the door open just a crack. He gave it a forceful kick, startling her.

Rake was not immune to the flattery, but every flirtatious remark from this woman made him feel more uncomfortable. He saw nothing wrong with her ankle and knew a lie when he heard it. After all, he managed to learn a few things as a law enforcement officer who heard many a whopper in his days from criminals trying to wiggle out of getting arrested. He couldn't wait for her to leave so he could continue his quest for Danielle with Eleni. Eleni obviously didn't trust her either and wanted to get rid of her. But Rita charmed her way into sticking around with this ankle thing. It made him curious. What indeed is she doing here? The Chairman's story also sounded like a lot of bullshit. He decided to play it out.

Eleni stood in the foyer, brown skirt flaring, one hand on hip, and the other holding a dripping bag of ice. Not one ounce of concern was on her face. She smirked when he almost dropped Rita walking on the slippery marble floor.

"Bring her to den," she commanded. "She can sit on chair for a few minutes," she said, pointing to an uncomfortable-looking bar stool in the far corner.

They entered a double-height room with an elaborate cathedral ceiling overhead. The room mesmerized him. The last ceiling he saw in this style was the reception room of the State Department building in downtown D.C. She furnished it in shades of white and blue with dark wooden tables that contrasted the light colors of the walls and upholstery. The floor to ceiling windows faced the back of the house, which overlooked miles of colorful countryside. The autumn hues contrasting with the cool colors of the room were breathtaking. The beauty spellbound him. He paused for a second, bewitched by the glamour of his surroundings. He then caught Eleni's eye, who was watching him warily. He turned and gingerly placed Rita on the plush white leather sectional. Rita smiled smugly at Eleni as Rake kneeled down before her.

"May I?" he said, motioning to her feet. "Forgive me, but I'm a little sweaty."

"By all means," she answered. "Are you a doctor?"

"No, I used to be an EMT," he lied. Although his FBI training included an intense course in First Aid, Rake's gut told him to keep quiet about his colorful government background. He didn't need to open another can of worms.

He removed her shoes and studied the foot she was pointing to. He poked at it, giving Rita the opportunity to let out some dramatic groans and winces.

"Oooh" she moaned loudly as he gently touched a section of her ankle.

"I guess we found it. Eleni, let me have the ice pack." He placed it on the tender spot.

"That feels so good," she said, closing her eyes

and lying back on the couch.

Eleni clucked. "Look at that. What? Chee moving in?"

Rake stared as Rita's breathing slowed like she was falling into a deep sleep.

In the distance, a phone started ringing. Rita's head popped up immediately, startling Rake and Eleni.

"Maybe that's Danielle!" she said, coming up on her elbows.

"Maybe you right. We get some news now." Eleni answered waddling quickly out of the room.

"Weird bird, don't you think?" Rita said as she watched her disappear towards the kitchen.

Not as weird as you, thought Rake, but nodded, pretending to agree. He kind of liked Eleni. She was fearless, and he liked fearless women.

"I hope this time, she doesn't come out with a shotgun. She should register that rolling pin as a lethal weapon with the Maryland State Police." Rita said, still staring at the door that Eleni disappeared behind.

A clock on the cream-colored wall was ticking. Rake noticed it was almost 4:30 pm. This chick was really wasting his time.

He stood up and said. "It served its purpose." Rita remained expressionless. She didn't get it. "So how's the ankle?" He continued. "Are you ready to go?"

"Ah, better, thank you. You're my knight in shining armor," she said, ignoring his last words while scoping the room. "This is some house. Great taste."

She changed the subject not so subtly, he thought, while looking around again as well. He tried to place the style. The room was a fascinating mix of contemporary and eclectic–very much like Danielle's personality, he thought.

"You know, I was told she used to work at our office in New York on the International side of banking. But they closed the office right after 9/11 and she came home." She said gazing back at him. Rake kept silent, letting her talk. "Branch managers don't live like this. I heard she built a fortune on her own, starting with some property she inherited. I never imagined she was this successful. You wonder why she stays with the bank."

She was looking at him for some kind of affirmation. "Don't you find that a little unusual? If I had this kind of money, the last thing I would want to do is to be a branch manager."

He looked at his watch and shrugged, hoping she would get the message.

367

They could hear Eleni continue to jabber on the phone, her lively unintelligible conversation filling the silence in the room.

"Well, Reek..." Rita said.

"It's Rake, Rake Harris," he answered with annoyance.

"Apologies. Well, Rake, where do you fit in all of this? By the way, I like your T-shirt" she said coming up on one elbow.

"Oh, um, thanks." He said reddening. "I'm just a neighbor. Just dropped by to say hello."

"Danielle's lucky to have such a friendly neighbor," she said, swinging her long legs off the couch balancing the ice pack on her foot. She didn't bother holding down her tight skirt, which rode up provocatively to her mid-thigh. Rake gawked a second too long. Shaken, he turned away and took a step back.

"... with such good timing," she said seductively.

Rita made him very uncomfortable, and that wasn't easy to do. Although she was attractive, it was in a dangerous kind of way. She was like the hot girl in school who always got whoever she wanted—one way or the other—not caring who she left in her wake.

Rake started running his hands through his hair as the feeling like he was cheating on Danielle started creeping up. Rita started talking again, but he wasn't listening. Instead, his gaze fell on the rectangular-shaped dark oak side table next to the couch.

"… and I thought her lifestyle was an urban legend, but I guess it's not. Neighbor Rake, are you listening?" Pausing, she followed his gaze.

Rake was looking at a small 6 X 4 frame with a black-and-white picture of what looked like a slightly younger, "30 something" Danielle and a woman about the same age with an eerie resemblance to Amelia Earhart standing in front of a small space-age looking seaplane. Danielle was holding a bottle of champagne while the other woman was giving a "thumbs up".

Rita leaned over and picked it up before Rake could get a closer look.

"Is this what you're looking at now?" Rita brought the photo closer to her, studying it intently. "Does she have her own plane, too? Ha! The name of the plane is St. Catherine, like that crazy fountain outside." She seemed utterly fascinated by it.

Something was nagging at him, but this time it wasn't Rita.

"Don't touch things!" Eleni yelled, coming into the room. Rake and Rita jumped. "Put picture down. Not yours."

"Sorry," Rita replied with a hint of sarcasm. She

returned it to its original place.

Rake was glad he wasn't holding the picture when Eleni returned because he had no desire to get on her bad side. However, he continued to stare at it from afar. Danielle has some kind of connection with a seaplane named St. Catherine, he thought. Was the name a coincidence, or did she name it herself because it's hers?

"Does Danielle own a plane?" Rake asked, turning to Eleni.

"No," Eleni answered. "No plane"

"Does she fly?" Rita piped in.

"No-fly," Eleni answered.

"So whose plane is in the picture?" Rake asked cautiously, hoping Eleni wouldn't go into a tizzy for being nosy and throw him out before he could get some information out of her.

"It's her friend, Ooilla's plane."

Rita quietly picked up the picture again and took another quick look.

"Aaach!" Eleni cried, grabbing the picture away from Rita. "You leave now. You have no more business in Danielle's house. Reek to take her out, now. Go! Go!"

"Okay, okay," Rake said, putting up his hands like he had to defend himself from a punch. "Geez,

370

what is it with these women from West Mendow? They're so aggressive!" he said to himself, remembering last night.

"I'm going. Don't worry." Rita announced getting up and handing the ice pack to Rake. He turned away while she straightened her skirt and fixed her jacket and hair. Picking up her shoes, she said,

"Thanks, Rake. Hope to see you around."

He watched as she glided steadily towards the door. "I see you're walking well on that ankle," he called after her.

Turning her head, she said, "You must have that magic touch." She winked, turned back, gave a backward wave, and exited.

"Stop looking at evil lady or I tell Danielle."

"I wasn't looking like that," Rake answered nervously, wondering if he looked that obvious.

"Humph," Eleni grumbled, putting the picture back in its spot.

"Eleni, I hate to ask, Rake said timidly, "but can I see that photo one more time?"

Bracing himself for the worse, Rake was surprised when instead Eleni started wringing her hands, visibly upset.

"Where is she, Reek? I don't tell evil lady anything. She no good. Do you see Danielle today?

371

I know I say she never say anything to me but not true. Danielle calls me hundred times - all day–do this, do that, make pastitsio, what's news, you know, who calls, who comes by, is there problems with business... but not today. And then lady comes around and breaks window to get inside. My son, call just now, tell me bank burn down last night. I don't know, I don't know."

Not expecting that, he felt sorry for the old woman–she was truly agitated. She probably knew Danielle better than anyone, and she sensed trouble right away. He reached for the photo.

"How does Danielle know Willa, Eleni?" Rake asked.

"Willa and Danielle grow up together here. Best friends when they young. Then Danielle goes to New York and Willa go to Navy. She is pilot."

"Where is Willa now?" Rake asked.

"I don't know. Somewhere, I guess. She not dead." Eleni said vaguely.

For some reason, Rake felt she knew more than she was letting on. "Is that Willa's plane?"

She hesitated a moment. Her shoulders sagged. "Yes," she said, her eyes burrowing deep into his. "Find her, Reek".

His skin bristled. That's all he needed to know. He broke the stare and took a long, hard look at the picture of Danielle and Willa making a mental note of all the details. He turned to ask Eleni if she thought they were together, but she had quietly vanished.

Instinct told him that the trail was heating up again. Alone in the vast marble foyer, he weighed his next move. Suddenly, the front door was blown open by a loud gust of wind, startling him out of his thoughts. The cool afternoon air blew past him like God Himself was sending him a message. What was it? A trail of leaves flew in, following the strong breeze. It looked like a tailwind, the kind that planes make as they take off. A plane. He was still holding on to the picture of the girls and the plane. Of course, he thought to himself, what else could get Danielle out of a jam? A modern-day warrior! Willa and her plane!

Chapter 27

It was amazing how three hundred dollars could turn an average cab driver into Mario Andretti, Danielle thought as they weaved in and out of traffic on the congested streets of downtown Washington D.C. She looked over at the name tag behind his seat. With her life in "Moe Miller's" hands at the moment, she could do nothing but lean back, close her eyes, and not watch.

Within minutes, her mind started wandering to the days when she used to travel throughout Europe–speeding towards an airport or train station not to miss her flight. Those tight schedules she kept didn't allow for any waiting time. If she missed a flight and was late for a meeting, she was doomed with those stuffy European bankers. And yet, what wouldn't she give to be in Paris right now on her way to a business lunch at Guy Savoy's- or anywhere else, for that matter.

Instead, they were in some nerve-wracking Washington D.C. traffic where traffics lights turned red and green while cars looked like they were cryogenically frozen in place. After what seemed like the Rover could reach Mars faster than the trip to the Bay Bridge, the traffic eased a bit and they finally reached the entrance to I-495. Cracking the window open to let in some air, Danielle's neck muscles loosened. She finally relaxed.

"Is that a burger in that bag? You gonna eat it? If you don't want it, give it to me. I'll have it," Moe laughed, eyeing her from his rearview mirror.

"Are you kidding? I'm starving!" She said sitting up and reaching for the bag she left on the seat next to her. She unwrapped it and greedily scarfed it down. "I forgot how hungry I was. I didn't eat lunch."

Danielle caught Moe's giant head, glancing curiously at his peculiar passenger through his rearview mirror. Did she give off a sense of desperation, dressed like a vagabond, offering him cash, and making him risk being pulled over while she stuffed her face?

"Traffic makes me nauseous. I was waiting to get out of it," she said, trying to explain her unusual behavior. Wiping the mayonnaise off her lips, she dug into the now cold French fries while gulping the diet coke between bites. She didn't want to admit she was trying to settle some "off the chart" nervousness as he weaved and honked his way towards I-50.

The crinkling of the used paper caught his attention again. "You must have been starving. You're so tiny. Where does it all go? You always eat like that? I eat like that and look at me!" he said, pointing a fat finger at his double chin.

Oh, oh, Danielle thought to herself. He was one of those annoying taxi drivers that liked to talk - a top ten in her "Irritant List". The shutdown process ensues.

Keeping it light, Danielle smiled and said, "Aw, you look fine. Hey, I think I'm going to try to get a few minutes' sleep." She shifted around in her seat to show she was trying to get more comfortable while hoping he got the message.

"You do look a little tired," he answered as he sped up on the exit ramp. "You want to hear some music? Listen to the news?"

"No, no news!" She replied forcefully. "I don't want anything. Let's just get to the Bay Bridge in one piece. You're doing great. Better you focus."

A light rain began tapping on the windshield. Danielle leaned back, trying to get comfortable against the lumpy leather seat. The tension in her body continued to ease as the swishing of the wipers made her drowsy. She remembered she used to call these interludes "catch-up naps in taxi hotels" during her international business trips. Some of the best memories she had were those bank trips to Europe, making deals, meeting clients, having fancy lunches and dinners, then catching up on her sleep in a cab on her way to the airport. Those trips were exhausting but also enchanting introductions to the good life. The bank taught her many things. The best, however, was giving a country girl from Maryland the taste of a first-class lifestyle. It made her crave more. The bank opened the car door. The desire was the ignition. Her parents provided the fuel with her inheritance. When she didn't make it in New York, thanks to 9/11, she put the car in first gear in West Mendow and sped off.

She felt Moe steering and dodging the traffic deftly. They were almost there. She didn't dare look at her watch. Eyes still closed, she heard the wipers pick up speed. The rain was coming down harder. It would not be a pleasant flight to Tilghman Island.

Off the Eastern Shore of Maryland on the Chesapeake Bay, Tilghman Island was still raw and real. It's one of the region's best-kept secrets. Normally, visitors to Talbot County would stop and stay at its more appealing neighbor, St. Michaels. As a result, Tilghman remained unspoiled by development and, some would even say, progress. Home to local anglers, Tilghman is still known for its oystering and fresh seafood catches. Around 800 people live on Tilghman year-round. There are a few restaurants and a smattering of hotels, but mostly, its lack of sophistication and charm has kept the weekenders and vacationers away.

It was the perfect place to hide out until she could figure a way out of this mess. It all came down to Willa. She had to make it to the Severn Inn to pick up Danielle. If Moe had to drive her the rest of the way to the Strangler's Point Inn; her whereabouts wouldn't be a secret anymore. God forbid something happened to him in the meantime, and that would be another murder they could pin on her. Her stomach churned. The burger she scarfed down a few minutes ago was talking to her about nerves.

Taking a deep breath, Danielle reminded herself that she had faith in Willa. Having been a former Navy pilot with her last tour in Iraq, the lady knew how to fly a plane in all sorts of treacherous conditions. This was a hop over a pond compared to whatever dangerous missions they ordered her to undertake. On the other hand, this wasn't a military exercise and 'Catherine the Great' wasn't all that great in major storms and high winds. She felt a twang of guilt about placing all her good friends in harm's way - Jen, the loyal accomplice, helping her escape from the police and now Willa, in a dangerous rescue like Danielle was breaking out of Alcatraz. They owed her nothing, and yet they were putting their lives on the line. Up to that point, all she did was throw her money around to make her feel like a better person. That was all going to change when this nightmare was over. From this moment on, she vowed to be a better friend while expecting nothing in return.

"Ach" groaned, Moe hitting his hands against the steering wheel. "Why the hell do these slowpokes hog the left lane?" Sitting up further in his seat, Moe deftly switched lanes, sped up and cut the slowpoke off with a chuckle. The guy knew how to drive a car.

379

And Willa knew how to fly a plane. She'll be there, Danielle was convinced, as she laid her head back and closed her eyes once again. Reliable from day one–a true blue friend from the first moment they met at West Mendow High. Danielle, of course, was the lifer. Willa was a transfer student from New York where her father was a big muckety-muck in the Attorney General's office. In 1989, he was tapped by the Reagan Administration to become some undersecretary of something or other and moved his family to West Mendow to live while he worked downtown in D.C.

As a former New Yorker, Willa's aggressive personality and acerbic humor quickly took over the school. This impressed Danielle to no end. In fact, it made Danielle very determined to move to New York if she could be just like Willa. And as Willa's star ascended, Danielle's diminished, and was ultimately dethroned as the "it" girl. But Willa was so cool and funny about it, that instead of being "fight to the death" enemies, they became blood-sworn friends.

Inseparable in high school, they finally had to say their goodbyes as they went off to college and Officer Candidate School respectively, where they both followed their passions–Danielle as a New York banker and Willa as a pilot for the Navy.

"It's dark out there..." she heard Moe say, interrupting her thoughts. His comments made her think about the time. Did she dare look at her watch? Willa wanted her there in an hour. She was cutting it close. He continued, "…this is going to be some storm." Her stomach started making some minor comments once again.

Danielle lifted her head and looked around. It had indeed gotten darker. The trees on both sides of the road were starting the hula dance. Leaves were blowing around like confetti thrown during a parade. The cab jerked sharply, avoiding another car who this time cut them off. Now Moe had her full attention.

Anxious and not knowing the area well, she asked, "Are we almost near Annapolis?"

"Yeh, we're on Route 50. We're close."

Craning her neck against the glass, looking out as far as she could, she sought the sky through the rain, hoping to get a glimpse of a sea-plane over the Chesapeake Bay.

She sat back, exasperated. She was tempted to call Jen with her new, cool untraceable phone just to see what was going on, but they were on radio-silence. It was hard getting used to being disconnected.

Moe let out another 'Ach' as the cab slowed down. Now it was the lights. "Annapolis, too many lights. Can't do my driving magic here."

Danielle saw the cars around them slowing down too. "No, no, no!" she cried, banging the front seat with her palms. "You've got to do something!"

He swung around to face her. He was a big man, in his mid to late fifties, with short salt and pepper hair, a thick neck, and two small dark eyes perched on a big, broken, crooked nose. "Watcha need... to catch a plane or something?"

His imposing figure was intimidating. "Well, yeh." She answered timidly.

"Which one–that sea-plane buzzing just off the Naval Academy?"

"You can see something? Yes, yes. That's her!" Danielle cried triumphantly.

"She ain't going to be able to do that much longer," Moe said with all seriousness as he turned back to keep inching the cab along. "The wind's picking up and that little ICON's gonna be taken straight out to sea soon."

"And you know that how?" Danielle said with annoyance, not really expecting an intelligent answer from him.

"Second Lieutenant, U.S. Air Force, retired. Flew three missions in Kuwait. I know a bit about airplanes, young lady."

"Sorry, my bad. Thank you for your service." She chuckled nervously. "Okay, give me a break. What's the probability that your cab driver knows much about flying?" she asked, trying to lighten the moment.

"You know, I'd rather fly than drive. But, not too many jobs for old navy pilots these days. Speaking of which, your friend and her seaplane just flew out of sight. I figure she can do one more loop and if you're not where you're supposed to meet in about ten minutes, she's gotta get out of here."

Danielle's heart raced. Shoot, she can't leave me here now, she thought. "Should I panic?" she asked, eyes widening.

"Well, let's see, I'm about to cross Ritchie Highway. I got a flashlight in my glove compartment. Open the window and shine it around upwards. It may catch her attention and let her know we're close."

The beam from the flashlight made a saber-like apparition in the approaching dusk. Drivers passing by stared as she craned her neck out the window, trying to spot Willa's plane.

"A little wet out there?" Moe snorted.

Pulling her head back into the cab, Danielle felt the water running down her face. She rolled her eyes at Moe's sarcasm but kept her arm out waving the flashlight, frantically hoping Willa would spot it.

"Point it more to the left. I see the plane coming towards us." Moe said, driving and watching simultaneously.

The word contortionist came to mind as Danielle strained to see the plane through the front windshield while her arm was hanging out the right window.

"Yikes! Look at that!" Moe said suddenly. A gust of wind seemed to carry the plane a bit off course, alarming both of them. "I can't watch."

"Better," Danielle said. "Just keep your eyes on the road."

"Is it going to land at the beach next to the restaurant?" he asked.

"I hope," Danielle replied.

"She gotta get down now! You taking off immediately?" Moe said skeptically.

Not wanting to divulge much to this stranger, Danielle pursed her lips and just mumbled an affirmation.

"You're a brave girl going back up in this weather. I wouldn't do it." He glanced over at her through his rearview mirror, eying her suspiciously.

"Look!" Danielle pointed up towards the plane, happy to distract him.

Willa was flashing her lights.

"She saw us!" Danielle felt instantly relieved. The plan had worked after all.

Within seconds, Willa was veering the Sea Plane to the left, heading towards Severn Beach. At the same time, the cab was pulling off the highway and heading in the same direction via Brice Point.

The Sea Plane was making its descent. Moe pulled into a public parking lot and they both watched in awe as Willa expertly landed the plane on the sand.

"That's some mighty-fine flying," Moe said admiringly as he flashed his brights.

As the propellers of the plane slowed down, the wind and rain picked up.

"You really gonna take off in this weather?" he said in disbelief. "Look, I'm a pilot and even I would think twice about it."

"Piece of cake" Danielle answered, trying her best to hide her nervousness.

Moe turned to look at her straight in the eyes. "You're nuts."

"That's not the first time I've heard that about me," Danielle said mischievously.

A broken branch slammed against the windshield, interrupting their stare-down. Danielle reached for the door.

"I better get going. Thanks for your help and your flashlight." A huge wind gust blew into the cab as Danielle scrambled out. She turned to grab the knapsack and saw Moe shaking his head, his expression full of sadness.

"Good luck!" he yelled, his voice barely audible against the cacophony going on at the beach. She had no time to think about anything except getting into that plane and getting out of here. She ran as fast as her out of shape little body could take her with one hand, keeping the baseball cap on her head and the other holding the knapsack with the precious computer inside.

The sand was really kicking up now, tearing at her face as she fought her way closer. She didn't want to look back in the event she glimpsed Moe wiping a tear, wondering if he was going to prove himself right.

Willa had lowered the steps and was standing at the door waving her to get a move on. "We have to leave now!" she yelled. "Move your...." The wind took the rest of the sentence, but Danielle got the point.

She clambered up the stairs and hurried to buckle herself in. Before Willa shut the door, she looked at the taxi in which Danielle arrived. They both turned and saw the driver standing outside the door in a salute. Willa returned a quick salute in response and shut the door. Danielle gave a quizzical look to Willa and caught the headphones

Willa threw at her while climbing into the pilot's seat.

"So, did you have a pleasant flight?" Danielle asked, knowing it was a bit of an absurd question. She watched while Willa checked and adjusted some gauges.

"Don't talk, okay? Just hang on. If we don't make it, at least I'm going down with my best friend," she answered while buckling her seatbelt, not meeting her eyes.

They grinned at each other. Danielle then sat back and watched while Willa skillfully moved the plane. She felt secure. She knew she was in expert hands.

The plane held steady as it taxied down the beach, turned, and sped up to take off. Danielle had flown enough with Willa that she knew in this weather her friend probably just had one shot at this. Trying to quiet the wild thoughts running through her head, she gripped the seat and hunched over. Out of the corner of her eye, she watched as Willa put more pressure on the throttle, hoping to outrun the wind.

"Okay- here we go," Willa said, biting her lip, a nervous habit she had since high school. Danielle subconsciously held her breath. The plane lifted, took a gust of wind on its tummy, but straightened out continuing its ascent.

It was going to be a choppy flight and Danielle was wondering if that whopper she was so crazy about an hour ago, was going to be making a comeback.

"I'm going to get higher to see if I can get out of some of this wind shear," Willa said. The windshields were flapping wildly, not doing much to help the visibility. "You can look up now, oh fearless one," she snickered.

Danielle slowly sat up and looked out the side window. They had just flown over the Severn River, passing Greenbury Point. The next landmark, Highland Beach, would come up shortly. At that point, they were going to be cutting over and following the western coast of Kent Island, passing over Poplar Island and on to Strangler's Point which was at the southernmost tip of Tilghman. Water surrounded three-quarters of the point. There was only one way in, and one way out. If the road was blocked, the only way to come and go was to fly or get on a boat. Willa had both. They both knew there always had to be a back door.

"You enjoying this?" Danielle asked as she watched Willa struggling to try to keep the plane level.

"I've flown worse," Willa answered tersely, not taking her eyes off the horizon.

Understanding it wasn't a great time to have a girl chat, Danielle sat quietly, hands now clenched on the handrails, and tried to think of something pleasant. But the circumstances and the craziness of the last couple of days made it difficult. Her mind kept flashing back to the horror she felt as she had watched the West Mendow branch of Capital National bank–the one she grew from nothing–burn to the ground. It was the turning point of this unbroken series of episodes– when the story went from circumstantial to hard evidence.

"Hang on." Willa practically shouted. I'm going to start the descent."

Strangler's Point Inn was a mere speck in the distance. Willa had to land St. Catherine on the water, then make her way into the plane hangar that was built at the end of the dock. At this angle, it felt like they were trying to shoot straight into a pinhead hole while being tossed around in a blender.

"Geez, I can't keep this girl straight," Willa said under her breath.

Danielle tightened her grip on the handrails. She glanced over at Willa, who was showing a little sweat on her forehead and upper lip. "You can do it," Danielle said encouragingly. "Thank you, Willa."

"Shut up," Willa snapped.

Hasn't changed a bit, Danielle thought to herself.

The plane lurched forward. Willa pushed the throttle all the way, starting a quick and steep descent. At the last moment, she leveled out the plane and glided smoothly onto the water. The waves slapped at the plane as she slowed towards the hanger. The plane came to a crawl, and Willa expertly steered it through the hanger doors. She then quickly shut off the motor.

After the racket outside, it was suddenly eerily quiet. They both let out an audible sigh of relief.

Willa winked and smiled at Danielle. "That was about the most excitement I had since that deer crashed through the kitchen last year. What do you think?"

"You know, Willa. This is exactly why I hate to fly with you. You have all the fun playing with your toys while I have to deal with the terror."

"Come on, let's get out of here and get us a Scotch. I can use one right about now." Willa said turning some knobs then unbuckling herself from the seat. "I can't wait to hear about your latest drama."

"Why do you assume there's a drama in play?"

"Well, you made me pick you up in the impending storm of the year, in the middle of the week, no time for questions. Your voice sounded funny, you showed up smelling like a hamburger, and most tellingly, you look like some dumpy

390

homemaker that just came off an overnight camping trip with a bunch of teenagers. Where did you get that outfit, girl?"

They had scampered out of the plane and were standing on a narrow platform inside the hanger. Danielle remained silent as she watched Willa secure the door and tie up the plane so it wouldn't float away.

"I look that bad?"

"You almost killed us and that's all that got through that thick head of yours? As Ricky Ricardo would say, 'Lucy, you got a lot of 'splaining to do."

Chapter 28

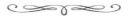

Still standing in Danielle's den, Rake realized that in his haste to loosen up and clear his head, he cleared it too much and forgot to bring his phone. He worried he could have been missing updates from Muckiss. Meanwhile, he was sure of one thing. Danielle was safe–at least for now–but she needed protection. He had to find her before anyone else did.

"Eleni, urgent. Where's the phone?" He asked nervously.

Eleni bustled him into the kitchen. Their shoes crunched on some broken glass as they reached a desk in the far corner of the kitchen. While Eleni began cleaning up the mess, he put the call into Muckiss.

"You got some news for me about your girlfriend?" Muckiss asked abruptly, not bothering to dispense with any greetings. "Murphy's apoplectic. He's ready with the All-Points Bulletin. He's convinced she's somehow at the center of this. The media are continuing to put pressure on him and the higher-ups want to see some "closure" if you know what I mean…"

Rake bowed his head and closed his eyes. He took a deep breath and paused for a second. He hadn't missed any recent developments in the meantime. Muckiss had nothing and was looking to him for some answers. Without saying as much, Muckiss also admitted that the FBI had lost her trail spectacularly. Now he wondered if he captured Danielle, would it be the easy way out for them? No apologies. They got her through Rake. Muckiss could save face for the Bureau. Rake did the dirty work. If he screws up, either way, they could pin it on him. After all, that was Murphy's modus operandi.

It didn't seem they had other suspects. Murphy, that old son of a gun, wanted a win and Danielle fit the bill whether or not she was innocent. He was gunning for her, alright, just like he took aim at him when he thought it was right to make his move. But where Rake gave up, Danielle was digging in. He didn't have the guts anymore, but the lady still fights. Murphy versus Mendow. This could be a match to rival the finals of Worldwide Wrestling. He winced at the thought. He wasn't sure who would survive.

He had to find her, but he needed help. Still wary of him, he decided to share his latest theory with Muckiss. Maybe the old-timer would do the right thing and help him bring her back, discover the truth, and calm the waters for everyone's sake.

"Look, I may have something. I don't know how certain this is, but I may have put a couple of pieces together that may help us track her down." He said pacing the perfectly polished wooden floor of Danielle's kitchen.

"Okay, let me hear it and it better be good because we're out of time," Muckiss said, taking one long sniff then letting out a light cough.

Rake stopped, brought the receiver around to his face and mouthed the word 'jerk' then put it back to his ear. He felt a little better. Clearing his throat, he continued calmly. "Apparently, her best friend, Willa, owns a seaplane."

"Geez, Rake, you've got to be kidding... She flew away?"

"No, listen. If Danielle contacted her, they could have rendezvoused somewhere and Willa could have whisked her off to some secret hiding place. If we can find that plane and find Willa, we may find Danielle."

Rake held his breath and stared out the kitchen window while he waited for his friend to respond. The tops of the distant West Virginia mountains were being touched by storm clouds rolling in from the West. Nearby trees shivered as the winds blew through. Flocks of birds were pushed from their perches, as if mother nature was forcing them to take shelter somewhere else. He waited some more. The silence on the other end of the phone felt eternal. He feared he lost his only hope to find Danielle quickly. He needed to give it one more shot.

"Pete, you still there? I said I think we can find her. I saw a picture of the plane in her den. It's an Icon A5–you know, the kind that can take-off and land on water and the ground. The registration number of the plane was pretty clear. You can track it down with that! It should be pretty easy. How many people fly a $400 grand plane around here?" he said louder–the frustration breaking through.

A few seconds passed. He heard two little coughs this time. Then the voice on the other end said, "Keep talking."

Rake let out a silent sigh of relief. This was a good omen. "Look, you know she did nothing criminal. She's just a train that's temporarily fallen off the rails. Let's find her, make sure she's okay, then ask her a few questions. I'm sure she'll cooperate." In reality, he wasn't sure of anything with Danielle, but he thought he sounded convincing.

Another pregnant pause. "Okay–tell me about the plane," Muckiss said, all business-like.

Rake smiled with satisfaction. This was good. "It's one of those amphibious planes where the wings fold so you can put it in a garage. Its state-of-the art. I've only seen a few of them. They can land and take off on the water and on the ground. Super cool, you know. The registration number is... uh," he stopped. After the big build-up, he realized he didn't write it down or memorize it. As he pivoted to return to the den to get the picture, he ran smack into Eleni.

"You looking for thees?" she asked, holding the framed photo out to him. "The picture of Willaki and Danielle?" He looked back to where she was cleaning and wondered how the old lady could move so quickly.

"Um, yes," he said embarrassed, reaching for the picture. He mouthed a grateful "thank you" and read the visible registration number on the side of the seaplane to Muckiss.

"Yup. That's all I need. Let's see if I can track this baby down. In the meantime, I'm going to give Dr. Place, the Chairman of the bank, a call to let him know where we are. That assistant bombshell of his keeps calling to see if we've located her. She keeps saying how very concerned they are for some reason. What's her name...? I have it here somewhere."

Rake heard Muckiss shuffling some papers. He spared him the trouble. "Rita. Rita Steele." he said, "and I didn't think she was so hot." Rake said with bravado. He gave Eleni a wink. She scowled, calling him "crazy man" under her breath.

"How do you know that? Have you met her?" Muckiss asked.

"We accidentally ran into each other about a half-hour ago." Rake told him the story, including some of Eleni's unorthodox but amusing security methods which had Muckiss laughing and even Eleni chortling.

"I'll leave those parts out when I call Place." Muckiss chuckled. He paused. "Ugh. I see The Murphy Man heading in my direction. Let me go so I can get away from him and get on this. It's probably our last shot before his hair catches on fire."

Rake handed the phone back to Eleni. She snatched it out of his hands. All the amusement from the last couple of minutes had instantly dissipated. "You think you big know it all, Reek. Make big deal. You so smart about plane. Why you don't just ask me where Willaki lives? I tell you if you think she's with Danielle." She glared at him and waved the phone in his face.

Taking a step back to avoid a potential smack in the head, he realized what a horse's ass he was all along. Of course Eleni would know. That woman knows everything. Why didn't he just ask her? "You're right, you're right. I should have thought of that," he said, holding both hands out for protection. These West Mendow women were driving him nuts. "My apologies. Please put the phone down," he begged, holding his arms up in a surrendering pose.

"You waste a lot of time with man on phone," she said, coming dangerously close with the phone.

Rake was just about to defend his actions and plead for forgiveness when his nose caught a whiff of a roasting lamb. Before he could stop himself, he unwisely uttered, "Mm, that smells so good."

"Aaach. You men are all alike. It's your stomach first…" she said, jabbing the phone into his belly.

He finally grabbed the phone out of her hand. "Give me that before you break my rib," he said, grabbing the phone out of her hand. "I love that smell. I had a moment of weakness."

Eleni cackled like a chicken. She appeared to be enjoying this. She was a formidable sparring partner- serious but good-hearted. She waddled away towards the oven, flicking her wrist like she was swatting a fly. "Enough"

"Wait!" Rake said, laughing nervously. "So where does Willa… uh… Willaki live?"

"Go home. Get changed out of sweaty, stupid clothes. Come back with fast car. I have address and food ready. You take to Willaki and Danielle. Both terrible cooks. Eat too much junk food and drink too much together."

Rake stood there like a tree planted in the middle of the kitchen.

"Why you wait? Go! Fee ye! Fee ye! (Go!, Go!)," she shouted at him.

It was pointless to argue with that stubborn old goat, so Rake ran out as Eleni busied herself in the kitchen.

Chapter 29

Eleni listened for the front door to shut, pulled out her little address book from one of the many hidden pockets in her skirt, and grabbed the phone. She licked her wrinkled index finger and quickly leafed through the pages. The book was old, brown and very worn, but it had every number of any importance to her on the planet. She looked for the private number of Strangler's Point Inn.

She punched in the number. The phone kept ringing and ringing at the other end. Either nobody was picking up or the lines were out–both of which always happened. She then tried Willa's cell, but she wasn't picking up either.

"A sto thiavolo!" she said to herself, cursing the devil. The clock showed it getting close to 5 pm. A dark shadow crossed the kitchen window, reflecting a transitioning sky. It was too early to go pitch black out there. The clouds and her bones were forewarning her of a severe change in the weather. She had to get a move on. Reek would be back any minute, she thought, acknowledging that an army couldn't keep that guy away from finding Danielle. The guy acted like a nerd but she knew there was more to him, but it didn't matter now. It was all about Danielle.

An idea struck as she pulled down some tin pans from the upper cabinet. The story could be Danielle. Contemplating this further, she took the lamb and the roasted potatoes out of the oven. While listening to the crust emit the last of its sizzle, she theorized maybe it was his job. Perhaps he was there to keep an eye on her. But why? The girl had her troubles these last few days, but she could always take care of herself. While she packed the lamb, Eleni thought about calling Jen. Jen had good intuition like Eleni, and maybe they could figure this out together. It wouldn't be the first time they had to do an intervention on their mutually crazy boss.

As Eleni was filling some Tupperware with Tzatziki dip and her home-made fish roe spread, Taramosalata that Willa and Danielle loved, she added a little extra for Reek in case he wanted to try it. Smiling to herself, she realized with that little act, her gut instinct already shook off the misgivings she had about him a few seconds ago. There were more positive traits than negative ones. He seemed passionate but good-natured, well-intentioned and strong. Although his age was definitely on the other side of forty, he still wore his masculinity proudly. Eleni was in her jolly eighties–and didn't care at this point about having another man around after her husband died, but she still could appreciate a good hunk of a guy when she saw one.

However, with all the positives, he was still a mystery man. But her worries about him weren't as bad as the uncertainties she sensed about the other lady who was there earlier. That Reeta really gave her a bad feeling with her crazy dramatics. Eleni's nose unconsciously wrinkled like a skunk just walked through the kitchen. That lady gave off a bad vibe. She made a mental note to bring out the Holy Water and sprinkle some around after Reek left. That picture with the girls interested her too. Had she also made the connection?

Pulling out a large wicker basket from the utility room, Eleni started stacking the pans of food inside. She also threw in a couple of bottles of Willa's favorite wine and a Sancerre for Danielle. The basket was full.

Within minutes, Rake was pulling into the circular driveway. Eleni was amused. He must have broken the record for showering and getting dressed. He emerged from the car wearing a navy blue blazer, khaki pants, and a white cotton shirt and trotted quickly up to Eleni, who was holding the basket waiting at the door.

"Here, give that to me." He said reaching for the enormous basket "Geez, this thing weighs a ton!" he grunted, stumbling back to his car.

"Ees nothing," Eleni replied.

"What? You didn't even break a sweat! Next time I have to move furniture, I'll remember to call you," he panted.

"Don't talk. You lose your breath." Eleni said

with a twinkle in her eye. "Be careful with basket. You don't want to wrinkle or spill anything. You look too handsome." She said as she walked with him towards the car. She noticed the flattery caused Rake to stand a little taller and puff out his already massive chest a little further despite the 3000-ton basket he was about to hoist into his trunk.

He put the basket down to open the trunk. "Honestly Eleni, how did you carry this thing?" he said tucking his shirt back in his belt.

"Greek women have superpowers," she said standing on her tiptoes to help him right his blazer on his massive shoulders. "We also know the future," she said, stepping back. "You like Willa and I know you like Danielle. You will spend evening with two ladies who like to drink and eat all night. You will have fun and my Danielle will be safe, okay? You get going!" she said, pointing that long, crooked finger at him again.

Rake hastily moved some stuff around in the trunk of his late-model black BMW, cursing the lack of space and trying to make room for the colossal basket. He heaved it up and let out a breath, thankful it fit. He opened the lid to make sure nothing spilled. The aroma of the roasted lamb and potatoes intoxicated him, and he bent in for a deeper inhale.

Eleni instantly appeared at his side and snapped the lid shut, almost cutting off his head. "It's for

Willaki and Danielle! Not for you to eat now!" she cried out, pushing him away.

He closed the trunk. "Okay, okay! Now, where am I going?" he said, suppressing a smile.

"Here," she said, handing him a folded piece of paper.

"What's this? Strangler's Point Inn? 1200 Tilghman Road, Tilghman Island," he read out loud. "Where the heck is this?" he asked, puzzled.

"Teelghman Island. Across Bay Bridge. Near St. Michaels! You don't know? Where you from?" she yelled, waving her hand at him in quick little short karate chop motions.

Scratching his temple, he suddenly remembered. "Oh, yeh! Man, I better get a move on. This could take me hours."

A loud rumble erupted in the distance. A burst of light followed, hitting the horizon.

"God is bowling. Just make strike, "Eleni said, throwing her hands up and looking at the sky.

"Great-perfect timing," he said sarcastically, following Eleni's eyes as she scanned the bowling alley in the sky. "It's a big storm. It's starting. Of course... just as I'm about to leave..."

They both looked at each other as drops of rain fell around them onto the driveway.

405

"Reek, you go now. I keep calling Willaki. She not answer before. No good cell phone out there and lines always go down in storm."

Rake looked at the paper to make sure she included the phone numbers. "I'll keep trying too. I hope this isn't a wild goose chase," he said as he got into his car, closed the door and started the engine.

Eleni tapped on the window as he was buckling up. "One more thing," she said as he rolled down the window. "You take this." From another fold in her brown skirt, she brought out a glass eyeball hanging from a safety pin.

"Holy Moly! What's that?" Rake exclaimed, shifting sideways, away from "the thing". He gaped open-eyed at the open eye.

As she dangled it in front of him, she explained it was an "evil eye" and that he should carry it with him to ward off evil spirits. "That place is full of mean ghosts and evil. I feel it. Willaki laughs and Danielle not afraid but it's bad place. Take this. It will protect you," she insisted, putting it in his hand.

Speechless, Rake put it in his jacket pocket. Finding his voice, he thanked her. "Okay. I'm good, I guess. Yes, I feel much better. Thank you." He nodded.

Leaning forward into the car, almost touching his nose with her round, determined face, she said, "Don't worry, I don't cast spells on you. You find my Danielle and bring her back. Keep her out of trouble. The devil works overtime trying to get her. But you don't find her, all promises are off!"

Right at that moment, a lightning bolt struck behind the statue of St. Catherine and a peal of thunder rocked through the landscape.

Eleni was done. She strutted back to the house, oblivious to the sensational opening number of nature's late afternoon performance. Rake shuddered as he watched her.

"What a piece of work you are," he said quietly after her. "Danielle is lucky to have you."

When she reached the door, she turned and took one last look at him. She gave the "be gone" wave and disappeared inside. Rake put the car in gear and made his way down the driveway. He gave one last glance in the rearview mirror and caught sight of St. Catherine, who appeared to be glaring at him as the sky darkened behind her. He could just hear her daring him not to come back without Danielle.

Rake turned on to Beatrice Lane and stepped on the gas, trying to ignore the sense of foreboding that was sweeping over him. Was it the jitters because he was out of practice and hadn't seen this kind of action since he retired or was he heading into something that even he, the great Rake Harris, may not be able to handle which was finding a woman like the unpredictable and exasperating Ms. Danielle Mendow.

Chapter 30

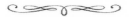

Rita watched Rake make a right out of Mendow's driveway. She stepped deeper into the thicker part of the woods, making sure it completely hid her. It was painful for her to be waiting there, hating the surrounding nature while watching the ins and outs of the Mendow estate in the last hour. But she had to be patient. Between the old hag and the hunky neighbor, she was sure someone guessed, just like she did, where Danielle was hiding.

As soon as he was out of sight, she reached in her jacket pocket for her cell phone and hit the speed dial.

The phone was answered on the first ring.

"Well?" said a male voice on the other end.

Swatting away some gnats that were getting in her face, Rita answered, "Her pal just pulled out driving like a madman. It looks like he figured it out too."

"He's a little late out of the gate. I'm almost over that frightful Bay Bridge. If it wasn't for this storm trying to blow me off the road, I'd be there to surprise the boogers out of her."

The woods grew darker and Rita shook something off that was crawling up her leg. The trees could only shelter her from the storm for a few minutes longer. "Listen, I'm out of here. You sure that guy you know at the FAA gave you the right information?" she asked while walking quickly towards the road.

The voice on the other end crackled. "Yeh, yeh. Makes sense. I remember that friend of hers. Willa. Tough broad. Used to drink me under the table, then wake up at the crack of dawn and run a 30-mile marathon."

Rita started to say something, but the connection suddenly went dead. "Shoot!" she said to herself as her heel caught on a tree root, almost toppling her over. He better not screw this up, she thought.

A strong wind blew some leaf dust into her face. She heard a crack and looked up just in time to see lightning shooting out of a set of distant dark clouds. The storm was closing in. An enormous explosion of thunder forced her to run faster. It felt like Mother Nature was on her tail.

She found her car where she had hidden it up the road, jumped in, and started the engine. Letting out a sigh of relief, she took a quick look at herself in the visor mirror, gasped at her appearance, removed some twigs from her hair, and backed on to the road.

It was late afternoon, but it felt like midnight. Wet leaves stuck to her windshield as she drove down Beatrice Lane. The road was slippery and her black SUV skidded a bit as she pressed on the gas.

The gusts of rain were making visibility almost impossible. She turned onto Cooper Street, which was already showing signs of flooding. Up to that point, she didn't know what she was going to do next–go back to the bank or continue on the quest for Danielle. But as soon as she passed the heaping pile of charcoal that was once the West Mendow branch, she knew what she had to do.

They were too far down that road together to stop now.

Chapter 31

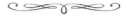

Strangler's Point Inn was the worst investment that Danielle had ever made. The thought of how much money it sucked out of her made her sigh as she looked up at it while she and Willa struggled towards it.

The waves slammed against the rocky shoreline, splashing the two of them as they hurried up the deck. The rain, coupled with the bay water, was soaking them faster than a cold shower.

"We need to hurry!" Willa shouted, her voice getting lost in the wind. She grabbed Danielle's bony arm and used all of her strength to pull her along. "Move it!"

"Alright!" Danielle shouted back. "I'm not that out of shape!" she yelled. In reality, the entire world was out of shape next to Willa, but she would never admit it. A tailwind came up behind her, which gave her a boost. Miraculously, this helped her get a few steps ahead of Willa with the added bonus of not losing her balance. "See?" she yelled proudly before stumbling on a small tree branch.

They were slowly getting closer to the old Victorian house. She could barely make out the white frames of the bay-facing windows against the brown clapboard siding as the darkness bore down on it. The rain and wind were pelting the house from all angles, tossing the plants and furniture around on the wraparound porch.

The grass underneath their feet was mushier than oatmeal as they slid and slipped their way up the great lawn. They hung on to the banisters like drowning rats as they pulled their bodies up the steps leading to the white wooden doors. The doorknob was stuck as Willa put the key in and tried to get it to turn. "Come on, come on," she said under her breath until it finally released, allowing the door to fly open. They both tumbled through. They immediately felt the warmth of the main room.

Laughing and shaking water off, Willa said, "It was easier to survive basic cadet training than trying to get you here."

Nothing had changed since the last time Danielle was there a few months ago, or probably within the last 125 years. Garish red velvet Victorian couches and wing chairs adorned the large room where guests entered directly from the front door. Round marble-topped dark wooden tables were peppered in between. The center of the room was overwhelmed by a large table decorated with a minuscule version of "The Winged Victory of Samothrace." Vintage magazines that nobody had touched since they were originally published were fanned around the statue. An antique rug with a busy oriental design took up most of the floor space. It did its job distracting the eye from the dark worn floorboards that peaked out from the edges.

The walls were covered in portraits of ugly people and landscapes from who knows where. Even the average person could tell that some were cheap reproductions. Local amateurs from the Tilghman Island Art Club painted others.

Doors led to all sorts of places–guest rooms, eating rooms, a kitchen, and an office. The carpeted stairway straight ahead on the other side of the room led to the second and third floors. Seeing them, Danielle remembered quite a few nights stumbling up assuming she had had one too many glasses of wine until she would remember that it was the stairs that were crooked and wobbly, not her legs failing her.

"Turn on the lights. This place is creeping me out already and I've just walked in." Danielle said wiping the water off herself and the book bag she loosened from her clutches.

Willa started switching on the little old lady lamps scattered about and then went over to the right wall and turned on the gas fireplace–the only modern, albeit kitschy, addition to the room in over 100 years.

"Aaaah" cooed Danielle as she moved closer–turning her back on the fake flames.

"You'll be feeling like a marshmallow in a minute," Willa said, taking off the flight jacket and boots. "By the way, what's in the bag? You've been holding it like it was a newborn. Can you put it down?"

"It's a long story that deserves a bottle of wine and potato chips."

"No chips, no wine," Willa replied, walking toward an old wooden drinks trolley and grabbing a crystal decanter. "Port? The alcohol is in the storage shed out back and there's no way I'm going out again while this squall is going on."

"Well, any Port in a storm then," Danielle said, laughing at her own joke.

Willa filled a snifter. "I'll take that as a yes."

"Hold that thought," Danielle answered while heading towards the stairs. "Let me change first. I feel like a Raggedy Ann right now. I'll be down in ten. There's so much going on that I have to tell you."

She had almost reached the second level when she shouted down to Willa, "Hey, I'm going to assume there are no guests staying here tonight."

"Of course there aren't!" Willa shouted back–her voice echoing around the empty Inn. "But maybe a few ghosts."

Danielle rolled her eyes and continued up the stairs. The Inn was a case study in Money Pit 101. There wasn't a month that didn't go by when she didn't have to shell out a couple of grand to keep it running. But she and Willa loved the place. In fact, Willa hated to leave the compound and only ventured out for necessities, to pick up a VIP guest that stumbled upon it, or an occasional walkabout with Danielle somewhere in this world. And for Danielle, it was her home away from home–a secret retreat that nobody, except Eleni, knew about.

Her rooms were on the third floor, facing the Bay. The creaky stairs and the dated wallpaper lining the walls of the wide hallway leading to her door brought her back into another era when life seemed to be much simpler. It was her happy place. The thought of spending some time with Willa at the Inn began melting the memories of what drove her here that day in the first place.

The door gave off a friendly creak as she opened it. The familiar scent of the bay mixed with years of mustiness immediately enveloped her. The tension in her body thawed. Despite the permanent odor, her room and the rest of the Inn were very well preserved and clean in the unlikely event anyone actually wanted to stay there. Danielle loved it for what it was–worn, comfortable, and in need of a good paint job. And if anyone dared to complain, she was sure Willa would fly them right out of here.

The room was toasty warm. She couldn't wait to slip into something dry and comfortable. She headed straight towards the dresser to find fresh undergarments and some leggings. As she was pulling out the drawer, she looked at herself in the mirror and cringed. Now, major repairs were required. She made her way to the bathroom, stopping first at the armoire for one of her softest oversized sweatshirts. She ran a quick tub, sunk into the warm, soapy water, shut her eyes, and drifted away.

The storm continued to wreak havoc on the island but Danielle felt like she was in a faraway place, safe in her deep porcelain womb. She cleared her mind and let the sounds of the outside world turn into a song being hummed by Mother Nature.

But within minutes, the water had cooled down, and the chill reminded her she owed "the story" to Willa who was downstairs probably on her second glass of port waiting impatiently to hear it. She quickly dried off, slipped on her clean clothes, ran a brush through her hair, and examined her manicure and pedicure, which had, except for some minor chips, miraculously survived the day. Passing inspection, she opened the door to go back downstairs.

It was at that moment, the Strangler's Inn went completely dark.

"You've got to be kidding," Danielle said to no one. "Willa!" she shouted. No answer. She called out again, "Willa!" The house remained still. She must have gone out to check on the back-up generator, Danielle thought.

Danielle felt her way back to her room to get some candles. She found two in her nightstand with some matchbooks and lit one. The room glowed with an eerie yellow light.

She returned to the hallway. A light flickered up the stairwell from the first floor.

"Willa?" she called out again. Still, there was no answer.

A bedroom door slammed behind her, causing her to jump. Her heart started beating faster causing her to feel it in her throat. She couldn't control the weird thoughts popping into her head about the spirits who were sometimes spotted haunting this floor. She turned instinctively to make sure there was nothing behind her.

"Okay, I'm being an idiot," Danielle said to herself, loosening her grip on the candle. Her eyes swept the hallway. Nothing appeared paranormal. Although she loved the Inn, she always thought this floor was spooky. After all, this place wasn't named the "Strangler's Point Inn" for nothing. Urban legends say it is haunted. The story starts in 1842 when Captain John Strangler built the place for his British bride, Laura. But she only lived there for about a week before she mysteriously disappeared one night in just her bedclothes. Supposedly, the dear Captain was consumed by his namesake and strangled her right in the same room Danielle had claimed. Apparently, she had become too friendly with the gardener, Henry Hogan. Other stories had her spotted in Baltimore, making a living roaming the streets. In any event, poor Henry went missing a month later only to be found washed up on the shores of St. Michael's, dead, with a rope tied around his neck.

For centuries afterward, some people who stayed there claimed hearing strange noises at night and witnessing the occasional apparition roaming the hallways. Willa and Danielle ignored the complaints. Hey, if they didn't like it, don't come back. Ghosts made the old place more authentic. When Danielle and Willa first flew over it, the place it intrigued them. They stopped in and had a word with the old man who owned it and the 100 waterfront acres surrounding it. He told them the story and complained that over the years the noises got worse and business was horrible. As a result, he couldn't dump the place fast enough. But nobody wanted to buy an old Inn with a sinister past, Danielle and Willa thought it was just perfect. Danielle made him an offer right on the spot. They loved the lore. Coupled with the remoteness, they decided it would be a perfect retreat.

It was one of the stupidest deals Danielle ever made (her attorney asked if she even looked at the pitiful financials) but she did it anyway and became a haunted Inn owner. Word of mouth about the mysterious new owners spread quickly and before they knew it, guests started asking to stay there.

That was the last thing the ladies wanted, so they raised the price to an exorbitant amount, hoping to keep people away. But economics is funny–the higher the price, the more curious rich people become and the Strangler's Point Inn became an underground hideaway for the very wealthy. The Washington elite discovered Willa's flying taxi and when they needed to quietly escape the craziness of D.C., they would call her and be able to disappear for a few days. Willa did not keep records, accepted any form of payment, and left her guests alone unless they asked. The guests counted on Willa's discretion, and Willa counted on theirs. There was honor among thieves and the military.

Danielle heard something scrape the floor. It sounded like a door had opened somewhere nearby. She felt the hairs on the back of her neck rise. A chill ran through her as she slowly and quietly made her way to the stairway. She stopped when she heard footsteps coming from the first floor. Holding her breath to listen closer, she thought to herself that it better be Willa making those scary noises. She wasn't in the mood for ghosts tonight. She stood dead still straining to hear further sounds.

A long minute passed. Nothing was happening. She continued tiptoeing down the stairs, hoping not to hit a loose floorboard that would reveal her movements. She hung on to the banister, careful not to take a tumble if something frightened her enough to make her lose her balance. She shone the light from the candle into the second-floor hallway.

All looked quiet. The storm outside was getting stronger. The force of the squall was causing all kinds of banging and lashing outside, but Danielle wasn't sure what was happening inside the Inn. Something didn't feel right. Not wanting to attract attention to herself, she blew out the candle and tried to make her way to the lobby by the indirect light coming from the gas fireplace.

Where was Willa? Danielle wondered. Why wasn't she answering?

The only sound was the rain pounding at the old parlor windows. She quickly scanned the lobby. The first floor looked the same as when she had left it, including the glass of port left untouched on the trolley.

Just then, a strong gale blew forcing air through the cracks in the walls causing the house to groan. The fake flame from the fireplace started playing tricks with her eyes, and she saw formless shapes in the corners of the room. A thud came from the Breakfast Room, but she couldn't quite make it out. Was it a chair moving? Something falling off a shelf?

"Willa?" she whispered loudly towards the doorway of the room. No answer.

She heard someone strike a match and smelled the Sulphur dioxide as it was burning. 'Oh my God!' Danielle's heart started pounding. 'Willa doesn't smoke and Willa said there was nobody staying here.' Her muscles tensed. Logical thoughts escaped her head and were replaced by irrational fears. With eyes darting back and forth, Danielle began walking slowly from the bottom of the steps to the front door, thinking about an escape.

A man's voice said, "Come on, Danny. How long do you think you would survive out there in this weather? Come back. I came all the way out here to see you and you're running away?"

Danielle froze. Her eyes widened. She felt her heart was going to explode from her chest. This was the second time in two days someone called her Danny. There were only two people that she tolerated when they called her that. And she reminded herself they were both dead.

Chapter 32

The wind ripped through the house as the back door to the kitchen behind the lobby swung open. "Hey!" Willa yelled out as she blew in, lugging a heavy box and a flashlight. She entered the parlor and put the box at her feet. Staring curiously at Danielle, who was staring back wild-eyed, she asked, "What are you doing standing there? You look like you've seen a ghost!"

"I... I..." Danielle stuttered, pointing to the Breakfast Room, "I... well, I heard something. Someone's in there lighting matches...Don't you smell it?"

Willa stood there sniffing. "Nope. Can't smell a thing."

Hands gesticulating furiously, she said in a loud whisper, "I heard a voice too."

"Yeh? What did it say? 'I'm a ghost. Cigarettes killed me.' Really Danielle, calm down. It's hard to take the weirdness, knowing you're still sober. You are sober still, right?" Willa asked, shaking her head. Danielle continued to stare at her, then started shifting back and forth. Willa's brow furrowed. "Okay, Okay. You know, sometimes, well, let me take that back, most times I think you are nuts. Let me assure you, there's nobody around for miles. It's pitch black out there, and the roads are badly flooded by now. Nobody can get out here now. But I know that look. You're not giving up until I go check it out."

Danielle nervously nodded her head up and down. Willa walked confidently towards the doorway of the Breakfast Room.

"You're right. Everyone thinks I'm nuts these days." Danielle said under her breath as she followed nervously behind Willa. She peered over her shoulders into the pitch-black room.

The light from the flashlight circled the breakfast room. There wasn't a soul–dead or alive–in sight.

"See? Nobody's here," Willa said with cool politeness. "And the smell was probably from a draft coming through the fireplace in here. Remember? This fireplace is original, which means the smoke is real and stinks now and then." She put her hand on Danielle's shoulder and came up close to her face. "I think someone here needs to take it easy."

"The voice!" Danielle implored. "I know I heard someone talk to me!"

"Yeh, well, I don't know about that," Willa said, rolling her eyes and backing away. "It's difficult to say..." she mumbled. "Hey!" she said cheerfully, "did we have a power outage or something? Why is this place dark and gloomy? Are the lights

426

working?" She went to work trying to turn on some of the petite crystal lamps that decorated the room. Exasperated, she kicked a wall, and the house hoping the house would light up like a Christmas tree. "Oh well. sometimes that works," she said, "I guess it will be candles in the wind for now."

Lowering her head, Danielle sighed, "You know, it's been a long two days." She walked over to one of the Victorian couches and plopped down. The soft red velvet pillows cupped her body, warming her and calming her some. Willa walked over to the drinks trolley and poured a sailor size serving of port into Danielle's glass before handing it to her. "All that? I'll be singing show tunes in an hour," Danielle said, snatching it eagerly from Willa's hand and taking a nice long swig. She closed her eyes and sighed like it was the best drink she had ever tasted.

"Good. You needed that. Now tell me, what the hell is going on with you?"

Willa had poured herself a drink and sat down next to her. Danielle took another mouthful and began the last two days' events. The story started gushing out quickly, beginning with Bill Smith's murder. She described the meeting in the Chairman's office, being followed by the black SUV, adventures with the flash-drive and climaxed with the fire at the Branch.

"And that was only Monday." She continued with the chase by some authority until she had to leave town. She confessed that she felt people were looking at her differently–suspecting her as an embezzler and murdering an old lady from the bank named Dolores.

Willa listened expressionless until she got to the old lady murder. Willa sat up straighter. "Hey! I remember Dolores! You used to talk about her years ago. Yeh, you used to call her that 'old shrew'. I didn't think you would bump her off!" She said excitedly, shaking her head and slapping her knee.

"Willa! I did nothing of the kind!" Danielle said with mock indignation. They both started laughing until they started to tear up. Danielle caught her breath and continued feeling the effects of a little too much port, the warmth of the electric fire, and her best friend. "In the meantime, I met this gorgeous guy who seemed kind of interested in me..."

"What?" Willa said, getting hold of herself. "All this happened in two days?"

"I know. Crazy, right? This hunk, Rake Harris, told me he bought the big "white elephant" house next door. You remember, the one I wanted to buy for Jen and her family because she just keeps pumping out those kids? Well, anyway, I never got around to it, but that's another story for another day. So, this guy moves in–and I didn't know it. That's weird in itself because I know everything, right? He shows up in my kitchen on Monday all sweaty and sexy and says he's retired and moved to West Mendow because he just wanted to get away from the hustle and bustle of the city. In between all the bank stuff going on, he had me over for dinner–well–it was a bit of a debacle because the fire department called me about the Branch and I had to run and I ended up at Sheila's with Jen and he walked in on us. So, I knocked him over with a table and Sheila pointed a rifle at him and then I kissed him in the parking lot." Danielle paused and took a deep breath. Tilting her head, she looked at Willa and said with a smile, "So what do you think?"

Willa's eyebrows nearly hit her hairline. She held up her hand and said, "Say no more. You are delusional...."

"No, no. I'm not! After all that, he called me the next morning and wanted to take me to lunch but then Jen gave me the umbrella signal and you know, 'No Questions Asked - No Hesitation'. I had to run."

Willa leaned back and crossed her long legs. "Let's stay right there for a minute. What, pray tell, makes you believe that he's still into you? From what I'm hearing, he may already be sorry he walked into your kitchen yesterday."

"I don't think so. You know, looking back, I don't know if he's interested or stalking me for some reason." The two of them nodded in unison, contemplating that thought.

After a moment Willa asked, "Does he drive a black SUV?"

"No, he rides a Harley," Danielle answered with a wink. They both took another sip of their drink.

"Nice. Okay, let's put Rake to the side for now. It sounds like he came along at the wrong time. What else do we have?" Willa said closing her eyes and rubbing her temple.

Danielle put on her banker's face and became all business, returning to her forte. "The flash-drive. Jen and I looked at it. We couldn't figure it out when we first downloaded it. There were a bunch of dollar amounts, dates, account numbers, and routing numbers. It wasn't until Suzanne, my regional manager, showed me the reports for my branch that we put two and two together."

Danielle took a second to think through her assumptions and find out whether they made sense before she continued. Her face got hot, and she was embarrassed thinking about the next part. After a big inhale, she looked down and said, "Apparently, there was a good amount of electronic transactions going through my branch that I was unaware of."

Willa's eyes widened. "Danielle, banker extraordinaire, was not in complete control of her little Kingdom?"

"Well, you don't have to rub it in," Danielle answered, looking up and crossing her arms. "Let

430

me continue so even you, village serf, will understand. All accounts in the bank are coded to one of the 120 branches of the bank. However, there are a few exceptions such as accounts for high net worth individuals who need privacy, some large corporate accounts that need special management, some old international accounts that are still on the books, and senior executives who don't want their salaries blabbed all over the place by some disgruntled low-level employee. In normal circumstances, all these accounts are invisible to the retail branches but can be seen at different levels on the wholesale side of the bank. Are you following so far?"

With eyes closed momentarily like she was picturing the scenario or taking a power nap, Willa kept slowly nodding.

"Now here's the kicker," Danielle continued as if everyone was just as enthusiastic about a clever money laundering scam as she was, "The transactions, both incoming and outgoing amounts, were going through accounts at my branch, but those accounts weren't coded to my branch so I couldn't see anything. They were coded to another division. If someone wasn't assigned to maintaining that division, nobody had their eye on what was going on! It's beautiful!"

Opening her eyes, Willa gazed at her, puzzled. "Let me get this straight. So, all this activity with the transactions was coming in and out of your branch, but you had no clue. Then suddenly, your regional manager tells you about these accounts and you're shocked. Sounds weird. Explain to me how, in the end, they were discovered?"

"Good question, village serf. Capital National has a peculiar way of coding. We can code the activity in one direction and we can code the profitability from a relationship somewhere else. Whoever set up the scam, wanted to monitor the business but didn't want to be seen making money from it because of... because..." Danielle was thinking it through as she was talking. "... because," her face lit up and her voice grew stronger, "they worked in a cost center, not a profit center, and it would raise flags!"

"Or, someone wanted to hide the activity but make her branch look good. Don't you monitor your profitability?"

That stung, thought Danielle. "Actually, we don't see those reports. That's the regional manager's job. We just know our transaction volumes and rankings. We don't see overall profitability." Danielle responded, lowering her eyelids and giving Willa the hairy eyeballs. "Plus, Mendow Enterprises makes so much money for the bank out of my branch that I assume it kind of all blends together."

"I don't know Danielle. It smells." Willa said getting up to pour herself another drink. Danielle got up and followed her across the room to the

432

drinks trolley wondering why Willa, of all people, joined the ranks of the suspicious.

"Come on, you don't believe me?" she yelled at Willa's back while rubbing a chill out of her arms and legs.

Willa busied herself at the drinks trolley, not answering. Finally, she looked up and said casually, "I know you didn't murder anyone, so that's out. I also know you don't need the money so I can't see you having embezzled the bank or continue to embezzle the bank. You are desperate for a boyfriend, so I CAN see why you're pissed about being caught up in all this right now and can't focus on trapping this guy, Rake. But I don't know why you were put in the middle of this. Whose accounts are they anyway?"

Before Danielle could speak, a form walked through the doorway of the breakfast room. Willa and Danielle gasped while taking a step back. They could barely make out the head which was covered by a shadow hitting it at the dubious angle.

"I told you!" Danielle said, whispering into Willa's ear. "There is someone here!"

"Who are you? And what do you want?" Willa asked the shape loudly while reaching for her flashlight on a nearby table.

A man's voice emerged from the dark form. The words came out slowly but playfully. "Hello, Willa.

433

Hello Danny. It's been a long time. Do you want to know whose accounts those are? They're mine."

Danielle stiffened. She thought to herself that it couldn't be because if it was, the place Strangler's Point Inn was indeed haunted, but it wasn't by the players of a three-hundred-year-old love triangle. "Frank?" Danielle said meekly.

"The one and only," Frank answered, taking a step forward as Willa shone the full brightness of the flashlight on him.

Danielle put her hand to her mouth. "You're supposed to be dead!"

Willa shook her head with amazement and said. "Incredible. You son of a bitch."

"Indeed," Frank answered, walking to the trolley and taking the drink out of Willa's hand. He held it up to his lips. But before he imbibed, he toasted the both of them. "Cheers, ladies! To the old days."

Chapter 33

The rain pelted Rake's windshield like it was trying to crack it. He could barely make out the lines of the Bay Bridge as he approached it. The windshield wipers on his BMW looked like tiny sticks trying to beat off the enemy fire during World War III. As anxious as he was to get to Danielle, he had to keep his car at 25 mph so he could at least make out the white lines on the road. It wouldn't help her if he were killed in a car accident.

He was concentrating so hard on driving that when the cell phone went off through Bluetooth, it startled him, causing him to briefly swerve into the left shoulder of the road.

Cursing to himself while straightening out the wheel, he quickly glanced at the caller I.D. It was Muckiss.

"Yeh," he said, pressing the call pickup button on his steering wheel while keeping his eyes steadily on the road.

"Yeh, yourself. Where the heck are you?" Muckiss grunted.

"I'm approaching the Bay Bridge…. I think. Anyhow, this storm is wild. I hope those two made it safely back to the island," he said while wiping some condensation off the inside of his windshield.

"They're fine. We're monitoring the area. No reports of seaplanes crashing into the Chesapeake," Muckiss replied.

"That's a good sign. That Willa must be one hell of a pilot or a real nut job to fly in this weather. I can barely keep the Beamer straight."

"Rumor has it, a little of both." Muckiss paused before he spoke again. "Rake, I'm calling you to give you a heads up."

Gripping the steering wheel, Rake prepared himself to hear that he had run out of time and they were sending the police out to Strangler's Inn to arrest Danielle. That Murphy. What was wrong with him? Hot dinner date and he has to make his custody quota before he rushes home? "Okay, Peter, lay it on me."

Muckiss cleared his throat. "Remember, you mentioned that Rita Steele was at the house with you because of the Chairman, you know, John Place was concerned about Danielle and they couldn't find her?"

"Yeh..." Rake said, dragging out his response. He sat up straighter, gripping the steering wheel a little tighter. A slight dread was creeping through his body. This was not the direction he thought the conversation with Muckiss was going to head.

"So I told you I was going to call Place to assure him we were on top of things, yada yada yada and that we assumed Danielle was safe but off our radar temporarily." Muckiss then paused.

"I remember, go on," he said carefully, trying not to let the anxiety show in his voice.

"Well, Place couldn't care less. He didn't care about Bill Smith, had no clue that Danielle's branch burned down, and started laughing when I told him the Mendow fell off our radar. The whole thing was such a joke to him. He said he was happy that Rita seemed interested enough to follow up and as far as he was concerned, that was good enough for him. Then he invited me for a round of golf at Congressional whenever and hung up. It was the most bizarre conversation."

Rake shifted a bit in his seat. Before he could offer an explanation, Muckiss continued.

"I assume you're still with me. So, I thought, well, the guy must be off his meds and the closest person to him that's still alive that I know is Rita herself, so I call her."

"Aah. The Vixen comes into play," Rake said knowingly.

"Curious you should call her that. Here's the thing with her. She never picked up my calls. I left her a couple of voice mails, but she never called me back. Suddenly my gut started telling me that something about her was just not right so I did some snooping and boom, it seems all is not what it appears."

By this time, Rake had passed through the toll on the Bay Bridge. He cursed himself for getting on the single-lane side. The glare of the oncoming traffic on the right meant he had to concentrate more on driving while listening to Muckiss, who was on a proverbial roll.

"Are you still there?" Muckiss asked. He was so eager to get on with the story, he didn't wait for an answer. "I called my buddy, Enzo, in New York, who worked on the original embezzlement case eighteen years ago before those bozos from the bank called off the hunt. He actually found his notes from the interviews pretty easily. The guy's really organized. He remembers talking to some employees at the bank, including your girlfriend, Danielle, who by the way, he noted, was pretty and very distraught about Bill Smith. Then he went down the list with me and we did a quick and dirty, "where are they now" exercise of the IRS database, (and don't you dare tell anyone about that). Everyone was accounted for except this nerdy, by the way, he was the one that said nerdy, not me, I don't judge, you know, Italian girl that worked in the Paying and Receiving area."

"Okay, go on. So what about this girl?" Rake had to admire this guy's investigation skill. He was tenacious. But then again, that's probably why he still had a job and Rake had been told to take a hike.

438

"Her name was Margarita Stilleto. Enzo said she was the homeliest duck you'd ever seen. Glasses, bad skin, big, heavy, front teeth that stuck out horizontally. An awning for a nose.... Could barely put two sentences together," Muckiss said dryly.

"All right, stop. I get it. The girl was ugly. Just tell me what happened to her?" Rake said with frustration.

Muckiss paused for effect. "Well, I don't know where she is at the moment, but you ran into her this afternoon."

Rake had to think. He didn't remember meeting anyone this afternoon except, except Rita Steele? Margarita, Rita! Stilleto, Steele! All sorts of crazy thoughts started racing through his mind. "Are you talking about Rita Steele?" he said incredulously.

"The one and only," Muckiss said, like he was introducing her to an audience.

Still confused, Rake asked, "She worked at the bank with Danielle in New York?"

The awful truth finally dawned on him. The revelation caused him to have some trouble concentrating on the road. "Danielle and Rita know each other from those days in New York?" Rake's heart started racing, hoping that Muckiss would say 'no'.

"Don't know," he quickly answered.

Rake hated to ask the next question, but he had to. "Peter, are they in cahoots? Did one of them go rogue?"

"Look, Buddy, if I knew, I would tell you. All I know is that Margarita the Caterpillar turned into Rita the Butterfly and that transformation probably cost a pretty penny."

His eyes shut for a split second. "Like ten million dollars?"

"Maybe." Muckiss replied, drawing out the "M" a little too long.

Rake's mind raced. "Did Rita take the money? Did Bill Smith know and lost his life when he emerged after all this time? Did Danielle think she was the next in line on the hit list and bolted? And how about that old lady? How was she involved?"

"Hey, slow down. I'm still trying to digest all this myself and don't know the answers to any of those questions yet. I do know one thing that Enzo slipped in. He always suspected that Danielle had something to do with it because it was her I.D. that was used to enter the SWIFT room and make the transfer. But Smith, before he disappeared, kept insisting it was impossible because she was supposedly by his side the whole time. Smith kept saying someone stole her I.D. and used it. Enzo thought that was a bunch of baloney."

"Well, I don't know. It's plausible." Rake said

indignantly, coming to Danielle's defense.

"Come on. I think everyone had their hand in the till that day and that may be the motive that led to murder–maybe two. You know, I don't care what happened on 9/11 to a bunch of money that could've gone to a beauty and brain makeover or build an agribusiness fortune. Ultimately, that money belonged to that unsympathetic lunatic, John Place, and it was his loss. But now I've got murders to solve and we need to know what's driving this."

The end of the Bay Bridge was finally in sight. Rake breathed a sigh of relief. He hated driving that bridge on a good day, let alone the almost four and a half miles dangling over the Chesapeake Bay during the storm of the century. In fact, it surprised him they hadn't closed it down to ensure nobody would fly off. Rake risked glancing at his GPS. He was about an hour away from Tilghman Island and the Inn. Bolts of lightning were stabbing at the horizon and the thunder was competing with Muckiss' conversation.

"What does Enzo think?" Rake asked, slowing down to avoid a large pool of rainwater that had formed as he continued east on Interstate 50 past Chestertown.

"Funny you should ask again about Enzo. He thinks there was a dark horse. Let me see..." Muckiss said. Rake could hear him shuffling some papers. He felt a twinge of jealousy. There was

Muckiss all safe in his office while Rake was putting his life on the line chasing what could be a fantasy. The good guys could be the bad guys and vice versa. Was he being played? He had to know more. "What's that supposed to mean by a 'dark horse'?"

"There was someone else. Maybe a ringleader or mastermind that was pulling all their strings."

Just then a gigantic bolt of lightning ripped through the sky, almost blinding Rake. "Geez, you should have seen that!"

There was silence on the other end of the line. The call had died. Rake tried to redial, but nothing was going through Bluetooth. The lightning must have hit a nearby cell tower, knocking out reception. He drove on in silence, hoping that Peter could reach him again.

As he pulled off onto Route 322, Rake mulled over this latest intrigue. He replayed the meeting with Rita, looking for clues on the kind of relationship she had with Danielle. He mentally reviewed the notes from Danielle's dossier that Muckiss had left with him at Starbucks. He ran about ten "what if" scenarios through his mind, but each one led him back to one place. They played him.

The road got darker and darker as the street lights grew farther apart. An occasional car would pass him going the other way, but as the weather worsened, this part of the eastern shore became a ghost land. He could smell the seasoned lamb and lemoned potatoes wafting through the trunk into his car, reminding him of Eleni and her last mutterings about that eyeball she gave him as he drove off. "Ghosts and evil things". Is that what he was in for?

His car started to skid on a patchy part of the road, so Rake slowed down to 20 miles per hour. A glaring light was reflecting off his rearview mirror. He glanced up to see a car behind him quickly approach. He wondered why the driver was being so reckless, traveling on this treacherous stretch of the road at such a high speed. The driver continued to speed up then passed him on his left hurling a big splash against his windshield, which made him swerve towards the right, almost falling into a muddy embankment.

"Road hog." Rake grumbled to himself. Rake always believed that people who drive big SUV's think they are infallible. Then he remembered that Rita Steele had a black SUV. Could it possibly be?

Rake could still see the red taillights in the distance, and he tried to catch up. Unfortunately, his little BMW with the balding tires was no match for the monster car in this storm, and soon it was out of sight. He was hoping his eyes were playing tricks on him and it wasn't Rita after all, but if it was, he better get to the Strangler's Inn pronto as these cowgirls could be heading for a showdown.

Drawing a long breath and saying a silent prayer that he wouldn't spin out, Rake put his foot on the gas pedal and watched as his speedometer started climbing. He kept his eye on the GPS to make sure he didn't miss the turn on to St. Michael's Road. His adrenaline started pumping like the old days when he was out on a case and didn't know what to expect. This was always the best part of the job. The action and excitement. The thrill of the unknown. Saving the day. Being a hero.

St. Michael's Road was coming up in a few hundred yards. Rake was so engrossed in his thoughts that he almost drove past it. He realized it a split second too late, tried to make a sharp turn, but the wheels skidded out from under him and soon he was taking a spin across the road and into a huge pool of rainwater that was flooding the ground across the way. Wipeout!

He was stuck in the mud, without a working cell phone, not a soul on the road, and in the middle of nowhere. Clutching the steering wheel, he looked up at the roof of his car and asked, "Can it get any worse than this?"

Chapter 34

Danielle continued to stare at Frank while questioning whether her mind was playing tricks on her. She reminded herself that she had attended his memorial service after it was confirmed that he was lost in the Twin Towers on 9/11. She cried. His parents cried. His friends cried. The few remaining colleagues who didn't perish that day cried. Yet, at this moment, he was standing in the same room as her.

Frank finished his port in one gulp, then closed his eyes. "Mmm, good job Willa," he said while putting his glass back on the trolley." You always did keep the best stash of alcohol in the city."

The ladies remained frozen, still paralyzed with confusion. Danielle opened her mouth to ask him why he was still alive, but Frank had in the meantime walked over to her, took her hands, leaned down, and planted a big kiss on her mouth.

"I've been waiting a long time to do that," he said gently while bringing her hands up to his lips and this time kissing her palms.

Her breathing quickened. She didn't know what she was feeling at this point. Was this really Frank? Her mind raced with a thousand emotions–anger, bewilderment, hurt, attraction. Yes, the dirt bag was standing right in front of her and he was still, after all these years, driving her insane. How could he still do that to her? It took all her courage, but she finally pulled it together. "Cut that out!" Danielle said firmly, finding her voice and pushing him away. "What the hell is your story? You pretend to have died and then come back like nothing happened? Who do you think you are? Patrick Swayze in Ghost? Do you really think you could walk back into my life after all these years and expect me to fall madly in love with you again?"

"If those beautiful blushing cheeks are any sign, maybe then yes." Frank grinned devilishly, taking a step towards her.

But before Danielle could respond, Frank was lying on the floor from a blow that Willa gave him with her flashlight.

"Did you kill him?" Danielle asked as they both stared down at him.

"Nah, I just knocked the jerk out," Willa said casually.

"Well done," Danielle responded, shaking her head from side to side.

"What should we do with him?" Willa asked turning her flashlight on and off making sure it was still working.

"I don't know, but thanks for giving me some time to think. I have a million questions." Danielle said, avoiding Willa's eyes.

"Look at me," demanded Willa. "I saw you, Danielle Mendow. You fell for him again. He burned you and it looks like he's somehow involved in this mess you're in–burning you again. The guy's a Wall Street scumbag. Always was, always will be now that he's back alive. He was good for those days in New York, but he's a loser now. Who fakes his own death, then comes back to haunt their ex-girlfriend? It's weird and creepy.

Willa handed the flashlight to Danielle. "I need to go find more candles. And Danielle? Don't even think about it. There's something up with him and you got to let go. He's a bad boy. Remember that." Willa warned, turning towards the kitchen.

Danielle looked down at Frank while she listened to Willa rummaging around the kitchen. Faint moonlight coming through an undressed window illuminated his peaceful face. His hair was still straight and long, like he was stuck in the 70's. Bangs fell over one of his two beautiful blue eyes as he lay there breathing (thankfully) heavily. He wasn't the tallest guy Danielle had ever dated, but his body was solid and she could see that after 18 years, he was still in great shape. She sighed. But Willa was right, as always, she thought.

Danielle straightened out his legs, which had crumpled beneath him, feeling the tight muscles of

447

his thighs under his black woolen pants. She reached under his shoulders to prop him up against the couch, giving her a chance to check if his upper body was just as solid. He was too solid. All she did was pull his black shirt out from his pants. She couldn't budge him.

"You're going to give yourself a hernia," Willa said, coming out of the kitchen carrying a lit candelabra. She held the light higher, surveying the body. "Man, the scumbag did always look great in black!"

Between the two of them, they finally sat him up and leaned him up against a couch. Exhausted, they sat on the floor next to him. Willa, the self-proclaimed expert on knocking guys out, gave her a medical explanation about how she hit him and insisted he was going to revive in a few minutes. "So when that happens, what are you going to do?"

"I wouldn't even know where to begin," Danielle replied honestly, rubbing her temples. They sat in silence for a few seconds, listening to the storm outside assaulting the house.

She tried to wrap her head around the thought that someone who she buried in her memory was once again sitting next to her, alive. Frank Giuseppe was supposed to be dead! It was confirmed that he was blown up during 9/11 in Tower Two when the first plane hit! Granted, they never found his body, but they assumed that he was there. Neighbors swore they saw him that morning, leaving for work. He worked on the floor that was slammed into by the plane. After that day, he was never heard from again. Everyone assumed his ashes were caught up in the air around Manhattan.

Danielle covered her face with her hands and went back in time. They were serious as boyfriend and girlfriend then. She was that rising star at Capital Bank International and he was a private wealth manager for the now-defunct Lehman Brothers–the successful and prestigious investment company of the day. They were the power couple among their friends. He made the money. She could move it.

They met where all the Young Urban Professionals, or "Yuppies" met in those days–the gym. They both worked out at 5:30 am every morning, Danielle on the bicycle and Frank at the weights. She had a great view of his biceps and hamstrings as he worked his muscles into taut ropes. When he grunted, she swooned.

After a few calculated "accidental" collisions, Danielle introduced herself, and from that day on, they were inseparable. Two years of blissful dating quickly passed, and Danielle thought it was just a matter of time before she would get a ring. But towards the end of the second year, Frank started changing. He was getting sick of working for the "nitwits" at Lehman and wanted to do his own thing. He kept talking about starting a business so he could be his own boss. But he had fixated on a venture he knew nothing about–making chocolate.

At first, Danielle was supportive, but after endless taste-testing experiments, she soon realized he had no talent for making chocolate. She tried to steer him into something that he was good at like sales, but he was obsessed with the idea of becoming a chocolatier. She didn't get it. He didn't even like chocolate.

Frank kept forcing his friends to try out his recipes. They were all adamant about how awful they tasted or looked. He tried ideas like "Make your own candy bar" or "Bizarre chocolate shapes" but each time he tested them, he received bad reviews. Danielle thought he was hopeless.

But he was driven by something or someone that she couldn't understand. After a while, she realized he would not give up, so she convinced him to go to Europe and study chocolate with the top chocolatiers of the continent. She packed him up in June for a two-month stint so he could be back in time for the finale of the summer season in the Hamptons.

The memories were becoming more vivid. She remembered getting ready to pick him up at the airport. Her hair was loose and her pants were tight. She loved her image at that time. Boardroom by day, vixen by night. She had missed him terribly. For two months, they had hardly communicated. Those were the days that international cell phone calls were expensive and you just didn't call overseas as much.

She was brought back to the present by a nudge on her shoulder. The 'memory remote' was put on pause. She looked at Willa who nodded towards Frank who was stirring.

"You never answered me. What should we do with him?" Willa asked, slapping the flashlight into her other palm.

"You're not knocking him out again," Danielle answered as she watched the man she used to adore opening his eyes and focus. She remembered planting a kiss on that handsome face while playing a reverse Sleeping Beauty where she was the lovely princess waking the gorgeous prince. Danielle leaned down. Willa must have seen the madness in her eyes and said, "Danielle, don't you dare. Don't you remember how awful he was to you at the end? One word. Airport. He really screwed you."

The words yanked her back to reality. She leaned back and squeezed her eyes shut, not to be tempted.

"You're right. A momentary lapse of judgment. I'm over it," she moaned.

The howling outside had stopped, but the power had not returned. The room was still being illuminated by the few candles Willa had quickly lit. The effect of the smell of the accumulating smoke hypnotized Danielle into a dream-like trance, and within seconds she was back to that last memory before Frank started stirring. She put the "memory remote" on play. She was at the airport. They had agreed to meet at the baggage claim of British Airways as Frank had connected through London on his way home. Danielle stared at the bags as they circled round and round on the carousel. Passengers were falling on them like crows on corpses, then dragging them off towards the exits.

The baggage claim was emptying. The silence was getting noticeable. She didn't see Frank. If he had missed the flight, he had plenty of time to get her a message. She kept checking her phone for a voicemail but nothing was coming up. She tried his American phone number and international phone number, but he didn't pick up. She waited another half an hour then went to the British Airlines counter only to find out that he was indeed on that flight.

She couldn't understand how their signals got crossed.

A live voice broke her reverie. "Did I die and go to heaven because I have two beautiful angels beside me," Frank said, rubbing the back of his head.

Danielle and Willa both turned to look down at him.

"L.O.L. You're still just as much of a jerk as you were eighteen years ago, Giuseppe," Willa smirked. "You're lucky I didn't aim that flashlight somewhere else."

Frank winced and laughed. "I deserve that, but not from you." He turned towards Danielle. "Have I told you how great you look?"

"Are you kidding? It's dark, and you were just hit on the head so I will not take that seriously." Danielle said, her face reddening. "You know, I'm beyond pissed. You've got a lot of talking to do–about two decades' worth–because I want to know why you faked your own death and then disappeared off this planet and most importantly, what happened to 'us'? And by the way, I'm over it, so don't get any ideas."

Frank opened his mouth to say something, then stopped. Pulling himself into a better seating position, he pulled his face closer to Danielle and said, "No. I'm not going there."

Instinctively, Danielle pulled her head back. "What?" she answered, confused.

Shrugging he said, "As much as I think you're still hot, I got over you years ago too so… no, no. Moved on." Frank said, continuing matter-of-factly. "I don't have the time or desire to explain anything to you. I am not here to make up or ask for redemption. You didn't believe in me, so that's that. I just want my flash drive so I can be on my way. I need to get out of here before you start to dismember me."

Danielle was stunned. This was all about that flash drive? Nothing else?

"Should I clobber him again?" Willa asked, raising her arm and gripping the flashlight.

"Tempting, but no," she answered, turning to Frank. "You're a real asshole, you know?" Danielle said to distract Frank to her so he wouldn't try to grab the flashlight from Willa and start a fight.

"I know. Thank you. Now, please get it so I can be on my way. I've got to go," he pleaded.

"I hope you get blown off the Bay Bridge," Willa said.

"I'll be fine but thank you for thinking about me," Frank answered, keeping his eyes on Danielle.

"Can I just ask you one thing?" Danielle said getting up.

Frank closed his eyes and answered with mock exasperation, "Well, if you have to."

Staring seriously at him, she asked, "Did you steal the ten million dollars from Capital Bank International on 9/11?"

Frank laughed in that stupid way he used to do when he was trying to cover something up. "How would I do that? I was killed that day, remember?"

"I thought so." She wanted to ask him how, but he quickly cut her off.

"All right, Danielle, that was your one question. Now please go get the flash drive," he said firmly.

She was just about to rise when she sat back again. "Can you give me one good reason why you are making such a big deal about that flash drive? I know what's on it. Even if I give it back to you, I can recreate it with all the statements."

Frank stared silently at her, then broke into his trademark roguish grin. "I guess it didn't take the payment queen long to decipher what was going on. Did you get to the end?"

Danielle caught her breath. She obviously didn't have time. Was there something on the flash drive that she missed?

"I didn't think so. We kept you running for the last two days so you wouldn't have the time, he said, laughing.

"What was in the end?" Danielle said, trying not to sound too alarmed.

"Bill Smith spilled the beans about the transactions and the whole dirty business. His conscience got the best of him. He wanted out, but he wanted to take us all down with him. I want that flash drive or else you're coming down with us."

By this time, Danielle was standing. She reached over and took the candelabra from Willa. The flash drive was in the backpack in her room, but she didn't want to give it up that easily. There were so many loose ends that she wanted to be answered, but the most important was finding out who killed her good friend, Bill Smith. Was Frank complicit in his murder? If so, he couldn't get away with it. Why did she have to help him? Why didn't she just dump this on the FBI to figure out? What could he do to her? Would anyone believe that crumbled mess on the floor? She had to stall until she could think of something that would keep him talking. She turned towards the stairs.

"Hey, where are you going?" Willa asked. "You will not give this loser the only evidence that could get you out of this mess?"

Leaning against the banister, she stopped and looked at Frank. "Do you want to come up and help me find it?"

Willa gave her a sharp look. Frank's chest started heaving up and down. She looked into his eyes, smiled, and then scanned his body like an MRI. "Come on," she continued, "it won't take long. I think I can find it pretty quickly."

She wasn't sure about the plan yet, but she thought that if she could somehow emotionally disarm him–maybe he would even tell her the truth. At least she deserved that. Frank smiled, stood up after a momentary struggle and took two steps towards her. Then he stopped.

"Ah, ah, ah. I know what you're doing," he said, shaking his head and pointing his finger at her. "It will not work." He turned around and sat on the red velvet couch–first looking to make sure he was far enough from Willa's flashlight. He settled in, crossed his legs and said, "Go!" waving her off.

Now she was pissed. First, did he really think that she would just trot upstairs, bring down the flash drive, hand it over, and tell him to have a pleasant life? If so, he was delusional. Okay, the vixen act didn't work. She watched Willa shaking her head and mouthing "stupid" at her. Danielle shrugged. They needed another strategy.

Danielle and Frank were staring each other down. "So you know Bill Smith is dead and before he was murdered he sent me the flash drive. You knew it put me in the middle of this, so you must know who killed Bill. You're complicit, Frank. Come on, admit it. You will not get away with it as long as I'm around. Are you going to have me killed too?"

"Enough, Danielle." He said glaring at her back. "It wasn't me. I had nothing to do with it. You're digging too deep. Let it go. Just do what I tell you and you'll be fine. You weren't meant to be involved. Bill made a mistake by sending you that flash drive," he ended punching his right fist into his left palm.

457

Willa put herself between Danielle and Frank to protect her. Frank held up his hands in a mock surrender, signaling he didn't mean to do her harm.

"Don't you think I'm entitled to a better explanation?" Danielle said, moving in front of Willa. "I'm tired, Frank," she said dramatically. "I was having a glorious life until this happened. In a few days, my world crumbled. Bill's murder and that stupid flash drive. I didn't need this. I'm on the run from the FBI, suspected of murdering both Bill and some daffy old lady from the bank, some nut in a black SUV's been following me all over the place, I've been receiving threatening texts that I realize was probably from you, my branch burned down for goodness' sake and they are throwing in arson. I find out my little universe has been laundering money for some chocolatier..." She stopped. Her heart was racing and she started breathing deeper hoping to calm her nerves. She saw Frank sit up a little straighter when she mentioned chocolatier. "Oh my, a chocolatier..." she repeated, taking her hand off the banister and putting them over her mouth.

"Danielle, don't..." Frank demanded.

Scowling, Danielle took a step back. With feet firmly planted on the red carpet, she held the candelabra to her face, hoping he would see how angry she was "Don't what, Frank?" she said with tight lips and creased eyebrows. "Connect the dots? It's a little too late for that. I get it. It's you. Frank Giuseppe. Joseph Franz. The inverted name. You're the chocolatier. You're at the center of all of this! The money was for you! You're the money launderer. You, Bill, maybe even Teddy Hudd, I wonder who else, had something going. Geez! And I was the pawn!" Danielle leaned against the banister, bowing her head. "I'm so stupid! Why didn't I see this?" she said angrily to herself.

Willa was quiet up until this point. "So I hope you're finally over him, hon, because now I'm ready to take him out with or without your approval."

They both turned to Willa. Frank closed his eyes and took a deep breath, like he was ready to bellow an aria. Danielle was about to say something but stopped. Their attention shifted to a noise coming from outside.

All heads tilted as they listened. A car was coming up the driveway. They all squinted towards the window as two headlights broke through the darkness of the lobby.

The car had barely stopped when the car door flew open and they heard footsteps rushing up the gravel sidewalk towards the door.

Willa turned frantically to Danielle. "Get out of here. Go hide until we know who it is."

"You're not going anywhere!" Frank said, bolting off the couch and grabbing her free arm.

Wax spilled from the candelabra and ran down her arm as Danielle lost her balance and almost fell down the stairs from the force of Frank's hold. "Ow! The wax is burning me! What are you doing? Let me go, Frank! This isn't funny" she said trying to pull away from him. Willa rushed over and took the candelabra out of her hand. In a martial arts move that would have made a ninja proud, she lifted her leg at the same time to jam it into Frank's stomach. What she didn't count on was that Frank seemed to learn his lesson from the last clobbering and was better prepared. He grabbed her ankle and held it while she fell on her butt.

Before Danielle could ask Willa whether she was okay, the door to the Inn swung open. Salt air and rain blew in. Everyone froze. They looked to see who was entering. A wet body pointing a tiny flashlight on a key chain was standing in the doorway.

"It can't be. Rita? Rita Steele?" Danielle said, squinting. "What in heaven's name are you doing here?"

Rita Steele walked in, shoulders pulled back, and looking like she owned the place. She pointed the flashlight from one person to another, trying to assess the situation. After a few seconds, she said abruptly, "Okay Frank, what the heck is happening here?"

Willa scrambled to her feet. "Who the hell are you?"

"Shut up, Fly girl. I ask the questions now. Frank, did you get the flash drive or are you reliving your wild party days in New York? Babe, whatever's going on here, we don't have time for it. I have some guy on my tail who'll be here any minute. We have to go."

Danielle's eyes narrowed as she looked at Rita, then Frank. She shook her head. "Babe? I don't believe it! You and Rita? How did that happen?"

He shrugged and let her go. "Just go get the flash drive, okay? It's too late. Fun and games are over. It's out of my hands now," he said, glancing over at Rita.

"You don't owe these two anything, Danielle," Willa said, pointing a finger at Frank and Rita. "You're both trespassing. I want you both to leave now."

Nobody moved. A demonic cackling broke through the darkness. "Are you kidding me? What are you going to do about it? You know I'm not leaving until I get what I want." She turned her attention to Frank, pointing the tiny flashlight at him. "You're right, Frank baby, it's out of your hands. I knew not to let a hopeless idiot like you take care of this. So I drove out here to make sure the job was done right. Now go find me a towel. I feel like a bucket of water was poured on me."

Finally, letting go of Danielle while quietly apologizing, Frank climbed the stairs silently, head

461

down.

"Well, that's pathetic," Willa said, staring at Frank and taking a seat on the red velvet couch.

Danielle, too, nodded in disgust and silently watched Frank disappear onto the second floor. She then turned to say something to Rita. It was at that moment, the power decided to go on again. The lights flickered first for a few seconds, then came on full blast. Danielle's eyes widened. Rita was pointing a small pistol at her.

"What's wrong with you?" Danielle cried out instinctively taking a step back.

Willa leaped off the couch.

"Back, Fly girl," Rita said, turning the weapon towards her.

Willa gingerly backed herself down on the couch. She looked over at Danielle, who was watching in horror. She shrugged her shoulders, held up her hands and mouthed, "I tried".

"What's gotten into you?" Danielle asked sharply, turning her attention back to Rita while blowing out the candles. "Since you like waving that pistol around, I assume you killed Bill thinking he had the flash drive. But you didn't know he may have had two copies. It was only after the meeting with the FBI in Place's office that you realized he sent it to me when they found my address on his body! Gross Rita! Do you really think you can get away with this?"

"Turn the question around, Mendow. Do you think you can get away with this? All roads - from Smith's murder, Kagan's unfortunate accident, the untimely fire, criminal banking behavior lead to you. I'm just here trying to save the day. Nobody suspects me. They suspect you!"

She had a point, thought Danielle. Frank and this maniac were trying to frame her these last two days! "And with the flash drives?"

"It will all go away. Smith's murder would end up unsolved, Kagan - an accident–the fire ruled a defective heater, and the criminal banking behavior will disappear because nobody will know about it since I have the flash drive."

"Aren't you the all-powerful," Willa said, leaning back and crossing her legs. Danielle looked over, eyes bugging out and lips pressed, hoping Willa would shut up and not set Rita off.

"More than you know, Fly Girl. Listen, one more word out of you and your girlfriend will not like you anymore." With her free hand, Rita combed her fingers through her wet hair, pushing it back. She looked a mess. Her mascara had run down her cheeks. Lipstick was smudged all over. Her face had that sad clown look. Her shirt collar was bulging up around her neck, further exacerbating the look. The tight black suit she was wearing appeared to have shrunk wrapped on her skin. The back tail of her white silk blouse had fallen out of her waistband and tangled around her hips. She needed to be kept away from a mirror or she would unhinge even further.

Danielle looked down at Rita's now destroyed Manolo shoes and shook her head in pity. Six hundred dollars had just gone down the drain besides any respect she had for her.

Although Willa appeared calm, Danielle was sweating. If Rita really already killed one person for the flash drive, is she so unhinged should she do it again? How on Earth would she get away with it? She'd have to shoot everyone!

The hand holding the candelabra started to shake. Her heart was racing. She wanted to think of something to do, anything, which would end this bizarre scene. If she went and helped find the flash drive for Rita, would it all end? How were Rita and Frank going to cover their tracks? These train cars were definitely off the rails.

She breathed harder. She felt her pulse racing. A little pain started throbbing at the top of her head.

"Hey, I got the flash drive!" Frank yelled down as he descended from the second floor.

Rita looked up, distracted by the voice coming from above.

This was it. Danielle had no time to doubt her decision. In a split second, she hurled the candelabra with the force of a World Series worthy fast pitch. She aimed towards the inside of the arm with which Rita was holding the gun. At the same time, Willa bounded off the couch and knocked Rita over. She went down hard. That was the good news. The bad news was that the force of the candelabra caused her trigger finger to get off a shot before the pistol broke from her hand. The pistol slid under an étagère across the room. While Rita was struggling with Willa, Frank came tumbling down, resting at Danielle's feet.

"Frank!" Danielle screamed, falling to her knees. Rita and Willa stopped struggling and looked up. "He's been shot!"

"Holy Crap!" Willa said, rolling off Rita. "Now you've done it." She crawled over to Frank and Danielle, Rita following behind.

Frank's eyes were closed. His head was leaning off to one side with his tongue hanging out and his knees twisted the other way. Both arms were spread out, opening his black jacket like bat wings. Blood trickled through the left shoulder pad.

"It looks like he took it in the shoulder," Willa said in military seriousness while peering under the collar of his jacket. "It's pretty bad." She quickly got to her feet. "The landline should work by now. I'm going to get the first aid kit and call an ambulance. Put pressure on it and don't let up," She ran off like a rabbit towards the kitchen.

Turning towards Rita, Danielle swallowed a sob and said, "You're such an idiot. You and that stupid gun! I bet you killed Bill with that thing too!"

"So what. Frank's still breathing. He'll be fine. He's better off than that old geezer, Bill," Rita laughed while scanning Frank's body. Danielle was following Rita's eyes. They both saw it at the same time. Frank's left hand still held the flash drive. Rita lunged first and grabbed it.

"Got it!" she said, gloating while rolling away. "I'm off." The tightness of her skirt gave her some trouble as she quickly struggled to her feet. Keeping her eyes on Danielle, she took a few seconds to straighten herself out.

Maneuvering her way towards the door, she said, "You know, I had nothing against you until Bill Smith got you in the middle of this. In fact, I thought you were a pretty good banker."

Of all times for Rita Steele to throw a compliment, Danielle thought.

"Hey, where are you going?" Willa barked, seeing Rita as she ran back into the room carrying towels and a giant box. "I got through. An ambulance and the police and whoever was following you are on their way. There's one road in and one road out. You're never going to escape so you better sit down and start picturing yourself in stripes."

"Yeh, like that's going to happen. Okay girls, got to run. I haven't had this much fun since my first date with Frankie the loser over there," she snickered. Then, like a bolt of lightning, she was out the door.

"What a piece of work. She won't get far." Willa said kneeling next to Danielle. "Okay, let go for a second. I hope you don't get squeamish around blood because you have to help me get this jacket off."

As Danielle labored, Willa slapped on some rubber gloves and pressed the towels against his shoulder to stop the bleeding. The rain had quieted down because they could clearly hear Rita's heels clicking on the driveway as she ran to her car. Within seconds, an engine started, tires screeched, and in next to no time it was quiet again outside.

"She's gone, right?" Frank asked through a pained smile on his face.

Danielle and Willa froze. "You're alert?" Willa asked.

"Okay Frank, you can open your eyes, you big faker," Danielle added secretly relieved.

Frank winced as he attempted to sit up. He leaned against the stairs and closed his eyes again tightly. "Although I'm in agony and will probably pass out soon, I just want to say that if one more girl decides to physically hurt me, I'm going to get

467

really mad."

"Don't worry. I don't want more of a mess on my carpeting." Willa said checking the towel. She looked at Danielle worriedly. "We can't let him fall asleep."

"Frank, can you hear me?" Danielle asked, getting close to his face.

"Yeh, yeh," he answered, keeping his head still.

"Do you want to tell me about Rita?"

"I'm not in the mood." He paused for a few seconds, then opened his eyes to see her staring menacingly at him. His head fell back, and he turned away.

Willa put more pressure on his shoulder. "You may bleed to death right now. It's time to confess."

Danielle tilted her head towards Willa and mouthed "Seriously?" with mock disbelief. Willa subtly shook her head, no. "Play it out," she mouthed back.

He spoke softly. His voice was weak. "Although I don't want to talk about Rita, I do want you to know I'm sorry for everything, Danielle. She started it all."

"What?" Danielle said in amazement. "How did you even know her?"

"We met at your bank's Christmas party. The last one. That one at Tavern on the Green" He made a sound - something like a snort. "Yeh. She was Margarita Stilleto then."

"Are you kidding? That little Italian girl with the greasy hair and glasses in the Paying and Receiving area? That's the same girl? I remember her as such a nothing. The guys in Operations used to call her Scooby-Doo, you know, after the cartoon dog." Danielle dropped her butt on the floor. Her mouth opened, but she didn't know what to say.

"I know. Hard to believe. But this kid was obsessed with me from the second you introduced us that night. In fact, while you got up to do the Macarena with all the other girls, she slithered over to our table, sat next to me, put her hand on my knee, and, well… you know, we were all pretty drunk… we kind of disappeared for a few minutes."

"You always were a slime ball, Giuseppe. I may revoke that promise of not hurting you again." Willa said, sitting closer to Danielle while she continued to work to stop the bleeding.

"Okay, Willa. You weren't a saint those days either. I remember a few times when… oooowwwww!" Frank screamed. "Stop leaning on my bleeding shoulder! Alright, alright! I was a jerk. Still am." Frank answered, trying to shift slightly away from the two faces breathing on him while trying to pull Willa's hands off his bullet wound.

469

"I hate you," Danielle muttered.

"You'll hate me, even more, when you hear the rest of the story, he said, glowering at Willa.

"You mean, it gets worse? Well, go on, keep confessing. This should be good." Danielle answered expressionlessly. Willa pressed a little harder again on his wound, evoking another swat of her hands from Frank.

"Anyhow," he continued giving up trying to control Willa's medical skills, "while you were all making fun of me and my passion to become a chocolatier, Margarita, was very supportive, very encouraging. She loved my chocolate. She kept me going."

Danielle and Willa gave each other looks of disbelief. "You know, we assumed at the time there was some evil force behind your craziness. Now we know." Willa said, checking his shoulder again.

"So let me guess. When you went to Europe to study, she followed you and the rest is history." Danielle said evenly. "And you didn't have the courtesy to tell me that there was somebody else?" she continued gradually raising her voice.

Willa made a move to press on his shoulder again, but Frank pleaded with her to stop. "Wait, wait. You don't know. She promised to fund my chocolate business. She said she had some money. She believed in me, Danielle. She believed in me.

You didn't believe in me. You were all about your own career."

The three of them looked down in silence. Danielle and Willa snuck a peek at each other and while trying to contain smiles.

"Okay, Frank. Finish feeling sorry for yourself and tell me what happened on September 11th." Danielle said.

He was speaking slower. His voice was getting softer and weaker. Danielle and Willa leaned in further to hear the rest. "I made it out of Tower Two by the skin of my teeth and just started running towards the river. There was a huge black cloud following me and I dove under a car so I wouldn't get caught in it. I was terrified and with everything going on around me I must have fainted because I lost consciousness."

"So you didn't die, but everyone thought you did because you let no one know you were still alive. The perfect time to disappear and start all over again." Danielle said.

"Yeh, something like that. When I came to, it was dark. I crawled out from under the car. It was pandemonium down there. Nobody paid any attention to me, and I started walking uptown to Margarita's apartment. She was ecstatic to see me. She thought I had perished too. Then she told me the deed was done. She got the money and was giving it all to me if we went into the business together. At first, I was nervous, and then when she explained how we would never get caught, I started seeing the opportunities."

Danielle interrupted. "She took my I.D. and got into the SWIFT room where she made the transfer. I assume you had gotten hold of it at some point during the time we were together, gave it to her to get copied, and snuck it back in time so I wouldn't miss it."

"Very good. You always had the potential to be a great embezzler, but Margarita beat you to it." Frank said with a weakened smile. "Anyhow, there was so much confusion that day. She knew you were the one responsible for the SWIFT Keys and that in the event the bank had to move to the backup facility, you would probably be in and out of the room several times. The plan worked perfectly. It took months to figure out the money was even missing. And when they figured it out, it was so embarrassing to your Chairman he just wrote it off and closed the books."

"If I remember, Margarita took a long vacation but stayed with the bank until we shut down," Danielle said.

Frank's breathing got heavier and they could barely hear him. "Yes, we agreed she would be 'business as usual' to ward off any suspicion. I would pretend to be dead so I could start all over again as Joseph Franz. She had made up a fake passport–don't ask–and I left the country within a couple of weeks. We had transferred the money to a bank in Latvia, and that's where I started my first factory."

"Frank! Stay with me! Bill Smith! How did he fit in with all this? We killed ourselves trying to trace it. He even left the country a couple of times, thinking he could track it down. And then he was gone!" Danielle asked while shaking his good shoulder, trying to keep him conscious.

Willa put more pressure on his arm trying to stop the bleeding. She looked at Danielle with deep concern. Frank grabbed her hand and held it. "Bill found me in France. I thought he was going to call Interpol on me and have me arrested. Instead, he asked to become partners. He became my chief financial officer." His voice was getting weaker. Danielle leaned closer to hear him. His warm breath made her shudder as he spoke his next words. "Bill Smith was the mastermind of the money laundering scheme. He chose you because he thought you may get hungry enough to join us after the bank demoted you. He had no idea who you were, Danielle. You didn't need us. You didn't need anybody. But the game was in play, and we couldn't change it without raising red flags. It surprised us you never caught on. Then Bill got cancer. The guilt was eating him up. He wanted to redeem himself before he died. He wanted you to find out, then do what you had to do. We needed to stop him."

His eyes closed all the way. Frank was trying to say something further, but Danielle couldn't make it out. He then fell silent. His chest was barely moving.

Danielle and Willa looked at each other anxiously. "Where the hell is that ambulance?" Willa said under her breath. "He's going down fast."

Chapter 35

Rake kept checking his watch. He was getting nervous. Not a soul had passed in the last twenty minutes that could help him. A rescue did not look imminent. The rain had let up somewhat, but his cell phone was still out. He was frustrated. He slammed his palms on the steering wheel. He needed to do something and fast!

But he hadn't eaten all day and his stomach was screaming, "Feed me!" He needed some sustenance if he was going to be out there all night. The hypnotic smell of the lamb in the trunk was making him dizzy. "To hell with Eleni's warning not to touch it!", he thought to himself. Like Eve's apple, the temptation of all that food in the trunk made him decide to venture out and bring some of it back into the car. Reaching for the door handle, he hesitated a second when the little eye she dangled in his face before he left appeared in his mind. He shook the image away. That little old lady's voodoo would not scare Rake Harris.

He opened the car door and immediately slipped into the brown mud where his car was held, prisoner. Cursing that he probably looked like a giant tootsie roll, he gingerly made his way to the trunk and popped it open. Water ran off the trunk door, giving him a heavier shower than the rain that was still coming down. But the misery did not outweigh the basket of food in front of him that shined like the pot of gold at the end of a rainbow. He loaded up with tins of lamb and potatoes. While digging around for some cutlery, he felt something odd. Lifting a cloth from under a tray of spinach pies, it surprised him to see a Ruger Precision rifle peeking out from underneath.

"The old coot," he grunted. Together with the food, he brought the rifle back into the car and placed it on the passenger seat. He didn't quite know what to make of it, so he covered it up with his raincoat–out of sight, out of mind. Hiding a rifle in a food basket wasn't normal, but then again, nothing about this assignment was what he expected. Didn't Muckiss say that he was just going to be "keeping an eye" on Danielle? Then how did he end up in the middle of nowhere, stuck in the mud with no form of communication during the storm of the century, almost run off the road by a sociopath who disguised herself as a banker, trying to save an innocent money launderer, and inhaling the aroma of the most delicious meal packed in a basket by an ancient lunatic weapon-dispensing Greek housekeeper?

A few stars were peeking through the clouds, signaling the storm was nearing the end. Rake sat in the driver's seat and chewed on the first bite of lamb, marveling its tenderness and taste. "Man, lunatic or not, that woman knows how to cook!" he said to himself. He leaned back, closed his eyes and sighed. A wave of romanticism overtook him. He mused how nice it would have been to have Danielle sitting alongside him, sharing the moment instead of her rifle.

The silence from his expansive surroundings magnified his loneliness. He took another bite to console himself. He had kept the radio off in the car for fear of missing the sound of a vehicle on the road, but he was now feeling very sorry for himself and wanted to hear a noise from another soul. He reached over, fiddled with the stations, and caught Al Green singing "I'm So Tired of Being Alone". How appropriate, he thought. He turned up the volume and closed his eyes.

A loud thump on the passenger side window rattled him. He opened his eyes to a piercing light flashing through the window. Instinctively, he slipped his right hand under the raincoat, grasping the stock of the rifle while trying to make out who was behind the glare. He leaned over to turn off the radio with his left. The flashlight turned off and knocked on the window again.

Through the glass, he heard a man's voice. "You, Harris? Special Agent Harris?"

"Who's asking?" Rake answered, getting a firmer grip on the rifle. From his years of experience, he knew a lot of weird people lurked in fields and this could be some sort of trick.

"Officer Toumey. St. Michael's police." The man replied, holding a badge up against the glass.

477

The guy sounded legit, but he wasn't sure. He relaxed a degree, leaned over and tried to get a closer look, but it was too dark.

Before he could say anything, Officer Toumey continued. "We got a call from your colleague, Peter Muckiss. He said he couldn't reach you and thought you may be in some kind of trouble."

Hallelujah, Rake thought to himself while he lowered the window. "Yes, I'm Special Agent Harris and thanks, officer. I'm stuck in the mud and..."

"Whoa!" Toumey said, sticking his head further into the car. "That smells delicious!"

A head full of brown slightly wet hair came in first then a round face that ran seamlessly with a neck-followed - all parts focusing intently on Rake's meal which he had resting on his lap. From what he could see, Rake thought Officer Toumey had eaten a few too many lamb dinners already and wondered if he was planning to push the rest of himself through the window.

Rolling his eyes, Rake said, "I'd love for you to join me, Officer, but I would prefer to get the hell out of here. I've got to get to the Strangler's Point Inn. I think it could be a matter of life or death" He said while packing away the dinner and opening the driver's seat door to get out. This time he gingerly stepped away from the car, watching his footing. But his attention was quickly drawn to the

478

furiously flashing police light. His heart started beating faster. Alarms were sounding off in his head. After twenty years in the FBI, flashing lights still did that to him. His gut was telling him something was terribly wrong.

Pulling his head out, Toumey noticed him staring at the car and said, "Yeh, we got to get a move on. Someone was shot at Willa's place. My partner and the ambulance are on their way."

Rake stiffened. "Do you know who it was?" he asked, alarmed.

"No. The phone call came from Willa and her voice was in and out. We just heard some guy was shot, but everyone else was okay. As soon as we got in the car, your friend Muckiss radioed in and told us it was imperative to find you. So, my partner, Bobby, and I split up. He's on his way to the Inn and I started looking for you. I'm surprised you didn't see or hear his car. It drove right by here."

Rake was embarrassed. He didn't hear a thing over Al Green's tribute to loneliness and couldn't believe he missed all the action. What a dope. At least it wasn't Danielle who was hurt, but probably some poor sod who was at the wrong place at the wrong time. Of course, the last thing he wanted to think about was that Danielle did it. She already had a growing kill count surrounding her that needed explanation.

They were in the front seat of the police car and

Toumey was advising the station that they found Rake and were going to head toward the Inn. The dispatcher said she had heard no further updates but he better get over there fast because she wanted nothing to happen to her dear friend, Willa. All the time, Rake was thinking about Danielle. What if she was the one that was shot and not "some guy"? Although relieved that she was now in excellent hands, he couldn't bear the thought that he didn't protect her enough to avoid getting into some kind of gunfight. Damn Muckiss. He shouldn't have trusted that team of his to pick up where he left off that afternoon. They probably couldn't keep track of an elephant taking a stroll down Rocktown Pike.

"Come on, get off that damn radio and let's go!" Rake said angrily, prodding Toumey on the shoulder. Toumey made a three-point turn back on to Route 50. As soon as they started heading towards the Inn, a black SUV, going about 65 miles an hour, cut them off, heading east.

"That's her! Stop the car! Stop the car! Turn back! I need something from my car! Now!" Rake yelled as he watched the black car tear off down the highway.

"Alright, alright". Toumey said with a suspicious look, implying that his passenger could be out of his mind. He made a quick U-turn, all the while keeping half an eye on Rake who was gripping the dashboard. The car had barely stopped when Rake bounded out, ran back, and opened the passenger car door. He grabbed the rifle, cocked it to make sure it was loaded, and said to himself, "She's not getting away this time."

Toumey's eyes were bulging out when he saw Rake run carefully with the rifle back to the car. "Um, Agent Harris. Do you want to explain what this is all about?" he asked.

"I'll explain as we chase down that black SUV. Let's get a move on before we lose her. She probably saw your lights flashing and maybe panicking."

Toumey appeared to be hesitating. Rake leaned over to him, got up close to his face and yelled, "Drive!"

This seemed to do the trick because, at that moment, Toumey stepped on the gas and shot off like his car was on fire.

The police car's siren was blaring and the one or two cars who were on the road slowed down and pulled over to let them pass. Rake kept his eyes out for the black SUV, but he couldn't see it. The trip to get his rifle must have taken maybe two minutes. He couldn't believe she disappeared in that short time.

After Toumey broke the news to his partner that he was in pursuit of some kind of suspect, Rake recounted the abridged version of the events leading up to the chase. Toumey agreed to put out an "All-Points Bulletin" for the Black SUV, hoping that some police officer or brave radio hack who was out on a night like this would spot her.

They also tried to patch through to Muckiss to let him know they were on the chase for Rita and get some more details on the shooting, all the while watching for any movement on or off the road. When Muckiss finally got through, he said he had no more information other than a third party radio relay that said they picked up a white male who was shot in the shoulder and semi-conscious. This allayed the last vestiges of Rake's fears while sparking an inexplicable twinge of jealousy as he wondered why Danielle was at an Inn with a guy who was shot. Unless she did do it... The thought brought a wicked smile to his face.

"You really think you can catch up to her?" Muckiss asked with a twinge of sarcasm in his voice.

"Yeh, why not? She probably shot that guy too. We've got to stop her. She's a snake," Rake replied, remembering his encounter with her that afternoon.

"Just making sure you're still on your game." Muckiss replied.

Rake was taken aback. That felt like a smack in the face. Muckiss could be such a schmuck at the wrong times.

"Peter, I have more game in me than Pacman!" Eyes shifting back and forth, Rake asked himself if he really said 'Pacman' but the thirty-year-old game was the only one he could think of at the moment. He heard Muckiss clear his throat and mumbled, "yes... ummm, okay. Watch out for Inky, Blinky, Pinky, and Clyde. They might be following you."

"Dick!" Rake muttered.

Embarrassed for him, Toumey avoided looking at Rake by obsessively adjusting his rearview mirror and taking glances out his window. They drove in silence for the next few minutes. In this weather and at this time of night, Route 50 was dark and dangerous. Toumey kept up the speed, but as time passed, they feared the black SUV was gone.

"That lady, Rita, she's a slippery one, huh?" Toumey said, eyeing Rake for a reaction.

"She's a probable thief and maybe even a murderer on top of being a snake. And who knows which criminals' money she's been laundering all these years," he answered, gazing intently out the window." She knows the FBI's got her number, and it sounds like she's unhinged. The lady is not only slippery but dangerous. I'm not even sure what we do with her if we catch her."

"Do you think we're going to have a shootout?" Toumey said worriedly. "You know, I'm married and my wife is having another baby in the next few months."

"Uh, Okay. But if we do catch up with her, I'm going to assume she's armed, and yes, it may come to that." Rake answered. His voice was more confident than he felt. Just like Toumey, he was in no mood to get into any sort of dangerous altercation let alone fire a rifle at Rita Steele, especially with this nice, young officer next to him who would obviously rather be home chowing down with his family. He hated conflict too. In fact, he could count on one hand how many times he actually got into a position like this, and when he did, he always had a team of agents with him. But they needed to catch her. She was not only a menace, but Danielle had to be vindicated.

The rain had stopped. The two-lane highway was littered with broken branches and leaves from the devastating storm. To keep his brakes dry, Tourney tried avoiding the flooded parts as best he could. They drove in silence. Tourney's face was a mask of concentration on the road while Rake kept searching for signs of Rita. The clock was ticking and their journey seemed hopeless. It was too dark. They were twenty miles from St. Michael's, and the chances of finding her were getting slimmer and slimmer. Although Toumey kept up the speed and was a pretty good driver considering the conditions, Rake couldn't believe that she was getting away.

"Damn!" he cried, banging his fist against the dashboard. Suddenly, Toumey's radio went on like Rake's hit caused it to work again. It was the female dispatcher from the St. Michael's police station.

"Hey, Toumey. I'm patching the FBI through again."

"Roger that," Toumey answered, giving a sympathetic nod to Rake. "Go ahead."

Muckiss's voice came in clearer. "Talk to me, Harris. What's going on?"

Rake was exasperated. "Peter, you tell me what's going on. You have better communications than I do. I'm driving around in the middle of nowhere. I can barely see a thing. These roads are a mess. I'm surprised we haven't crashed into a tree yet. Rita the Wretched has gone poof."

"Yeh. Well, she is definitely a slippery one. Anyhow, I may have something, but it's not much. The guy they brought to Easton Hospital's name is Joseph Franz."

"The chocolate guy?" Toumey interjected excitedly.

"Who's talking?" Muckiss said with annoyance. "Rake, can you tell whoever is in the car to keep quiet? I don't need everyone badgering me. It's enough I have Murphy on my back..."

Rake held a finger up to his lips and gave Toumey a wink. Toumey gave a mock horrified look, mouthed an "I'm sorry" and focused on the road.

"Okay, so the chocolate guy was shot at the Inn. Where's Danielle?"

"She's fine. The police have her now. She insisted on going to the hospital. We had a long talk with her. She told us everything. That woman's got a great mind. Quite a gal. I can see why you were smitten."

Toumey looked over and mouthed "way to go".

"Just keep driving, okay?" Rake said, staring back. "And Peter, I'm not smitten. She's a great gal but it was a job," he continued trying to sound convincing. Muckiss didn't have to know everything–that nosey S.O.B. Meanwhile, Rake wondered why Danielle was so interested in this guy that she followed him to the hospital. Was this his competition?

Muckiss cleared his throat. "Yeh, alright. Anyhow, your girl, I mean Danielle, gave us the whole lo-down on how Rita Steele did it. At least on the banking side. We're not sure who she was laundering the money for but Danielle was so pissed about the whole thing she offered to help us figure it out."

"Banker by day, spy by night." Rake said, smiling to himself.

"Yeh, something like that," Muckiss replied. He paused. "You know, Rita's gone. You're not going to find her. She's too slick. She probably had that escape route planned even before she got to the Inn. Why don't you give it up? We'll find her. I know Murphy's going to be pissed because he doesn't have the suspect in custody from the Willard murder. He hates loose ends. You just can't have someone being knocked off within feet from the White House. You know, too many conspiracy theories. Got to nip those fast. I'm not going to tell him it is what it is, but it is."

Rake shook his head. He didn't want to give up. He looked over at Toumey, who was smiling. The guy probably couldn't wait to turn around and head home, he thought. But Rake was mad at himself for everything that happened - letting Danielle out of his sight, being duped and "one-upped" by the serpent, Rita Steele, getting stuck in a ditch, having to be driven by this junior police officer who would rather be home watching cartoons with his kids. No wonder the FBI asked him politely to take his retirement. They think he doesn't have it in him now like they thought he didn't have it in him then. But he was going to show them how wrong those morons can be.

"Peter, I'm going to finish this. Any way you can get some choppers out here to scout the fields?" he commanded.

"Are you kidding? You don't need to do this, Rake. You may get hurt. We'll take care of it. Go home." Muckiss implored.

"I'm not a screw-up, Peter. I've got to do this. I need to go out knowing that I didn't give up and did the right thing. I'm going to find her," he replied.

"No, you're not. Come back. It's not in your hands anymore," Muckiss said.

"What if you don't get that slithery beast woman? She would have gotten away with murder and all sorts of crimes. She's smart. If we give up now, she'll disappear forever!" Rake replied insistently.

"Murphy's going to blow a gasket. You're not an agent anymore. You're just an independent contractor. You've fulfilled your contract. Danielle is safe. We know the culprit and we'll find her."

Rake lowered his head. Toumey slowed the car down. He turned towards him and said quietly, "It will be impossible to find her tonight. She could be hiding anywhere on the Eastern shore at this point and the dark car doesn't help."

A female voice broke through on the radio. "Ah, Big Sam, is that you?"

"Who's that, who's that?" Muckiss shouted. "Who's hacked our line?"

"Yes, who IS that?" Rake added, staring at the radio.

"Hey, Willa!" Toumey answered. "How'd you get on this frequency?"

"I have my ways. Is that you on Route 50 about ten minutes out of Cambridge?" Willa asked, her voice coming on surprisingly clear.

Rake glared at Toumey. "Big Sam? Willa? What's going on?"

Muckiss burst in. "Who's Big Sam? Isn't Willa that lady that owns the Inn? Why is she on this radio? And how does she know where you are?"

"Can you tell that guy who wants us to quit to stop yapping? He's so annoying–like a mosquito in your ear. Look out your window. I'm flying over you right now. I've been following you for the last ten minutes."

Toumey and Rake brought down their windows simultaneously and looked up. Willa's seaplane was gliding overhead.

Rake laughed. "Willa, you're a woman after my own heart!" he cried. "Peter, we'll get back to you."

"You people are out of control out there. I'm staying on. God forbid something happens and we have to dig you out of trouble." Muckiss replied, rather irritated.

"Peter," Willa said. "Keep your hat on. I've been around this hay bale a number of times. We'll find that 'you know what' and make you look like a hero. Okay boys, keep driving. I've got your backs."

The seaplane flew out of sight. Toumey picked up speed again. Everyone fell silent. An eerie stillness was in the air. All eyes were busy searching the road and surrounding areas.

"Rake Harris?" Willa asked, startling him. "Danielle's crazy about you."

Toumey tried to suppress a smile. Muckiss was heard clearing his throat. Rake went red.

"Thanks, but can we save all that for later?" Rake asked.

"Just saying. It's kind of boring up here. Thought I'd offer something for you to look forward to after this is all over." Willa replied.

An awkward quietness ensued as they kept driving. It felt like everyone had something to say, but nobody wanted to say it.

"Any luck?" Rake asked after a few minutes.

"Nada," Willa replied quickly.

"This is hopeless." Muckiss was heard saying. "Look, I'm really thankful to all of you for trying to help but really... I have a whole agency that will be stepping in. You are all putting yourself in danger now. It's getting late. I'm sure everyone's tired and wants to go home. She's disappeared. You all need to stop right this minute and that's an order. We're not playing a game. This is real life."

"Got her," Willa said.

Rake sat up. "Where is she?"

"Are you sure?" Muckiss said excitedly.

"Yup. I see her Black SUV parked behind a Holiday Inn Express right outside of Salisbury. She's probably around there somewhere. She can't get far in those wacky shoes and tight ass clothes she was wearing."

"Okay, I'm on it. Willa, this would be a miracle if we could nail her tonight. Stay with me." Muckiss said. Rake had never heard him so animated.

"You got it, boss," Willa replied.

Speaking to Rake in a more serious tone, Muckiss said, "Okay, Buddy, you're back in business. Can you get over there to coordinate? I'm going to make some phone calls. Ask the officer you're with to alert the local police and have them meet you there. Tell them we're going to assume she's armed."

"No problem." Rake replied, taking a deep breath. He had to hand it to Muckiss. He was giving him a second chance to prove himself. Tonight, it felt good. He had Danielle to come home to. He turned to Toumey. "Are you ready to be a hero?"

Toumey looked like he was about to puke.

"Let's go get her." Rake said, picking up the rifle.

Chapter 36

Final Chapter

One Year Later

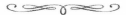

Danielle dislikes being philosophical. However, there comes a time in one's life when you just can't help it. Here she was standing on the balcony of her winding staircase in her own mansion and looking down at a grand party. It was like a scene out of The Great Gatsby. Her hands casually rested on the railings. Her head was tilted to one side while her body swayed slightly to the music. She looked perfect. She felt perfect. She was experiencing the greatest feeling of self-satisfaction she's had so far in her life. There was, however, a slight apprehension that she may kill herself going down the stairs in her new Manolo Blahnik shoes, but she tried not to think about it. It always came down to the shoes. Other than that, life was good.

The scene below was a blend of music, laughter, clinking, and chatter. Reds, blacks, purples, and whites whirled together, creating a holiday flag in constant motion. The four-piece band flown in from New York was playing Sinatra. Danielle closed her eyes for a moment to soak in the timeless masterpiece of one of her favorites. She hummed along, lost in the moment. "That's life, that's what people say, you're riding high in April, shot down in May, But I know I'm gonna change that tune. When I'm back on top in June..." It just doesn't get any better than this, she thought to herself.

Over the years, Danielle's holiday party had evolved into the most coveted invitation of the season and morphed into a life of its own. The elite of Maryland and beyond came to be seen and see while snatching at Eleni's home-made hors d'oeuvres and grabbing at the trays carried proudly by the West Mendowans who needed some extra money to get through the holidays. Everyone came together that evening. The catering was a town affair highlighted by the temporary truce between Eleni and Danielle's favorite restaurant, Sheila's. One night a year, Eleni allowed Sheila's to cater part of the buffet table, which included an ample supply of Tuna Salad and potato chips as an homage to Danielle. The other half was, of course, Eleni's barbecued lambs, pigs, and goats that she spent days preparing in a pit in the backyard.

It was a global disappointment when Danielle had to cancel last year's party due to all the clean-up required to get rid of the Frank and Rita stink that was attached to her. But she made up for it this year by going all out. She even tried to get a few of the Rockettes to come down, but there was a conflict with their own holiday show.

The music continued as Danielle's eyes followed the women dressed in their glamorous gowns, flowing in and out of the main floor rooms. She smiled to herself as she watched them pretend to search out the powder room, but secretly snooping to glimpse the latest Mendow interior design projects. The tuxedoed men, meanwhile, focused primarily on each other, back-slapping, deal-making, and networking while knocking down any alcohol within sight. Danielle checked her Rolex. In an hour, the party was going to get very animated and noisy with some of the less inhibited taking to the dance floor and getting a little silly. But what happened at this party stayed at this party. It was always the unspoken rule. There were enough security guards outside to keep out an advancing army let alone the few journalists who always tried to crash.

From her perch, Danielle caught sight of the newly elected governor (thanks to her), who waved. She blew him a kiss, which he caught with his right hand and placed it on his heart. He then quickly scanned the room, looking for his wife to make sure she didn't catch that little exchange. Danielle saw him breathe a sigh of relief when he located her, oblivious to the surroundings as she dug into the shrimp bowl.

The front door was continuously being opened by Eleni's handsome and virile sons, who looked spectacular in the new Armani suits she bought them. They greeted each guest cheerfully like they were part of the family – all part of the show. It was another successful Mendow bash! There was plenty of booze, food, and gossip, and of course everyone wanted to hear the finale of the biggest money-laundering scam of the last decade. In her mind, it is the greatest story ever told - the fall and rise of Capital National Bank and its new owner and chairman, Danielle Mendow.

It was hard to believe. She followed her dreams, trusted herself, and never gave up. In the end, she got what she always wanted. Six months earlier, in a quiet ceremony on the top floor of the Capital National Bank headquarters in Washington D.C., she wrote a big fat check to ex-chairman, John Place, in exchange for the keys to the bank. With one signature, it became officially owned by Mendow Enterprises LLC. The once lowly branch manager, banished back to her then dying hometown by forces out of her control (although she always suspected that empty-headed twit Teddy Hudd had a hand in it), was now ruling the roost.

Oddly enough, with the additional notoriety she received by uncovering the horrific but admittedly quite clever financial crimes and solving the double murders of Bill Smith and Dolores Kagan, not only did the bank get some much needed, albeit dubious, exposure, but Danielle's private businesses flourished. Go figure- it seems any publicity is good publicity. With Rita's and Frank's apprehension and soon-to-be conviction, West Mendow was firmly put on the map - the upshot being good business for everyone.

A momentary hush settled on the crowd as all heads turned to gape at a tall, long-legged blond woman who entered the house wearing a white satin body-hugging gown, a white stole, and a glittering diamond necklace that stopped at just the right place on her décolletage. Her arm was being held by an equally tall, blonde, very handsome man in a Zegna Tuxedo whose bemused grin verified his awareness of what a striking couple they were.

It was work, Danielle recalled, grooming that now stunning woman from that awkward young teller she hired a few years ago, but it had to be done. When she bought the bank, she asked the only person who understood banking, like she did, to help her manage it. As soon as her attorneys finished the due diligence, she asked Jen to take over the bank's operations. But there was a condition. Since the girl rarely got out of West Mendow, having been born and bred there, and was so busy with her ever-expanding brood, she was a bit rough around the edges. When Danielle offered to quadruple their family income, she made it conditional that she had to follow not only Danielle's management style but her personal style.

It was a no-brainer. Three seconds after the offer, Danielle had a new Chief Operations Officer.

As soon as she jumped on board, she went to work with the Feds to clean up Rita's mess. Jen tackled the bank's involvement in the criminal operation with zeal. She uncovered so much that it was going to take years to untangle the criminal racket. Apparently, the bank was just a small part of the illegal activities which involved Rita. A new investigation started at every turn.

In the meantime, Jen's exposure to a global money-laundering scheme was an education on its own to the lifestyle of the rich and devilish. The investigation had her going everywhere–flying first class, staying in five-star hotels, running around in a Paris wardrobe, having dinners at 3 star Michelin rated restaurants, and so on. It didn't take long for Jen, who is a very quick learner, to catch on to the act.

Coupled with some elocution lessons and etiquette training, Danielle now had a brilliant, loyal, trustworthy and sophisticated partner that could help her build new relationships all over the world while running a flawless back office.

Danielle watched as Jen quickly absorbed the scene and then looked up to find her. Danielle winked. It was a well-timed entrance. Jen smiled back. Her husband received a quick peck on the cheek and a slight shove that sent him away while she went the other direction to work the room. Danielle watched with pride as Jen gracefully made her way to the Chairman of the Securities and Exchange Commission who stood by the kitchen door devouring Eleni's dolmades as soon as the trays came out.

Two hands came up from behind to rest on her shoulders. Strong, confident fingers began to slowly massage her neck. She closed her eyes as a warm breath caused a tingle in her left ear. Moist lips bit softly on her earlobe.

"Mmmm." she groaned, bringing her shoulders closer to her neck. The electric charge was slowly making its way up her spine. This guy had all sorts of hidden talents she was discovering, she thought to herself.

"So, what's your name again?" she asked softly, her eyes closing as her thoughts floated back to moments ago when they were in each other's embrace.

"Ha, ha" Rake answered, twisting her around and quickly planted a wet, gooey kiss on her lips. "You're a piece of work, Miss Mendow," he said, taking a step back and flashing her that signature crooked grin.

"By now, I think you can call me Danielle," she said coyishly. And you're what I've been waiting for all my life, she thought to herself. But she would not let it on yet. Although Mr. Rake Harris was close to perfect, she had to be convinced he could handle her. Sadly, she learned over the years, few men could.

She turned back around before her emotions gave her away. Hearing him sigh, she changed the subject.

"What did Muckiss want?" Isn't he on his way?" she asked. A few moments ago they were enjoying some private time when they were rudely interrupted by the incessant ringing of Rake's cell phone.

"Yeh, he's on his way" he answered, his voice more business-like as he came up beside her. "But he had some last-minute changes to make to the case on Rita and Frank."

Danielle's heart started beating faster. News about the case always made her a bit nervous. Rita and Frank were the only two people still alive that totally duped her, and she was still looking to get her revenge. "Well?" she asked, drawing out the question. "What's the bottom line?" For the sake of the bank and everyone involved, she was hoping this ordeal would end soon. "Come on, talk! The suspense is killing me!" she cried, giving him a playful punch in the shoulder.

"Not so fast, baby doll." Rake answered, grabbing her again and leaning in for another kiss.

Pulling her head back, she said, "One-track mind... Is that all you can think about? Cut the Bogart stuff. Tell me now or you're going over this balcony headfirst into the Spinach dip!"

He chuckled silently, his head bobbing back and forth with his mouth slightly open. She blushed. The look was so adorable, she could think of nothing else than dragging him back into the bedroom. Of course, she didn't want to let on that she had a one-track mind as well. Instead, she pressed her lips and narrowed her eyes, trying to convince him she was really mad.

The band started playing a bluesy version of Sam Cooke's, "Nothing Can Change This Love". The playful mood changed. They both stood quietly listening. Danielle swore she saw Rake's eyes glisten.

"Rake," she said quietly, her pretend anger gone.

"I know," he replied, looking down. "Not to change the subject, I still don't know why you said 'no'."

Turning away, Danielle inhaled. "Let it go for now. Just give me some time, okay? We'll know soon enough." She looked down at her guests again, trying not to meet his eyes. She waved back to the Vice-President's wife, who was dancing with The Rock. Without looking at him she asked, "Rake, can you just tell me what's going on with Rita and Frank? Will they be wearing a ball and chain soon?"

Rake was silent for a few seconds. She could hear him taking some deep breaths. Danielle wondered if he was going to keep pressing her. Thankfully, he moved on before she said something that later on she would regret.

"Ok. As you know, Rita was booked for the murders of Bill Smith and Dolores Kagan. Once they suspected her, they found all sorts of DNA and clues pointing to her–not you. They also charged her with a whole litany of financial crimes, attempted murder, kidnapping, weapons charges, well–let's just say the list is almost endless. Net, net–she is going to be spending the rest of life behind bars."

"Old news, Rake. We learned that month's ago." She said impatiently.

"News flash. Frank agreed to testify against her for a more lenient sentence."

"Finally! I couldn't believe that guy was holding out. Really. He had nothing to lose at this point." She said nodding her head in disapproval. She still couldn't believe she once had feelings for that guy. Was she so blind to his bad moral character? How could she allow those looks and charm to overpower her? On the other hand, if it wasn't for Frank, she wouldn't have hit rock bottom and learned to fight. He gave her grit and Josef Franz Chocolatiers for practically nothing. And, if it wasn't for Frank's desperate need for money to pay for his criminal defense and the civil suits, Danielle wouldn't have been able to buy it for a song. Although the market was surprised by that move, little did they know that after all the illegitimate business was cleaned out, it was actually a great company with a lot of financial upsides.

"Anything else? You were on the phone with him for quite a while," she continued.

"Muckiss finally accepted my resignation." He answered flatly.

She straightened up with a jolt. Beaming she said, "Wow! That's the best news I've heard all night!"

"I know." Rake said, not matching her obvious glee.

She looked at him curiously. "Regrets?"

"I have a few," he answered with a smirk.

Laughing, she said, "Don't go there. Sinatra will always do it better." She moved her hand over his as he held onto the balcony. Now it was time to pop the question. "Rake," she said, staring lovingly into his eyes.

"Danielle?" he answered, gazing adoringly back at her.

"Rake, will you be the C.E.O and President of my Chocolate Company?"

They had talked about this many times but Rake, rightly so, would not give in because of the obvious conflict of interest consulting with the Feds while running the company they were investigating. In addition, he wanted to see that the chocolate company was completely severed and exonerated from illegal activities or future liability for civil and criminal charges. Muckiss had made that part official a few weeks ago. But Muckiss didn't want

Rake to go. He was hoping he could get him to come back to the agency if he could prove to Bob Murphy how valuable an agent he would be on future financial crimes cases. But in the end, Rake's insistence paid off.

"I do." Rake said solemnly.

They stood silently looking at each other for a while. Danielle understood Rake was hoping for a different question, but this was it for now. Danielle got Rake safely ensconced in her web. And with his new salary, he could easily afford to continue as her neighbor and date her in style.

"This is great," she said merrily breaking the silence. "I already started moving the headquarters from Germany to West Mendow so we don't have to be apart too often."

"Yeh, thanks." Rake said – a hint of disappointment in his voice. "But I hope the next time you make a decision like that, you consult with the guy wearing the pants, okay?"

"Oh, of course!" Danielle answered, making a mental note to take a step back remembering that men have egos. She turned away so Rake wouldn't see her roll her eyes.

Visible floor space at the party had disappeared as more people arrived. The noise level had risen to the point where people couldn't hear each other without shouting. She recognized a few more faces as she tried to place names to the bobbing heads. She noticed Teddy Hudd with his thumbs pressed to his temples rubbing hard, cornered by Willa who was close-talking incessantly at him.

On the other side of the room, Eddie, the new manager of the rebuilt West Mendow branch, was grabbing at the microphone while trying to harmonize with the band's vocalist who was in the middle of singing Marvin Gaye's, "Let's Get It On." Danielle made another mental note never to let him live that down.

Rake draped his arm around her shoulder. "Have I told you that you look ravishing tonight?" he said.

"Yes, about a thousand times," she answered, relieved that business was over and they were flirting again. She knew her red silk gown with the low cut back shaped her petite figure in the right places. It was tailored to the centimeter. The right amount of cleavage and leg peeked through while the Manolo Blahnik shoes finished off the outfit perfectly. She had her hairdresser, Mimi, tie up her hair into a perfect French twist and her make-up was done by the same person who did the President's wife. The overall effect was to make sure that when she walked down that stairwell, everyone would gasp in awe or gasp in horror if she tripped instead on those ridiculously impractical heels. Regardless, she would have Rake Harris in his Hugo Boss Black Tie on her arm. If she wasn't impressive enough, he would complete the package or hopefully save her from breaking her neck.

"Are you ready to make your entrance yet?" Rake asked, holding out his arm.

"I think it's time," she answered, glancing at her Rolex. "Elton promised to stop by and play some Christmas carols for us and I wouldn't want to miss that," she said, putting her arm through his and turning towards the staircase.

A slight tug pulled her back. "Elton? As in Elton John?" Rake said, as his forehead contracted and his lips remained parted. She looked at him curiously. "Of course! Who else would play for us?"

He was still standing there as she pulled away and approached the top step. She turned her head, put her hand on her hip and said, "Are you coming?"

He walked up behind her and locked his arm through hers. He looked at her, speechless. She put her other hand under his chin, guided his face towards hers and planted a kiss on his lips.

"Welcome to my world, Mr. Harris.", she said, breaking into a wide smile.

Studying her face for a minute, he shook his head slightly like he was coming out of a trance and pulled her closer. "I'm ready."

"Hold me tight then, okay? Just don't let me fall," she whispered in his ear as the music stopped and her guests turned one by one to watch her make her entrance.

"Never," he assured her as they took their first step together.

Made in the USA
Middletown, DE
05 February 2022